Hal,

May you
beyond your dreams .

# Intimate Strangers

A novel

By

Reginald Smart

authorHOUSE™

1663 LIBERTY DRIVE, SUITE 200
BLOOMINGTON, INDIANA 47403
(800) 839-8640
WWW.AUTHORHOUSE.COM

First published by AuthorHouse 01/11/05

ISBN: 1-4208-0723-4 (sc)

Printed in the United States of America
Bloomington, Indiana

This book is printed on acid-free paper.

# TABLE OF CONTENTS

# BOOK I

# Chapter One

It takes a man a long time to grow up.  Eric Johnson's growing up between thirty and forty-five was quite an odyssey.

### 

She was Malay or Indonesian.  Eric wasn't quite sure.  Had he not done that teacher exchange year in Singapore he simply would have been puzzled by the slightly Negroid, somewhat Chinese facial structures.  He certainly would not have given her a second glance the first time he walked down the aisle to the plane's rear toilet.  But the exchange year had modified his notion of feminine beauty.  With such memories he had appreciated this passenger at first glance.  In his now Asianized judgment, she seemed perfect – much more interesting than those vacuous-looking interchangeable women called supermodels in London, Paris and New York.  The smooth, clean lines of her face, crowned with straight raven hair pulled back into a fanciful bow, transported him back to the kind of (now appreciated) beauty which at first had seemed beyond his taste.

His habit of stopping in full stride and turning to "take in" something beautiful always embarrassed his wife Frankie.  In her company he now restrained himself, but the habit still discomforted his best pal, Michael.  Michael's reprimand "There you go again, you lascivious coot," always got the same response.  "It's got nothing to do with sex.  I just appreciate beauty.  You know that.  You know that I feast my eyes on anything beautiful, not only women."  Michael would smile indulgently and say

1

"Yes, I know. But other people don't know that you can be equally engaged by the shape of a tree or the colors in a garden. I admit sex is only one part of your thing about beauty."

Today Eric found himself wondering what this Asian woman could be doing here, on a plane from Denver to Boston. She is not just a visiting student; she must be twenty five or so. "This is another of those situations," he found himself muttering, "I spend the whole trip wishing I could get to know a woman who attracts me so strongly that I have to readjust my pants, and then we're there."

Who knows what went on unconsciously during that appraisal? What is going on when any man eyes an attractive woman? "Sex" is and is not the answer. Yes, of course the sex drive is operative. But after we have acknowledged that Freud was onto something, must we not also ask: "Is that all?" When a penis is welcomed by other warm flesh, what else is happening? What else is sought, is found? Such questions seldom occur to men; they had never occurred to Eric. But they would, as he grew to full manhood, for such unusual questions did occur to him when he let them.

She had noticed this attractive man. His six feet of well-built, obviously-athletic frame supported an open face topped by a dense head of black hair with the slightest touches of gray around the temples. He had no idea how he looked to women; they made him uncomfortable even as they fascinated him. He also had no idea that women see out the side of their heads. But this woman had found herself thinking. "That's the kind of American I'd like to know."

At the same time Eric was berating himself. "What's wrong with you, Eric? It's now or never!" On the next pretended toilet trip he caught her eye and proffered his best big smile. She immediately turned away. But with an inner voice saying "You can't back out now," he awkwardly plunked down beside her and heard himself saying, "Excuse me for asking, but aren't you South East Asian?" Even while hearing the question as too stupid for a teenager, let alone a professor, he was also thinking "No one calls themselves that." Thus, without pausing for breath he continued "I meant to ask where you are from in South East Asia."

Eric was looking at her so intently that she had to respond, "Indonesia. But how did you guess?" Had this been just another guy coming on to her she would have ignored him as she did those who appeared most days of her life. But this man looked different, interesting.

2

"I worked a year in Singapore," he explained, "as an exchange teacher. I got to know mostly Chinese but also a few Malays and three Indonesians — enough never to confuse the Chinese with the others."

"The others?" she teased. He was about to show his supposed erudition (without realizing it would display the opposite), but she saved him with a chuckle, sustained for enough time for him to join in. Then he realized he was doing something without precedent because he never laughed at himself. And furthermore, if it accompanied a gaze into fathomless dark eyes, he could think of nothing he'd rather do.

She interrupted his fantasizing with the query: "So you're a teacher?"

"Well, a bit more than that. I'm a professor."

"So young! In my country the professors are all old."

He backed off, his basic insecurity surfacing in the realization that he had exaggerated his status. "Well, I am actually an assistant professor of political science."

"Really? That's what I'm interested in. I got my degree in Indonesia, and my major was political science. I'd love to do graduate work in the field. In fact, I've even got a thesis topic."

"You're not serious?"

"I am. You see, I come from Aceh in Sumatra. It's the northern most province and very different from most of the so-called nation. My parents sent me to a Catholic high school in Medan, and then I did my degree in Djakarta at the Polytech. About half of my professors had U.S. doctorates."

"Yeah, but?" He paused. He didn't want to insult her. But really, how could she with only an undergraduate degree, from God knows what kind of an institution, presume she could even begin to formulate an acceptable thesis topic. Most quality schools would laugh at her.

"You don't believe a woman from Aceh could be doctoral material?" The question came with a smile, half challenging and half joking.

"Well, what's the topic?" He attacked, hesitantly.

"The role of women in the Gerakan Aceh Medeka, the GAM movement for independence of my region."

3

"What is GAM?"

"It's an organization formed five years ago, by a man now in exile in Sweden. The government calls it the GPK, which translates as "the gang of security disturbers." It's really a very old movement, the modern part of its life going back to the attempt to make our country a formally Muslim state in the fifties. We were the leaders of the Darul Islam movement because our little state is the most truly Muslim in all Indonesia. In fact, the faith first came to the Indonesian islands through our people, sometime around the year 700. And we have kept the faith pure ever since unlike the strange mix of Hindu and Buddhist elements you find in most Indonesians' brand of Islam."

"Yeah. I've never heard of any of this. But go on. What's all this to do with women?" He tried to mimic her teasing smile.

"So you heard that, huh? The fact is, women in my province of Aceh are what The Prophet (Peace be upon Him) thought women ought to be. We are fully equal and, more often than not, women have been the leaders. You remember that Mohammed (Peace be upon Him) was really just a manager for an enterprising, rich, older woman who became his wife. Without her we might never have received the Divine message which makes up the Koran."

"Of course," pretended the professor.

"Well, there was no really big problem under the Dutch. They simply left us to our own ways. Some, like my grandparents, did well after being educated and became managers for Dutch companies which grew and exported spices. The people of Aceh were even given special status when Indonesia became independent in 1949."

"Interesting!"

"But then the government started to populate us by 'transmigration' from Djakarta and Surabaya – people who were as secular as most of the nation. These newcomers were also excited about the big money offered by Mobil when they came to Aceh in 1971. Since then, things have become worse and worse with terrible repression, atrocities, and killings as well as awful pollution of our beautiful forests and mountains."

"I hear you. It sounds as though this is an issue you are passionate about."

4

"It is more than an issue. It is my family, my home, and my sense of who I am as an Acehnese woman and as a Muslim."

Eric didn't know how to respond to all of this. To him Indonesia was a blur of hundreds or thousands of islands and a population nearly the size of the U.S., which made it the sixth most populous nation in the world. He could recall something of the dictatorial reputations of Sukarno and Suharto, and that the former had led them to independence just after WWII. And that's about all he, a professor of political science, could have said if asked what he knew about the country from which this very bright, delightful, and lovely woman had come. He changed the subject.

"I recall," he launched into safer waters, "how fascinated I was by your dance called the Joget when I saw it a couple of times in Singapore."

"Really? It's my favorite form of relaxation. In fact, it's more than relaxation. Something happens to me when I joget. Without physical touch, you harmonize with your partner. For that to happen there has to be some communication which is more than physical. I can do it for hours."

"But why don't you get confused?"

"I don't know, but we never do. You should try it some time."

"I suppose it's part of being Muslim?"

"It enables us to move to the music and to socialize without the sexual stimulation of your Western bedroom behavior in public, excused by some nice tunes or rhythm."

"Wow! Looking at you, I'd never have guessed you would have those kind of feelings about this country. You seem to fit this country so well."

"I guess it's just that dancing is my favorite activity. What do you really love doing when you're not being a professor?" Again the teasing smile that threw him into confusion even while it delighted him.

"That's easy. Two things. Playing with my daughters and being in the White Mountains."

"So you have a family. You don't wear a ring?"

"Oh! That means nothing although my wife wishes I did. But I think it's stupid. My Dad never wore a ring, nor his Dad, so why should I? But my twin daughters – they are unbelievable. They have just started talking. And you should have seen how they crawled up till a year ago. I expected they would wear out the seat of every diaper the way they scrunched along at walking pace. But a few weeks later they could run. Isn't it amazing?"

"You're very fond of your children?"

"Yes, and of my wife Frankie. We have a great marriage."

"Lucky you. I never see my husband. That's why I'm here en route to Bangor, Maine. If I didn't go where his work takes him, I'd never see him. On landing I have only forty minutes to connect with the flight to Bangor. My husband has business there and said I might like it. So here I am, on my way to eat lobsters."

"Too bad. I was hoping I could offer to show you something of my city." Then, realizing he needed to return to his seat for the arrival in Boston, "So here's my card in case you do have time on some future trip."

"If Allah wills," she smiled, adding impishly, "With a little push."

### 

Eric Johnson was an attractive man – a tall, tanned, athletic type who carried himself with an air of confidence which reached out to people in a big smile and just the right words. On campus co-eds ogled him. Female administrative staff met his every request because he always expressed interest in their well-being — after finding something to appreciate in their appearance. Moreover, you could not ignore his presence. A palpable intensity demanded acknowledgement, never obtrusively but undeniably. There was also just enough hint of the passion with which he lived most of his waking hours to energize any with whom he talked. Yet none could claim to really know him. What lay underneath that pleasant, agreeable, vital persona? What lies under any skin of any "nice person?" If we do find the answers, can we judge them? By what criteria? By what right?

He saw himself as an accomplished achiever who was now reaping the rewards he felt he deserved by his thirtieth birthday. In moments of uncertainty he had a litany, "I've worked dammed hard for what I am. I'm known and respected professionally, and I am beginning to be known nationally. I'm a good teacher: My students respect me, and the outstanding ones flourish in my classes. I'm a faithful husband. I'm a

6

good father to my two girls. And I do my share of volunteering and helping others. I think my mother would really be proud of me." He had no clue that such exaggeration of achievements was his mode of repressing a basic insecurity of which he was quite unaware.

His wife Francine, or Frankie, had a somewhat different perspective. While she continued to adore the man she married six years ago, she did have some thoughts which he might not have been pleased to hear. She confided to her best friend Christine "Sometimes, I feel that nothing really matters to Eric except achievement. Oh, I know his goals are to change the world, but I ask you! He doesn't have a clue about how people really see him, and I do! At the faculty barbecue, I overheard a couple from the department call him a self-serving egotist and an arrogant bastard."

"Some people can be mean and perhaps jealous," consoled Christine, gently touching her friend's hand."

"Well, I've been thinking more about it," Frankie plunged on, "And I've realized there is some truth in what they say. He certainly is brilliant and he knows it, and he never hesitates to demonstrate it in conversation. And he never hides the fact that he suffers fools very badly, but – well, I guess sometimes he makes me feel a fool. You know, just little put-downs. He often just shrugs his shoulders and turns away when I say something he thinks doesn't matter or isn't worthy of his attention. And I do find myself in a bit of a bind when he comes home feeling whipped and wants sympathy after something said by other faculty members. Sometimes I agree with them. Yet somehow I feel that I should loyal, cuddle him, and make it all OK. But there is no way that he would have any of that. He is compelled to put up this big front and to hide the little boy he fears himself to be. He has to act independently of everyone and especially of me emotionally. He seems to think that to be a real man he must be completely self-sufficient. How do I take care of him?"

Although Christine was inclined to remind her of Eric's behavior when Frankie gave birth to a stillborn infant a year ago, she thought it kinder to respect her friend's feelings. But really, how could a man just go off to give a speech somewhere on the same day as their son came into the world stillborn? Moreover, Christine alone knew that the conception had been a secret gift to Eric. When the twin girls arrived, Frankie had detected just a hint of disappointment. He had so wanted a son. Because sex wasn't a big deal for her and so happened only weekly, she had gone without the pill for many months after her decision before she was able to greet her husband one evening with a festive looking dinner table. In response to the questions "What's the occasion and where are the girls?" she had been able to answer "I'm pregnant again and keeping my fingers crossed that I'm going to give you a son." And he up and flew away for a conference the afternoon she lost it. Men!

Frankie and Christine were a matched pair. They had met at Smith in a freshman seminar and had roomed together for three years. Although Frankie was a tall, brown-eyed brunette and Christine was a short, blue-eyed blonde, they had a great deal in common. Perhaps because of class, New England parents, peer influence, or affluence both girls always looked preppy in coordinated, dun-colored mid-calf skirts, proper blouses, penny loafers, and understated make-up. Christine's never-cut locks were tied back with a few strands flying in the breeze around her clear-skinned forehead; Frankie's hair was always perfectly cut in a conservative mid-length style. But temperamentally they were very different as often happens with closest friends. Although Frankie was slightly unsure of herself, she was honest to a fault and when aroused could be quite forthright, incisive, and sometimes cutting. Christine's nervous habit of playing with her wayward strands of hair combined with her bitten-to-the-quick nails to betray an edgy tense woman whose uncertainty caused her always to wear over-sized garments so that her voluptuous figure would never be noticed.

Right now, after adjusting the one displaced hair and biting what was no longer left of a fingernail, Christine cautiously edited the thoughts about Eric's behavior into the response "Have you two seriously talked about finding a good marriage counselor? No, I'm not saying your marriage is on the rocks. It's just that I so wish you were as happy as you were during your first few years together."

That remark reminded Frankie of the Thanksgiving dinner at the U.S. consulate in Singapore. She and Eric had just finished their degrees; hers in pediatric nursing and his in government. They were in the Peace Corps. She was nursing in the general hospital and he was teaching at a high school. For her it had been love at first sight. It was probably his incompetence as a social being that had made him seem so safe. She found herself wanting him to ask for a date, but that didn't happen.

Back in Boston a year later they bumped into each other Christmas shopping in Filenes. She would have noticed him, even if she not known this well-built, good-looking-in-a-rough-way guy whose intensity expressed itself in his whole physique. You felt he knew what he wanted and where he was going. She had been impressed in Singapore by the image of social incompetence as she now was by the image of a strong, competent man. Perhaps it was the combination of strength and weakness which captured her heart.

That day in Filenes, Frankie took the initiative and suggested a shopping break for coffee. In the excitement of discovery and safe disclosure they found they shared values: a conservative religious upbringing (and a thoroughly secularized reaction to it) and a passionate concern for economic justice. "It's so rare to find anyone who gives a damn about the poor in the Third World" he almost spat out, an explosion whose intensity she both envied and loved. Born in 1952, both had grown up with Viet Nam in their living rooms, its killing fields uncensored and unedited. While the violence had horrified both of them intensely as children, it was later as college freshmen that the shooting of fellow students by Americans at Kent State University had radicalized them. No longer were matters "international" the hidden domain of specialists. They both had acquired a lifelong passion concerning peace among The Family of Man, treating as their bible the volume of photographs with that title. With so much in common and with sex sufficiently on the back-burner to make both very comfortable, it had been no surprise to Christine that they married although she suspected that only Frankie was really in love. Two years later the twins arrived, and Frankie had been a homebody ever since.

The girls' birth should have been an epiphany to Eric. It could have been, had there not been so many "important" matters commanding his time, his thoughts, and his viscera. Watching their emergence he had been filled with wonder, awed as never before. In that moment he lost all sense of self as first one, then the second emerged. For a brief time he looked into his wife's eyes in a new way until he was forced to respond to the nurse's request for "some room here." An hour later, waiting the chance to join the three of them, propped up for his camera's eye, the challenge had struck. 'How can I be adequate as a father of these two girls?' He thought of other men in his shoes and found no inspiration. They were hostage to their own needs, not to their progeny. Their children were held up as tokens, even proof of what they wanted the world to believe about themselves as fathers, but mostly as men. He found himself praying 'Eric, don't be like them. Love your children for themselves, not as reflections of you.'

From those thoughts he had moved on to ask himself how he might show his love for them – next month, next year, or at age fifteen. Love was so vague and abstract that it eluded his conceptual skills. His wife could have helped. Frankie could have told him that love is how you are with another, having little to do with intentions and nothing to do with definitions.

Sadly, by the time this reverie ended he had become lost to the true, glorious wonder of the birth moments. In the struggle to overcome an unacknowledged insecurity by achievement and preferment, he never allowed those moments to return. As the infant girls grew, his determination to put them first slowly faded. These days it made Frankie very sad every time she saw him struggling to meet the four-year-olds where they were, only to admit defeat with the rationalization "I have to get back to my study."

### 

To celebrate his return after a week away, Frankie's mom minded the girls while Eric and Frankie went out to dinner. To mark the occasion, his inevitable gray or beige polo neck was replaced by white, and Frankie had dressed up her normal quiet attire with a Hermes silk scarf printed with Van Gogh's Irises. They were barely seated before Eric began effusing about "this intriguing woman I met on the plane."

Frankie sighed. It was unnoticeable but expressed her continuing disappointment. Eric had been quite agreeable about celebrating his return. But now, instead of being with her, he wanted to relive part of his trip. "Oh well!" she uttered it under her breath. Then her activist propensities and memory went into high gear and she responded. "I've heard of that Mobil stuff in Indonesia. My friend Christine was telling me about it. There was a big article in The Christian Science Monitor. I got hold of a copy and read the whole thing. It wasn't just about Indonesia and Mobil. Our thirst for cheap fuel gets us involved in places you never hear about otherwise."

"You can say that again!"

"Apparently Shell is causing all kinds of trouble in Nigeria. One of their best-known authors has been arrested and is on trial for something like treason – just because he has spoken strongly against the damage which their foreign-owned extraction industries are doing to the jungles, the air, and the social structure."

"What about the social structure?"

"Well, you remember the way Singapore had so many expatriates from India who would see their wives and children back in India only once every three years? What is apparently happening in Nigeria is that men flock to the new industrial areas hoping for a job. They leave their families behind with grand promises. But the jobs are fewer and lower paid than expected, and families never see them again."

"You know, that's another great example for that course I'm proposing on Third World/Our World Politics. Thanks."

"I really get very upset about that mindless exploitation. In fact, every time put gas in the car, I find myself wondering what my cheap fuel has really cost. You know, what has it really cost some of those wives and children? Will their kids grow up as well as ours?"

"Well, I don't think it's fair to make it all as personal as that. I'm sure the Mobil and Shell shareholders want for their families the same things you and I want for our own family. So why pick on them?"

"Why not, when we Americans enjoy so much? Especially if what we enjoy is at the expense of the poor of the earth?"

Eric was unusually silent as he gazed at his wife. He had thought her the perfect mate from their first meeting. She had convictions. She was prepared to put herself out there and take the consequences. And she could think. He had forgotten. Now he was pleased that he could be having this kind of conversation with his own wife. He hadn't realized that her world was also still expanding. "The twins are really lucky to have a mother like you, was how his appreciation was expressed.

"I don't think I've ever told you how guilty I felt all the time in Singapore. We had so much! And that Thanksgiving dinner! Do you realize each of us ate almost a week's food by Malaysian standards? Why should we have so much when others have only a fraction of what we have?"

"I know. I feel the same. We are ten percent of the world, and we consume ninety percent of the world's production. It's wrong. But we can't give them what we don't eat. Remember Mom used to say 'Think of all the starving Asians.'"

"That's why I think your commitment to get globally-oriented courses going is so great."

"That's not going to be easy. I thought I'd start by proposing a course on foreign aid. That might seem a bit relevant because our government is already committed to it, and the topic comes up in Congress every couple of years."

Frankie was really warmed up now, not only by the topic but by the positive feelings surrounding their table. This seemed a good time to give at least a hint of her feelings about another topic. "You said this Indonesian wants to work on the role of women in revolutionary activity?"

"Yeah."

"What would you think if I said I was going to start up a radical movement here in Massachusetts that would upset our state government?"

"I'd say you were crazy. You've got the girls to worry about. You've always said they come first."

"But what if the issue was about state policies which damage the health of prepubescent girls? Would that not be part of my being a responsible mother?"

"Yes. In a way. But it would be irresponsible if they ceased to be your prime attention."

"Even after they start school?"

"Yep!"

"Well, you'd better think about that for the next two or three years, because what I'm reading in medical journals these days convinces me that someone has to do something soon. And I mean a lot more than writing an occasional letter. I even dream of starting a movement of mothers like me. When it's your own kids at stake, I am convinced that it is surprising what you can do."

### 

In the following week at his folks' cabin on the shore of Squam Lake, Frankie idly watched the girls playing on the tiny piece of sand they called "our beach." She speculated what Eric's response to her political activity might be in a few years. Then smiling to herself and at the girls' simple delight on such a balmy August afternoon she told herself: "He'll come around." He had in other ways. She recalled his total inadequacy in all matters domestic when they married. His mother had always waited on her kids hand and foot. But he had taken some responsibilities late in her pregnancy and even learned to put together a spaghetti and salad meal during the first few weeks after the twins' arrival.

At the same time, Eric was working his way up Mount Whiteface, a half hour away. The climb is not technical, but neither is it for wimps. In addition to the plain physical satisfaction strenuous exercise seemed to restore his emotional equilibrium. Such times alone also provided the time to get it together, without the interruptions and demands of the rest of his life.

He told himself that the feminist talk over dinner the other night had troubled him. His mother had been a great mom, and he put it down largely to the fact that, apart from her church work, she had given her whole life to her family for 23 years. Why shouldn't Frankie do the same? If his career plans were fulfilled, they would be able to get along independent of her family and without her working by the time the girls were in first grade. Maybe they would not be in her dream home, but it would be better than they now had, and one that they could afford with a family loan of the down-payment.. Then I could give all my energies to making education the major factor in benefiting all humanity rather than the few.

As always, he pushed himself to climb until short of breath, then to rest until his pulse slowed down to normal, then repeat the process. No matter if others seemed faster. Usually he would pass them later on, for they didn't have the sense or experience from boyhood which told him that listening to your own body is basic to hiking in the mountains. Soon his altimeter told him he had climbed slightly more than a thousand feet from the trailhead. The air felt a little thinner and was certainly more clear, and the sky was bluer. This is the life, he told himself. Fancy just lounging around down there by the lake like Frankie suggested. That's her choice. So be it. And it does work out for the girls. He seemed oblivious to the fact that it also suited him perfectly.

So in this kind of emotional freedom he sat down on a smooth rocky outcrop and allowed his mind to wander, something he never did in the city. The vista stretched to range after range almost endlessly. Mountaintops, he thought, command that we see bigger than we even dream. They brush away the immediate; the only limits are within us. There, for a time, we can slip the bonds of earth and dream. Oh how he loved being up here.

On this kind of exposure, only the oaks seemed to do well. This contrasted to the deep birch and maple woods through which he had passed. He mused at a nearby rock. No sculptor could ever produce the way those curves seem come together and then abruptly change. It's so wonderful. A chipmunk showed its curious face inches away from where his head rested on a rock. "Good-day and how are you?" said Eric. And as it scampered happily away to find something more edible he called out "Thanks for welcoming me. And good digging!" Then he closed his eyes, the better to hear the distant woodpecker's rat-tat-tat and the nearby junco's "twit twit" he felt completely connected to everything about him.

As usual when he allowed this to happen, he found himself reviewing "How's it going?" The answer was, "Very well." He was doing well in academia and had some great things to propose during their all-day faculty meeting in exam week in December. Although the meeting was still four months off, he needed the time to plan a presentation that would convince them to OK the department branching out into a more global approach to the discipline of political science.

The girls were doing great. What a thrill every time they went for a picnic. How proud he felt every time someone said "What beautiful girls!" He didn't even mind if they added "You can't be their father?" which he thought was a reference to his youthful physique.

After a long internal silence, Eric considered how things were going with Frankie. That was more difficult than the big cosmic questions. She's the perfect wife. Everyone says so. She certainly has created a wonderful nest for us all out of limited resources. I wish I earned more so she could get that other furniture for the family room. And it's great the way she has mastered Indian and Chinese cooking sufficiently that I no longer have these pangs of nostalgic hunger for the delicacies of Singapore. But I long for some real Hokkien Mee. There is something about the real stuff, cooked over charcoal, flaming as the man throws the oils and spices into the wok. So I guess I shouldn't complain, even to myself up here, about the fact that I am sexually very frustrated a great deal. But gosh! It was so difficult when my most beautiful student, almost my age, came to my office in a see-through dress, with nothing but pants underneath. Come on, Johnston. You know that you wouldn't have done anything, even if the college policy hadn't forbidden you to meet alone with a student behind closed doors.

After a long time of mental quiet, he found himself thinking about his courting days with Frankie. What a time they had at her place! Never had he known such glorious chaos. Her Mom seemed to instigate a lot of it in the large crowd who always seemed to be staying over or putting up here while they look for something that suited them. Why doesn't Frankie do that? I must ask her. I really did expect our home would be a home to others and it isn't.

### 

"You look all aglow!" and "Daddy, daddy!" came the greetings as he returned. "Have a great hike?"

"I certainly did. It was just wonderful up there. Such a great place to get things in perspective. And the rocks. I'd never quite seen them as I did today."

"Any revelations?" Frankie inquired of this handsome man who still made her think about him a dozen times a day, especially when there was that flushed face after a day in the mountains. She was really quite envious of the fact that he got so much from being up there, without her. Her envy shaded into resentment, then into pride, then into a sense of common purpose. But why did his single-minded devotion to justice in human affairs have to be so exclusive? Why did his profound dedication to the good of humankind exclude his family for so many hours of each week, even during vacations? Why, she asked herself, can we not be working really together when we want the same things? It just makes no sense! But I love him so.

Not having a clue to what she was asking he just replied, "Nothing new." Disclosing what had transpired in his mountainside self-talk was not only a matter of would not; for Eric it was also a matter of could not. He might have been highly intelligent and marvelously articulate, but none of us can verbalize those things of which we are not aware. And there was so much of which Eric was not aware — within himself, in others, and in their reactions to his own words and behaviors. Perhaps few realms were less explored than that great continent which spread so wide below Eric's consciousness.

### 

15

"I'm going to fix up that pressure problem in our well that has bugged us for so long." Eric announced at breakfast the next morning.

"Who are you getting to help you?" asked Frankie.

"I don't need any help."

"You do. You need a plumber."

"Whatever for? There's a leak where the pipes are joined that go down into that well. I'm pretty sure it was not tightened up by the plumber when he replaced the pipes. I could get him over. But I can do it."

Frankie gave up. Eric was competent, and any suggestion that he needed someone else to help was always greeted this way. So be it!

Not thirty minutes later she heard calls, as if yelled from a distance: "Frankie! Frankie! Help!"

She ran the few steps out toward the calls and the well, then stopped in her tracks, and laughed.

The well was "topped" about two feet above the ground with a continuation of the stone walls which went down to some three feet below the lowest level in the dry seasons. There, sticking up above the stones was a pair of legs flapping helplessly. A voice came from a head which must have been five feet further down.

Calming her inappropriate reaction, she hurried the last five steps and peered in beside the squirming tensed body, asking in her most concerned voice, "What's wrong?"

"You can see what's bloody-well wrong. I'm stuck!"

She couldn't help her response, "Would you like a hand?"

"Don't be so ... Just get some steps to put your feet at the same level as the top and give me a bit of a pull. I'm sure that's all I need to get back out."

Five minutes later, as if to say he had done it alone he added "There, it's all fixed."

But she couldn't resist "Sure is, once you're out!"

16

Eric did not appreciate the way Frankie told the story to the girls or the hilarity in which they joined their mother. Thereafter, whenever he proposed any job, one or the other would ask, "Do you want me to hold your legs?"' It took more than a year for him to share their humor.

# Chapter Two

He answered the phone in his office, "Professor Johnston here."

A woman's voice asked, "<u>The</u> Professor Johnston?"

Irritated at being interrupted in the middle of a conference with one of his better students, Eric snapped, "That's who you called, isn't it?"

"Actually," came a voice which he now recognized, "I wanted to speak to Eric Johnston."

The voice was so pleasant that he felt guilty about his abruptness, "This is he, but I'm not sure . . ."

"This is Minah, the Indonesian woman who so enjoyed talking with you on a flight to Boston two years ago."

He chuckled, "Both the professor and Eric are delighted to hear your voice, Minah! But how come?" Then, remembering her teasing remark as they said goodbye that day nearly two years back: "Is this Allah's doing? Just excuse me for a minute and I'll be right with you." Turning to Annette Cartwright, one of his best majors, he asked, "Would you mind giving me five minutes to answer this call, please. Then I'll be able to give you the time we need to figure out the best plan for your senior courses if you want to go on for graduate work."

"Of course, I'll be just outside when you're through," Annette replied, only too pleased to be able to do something for the mentor who always made time for her and treated her as though her concerns were the only thing in his life.

"Now I'm back," he said, picking up the phone again.

"I hope this is not an inconvenient time, but I simply had to call you now that I'm in Boston."

"In Boston? On your way through again?"

"Oh no. You remember I said I was going to do a doctorate in political science?"

"I do."

"Well, I'm enrolled to start at Tufts in January. They really liked what I said I wanted to work on. So I moved from Denver last week and am sharing an apartment with another Indonesian student."

"Well congratulations. Tufts has a fine political science department! Not quite the equal of my Harvard one, of course, but still quite excellent."

She mimicked "Of course!" and he found he couldn't resist chuckling again. It seemed like a continuation of that high they had shared "hanging in the sky" from Denver

Eric regained his equilibrium, "You're into four courses then and for the following two semesters to get your master's. And a couple after that before you get onto the thesis? That's normal. It's a real grind. But I'm sure a tough woman from Northern Sumatra can cope. But what about your husband? What does he say to all this?"

"That's another story. And I'll tell you in a moment. But about the time and the masters requirements, Tufts was quite impressed by what I had done for my honors degree in Djakarta, and they were very interested in what I plan to do eventually, back home. To write a dissertation about such a topic really impressed them. The bottom line is they have given me quite a lot of transfer credit and are not going to require any masters thesis."

"You are a favored one."

"Yes. I think so. And I'm very grateful. So what point was there in exploring any more schools? But you asked about my husband. That's the sad news. We had a terrible car accident. And I was in hospital for weeks and then in physiotherapy for nearly a year. But he was not so lucky."

"He was not . . .?"

"He was killed outright."

"I'm sorry, very sorry for your loss." His mother had taught him the right things to say even though his immediate thought was "What a beautiful young widow? She's calling me! And she's right here in Boston."

"Thanks. We don't always understand the will of Allah, but we must accept it. And I do."

Eric didn't know what to say next. He had never felt quite so confused. He should be thinking about life and death, yet his feelings were nearer to those surrounding his first high school dance. After a long silence, he blurted out, "Coffee! Would you like to have coffee sometime?"

Her response carried just the right sound of surprise, as though she had never expected this to be more than a formal greeting, "Why, yes, if that is convenient for you." She was not about to confess she considered him to be a real "find." The truth be told, she had not met a single American who had both an intellectual and a gut understanding of what it was like to be from a poor nation. Many said they understood, but they had not lived there, and they certainly did not look at her intensely as she shared her passion about the injustices of global economics. She was delighted at the thought of a local friend who empathized with her. It never occurred to her that his intense listening was more a matter of style than of substance. Nor did he.

His mind was racing through the possibilities, and the fantasies, about what might come from this out-of-the-blue development. On the possibilities level, he immediately thought of dancing with her. He could just imagine what it might feel like to hold that body. Then he realized "but she's a devout Muslim, so it would have to be the joget." His mind then went into neutral, idling without motion in any direction. If asked what he was feeling, he would have told you what he sensed in his body – an unusual level of energy, even excitement. Further inquiry would have elicited nothing other than "I can't think about anything else but that delightful woman" or the more Freudian "she has such lovely breasts." His idling mind came up with nothing more than the sensation: I feel just great!

###

Because fantasies often determine the direction of a conversation, they had finished coffee and were not long finished talking about the details of her accident and the miracle that she was even walking today when he asked, "I'm surprised how well you walk, given all that had to mend. Do you think you will also get back to dancing? I know it means so much to you."

She looked touched, as though she hadn't expected empathy from this man, intelligent and attractive though he was. The boyish naivete concerning his own emotions and his motivations appealed to her, although she felt he needed some help in channeling his enthusiasms if they were to produce rather than destroy. All this flashed through her mind intuitively as she voiced the words: "Honestly, I don't know. But I'm sure going to try," a little bit of uncertainty crept into the normally radiant smile.

He liked that. And it made him confident enough (God, what am I doing?) to ask: "Look, I have an oddly timed class from six to eight Wednesday night. What if we go to Tommy's Place and see how it feels."

"What do you mean?"

"Well, Tommy's is a place where there's great music, good drinks, and not too much noise. It's also away from the college environment. Remembering the Islamic issue he added, "Maybe you could teach me how to Joget. I'm no dancer, so there's nothing about ballroom skills I would have to unlearn."

### 

Wednesday they went. And they danced the joget. Neither could believe the power of their experience. Because she knew what to do and felt the strength had returned to her body even if the flexibility had not, they had barely started to sip their drinks when she arose and ordered, "Come on. Here's where we see if you can walk your talk, as they used to say in our exchange program. Or at least, if you can dance it."

"But . . !" he started, but was cut off with

"This one is slow. If you start out with a slow set, it will be easier."

She could not believe herself as she took two paces and turned to face this very confused professor who had such need to be in complete control. Poor thing. He looked so forlorn. Her body was already moving with

21

surprising ease and a grace that he associated with the movement of wild things but was too rarely seen in humans over the age of nine. She gave him the most encouraging smile he had ever seen and said, "Just watch me with every ounce of you, listen to the music, and let your body mirror my movements." The unintentional seductiveness of that smile was all the encouragement needed.

Eric could not believe what happened. As one who loved physical activity and music, especially its rhythm, he should have been less surprised. For almost as she spoke he found his feet and hips moving, not in some haphazard way, but with hers. In fact his body quickly began to feel as though it were part of hers. He could not say whether he was copying her or she him. The movements were all natural, not the sexually exaggerated forms so current in Western dancing. Every part of her moved, without exaggeration and without effort, responding to the music – its ebb and flow, its minor changes between dominant beats. He found himself chiefly aware of Minah and her body and only minimally aware of what he was doing. If a shot had gone off in that room, he would not have heard it.

"Wow!" was all he could say when he sat down at the end of that quiet set.

She glowed. "Now do you see why dancing was the most important thing before my accident. But don't sit down. You're ready for this fast set they're just starting." How could he refuse? He felt that, without intending and without any effort, he was somehow responsible for a glow in this woman's whole being which he had never seen in anyone previously. And just because we danced? And what happens as I look into her eyes and cannot let go for an instant, am lost and yet so found, so safe and so warm. With more self knowledge than was yet available to him he might have said: "Isn't it wonderful how certain we can be that we have found what we were looking for?" Or again: "We are as connected as I have only felt with nature."

### 

Little wonder that the following Wednesday Frankie had dinner early with the girls because "Eric is working late at the library after his evening class." It became a habit, justified by "only in the evenings, at the library, can I get some things done."

###

When they weren't dancing and some of the time when they were, their conversation would have seemed weird to most listeners. Time and again they would come back to the issue of the rich nations and the poor nations. "I share your resentment," Eric would assert, quite sure that he was coming from the same place as his gorgeous partner – with whom he held hands at the table but never touched when they danced. "Really odd!" was a common, barely audible comment from patrons nearby.

### 

"No you don't!" was Minah's usual response when Eric claimed to share her feelings about global inequities. She was testing the impression of empathy he was so determined to give.

"How many Americans," he would defend himself, "have you met who feel as passionately as I do that we should do much, much more for the poor – in Southeast Asia, Latin America, Africa, and so on?"

"That's not the point. We don't want handouts of your surpluses. We don't want gifts we can't move from the ports because we lack roads. We don't want to be helped out. We want to be enabled to help ourselves."

"You don't have to get so angry with me about it. I'm on your side."

"I wonder. Why do you think the U.S. gives anything away? Certainly not out of compassion for kids suffering malnutrition."

"That's what our representatives say when the issue is debated in Congress."

"But who gets the aid?"

"I don't know what you're getting at."

"Which nations get the aid is a matter of whose side they are on in the Cold War."

"Well, yes, as I think about the recipients I certainly don't see any pro-Communist countries on the list, no matter how poor."

"That's just the point. The votes are there because in Washington committees and in its hallways, they all know that the real agenda for aid is to export The American Way."

"What do you mean, The American Way?"

23

"I mean the expansion of human rights and democracy."

"And what is wrong with that? It's precisely what most poor nations lack and need. Look at what Soekarno and Suharto have done with your country. No poor nation will ever get on its feet until its citizens are truly free."

"Do you know something, Eric? I think that when you propose a course on foreign aid" and again with the mischievous, adored giggle she produced at the strangest moments, "you should invite me in one day as a guest lecturer."

"And get myself fired?" He teased her in return. But she was quite serious. She also realized he could not begin to hear what she wanted to say. No aid is acceptable if it comes with the condition of surrendering the basic values of one's culture. Hers come from Islam. No help is really help if, even inadvertently, it takes away from people their self esteem, their sense of worth, their equality as humans. She wanted to say that Americans must learn to respect others' values. That they must learn to co-exist with values different from their own. That they must learn to co-exist with values which are even antithetical to their own. But she knew he could not hear such thoughts. So she left it for another day, thinking that, for the moment "ti d'a pa", as they say "at home" when they are content to leave it until tomorrow.

# Chapter Three

Some weeks later Minah began: "Eric, I know you're happily married, but I want to ask something very unusual. I guess I can ask it largely because you are married. Any single guy would misunderstand what I'm about to say."

He returned her intense look, his whole being on the edge of the chair: "Go ahead."

"Could we become intimate friends – without it getting sexual, that is?"

For a second time with this woman the highly articulate Eric was speechless. All that came out of his mouth was a strange variation of "Uh?"

"I know," she explained, "that there is no model for intimacy without sex between a heterosexual man and woman, but it seems so stupid. Doesn't it? So?"

His thoughts were not platonic. He could not imagine not wanting her the more if they became closer. No artist, he always scribbled or sketched on table napkins, and of late found himself drawing curved lines all over them. To others they would have been nothing but scribbles; to him they represented the curves which were peculiar to her body, shoulders and head, the shadow of her breasts, the relation of waist to hips, and so on. But he was not about to admit any of those fantasies to her. Instead, with an appearance of buying into her idea of a potential experiment in male/ female relationships, he found himself saying, "I have an idea. Let's go out to Walden Pond for the afternoon, say after my noon lecture Thursday? Then we can talk there without interruption, and privately. It would be wonderful if what you say were possible. I'm willing to try."

### 

Leaving the car and starting around the famous "Pond" he said, "Well, here we are. Let's go that way!" He pointed towards a path which looked excellent, but was marked 'Path temporarily closed. Access forbidden'.

"But the sign says. . ." she began.

"Oh! That's for others," he casually dismissed her hesitation. "I know what I'm doing. I come here all the time. There's one muddy section, but that's all."

Having already taken charge, he asked as they set out, "Where do we start?"

"Why don't you start, and tell me all about yourself?" she replied.

He could not believe the next thirty minutes. He talked non-stop, beginning with several stories about his warm, close, but somewhat standoffish New England family – his perfectionist, religious mother, his ever-busy father. He recalled with some hesitation that he had never felt he was good enough to merit his mother's approval. ("If I got ninety-eight, her inevitable response was 'Why not one hundred?'") By his standards, he then modestly went on to talk about achievements: valedictorian, leader of the high school debate team, star of the regional Battle of the Minds, the number of colleges that had vied for his attendance. "All through academia," he began to wax eloquent, " I've had a growing sense that I'm in this world to do something big." He could not believe he was voicing these thoughts. "Governments are all so parochial, and representatives are so concerned to please the voters. Why? Because they simply don't know the big picture. And why don't these intelligent people know the big picture? Because teachers in high school and college never share it. They simply prepare students to fit the status quo and please. The world can be different, and I'm going to influence education so that decisions are more informed and more concerned with the total picture." His assumptions about the need and the desirable direction of change accorded with her own. His solo heroic approach, however, seemed sadly immature to this woman with 'on the ground fighting experience.' But he has a vision, she told herself, and that's the start.

"What about girls during your adolescence?" she interrupted when he appeared ready to launch into his specific professional goals and attainments. There was a long silence. She was quite content to let that be, certain that important things were rumbling around, perhaps unmanageably, within her new friend. There was no hurry.

He recommenced his recital, but now it was a halting male, not a successful professor, who hesitantly ventured a disclosure he'd hardly made to himself, let alone to any other: "I have real trouble with women. I've had a strange history with women. I guess you'd have to call it unusually repressed. I've always been very attracted to them, gone out of my way to please them, sought their company rather than that of guys, and had their kind of interests – music, ballet, literature, and art – rather than the Red Sox, football, and all that stuff. But," he felt he had to add, "I've always been a good swimmer, tennis player and fanatical hiker."

"And?" she helped him to continue.

"Well, you won't believe this."

"Try me."

"Well, for all my smoothness with and interest in women . . ."

"Go on. For all your enjoyment of their company . . .?"

"Yes. For all the enjoyment of their company I was a virgin when I married. In fact, we had been engaged for months . . .I had done lots of necking with other girls before and even more with Frankie, you know, in the back seat, out by a brook, up in the mountains, on front porches," again he subsided into silent reverie. Or was it more? For some reason quite beyond him he revealed: "I remember my first French kiss. I was nineteen, and thought I had done lots of kissing. But this young woman was a senior that I had been obliged to partner for a dance. When I showed her to her door she made it obvious we might kiss. Her mouth was open, so I opened mine. She put her tongue into my mouth, and so I did the same. I was so stimulated I said a quick good-night and never saw her again."

"You were saying that you were a virgin when you married?" Minah helped.

"That tells you a lot about my upbringing, doesn't it? In all my playing around I had no difficulty in controlling my sexual urge because I didn't feel any. In fact, I had been engaged to Frankie for six whole months, with lots of petting, before I was conscious of wanting copulation. And I know I was normal because , once married, I found my appetite for sex was far greater than hers. So there was something about my upbringing that would not allow me to acknowledge what I wanted. Wow!" Eric paused. "I can't believe I've told you all this. I think it must be your turn." A therapist might have enabled Eric to surface the realization that he had felt "safely known" by a woman for the first time in his life.

She sensed what an effort as well as relief this disclosure had been for Eric. She sensed that he had never disclosed most of this to a living soul. But he had to her. For the moment, no more pressure. He needed to be quiet with this unprecedented situation – of being vulnerable, without pretensions, in the company of a woman.

Related memories from her life welled up. There had been major gynecological problems in her history which she had never shared with any man. Her reproductive problems (could she really even call them that?) had been seen by Mahmud as a divine punishment for her refusal to be as submissive as any Muslim male expected a woman to be. Now she found herself beginning her sharing at this most sensitive part of her story.

"Well," and she hesitated. "Your statement has pushed me back into the most painful part of my own story. I guess if we are to be as open as I want us to be I'd better tell you about that." She told how, in her late teens, a uterine infection had been so mistreated that she was unable to bear children, and that this had not been shared with the wealthy, charming, much older Mahmud with whom her parents had arranged marriage.

"I cannot believe they did not tell him. What could they have been thinking of? Of course he wanted me to bear his children, many of them, ideally. So when the first year of our marriage had passed, and I had not become pregnant, he insisted that I get the advice of a gynecologist. I went to a well reputed woman and reported back that there seemed to be some reason why my eggs were never fertilized. He was livid. 'Are you saying it is my fault? My former wife died bearing my seventh child? It must be you that's at fault.' So I paid another visit to the doc and reported that further tests showed that I had a problem which was inoperable. He never did learn that the problem preceded our marriage, but neither did he ever forgive me for not giving him a second set of kids."

"How did he express that?"

"Do you really want to hear that? I don't know that I can bear to recollect the details."

"Perhaps another time," he surprised himself saying with real concern that would have surprised his wife because she never received such consideration.

Changing the subject, she went on to enlarge on what she had told him on the plane about her Aceh background with its strong, independent women and its anger at Mobil's exploitation.

Then to his own surprise and in words which fed her deep hunger, he found himself suggesting, "Your marriage must have been a terribly lonely one?"

She stopped, and looking deeply into a face that she wanted to be really sympathetic, she whispered, "No one will ever really know." She turned away, perhaps to hide the damp cheek, and he found his arms encircling her from behind. This was not sex; this was basic caring about another's pain which at that moment seemed to fill his chest to breaking point. They stood in silent stillness. As she started to turn his hands dropped and two sets of eyes gazed into deeps beyond all words. For how long, neither could have said. But when they moved on, it was hand in hand, like a small boy and girl. The silence said more than any words he had ever spoken.

She eventually broke the silence with something unexpected. "I have to tell you that I did not expect the depth of feeling that I am experiencing in you."

"And," he interrupted, "I have to say that I did not know I would say the things I have said, and I would never have expected to find anyone who would treat me with the level of acceptance which I have felt with you."

"So we're intimate friends?" she asked with confidence, needing to verbalize the obvious because it was so obvious and so wonderful, even while it was almost unbelievable.

"Sure are."

"Then," she parried with that teasing look, "I have one more thing to ask."

"Which is?"

"May we make a pact? That each may ask anything at all? And expect an honest answer?"

"You don't ask for much, do you? But I supposed you warned me about Aceh women."

"Well, are you willing to do that?" she pursued in a voice which was far less demanding than her normal style.

"What do you think?" he teased, making his response obvious.

At the end of the afternoon he hugged, then kissed her. From his perspective, it was a tad more than a brotherly expression of affection.

### 

Minah's return to her friend Rugayah's apartment was greeted with the demand, "You look like the cat that's swallowed a goldfish. Come on. Tell us. What's it all about?"

"Something really wonderful," the words just tumbled out. "I have a real male friend. A real friend. We just talked and talked and talked, about all kinds of very personal things. He was so open. And I felt I could be too, and safely, without feeling I had to protect myself from sexual advances. No hokey pokey! Isn't that the way they say it? Anyhow, the wonderful thing is that I now have an American male friend, safely married, with whom I can learn about American men before I run any risk of involvement with one of them. I've had one awful marriage, and I am not going through anything like that ever again."

"Just a moment. Slow down. All you told me about this afternoon was that you were going for a walk around Walden Pond. Anyone would think, to hear you, that you'd met the ghost of Thoreau and had been spirited off to another dimension where you met a person quite beyond anything I have met."

"Well, it's like this. I've had coffee a few times with Eric, the professor I met on the plane two years ago. He is attractive and highly intelligent., When he's with me, to his surprise he is real fun. He's funny too. He doesn't mean to be. It just happens. And when I laugh at him he sees the humor. I don't think that has ever been part of his life, as a stuffy, straight-laced New Englander."

"Sounds like a great date to me. Could he even be Mr. Right?"

"Not exactly. At least not now."

"What do you mean, not now? All the words you have used, combined with the glow all about you, looks very much like Mr. Right has entered your life."

"Well, I guess he has. I could imagine Eric in my life, always. He needs someone like me to help him to be more realistic and to strategize. Together I think we could make a big difference in lots of ways. Of course, he's also very responsible, or he wouldn't be in a home of his own with twin daughters and a wife. I can just see us . . ."

"To hear you, I would think you had just had a proposal, but then didn't you say something about him not being Mr. Right *now*, or something like that?"

"Yeah. I did. Right now he is married with twin girls, and believes he still loves the wife who gives him a little of what he wants. But I doubt whether she provides any of what he needs most."

"And you could? Don't be crazy."

"I know. One minute I say it's platonic; the next I start to dream. Anyhow, that's not what today was about. Today was one of the most wonderful in my whole life."

"Tell me more."

"I decided he was a potential platonic friend, and the walk was to explore that possibility. It was a risk I decided to take, because I'm so tired of the way these Americans come on to me. It worked. It worked. We even ended up with a promise to ask and answer anything which comes into our minds. And he will. And I will. And it's wonderful."

"I just hope you don't get hurt," was the caring response of her friend almost an hour later.

### 

Eric was in a daze. So much had happened in just one afternoon. He had spent the most incredible afternoon with the most beautiful woman. It had been an afternoon beyond anything he had ever dreamed. She had filled his every sexual fantasy since that first Thursday afternoon coffee.

Every time he laid eyes on her he found he feasted on her from the top wisp of raven hair right down to the daintily shod toes which always peeped out seductively from the sandal style of shoes she wore – so different from the practical clodhoppers which, truth to tell, always annoyed him. Because any Indonesian woman would take such male appreciation as no more than a compliment, Minah responded to Eric's appreciative glances with innocuous smiles. He read them otherwise, finding the toes especially stimulating and viewing her smiles as a sexual response.

But that was before this afternoon. He had held her in his arms. She wanted to be held. They had even kissed. "I don't believe it," he told himself. "This is what Romeo must have felt. First the joget experience! And now this?"

Slowly, very slowly, the physical replays of the afternoon gave way to the rest of the afternoon's events. He found himself recalling all the topics and all she had said. It all felt so good. He recalled her tears. What had he said or done that allowed her to be so expressive? Such a public display was quite beyond his experience. He had triggered it. That much he knew. But how? Not to worry, he told himself. He found himself elated by it even though it was beyond his comprehension. The mystery made it even more of a high.

When she had proposed an "intimate relationship" he had been unable to suppress a sense of sexual excitement. What else does that word mean to a man like Eric? Eric and Minah certainly had different things in mind when she used the word. Now that he had experienced intimacy without sex, would it still qualify for that platonic label? The fact was that to Eric, every word and every confidence had been as much a symbol of sex as had the gentle touches which had so stirred him. That the stirrings had not all been sexual passed right by him, unnoticed. The walk did nothing to modify his conscious definition of the word 'intimacy.'

Only when half asleep, well on the other side of the bed from Frankie, did he realize that never, no never in his whole life had he so trusted another human being. The things he had disclosed were such that he hesitated to look at many of them. Yet he had held them out for her to see, hear, analyze, and . . . that was beyond him. But not since his early teens had he felt so secure, so safe, so certain that the world was totally good, and benevolent, particularly toward him. As sleep took over, all he could think was, 'It feels so, so good.' He also fell asleep conscious that his penis felt so, so hot.

32

# Chapter Four

Subsequently their meetings took place every Thursday afternoon immediately after his noon lecture. Each week they would talk and argue, particularly about what she insisted was "U.S. exploitation" and "colonialism of the mind".

A month after the Walden Walk Eric had an idea and called Minah suggesting that she might meet him at his office. It was easy to find, for this campus had clear signs everywhere and his second floor office was equally accessible. The stylish gilt name plate on the door indicated that this was indeed the door to the "assistant" professor's domain. So smiling to herself and without hesitation she knocked gently and heard an immediate warm invitation, "Come in." She was hardly in the room when he was on his feet, closed the door and enfolded her in his arms. He did not attempt to kiss her but settled for a big bear hug. The embrace felt so warm that Minah simply let herself be, safely held, by a man she trusted completely. It was not the welcome she had expected although she admitted to herself that she liked it, very much.

At the same time, Eric could not resist the temptation to explore and his hands slipped down, first just inside the elasticized waist-band of stylish slacks, then gently moving back, forth, and around over silky underwear, luxuriating in the feel of the skin and the form which the thin material enhanced more than it veiled. Yet his hands ventured no further fearing that his action might be seen as 'going too far.'

Minah was in a quandary. This was the same man with whom she had felt so safe. She had been confident that this was developing as an intimate but completely platonic relationship. There were so many reasons to believe that was so: his avowed happy marital state, his lack of pre-marital sex and no history of affairs. Yet why were his hands where they were? And why was the door closed behind him?

At the same time two feelings were welling up inside her. The first was the easily acceptable, indeed eagerly desired feeling of being cared about. It was possible to talk to Eric as she had never talked to any man before, not even the older brother to whom she had always been the protected "little" sister. The last weeks' coffees had been a continuation of the easy disclosure and discovery of things about each which had never been shared. And with all her heart and soul, she wanted that to go on.

She ventured into second feeling with real apprehension. She liked his hands there. Their movement gave her whole body a wonderful glow. Something deep within was saying, "Go on."

Nevertheless, she demanded, "What are you doing?"

Yet she did not move for the words "Telling you that we are both completely safe, together" were just sufficient to allow continuation of the pleasure.

Then came a long, rich silence for him and a complex set of wonderings for her, which climaxed in her comment: "There's something wrong with your marriage, I think, or you wouldn't be doing this."

With his hands continuing came a terse denial, "There's nothing wrong at all. My marriage is central to my well being. And to my daughters'. There's nothing wrong with it and I'd never do anything to damage it."

There were many things she could have said, but it was not in her cultured nature to discomfort another. She knew with deep certainty that Eric lived in a different world from women, while being deeply dependent upon them. Nor would argument have been in harmony with the deeper need and long-term desires which had begun to surface – since the Walden Walk – that, just possibly, she might one day marry this man. So, for many reasons, some quite unconscious, she was relieved when he relaxed his embrace, and they both sat down.

"What is your take on Congress's action of reprimanding the President?" She asked, knowing this was a sure way to get Eric's attention going in a new direction.

"You mean for using federal fund to mine Nicaraguan harbors without any declaration of war by Congress?"

"Yes. Will you mention it in your Introduction classes?"

"Why should I?"

"Why should you? Sometimes I can't believe you, my dear. They, your poor brainwashed kids need to know that this nation is doing that kind of thing all the time. And you have every obligation to point out in a political science course that these behaviors, as demonstrated by people like the honest patriot Colonel Ollie North, are against your constitution, and they make us in the Third World despise you."

"Wow. You really are into it today. But thanks for jogging my conscience. I really do owe it to them to make use of this topical example concerning the War Powers Act."

When they stood to leave and exchanged a simple hug (to her relief and some disappointment), she was surprised to find herself open to his next words: "Do you know that the Seneca tribe of Indians lived right here for two thousand years, at least? I've got a crazy idea."

He paused, seeing the puzzled look at mention of Indians. But the look was about more than Indians. He caught the uncertainty in her face but plunged on: "Would you humor me? Next Thursday I thought we could play a game, of re-living their life, in a campground not far from here."

"What? You are crazy. What for? How?"

"Just for the hell of it!"

Without understanding what was involved and in a state of considerable confusion, which state right now she just loved being in, she found herself saying, "OK!"

Gazing down at her in delight, he was again completely lost in those dark pools just below his, an experience unprecedented with any other woman. Thus submerged, her voice surprised him saying: "Lots of the Koran can be interpreted in a number of ways, but not the surah which condemns adultery. That is absolute. And I am a very serious Muslim."

"I know that and respect it fully," came his reassurance.

### ###

The following Wednesday evening it was same time, same place, same dancing, with a certain tension between them which was new. Given today's headlines it seemed unavoidable that he opened up a conversation about the Ayotullah Khomeini. But Eric was brought up short by a simple question: "Just where do you get these ideas about Islam?"

"Well . . . ," and he paused, not wanting to admit that the popular press was his own chief source. The pause was her entrée, and he found himself being lectured by a stern teacher:

"Americans seem to assume, and their reports play upon the assumption, that Islam is some terrible, uniform fanaticism shared by a fifth of the human race. They also seemed to assume, until this whole business with the Shah's expulsion from Iran, that all Muslims are Arab. Only one quarter are Arab. And as for being all the same! Why, the Ayotullah himself claims that he has had revelations from Allah."

"Really? I'd always been told that Muslims hold that the last and final revelations were given to The Prophet."

"That has been generally taught to us, yes. But the Ayatollah is something again. He claims his revelations supersede some of the teachings of The Prophet (Peace be upon Him)."

"You're kidding?"

"I am not. Your papers have been full of stuff about Khomeini ever since I arrived here, which was just after he returned to Iran in 1979, from exile in Britain. And it's all sensationalistic. You know, the approach that keeps people excited, without helping them to understand the dynamics of a situation. I guess you have to do that to keep people buying. But it's sad."

"I agree. So educate me. What has been going on in Iran?"

"Do you have an hour?"

"Well, what about half?" he smiled.

"OK. Here's the short version. But I have to go back to the roots of the situation in Iran – when it was completely controlled by outsiders."

"A few years?"

"Oh no. The roots of the present situation go back to the great days of the British Empire and all that. Being used and belittled for six, maybe even eight generations creates a deep anger kept alive by memories within your own family."

"Yeah. I know. I even got a whiff of it when I was in what is now a very independent Singapore. We'll all be living with the fruits of colonialism for many, many years."

"In the early 1800s, Britain made an arms deal with Iran as a safeguard against Napoleon moving towards their "crown jewel" colony of India. That deal made the Iranian people completely dependent and more impoverished than they had been but without any of the goodies that had been given to real colonies like India."

"You mean the Brits took but invested nothing?"

"That's about it. The only residents who had anything were either British or Russian. Even cottage industries were undermined. Merchants, who had long operated camel trains, were put out of business by new rail lines and the telegraph. That went on for a whole century."

"Then?"

"The merchant class started to rebel at the beginning of this century, supported by the Ulema."

"What's that?"

"The Ulema is the name given to the learned men of Islam, who are considered the guardians of its legal and religious traditions. For a whole century they were of various persuasions. Some like Karim Khan studied the Western tradition, and his follower, the Bab (which means the gate) produced a new scripture. The Bab even had a woman preacher in his following who removed her veil as a symbol of the end of female subjection and the end of the old Muslim era of the traditional law, the Shariah. His followers saw him almost as a messiah and created great unrest until their leader was executed in 1850."

"Doesn't sound like my preconceptions of Islam at all."

"Their battle for justice did not die. It spawned two quite different movements- the one we all know today, the Bahais, and a broad movement in this century in which clerics and laymen, secularists and mystics, believers and atheists joined to challenge an oppressive regime."

"That variety is hard for us to believe, given the media image of Khomeini as such a single-minded spokesman of a faith we can't critique."

"I'll get to him in a moment. A couple of other big things happened before he showed up. First, Turkey became a fully secular society under Attaturk. The Persian Ulema pushed for a change of equal proportions, but with a constitution based on the Shariah, but they lost. A new Shah sold out completely to Western oil interests. This was followed by a new constitution under Reza Khan which was more ruthlessly secular than Turkey's. But religion was still around, ready to rise as soon as the limitations of this new regime became apparent."

"When did that happen?"

"Not until the 1960's. By then the gulf between rich and poor had increased enormously. Because of the Savak, the secret police, fear ruled the lives of most, and the great majority of Iran's population felt as though it had become a foreign country. Qum had become the center of Islamic scholarship where one brilliant teacher, Khomeini, was brave enough to speak out against the Shah. A riot ensued, many were killed, and he was arrested. Student pressure gained his release after only a week, but he went right on preaching, and was arrested again."

"He must have been like a Martin Luther King."

"I think not. He was not impressive by your standards. He was a very inward man, for before all else he was a mystic. He was convinced that social change had to happen, but that it would be worse than useless unless it was also accompanied by spiritual transformation. Shiites always recognized he was a mystic by his withdrawn look and the monotone in which he spoke and even preached. Everything I've read says that he felt he had just finished the requisite "journey to God" when the Shah set the Savak upon the people. That made him ready to begin the activist part of his life – what he called the 'outer Jihad', to distinguish it from the struggle to align one's total being with the will and the spirit of Allah. He called that the 'inner jihad'."

"I don't get you."

"It's the battle within oneself to control one's social action so that it has the effect of Ghandi's 'soul force,' really changing things to be as Allah wants. For five years now he has been trying to get diverse factions to work together, but with little success. The students who thought they were helping at the U.S. Embassy really hurt his efforts more than they helped, initially throwing a bad light on our faith. He is doing all he can to keep the people on a spiritual path while they try to change their nation. He has pushed through much legislation to help the poor by creating organizations which provide employment and improve their self-esteem. But he is not the government head; he is the supreme spiritual leader. The head of state is Rafsanjani. I profoundly admire the Ayotulloh."

"Wow! I see you do! Thanks. I'll have to get into the related literature. Hearing you makes me feel so ignorant about matters which are so important to my country nowadays. And me a professor of political science!"

### ###

Frankie and Christine met for lunch every Tuesday. Frankie found herself feeling quite defensive when Christine asked, "What's with Eric these days? He seems very quiet and more critical concerning little things you do than I've ever seen him."

"I wouldn't say that!"

"Come now!" Christine persisted. "He even glared at you when you told him we might be a bit later than usual. That's absurd. Is he having an affair with one of his grad students? You know how common that is. I'll bet they are all crazy about such a good-looking professor. And I imagine he is a very good if demanding teacher, just the kind that would turn on one of those older students. You know they're almost our age."

"That's absurd. He'd never do a thing like that," came her quick defense. But it started a fresh stream of thought. She considered for the first time how easy it would be for him to play around. I have no clear idea of how he spends all those other hours when he is not actually in the classroom. That night she dreamed of being one of his students. It was horrible. She could not understand what he had just explained. She had to ask. But he answered every other student before attending to her question, and when he said, "Now Francine, what is your question?" the period ended, and she awakened in confusion.

Eric himself awakened with unusual vigor the next morning but feigned sleep for half an hour after Frankie got out of bed. As he approached the breakfast table he sensed that Frankie looked ready to make demands. He had no idea of her troubled sleep, his own mind being full to exploding with dreams about what might happen with Minah later that day. Yet for all his preoccupation, something told him that he was likely to be engaged in a long, uncomfortable, demanding conversation over coffee. That was the last thing he wanted. His behavior slipped into automatic. Perhaps that explanation is too kind. Eric certainly would not have acknowledged the accusation that the next few minutes were manipulative; they were really one of several ways in which he routinely controlled his wife so that life together demanded less of him.

Although his spirit was singing within, when she placed the eggs and bacon before him his "Thanks!" was very quiet. Instead of immediately picking up the utensils and eating ravenously, as was his custom, he paused, head bowed.

"What's wrong?" his caretaker inquired.

"Nothing," was accompanied by no eye contact; it appeared that the raising of his head would be an effort. Then, slowly, and still not touching the food, "I feel off, this morning."

"That's no good. What's wrong, darling?"

"My neck is just awful. I must have the wrong pillow or something." With these few words he affected an even more pained posture and began to play with the food as though his debility was so great that food held no interest.

"You poor dear," came the predictable words from his rescuer wife, who had completely forgotten her own concerns as she was seduced into consideration of his. The meal passed just as Eric wanted it to do, and he drove off feeling on top of the world.

# Chapter Five

Later that day Eric collected Minah as arranged, and in an hour they were playing around with a mini tent. She then watched as he took two inflatable mattresses from the trunk, unscrewed their valves and, as if by magic they thickened and grew straight. He then slipped each one into a cover and pushed it into the tent. Dazed, with a little voice asking what am I doing here, she stood back, as if to say, this man and his tent has nothing to do with me.

"Come" he invited, and she followed as they crawled into a space which was just big enough for the two pads and their occupants. "Oops! Forgot the pillows!" He was quickly gone and back again.

With the smile of a little boy at play, as if addressing another eight-year-old of the opposite sex, he announced, "Indians never wore clothes on a day like this." She should have anticipated this, she told herself. What was she to do? Why had she come this far, on a "little boy" adventure with a man whose penis would obviously outmatch his feigned maturity. But wasn't his unawareness of dynamics part of his attractiveness to her? Yet another part of her was suggesting that very boyishness might be a superbly crafted piece of masculine manipulation. While granting the possible element of truth in all these thoughts, two feelings dominated her being. First was the absolute certainty that the man who had disclosed so much on their Walden Walk was to be trusted, albeit into very strange territory. And second, that she wanted this, whatever it was – or almost.

Lack of headroom seemed no impediment, for in no more than twenty seconds two bodies were stretched out on their backs, stark naked, looking up through the tent's vent hole into deep blue heavens. That sky offered no

41

comment upon what it saw below, where two people shared the sensation of having been deposited right through that hole into an uncertain world where they were quite alone. Both felt quite uncertain about what they, or the sending gods, would do next.

This breathless touchdown was followed by an awesome quiet, a quiet which neither seemed eager to break. The situation was so unbelievable that both felt quite out of body, yet each acutely aware of their own nakedness and of the other's. But to move would break the spell. So they just lay there – perhaps for ten, perhaps for twenty minutes. This crazy situation was all his making, he should have called the next move, but they had reached the end of this boy's conscious fantasy. It was she who eventually broke the silence, with a half-question, half statement: "You like my breasts, don't you?"

Both knew this to be true. Whenever together his attention alternated between her face and the cleavage which two delicious scoops created, made the more obvious by her choice of fitting knitted tops. She had always enjoyed his staring – had even wanted it as from no man she had ever met. The enjoyment was the greater because he seemed to believe she did not notice – to such a degree that she uttered many an unexplained little giggle. She certainly never considered visually challenging those looks, which sometimes went beyond ogling, to the point of visually undressing her. At the same time, he had always felt self-conscious about that behavior, for in ogling every other attractive woman, he had never fantasized them naked. Now, with her words, he felt freed to express the pleasure he felt in just looking directly at that part of her anatomy. Indeed, he had come to ask himself, have I ever seen another human creature quite as beautiful as this one?

"Whenever I look . . ." he started.

"Don't!" She interrupted. "Don't tell me! Show me!"

With this permission, he raised himself on one elbow and used the other hand to barely follow the curve of one breast, then the other. "Yes." Was the only sound from her.

Looking at one nipple pointing straight up at him he began to reach for it, but a better idea intruded. Ever so gently his tongue moved around the aureole, time after time, around and around. Her bosom rose and fell on the waves of her deepened breathing. The central focus seemed too precious for speed, demanding that he waited – forever it seemed to her

42

– until at last his tongue reached the center of its orbit. When his lips enclosed and held the very large nipple she gasped.

To kiss her he had to be over her. She drew him down so that every inch of skin was to skin. "Shhh" was all she said and their mouths melted together – ever so softly and naturally, as if they had been known to each other forever. But his penis, touching her belly, was saying something more. As he raised his body off hers and partly kneeled back her hand moved to cover her pubic hair.

Eyes asked eyes, "What?" "Why?"

Eyes answered eyes, "No."

"You asked me to caress every inch of you?"

"Yes."

"You responded so . . ., I don't know how to say it. Ardently? It seemed this is all just as wonderful for you as for me?"

"Yes."

"But now you say . . . ?"

"No! That's right. We talked about this on our wonderful Walden Walk. The Prophet (Peace be upon Him) reported Allah's clear command concerning adultery. And no matter how much I want you (and I do, I do) no matter how sincerely you might even love me, I am not your wife."

"But, but, be sensible. You want me?"

"Yes."

"You want me as overwhelmingly as I want you?"

"Oh yes, with my whole being. I've never really wanted a man before now. Certainly not that old bear my parents pushed me to bed. But with all my heart I love you. And I want to say that with my body and soul."

"Then . . .?"

"Then you must acknowledge that I am Muslim. Islam means submission. Not to you, to Allah. No matter how I feel, or how you feel. It is what must be. Or, I suppose, it's what can't be, as long as, in this country, you are married to another – even though I'm a widow."

43

There was silence for a few minutes, he still kneeling over her. Then she stifled a little giggle.

"What?" He demanded. "What's funny?"

"Look," she explained, and there was no doubt about where she was directing his attention. "He accepts it."

In a different mood in the car she asked: "Have you always been a crazy man?"

"What do you mean?"

"The whole idea of today! That was really crazy. It all took me back to when I was little. We used to dream up all manner of situations. Just in words. We had a game that required the other girls to come up with the best – I guess you would call it a follow-up – to the situation one of us had described."

"That sounds fun. We never did anything like that."

"So today was out of character for my professor?"

"It certainly was. I don't know where it came from. I have never done any crazy fantasizing, not even as a boy. I guess you must have tapped something in just the right way. I don't know how to say thank you adequately."

Nor did she.

### 

The family room was their haven. With the kids tucked in and a good home-cooked dinner proudly presented by her and really appreciated by him, Francine and Eric were settling down for a quiet Wednesday evening. She felt quite pleased with the way their home was coming together. The rug on the oak floor had been such a bargain, and it was just perfect. Its frayed edges and two worn spots didn't detract; they made it look like a real valuable bit of old Persia, even if she'd only paid $100 at the consignment shop. It was a good fit with Eric's recently acquired adjustable leather chair and Mom's expensive cast-off sofa. But those brick and board shelves along one whole wall and around the corner! She remembered his pride: "Look how professional the edges look. You'd never guess they were plywood." But they had to go. This was not the way she had grown up, and it was only his need for independence which prevented her from accepting what her parents so badly wanted to give them. She dreamed of getting most of those books into his office (at college), or into his study in the attic. Then she could buy that armoire and matching piece which would complete the décor just the way she wanted.

He interrupted her review: "Is that the girls? I thought I heard a little whimper. Why don't you go look?"

"Why don't you? You're their parent as much as I." She made for the girls' room down the hallway, thinking "Why argue? That's a man for you."

"Jennifer is rubbing her ear again, and says it hurts," she reported. "She's been pulling at it all day, and I just dismissed it. Suppose I don't want to deal with another ear infection."

"And now?"

"I just stroked her forehead and whispered 'Go to sleep. It'll be fine in the morning.' I'm sure it will be."

But half an hour later a tiny plea penetrated his review of that morning's meeting: "Daddy! Daddy!" Frankie hardly needed to catch his eye with a non-verbal "Your turn!" before he was on his way. He returned almost as fast as he had left. "She's burning up. You've got to do something!" and passed the shivering bundle into his wife's arms.

The thermometer screamed at them: '103!' "You get the Tylenol, I'll run a tepid bath to help cool her down," ordered the efficient part-time nurse. "I guess I was just wishing she wasn't running another of those ear infection fevers."

"I don't believe it. You a nurse, and you let wishes get in the way of responsibility. You would never have done that in the hospital."

"My dear, you wouldn't believe what we sometimes did on the night shift. But right now, let's hope that she will sleep the night through so we can get her to the pediatrician first thing in the morning. Or, I suppose to be realistic, in the afternoon, for that's when his office hours are. He spends the morning at Children's Hospital."

Only at breakfast, with one very concerned little girl trying to comfort her whimpering sister, did Frankie raise the issue: "Who's going to care

45

for Nicole this afternoon? It is bound to be a wait. I don't want to take them both in when Dr. Ruskin examines Jennifer. And Mom is out of town, visiting her sister in Florida until Saturday. Could you get away? Do you have any classes Thursday afternoon?"

The response exploded silently within him: Thursday! Damn! What do I do now? This is the day I meet Minah after my 12 o'clock class. How can I let her know I won't be at Tommy's Place as usual?"

He found a solution: "I have to get into the office for an early appointment, so I'm going an hour early to beat the traffic." Two minutes from home, a phone booth enabled him to get Minah on the phone before she left for her first class. Predictably, she immediately agreed that his daughter must be his first concern. "See you next week, then," came the cheery end to the conversation.

# Chapter Six

Most of their subsequent meetings included physical intimacy, but always short of copulation. They found more private and comfortable places, the most frequented being Minah's apartment, for her friend gladly adjusted her schedule to leave it to them early some Wednesday evenings, as well as Thursday afternoons.

"God, I'm grateful we can come here," came from the man lying naked on the bed, watching the just showered Minah walking towards him through the bathroom door. "Stop right there, if you don't mind. My being here and able to look at you like that is something I could never have even fantasized. I'm sure there's no more beautiful body in the world than the one I'm looking at right now."

She was aware that her nipples had hardened in the seconds that he had been drinking in her every curve and hollow, even her slightest movement. Perhaps I should not enjoy this so much, maybe not at all, were thoughts quickly dispatched. I feel like a queen, that this body was made to be adored – by this man. Oh, how lucky I am. And then, remembering their first meeting, she smiled at the thought of what a tiny "push" by her had been required to bring them together, albeit together in a way far more consequential than any in her mind as the plane landed that day in Boston.

As she lay down next to him it seemed natural for her head to be on top of an arm which curved perfectly around her neck and was just the right length to cup one breast. She was barely able to take in that reality when his other hand was in her crotch, one finger tenderly seeking, seeking. And she felt SO warm.

In this position they simply luxuriated for a long, long, time. When they did move, it was for the longest, deepest kiss she had ever imagined. What she could not believe was the ease with which it all took place. This man was no self-styled 'stud' who had slept around. He had always been an uptight New Englander with a sadly repressed sex drive. "But I have freed him!" she exulted silently.

On his arrival they had exchanged no comments of any moment. She had simply said "Make yourself comfortable" while pointing toward her room, "I'm going to take a quick shower." He could think of nothing but to disrobe and climb onto the bed where he had listened and watched like a starved teenager. Now, twenty minutes later, their most immediate hunger somewhat assuaged, another aspect of their relationship entered the room.

"Did you see the news about Beirut?"

"How could I avoid it? On every newsstand! In every broadcast! 243 dead! Can you believe they could drive the truck close enough to kill that many? I thought the US was wary, with all sorts of precautions, after the Iran hostage business."

"What I want to know," posed Eric, "is whether this constitutes an informal but very real declaration of war by Islam."

"What? What do you mean 'by Islam'? That's absurd."

"Well it certainly looks that way. Here are a bunch of US soldiers guarding the Embassy in a country which is mainly Arab with a notable Christian majority, and some Arabs crash through the barricades of what is, by international law, US territory."

"Wait a minute, my love. Let's get a couple of things clear. A minor one is your strange notion that their population is Arab and Christian, as if those were quite different."

"Well, they are."

"No way! The Christians in Lebanon are of various denominations, but they're almost all Arabs. In fact the Marionite Christians are an Arab branch of Christianity."

"You do know a lot," was all he could say.

"But the important thing I want to say, the thing I am really reacting to, is your identification, your equation of Islam and Arab. That's absurd. It is true that most Arabs are Muslim but, and this is the main thing, only a minority of Islam is Arab. By far the majority of that fifth of the world that holds our faith is to be found in my country, in South Asia, and in Africa. None of those peoples has anything Arab about them."

"OK. So?"

"So don't go suggesting that the action of some Arabs is representative of Islam. Some Arabs are part of Islam, but they don't represent us."

Affectionately pulling her to him again, he meekly whispered, "Yes dear."

### 

And so it was every time they managed to be in his office behind the closed door, or in her apartment. Such moments combining physical intimacy and the education of Eric in global politics even occurred when they were confident of privacy through the Fens, that wildly natural area was adjacent to the Boston Museum of Fine Arts, only a mile from her apartment, and less from the coffee shop. When the weather was good the outdoors was preferable to any of the other places. There they had some privacy and the freeing environment of nature.

In the middle (she hoped) of a long embrace (with mobile, searching hands) on one such occasion she mischievously asked, "Have you always fancied yourself as the great lover?" There was no problem with this as tease, but now, neither was there any problem in exploring the answer within himself. The intellectual question took his mind off the other growing problem – a new level of sexual frustration.

"Well, I have to admit that my level of sex drive is so much greater than I had ever dreamed when frustrated by Frankie. That was minor compared to this."

"But it fits."

"But it fits? With what? What do you mean 'it fits'?"

"It fits with your attractiveness. You are one very sexy man. You exude vitality. That is what really made me respond on the plane. Didn't you realize that? I felt sure, before our Walden walk, that you had always

49

known that women are attracted to you. I watch the way they notice as you walk by, or at Tommy's. I bet all your female graduate students have bets on who can lay you first!"

"You're kidding?"

"No. This is very true. You are tall, with strong musculature. You have an interesting, face, with strong features, and you have a smile which invites people to join you in enjoying life. And you are so intense, in walk and talk, that you are almost yelling: 'Let's all really live. Come on! Wake up! Life is grand!' What woman wouldn't fall for such a combination?"

"Oh. Go on. You're not serious. Remember we vowed to give honest answers?"

One direct look and he realized that his skeptical response had been taken as an affront to the sacredness of this relationship to her.

"I apologize. And I am delighted." Then, mimicking her style of tease: "I'll have to test this attractiveness on another woman some time."

For that he was silenced in the most enjoyable way, reminding him of that senior's kiss in college, but much nicer. All of which completely changed the subject.

Then, out of the blue, as happened so often, he introduced another topic. "I had a great session today with Annette, my favorite student."

She eyed him for a moment, then teased, "I'll bet you did - just as when I visit your office."

He was about to retort in defense when he caught the faint twist of her top lip, and they both dissolved in laughter. "It was a great session," he began again. "She's looking to graduate work in our field. She's really into international politics, and so I told her about you."

"What do you mean? What did you tell her about me?"

"I told her you were doing a degree at Tufts which ties into your activism back home. She was fascinated to hear about Aceh, and especially about your freedom movement. She wanted to know where she could learn more about the role of Mobil in Sumatra, and wondered what the ties are to the Indonesian military. I told her I didn't have a clue, but that I would introduce you so that you could ask her yourself."

"You did what?"

"I told her she would get all the answers she wanted if she asked you directly. You have all the facts, plus first hand experience. Plus a different view from the one which is hawked by our officialdom, and theirs."

"You did what?" Minah demanded even more loudly this time.

"That's what you asked before, and I've just given you a summary of my conversation with her - with Annette."

"And who is this Annette?" came inquisitorially.

"What do you mean, 'Who is she?' I told you. She is my best graduate student, and she'll go a long way."

"I had thought I understood you Eric, but you continue to surprise me."

He cut himself short after the words "Well, I try to keep . . ." when he caught the steely set of her mouth. "What is it? What have I said?" There was real fear in his voice, but no glimmer of understanding what was out of line.

"I really can't believe that you are a political science scholar. Have you forgotten all you ever learned about how the games of politics are played?"

"Whatever are you talking about?"

Again she looked at him – at this man she so loved – now with some horror on her face. "You don't know what I'm saying, do you?"

"I don't have a clue."

"You are such a boy. You don't know this Annette, do you? I mean, you don't know all her connections, her family, their politics, their possible connection to Mobil? You cannot be certain what she will do with the facts you gave her about me?"

"No," came a little sheepishly, betraying the first glimmer of awareness of what had so disturbed her. "No, I'm not sure about any of those things. But she is a fine young woman with high principles."

"That, my dear professor," she began to lecture, "is not the point." He now looked the little innocent in an adult world. He rarely considered the consequences of talk, of sharing, of questioning. His own motives were pure; why ascribe anything less to others? As if reading his thoughts she continued, "Without knowing, you could have hurt those I love most dearly; you could have jeopardized their cause. And did it never occur to you to ask me whether I would mind if you shared these things with her? Or if I would be happy to meet her and answer her questions?"

He was no fool. Put thus his actions were thoughtless, possibly harmful, and certainly embarrassing to this woman he loved so much. How could I be so insensitive? was all he could think as she kissed him gently on the cheek and turned to leave.

### ###

If asked to express his idea of 'family', Eric would have answered very quickly: "The girls" and "Thanksgiving at Gloucester".

During the forty-minute drive from Needham five-year-olds Nicole and Jennifer spent most of the time fantasizing the meal. "I'm going to have four different pieces of pie," boasted Jennifer.

"And I'm going to have five different kinds of ice-cream," countered Nicole.

Frankie turned the talk to "Who do you think will be there?" and in no time they arrived.

Who was there? Well, if you counted, and Frankie's mother Edith certainly did as she planned seating arrangements, there would be thirty-eight.

"Only thirty-eight? Last year there were nearly fifty."

"Well, forty-seven to be precise, but my brother Tim is working in Germany this year, so that's five less. Then Amy's husband won't be there because they're divorced. Oh, and my Uncle Andrew and Aunt Martha aren't well enough to travel up from Florida. And don't forget that Dad's elder brother died this year. And then, when you add Michael and his wife Mary from college, and Eric's friend from Iran . . ."

"You get," interrupted the precocious Nicole, "thirty nine. Does Gran know she's counted wrong?"

"It won't matter."

"It never does," laughed Eric.

It was a big house, a great sprawling place with verandah all around, quite open now because the screening which converted half of it for summer use had been stored for the winter. Inside, you felt like you were in a guest house, with the same old-style furnishings, but with the addition of galleries of photos at every second turn between large, ornate frames which contained paintings which had been darkened almost beyond recognition by age and dust.

The women seemed to head straight for the kitchen, bearing six kinds of pies, four hand-churned ice-cream makers, and prepared ingredients as well as the bags of dry ice. The latter was essential to the making of what several would always declare was "the best ice-cream I've ever tasted." All fifteen children anticipated the production as well as the eating of that product, arguing about and competing to turn the handles – until it became too stiff, first for "the little guys", and finally for all but the "big strong guys."

It was a mystery how eleven mothers all fit in the kitchen, or how all seemed to find a job. At least, all except Aunt Mary who quickly whisked Amy off upstairs for the "chat about your new life" (as a divorcee) which she no longer need postpone and which poor Amy could no longer avoid. The others, assisted by or perhaps assisting Edith's housekeeper and her sister (imported for the day chiefly to do dishes) seemed to be busy either in making the gravy and other extras, or checking on the table details which "Edith never does take enough care about", as her younger sister whispered to Frankie. The stuffing, tying, and trussing of three enormous turkeys was always a test of debating powers, wills and skill. Once the oven gave off their characteristic odor the poor birds were viewed and poked so many times that it was a wonder they ever finished cooking. But eventually the order was given to "Go and find the children and tell the men it's time to sit down."

"The men" could have been taken from a period photo – except that one lacked the required suit and tie. That exception was the academic in the tweed jacket and his 'best' polo neck. Three older men were smoking, while the younger ones seemed to be doing their best to avoid the lethal clouds which billowed from Uncle George's customary cigar. Eric was so involved in holding forth on "the latest fiasco in Washington" that he hardly noticed the noxious environment he would otherwise have avoided like the plague.

The children were not so concentrated. Terrance had fallen in a puddle and looked like it, while Nicole was last to appear – after her dad went off to the old tree house which he knew to be her favorite spot in Gran's small, but densely wooded "natural garden." Seating them could have been chaos would have been, had Gran not been the supervisor: "Any six here, four there and five there," she commanded, quickly ending any disagreements or complaints with "That'll be fine. You'll still get fed." To the surprise of all the younger parents, the children cooperated. "There's something about her," was the only explanation they could produce between them. But their gratitude knew no bounds.

Edith's husband, now eighty four, still expanded visibly as he rose in response to her "Now ask the blessing, will you please father?" Somehow the two paid help saw to it that everyone received more than they desired –of every single part of the menu – eventually to the accompaniment of groans, real and pretended (to tease Gran), at which time several took a break in more relaxing positions and places "to make room for dessert". The break was needed, in any case, for the eager youngsters to turn those five handles – until the going got tough, at which time fathers' strong arms were recruited to finish the ice cream.

Just when second cups of coffee were almost finished, today Eric, but usually his brother-in-law Basil called, "Time for football!" Eric's Iranian guest Ahad looked at Eric questioning, and was told that this always comes next. After much talk the teams were finalized, with two able males on each, to be backed up by four who did little more than walk, three feminists determined to show the guys a thing or two, and six or eight children apiece. It was bedlam - but great fun. Except for "a slight mishap" which was unavoidable as long as testosterone even dribbled through the systems of eight males.

A later walk, in the dusk, ended in the one great living room where the youngest were now getting testy while the three of Edith's generation were ready for a little peace. Eric was always one of the last to leave. He really wanted to stay forever. His feelings during this annual celebration - here in this house, under Gran's bounteous auspices - were among the most treasured in the whole of any year. "It's always so great. Thanks Gran." So, with hugs all around, and that still took fifteen minutes, they were in the car headed home.

While Eric would have given two answers to the question of his image of "family" – "the girls" and "Thanksgiving at Gloucester" - if you insisted he give just <u>one</u> image of his ideal, he would have replied, without a moment's hesitation: "Thanksgiving at Gloucester." Without knowing it, more than anything else in the world he wanted the warmth, stimulus, acceptance and safety of a big sprawling family, from which you can go at will, and to which you can always comfortably come back. In that situation there was no uncertainty, no fear of the unknown future, of what some "he" or "she" might do which would endanger, discomfort, or even destroy. In that situation there was "everything" which made life worthwhile. Where else could one be so free from fear, and sated by that for which, though undefined, he had the deepest yearning? He treasured what he had (at Needham, with the girls), but he wanted much more, even while he knew it would never be his lot. But was it the actual situation for which he yearned? Or was it something more abstract, yet also more concrete, which the person of Gran symbolized? It would take a very grown man to make such a distinction, while one fully grown would know it was vain to make such an attempt.

# Chapter Seven

Two weeks later, Eric and Minah had enjoyed their customary Wednesday dinner and were ready to leave for Tommy's Place. Their food had been good, but not the service. As the slovenly waitress left their table with her tip Minah asked, "In line with our agreement about asking each other about things, I have a question – or maybe two."

"Fire ahead."

"Why did you give her a full ten percent tip when she has been so unsatisfactory?"

"I don't know. It's the thing to do."

"And why did you tell her 'Thanks so much!' with your best smile?"

"My Mom must have taught me."

"Alright, let me try a different wording – of what is really the same question. Why do you treat men so differently from the way you treat women? It's the case with your students – there are always women waiting to see you, and never a man. When we are leaving a gallery or a store you always give a woman a big smile and an effusive set of comments – almost like you are trying to talk her up, but I, of all people, know that's not the case. But if it's a man who has fallen even slightly short of the attention you feel is called for you are quite gruff. Why the difference?"

"You do ask hard ones!" He tried to escape into their usual light banter.

"No. Really. I want to know. I want to know you better."

"Truthfully, I just do not know why. In fact, I didn't even know that I treated the two genders all that differently."

There was silence for a few minutes before Minah asked: "Sometimes, when I have really won an argument with you, or demonstrated that I know more than you do about a particular subject . . ."

"Never," he tried the teasing approach again.

"Oh yes, from time to time. Anyhow, when that happens, there's a long silence. Sometimes for minutes, once for a half hour in the car. But never, never have you just told me not to be so arrogant, or anything like that. I thought you were angry at me that time in the car. But after a long silence you just 'returned' as it were, with a big warm smile and a new subject. It left me puzzled."

"I don't know . . . didn't know," was all he could say.

"And then, there's the way you talk about Frankie. Do you say to her the kind of things you say about her, to me?"

"Wow! You are into the awkward questions today. Well, yes and no."

"Yes and no?"

"She says I just go off into a gray silence whenever I get mad at her. I say I'm not mad at you. She says 'Liar!' Then I find something else to do."

"Sounds just like you were with me that day in the car."

"I don't think I'm ever mad with a woman. Well, except Frankie. I do get mad at her, as you have heard. But I never blow off at her."

"So what does happen to your strong negative feelings towards women?"

"I don't have any."

Minah lapsed into silence to consider what had been said. They were now full circle, with Eric contradicting himself. Pointing out that fact would gain nothing. And clearly Eric himself had no answers to what puzzled her. Nor was it simply an academic question. His relationship with Frankie might well be replicated with Minah herself, if her dreams were realized. And she wanted something much more, much better than male silence and withdrawal in times of domestic conflict. Moreover, she wanted her man to be out in the open with her, not hiding behind some wall he built whenever that was the most comfortable 'out'.

She had also started to wonder about the charm he always laid on with women –as if something compelled him to please them – even that unsatisfactory waitress. But there was no way she would push this any further today. For now, warm smiles and touches, all completely honest, were the best forms of interchange.

At the same time as she was lost in thought, so was he. Was it true that he treated the two genders so differently? To be honest, he could not recall one female (except, of course, Frankie) towards whom he had felt anger or even annoyance. Didn't he get along famously with the departmental secretary, and with all the female work-study students? Who were certainly much more reliable than the guys. Come to think of it, the women assistants in the library were always pleased to see him, greeted him warmly, and gave him superb attention and service. No, he concluded, Minah must have it wrong. But he decided not to say so just now.

Then, each having settled the matter within themselves, without a word, they now joined hands and left the restaurant, embarking on a fresh topic of conversation, Minah waiting for another day, and Eric all unknowing that this matter would become the center-piece of the biggest change in his life.

### 

"I'm having difficulty dealing with discombobulating differences."

"You're what?" asked his puzzled colleague, Michael.

"It's been on my mind for weeks. I only just came up with a name for what troubles me. Not just for anything that's different, but for those differences which really throw me for a loop. A good expression for being thrown for a loop is to say that you're discombobulated. It's also a good way to make the point that it is a very confusing state. It's more than a mental confusion; it's a mess that makes me unsure of myself. I want out of it."

"So then you just had to state it in a more striking way?"

"Sure. Why not? But seriously, I have to deal with this problem – the upset which these differences cause. There isn't any option."

"OK, you have my attention. What differences, and how do they upset you?"

"Well, I started out life where we all start, acting as if everyone thought as I do, wanted the same things, would die for the same things. My world as a child was a safe, predictable place. Everybody around me understood what I said, why I said it, why I was happy or sad, and so on. My view was that anything that did not fit, ought to. Sure, there were variations in taste, and differences of opinion, but I could just shrug my shoulders and ignore them. Basically I would have to say I was quite intolerant. The product was a youthful Eric who knew who he was, and how the world worked. At the end of high school neither identity or meaning gave me a problem. Both were given by the culture and accepted by me without question."

"We're all that way as kids."

"Yeah, and it's a wonderfully secure world. It makes sense. And it tells me clearly who I am, and where I stand in my world."

"Until something, or someone, really upsets the assumption that all good folks are like this, think this way, etc.?"

"Exactly! Well, for me, with noble ideals about helping others, I studied other cultures, wrote papers about human needs in the non-Western world, read news items, and got the Peace Corps bug. I decided as a sophomore that I wanted to make the world a better place, and couldn't wait for graduation. I was going to spread the good American life. For two years, I would contribute to that by service as a teacher in Singapore."

"And that's what led to this upset?"

"Well yes, a bit then, but more now, through my relationships here after returning. But first, what happened there. In Singapore I did meet real differences, real otherness."

"How did you get comfortable with them?"

"Some differences really upset me for a while – like Singapore's limitations on freedom, and the beating of some found guilty of quite small offences. But for the most part, I opted for a comfortable kind of tolerance. You know, just in my head, not in my gut, because it cost me nothing. I soon learned to shrug my shoulders and say "That's their way. They'll see the light in time. They should. I also feel I should help them do so."

"Pretty superior, weren't you?"

"Absolutely! I had, and still have no doubt that our Western heritage is the way it was meant to be. For the individual our ways lead to greater happiness and fulfillment. From all I know, that makes sense – of history, of human nature. What I have learned, particularly by being in another country, is that those people "out there" are not the same as me, and I am now a lot clearer on whom I am. I guess mainly by contrasting what we stand for with what they seem to live by. Moreover, this is my world, and I like it. So do all the people I care about."

"Present tense? I thought you were telling me what was, in Singapore, but has now changed so that, as you put it, you are discombobulated?"

"Yes. It's Minah who has discombobulated me. It's a new experience, in spite of my having spent a year in Singapore. And it has nothing to do with love. Or almost nothing."

Michael could not resist the comment: "Discombobulation is surely a new word for it!"

"No! Seriously! Until I met her I never thought twice about whether they, in Singapore, might have a clue about how the world fits together and what the good life looks like."

"How has meeting her changed you?"

"Well, these days when I hear someone criticize Muslims I take it personally. I feel as though they are criticizing me. I cannot prevent myself from defending them. It seems only fair, if they can't defend themselves."

"Sounds like you really identify with Minah, and by extension, with others who share her faith, Islam."

"That's right: I think of her, of what she would be feeling if she were present. And I talk on her behalf."

"Sounds like she's part of you."

" Given the great arguments we have about her faith, I can't believe that. But maybe she, a Muslim, is now part of who I call myself, of what I am, of my identity. If I were to shut up on those occasions I would not be true to myself, to who I am."

"And that's discombobulating?"

"Very; because I'm not the person who went to Singapore, so certain of Western superiority in every way."

"I have to say this all makes lots of sense to me, a Francophile. My time in French West Africa was only brief, but I love Paris. I get so defensive when Americans start to tear the French apart, I just have to defend them."

"Sounds as if we are both in about the same place. It is discombobulating, isn't it?"

### 

Concerning Eric's sex-life at home, though something must be said, the less the better. Frankie was accommodating to the increased frequency of Eric's demands. She behaved as she had been taught that 'a good wife should,' but with growing puzzlement. Indeed, in one weak moment she found herself blurting to her friend Chris that "Men are such animals." In bed, Eric found himself aggressive and sometimes rough. While inside her he vacillated between imaging the true object of his unbearable craving and anger that this body beneath him was keeping him 'quarantined' from the woman he loved. In a word, it was a bad scene.

During the next few times Eric and Minah were together he simply controlled himself. He determined that he would not get into it again with this 'submissee.' If there isn't such a word for one who puts the will of Allah first, there ought to be. He would not get into it about the frustration of their mutual yearning. But the occasion did come when the dam burst - in anger at Minah:

"You are so inconsistent!" he blurted, without any preamble.

To her the words came out of nowhere, and her expression was a mix of confusion and hurt. Eric had never been other than gentle, except when very confrontive about impersonal issues on which there was a disagreement or a misunderstanding. She felt hurt at the tone in which these words were delivered. There was real bitterness in them. The accompanying look said to her: 'There is a wall between us. You put it there. But I'm the one who is excluded. How could you?'

Insightful and skilled as she was in listening she sought to hear him out, and to understand these feelings, so alien to everything that had brought them so close and so trusting; in fact, so perfect that she could not believe how Allah had smiled.

"You're referring to . . .?" giving him room to end her question.

"I'm referring to the fact that one moment you give me your very self, your soul - as if this is quite acceptable according to the Koran. The next moment you tell me that I must divorce if we are to copulate. One moment you give me your body so that we are really more physically intimate than I have ever been with my wife. Then you tell me that the one, small step beyond that is forbidden."

"Is it such a small step?"

"In one sense, in the sense of which I am speaking, yes."

"Well then, why the fuss? If it's such a small step?"

He almost screamed "damn you." but substituted a long silence, during which they slowly relinquished the strands of touch which symbolize connection, or the loss of it.

# Chapter Eight

It was a full-day meeting of the department, during exams, when every student was pulling an all-nighter either to cram or to complete a paper, and none were looking for professorial guidance. All staff proposals had been read in advance. Early afternoon they came to Eric's part of the agenda. He knew just what had to be said. He was completely confident about its rationality. No doubt about his colleagues' agreement clouded his horizon as he did the customary throat clearing. He was about to lead his department toward a better world, even by this first small step.

Eric began with an impassioned statement about what he had seen of poverty in Southeast Asia, and how guilty he felt that all of us here have so much ("We spend more in a week than they do in a year.") In his mind, This established the need for the course.

"So here is the outline of what the course will cover:

1. The Marshall Plan and Macarthur in Japan

2. Early unilateral aid

3. The proposal that 'trade is aid'

4. Aid as part of the Cold War

5. Our aid efforts compared to other nations

6. The role of Non Governmental Organizations

7. Technology sharing as aid

8. The work of the United Nations Educational Scientific and Cultural Organization (UNESCO), the International Labor Organization (ILO), and the World Health Organization (WHO)"

Considering he'd said enough to start a conversation, he sat down. What followed left him gasping. His least favorite colleague, Beverly Thompson (characterized by his friend Michael as "The only man on campus who wears a skirt") was on her feet and making it very clear where she stood on this proposal.

"I have seven criticisms to make of Dr Johnson's proposal for a new course. After hearing them I believe you will agree that it is not worth the time of my Curriculum Committee to even study his proposal. My reasons are:

1. Your real aim, Mr. Johnson (she was clearly demeaning his doctorate) is to encourage bleeding hearts. So why not admit that openly?

2. We all know that the days of the aid craze are over, because it has been shown to be useless.

3. This nation now has better things to do with its money, here at home.

4. I know that the UN peaceniks say we should have taught more about Southeast Asia and then the US would never have bought into the mess which France had produced. But we're not a colonial nation with colonies we need to help so that we can continue to use them like Britain and France.

5. Our kids would be better served to learn about the politics of aging, or water in the West, or how lobbying is organized. We ought to have more coverage of these and many other domestic topics.

6. You personally are not qualified by your graduate education to teach in the global arena. So stop trying to make a name for yourself as an innovative professor and help us get the essentials of politics well taught to all. And encourage our majors to dig deeper into American soil. There's more than enough there – and it fits our competencies.

7.  Finally, if you were to teach this course, who would pick up on the sections of Introduction to Government you'd probably want to drop to fit your course load?"

"So," she concluded, "I move to table the proposal."

"Seconded!" came a chorus of agreement.

"One comment," injected Michael, Eric's only real friend in the department.

"You are out of order, Mr. Gibson, but be brief."

"I wanted to say that if we were to follow Beverly's reasoning, we would fire tenured people every decade or so and replace them with specialists in matters which are important but have arisen since they were hired. That's all till later."

Michael's suspicions about Dr Thompson were close to the truth: In his mind, she was "a masculinized woman", who was determined to come out a victor in the race for academic preferment. She simply knew that men were only interested in one thing, and that they expected to dominate in academia as everywhere else, and that there was no way she was going to let this happen any time she could prevent it. Moreover, Eric's style of speech and bearing got under her skin even more than most – he seemed to make such a point of being "male" that she felt it demeaned all women. How often, as they passed in the hallway did she find herself asking, "What self-respecting woman would live with such a man?"

For that time, over that particular issue, her wishes won.

### 

His steps were heavier than usual when Eric walked in the front door of his home that evening. When the reverberations from its banging had ceased, a small voice from the kitchen ventured, "Bad meeting?"

"Are you kidding? Those so and so's can't see the woods for the trees. They wouldn't care if the whole world went up in flames as long as, by some way or another, it didn't affect them. The selfish bastards!"

"I wish you wouldn't . . ."

"Wouldn't what?"

65

"I wish you wouldn't swear that way, at least when the girls can hear you. And you're so angry. They are a bunch of brilliant people who must have good reasons for the opinions you see as 'selfish'."

"There you go, taking someone else's part. You are supposed to be my wife not their support team, when I walk into my own home."

"I'm sorry I came across that way. What happened?"

"I don't think you care."

"Of course I do. I really do. So they voted down your new course proposal?"

"Yeah! Eight to two! Only Michael supported me. And you should have heard the way that bloody Beverly tore into me. She started by taking apart the data about demand and student interest and the course load issues. That was just understandable. But then she became personal. It was she who led the attack. The others seemed to feel they had to go along. I almost felt they had ganged up on me in advance. The narrow-minded, self-centered, xenophobic bastards!"

"Eric, the girls!"

"Damn the girls. I'm sorry. I didn't mean anything about the girls. It's you. Here I am, wounded personally, even while my finest plans are scuttled, and all you can talk about is what I say in front of the girls."

With that he had stamped off to the bathroom, only to reappear when the call from a little voice the other side of the door said, "Daddy, mummy says dinner is on the table."

### 

How different he felt when he heard Minah's telephone voice saying, "Sure I can get to coffee at three."

"You look so grim, so unlike yourself," were her first words after their warm, appropriately brief embrace.

Looking into her eyes he saw her need – to understand, to support, to help – and felt different in an instant. Proof that he felt different, different from the way he had ever felt in a moment of disappointment, was the statement which came without thinking, "I so need you. I so need you to help me with the fact that I seem to be unable to get them to hear me."

66

"Who? Your departmental colleagues?"

"Yeah!. They just seem to have their minds made up before I open my mouth, so I never even get a fair hearing."

"Tell me what happened." As the coffee was slowly consumed, and long after the clientele had changed not once but twice, he talked and she listened. After more than an hour of history, going way back to his first days in the department, during which she nodded, smiled supportively, and gave those sounds which indicate the listener does care, she asked quietly, "So what are you going to do differently to turn this around?"

That question had never occurred to him before. From Frankie, it would have brought a defensive listing of the need for 'them' to change. Now it brought no defensiveness, but several practical thoughts such as "Perhaps I should always share my developing ideas one-on-one in advance of a meeting, and perhaps even build in a suggestion which one or two might make."

All she did was smile, reach across to take his hand, and look at him.

###

The next afternoon Eric spent walking around The Fens. He could not believe that life could be so difficult – so much beyond him. Minah's suggestion was so obvious to her, so simple. Why had it never occurred to him? Of course he would act on it. With that matter 'in place' he walked on, his mind a blank.

One rabbit chased another right across his path, sight unseen. Even the raucus call of a blue jay failed to gain his attention. The cold marshes were more aware of the ducks foraging among frost-bitten weeds than the walker with head down and shoulders slumped as if carrying the whole world.

Nor was he any more conscious of the world within. The brief argument with himself to act upon Minah's suggestion had given way to – nothing. Eric could not have told you what was going on, why he was walking, or whether he was experiencing anything at all. When the lowering sun caused him to glance at his watch it came as a shock to realize he had been there three hours, thinking of nothing.

Something clicked on in his brain and forced the question: Why? Of course he was there because of the question of what to do about Minah.

This pain was more than anguish; it was tangibly physical. There was guilt too. There was anger at the universe. What should he do? What could he do? There must be a solution. Yet he could see none. Insofar as he could feel, or think, he knew only one thing: he could not have what he wanted more than anything else in the world.

It was not just sex. Sure, that frustration had become unbearable. But when he allowed thoughts to surface they would alternate between desire and something else. Her smile as she took his hand alternated with the feel of her body – which was almost but not quite his. The warmth of her smile could not dispel the pain of sexual frustration; but neither would the warmth disappear. When he reached the point of censuring his lascivious anger her smile would appear before him, bringing that assurance about overcoming any recalcitrant committee.

He found himself re-living the night they had first done the joget. Then the Walden Pond Walk re-surfaced, with the incredible experience of vulnerability coupled with being so, so safe. For a space there would be peace and he wanted only to lose himself in it. But the hand and the smile were not dismembered: as its owner slowly materialized in his mind he felt her total presence. And with that phantom came pain.

Because he could hardly see twenty feet ahead of him he now looked at his watch and exploded with a "Damn! Frankie will have dinner waiting any minute now!" Four hours had produced nothing. He was no clearer about this ultimate frustration than when he had started walking – except that it was now quite dark.

### 

That evening, over dinner at home, he re-opened the topic. "I've been thinking about yesterday's meeting."

"Mm?"

"I've been thinking about who I should approach privately. Do you think I could get away with that? After the vote? And who? Who do you think would be more open? You know, apart from Michael, who would be more ready to talk to me – if I made an appointment to do so?"

He looked at her in a way she hadn't seen before. He's really asking some-one's help, she thought. Whatever's come over him? And he's not carrying on about 'those bastards' for days and days, as he usually does.

68

"What about Jonathon? I know it may be odd to start with the chair, but he is the one who pushed most strongly to hire you in the first place. But don't make an appointment. Just lounge into his office with your coffee mug when he's obviously not busy. And just let the conversation happen."

"Do you really think I could do that?"

Even while thinking, "Who is this man, my husband, asking my advice, and ready to take it?" she reached out to touch his arm, gave a reassuring smile, and said, "I'm sure you can."

### 

After the customary niceties of introduction Dr Miriam Kendall asked, "So what brings you here, Dr Johnson?"

"The main answer is the fact that I need someone to bounce some thoughts off. The reason I have sought out a woman therapist is that my problems – at work and of the heart, are women. There's a bitch of a colleague, a virtuous wife, and a wonderful Muslim woman."

"An interesting group! Tell me more about them."

"The main issue is that Minah, the highly sophisticated Indonesian woman who wants me, but won't . . . you know. I need to talk about that and hear some reactions from a neutral party."

"And your response to Minah's position?"

At this point Eric launched into a long tale of their meeting, the subsequent intellectual and sexual magic between them.

"So she's demanding marriage?"

"Well yes and no." A nod encouraged him to continue. "She never said a thing about marriage until . . . well, until we were petting heavily, and . . ." Another nod helped him say, "and she refused to have intercourse."

"So that's against her principles, but not against yours?"

"That's about right."

"What would be the cost of giving her up?"

"You've got to be kidding. I thought you would have guessed she means everything to me. She is what I have always fantasized: she hears

69

me, makes me laugh, even at myself, gives me the encouragement I need for my work life. What more could I ask?"

"Well, what else is there that matters in your life?"

"Oh, my girls! I have twin daughters, nearly five. I guess that is the element that is so confusing. Minah thinks they could be equally shared with us and Francine. But Francine would never go along with that."

"So the choice comes down to?"

"What do you mean?"

"Are Minah's unique goodies as important to you as your girls?"

After a long silence, Eric asked: "What else have I not considered?"

"The most obvious thing is the uncertainty of how a long-term relationship, a marriage that is, with Minah would really work."

"I'm sure it would be wonderful."

"But are you?"

"Well, I s'pose that's wishful thinking. I would have said the same . . . no, I did say the same thing about being married to Frankie, in advance."

"So?"

"You're suggesting that the choice is between a total family package that I have and know, and an uncertain life of – perfect bliss? He was surprised that he had the same kind of slight smile that had only developed since meeting Minah.

More surprisingly, he now found himself saying: "And there's the whole Will of Allah thing. Who knows what issues would hinge on what Allah demands, or allows?"

"Who knows?"

Another long silence was again ended by the client: "But one thing is certain, Allah would trump me every time."

Miriam Kendall did not know, and it had been beyond Eric's self-knowledge to tell her that this session, and its impression of "advice" fell far short of dealing with the real issues, with those realities inside Eric

70

which did and would continue to determine his happiness. But was that so unusual, for anyone in their thirties? Especially if the person is a man?

### 

"I knew all along that a man and a woman could not have an intimate relation without sex, at least not if they were both normal. We are normal. Look where it's gotten us. I want our deep relationship, but my sex drive won't let me have it without satisfying it too."

Minah simply looked at him. "Do you really think Allah wants my natural functions (which he created, by the way) to be in such distress?" More silent looks.

When she did speak, it was neither to counter his assertions nor to answer his questions: "If we were married, I'd so love having the girls with us half the time. I can just imagine how we would spend the days at the New Hampshire cottage, on the beach, and out on that sailfish you talk of buying. Jennifer especially, from all I've heard. It must be hard for her to be so passive, when her twin is a cheer leader type, and all that. I could give her the solo attention I'm sure she would like. I'll bet she would be a whiz at chess, which I just love. And to be able to shop together. I've always dreamed of the daughter I can never have"

While Eric bristled at some of the implied criticism of his and Frankie's parenting in that statement, he found himself imagining this combination of the two things he wanted most. Yet the words in Dr Kendall's office kept creeping into his mind. It would not be that easy. There were no assurances. And if it's between my family and the Will of Allah?

"Eric," and taking both his hands in hers she looked up into his eyes and said: "I do love you more than anyone I have ever met or could imagine ever meeting. I want your happiness as much as my own. I want your body as passionately (and with as much frustration) as you want mine. So there's got to be another way."

"I see that. It's not fair to just go on this way. I treasure every touch, every kiss, but I almost resent the stimulus much of the time away from you. So I'm probably a bigger bear with my students, and at home. The last thing I want is to be bad for my girls."

"Well then, my love, let us agree that we will make a decision very soon. Say, at the end of the month? That's three weeks away."

###

The smiles with which they greeted each other a week later had an unprecedented quality. Hers were filled with question marks, his with confusion. Their hug was an attempt to meet both needs, and for moments all the uncertainties disappeared in the comfort of this relationship which had come to mean so much to both of them.

She was confident of her intuition that Eric wanted a lot more than sex, even though he acted as if sex were the desert water which mattered more than anything else. He was so vulnerable, yet so unaware of the fact. He so needed a mother, but in an acceptable form to whom he could acknowledge that need without becoming less a man. He so needed confirmation of his commitment to the poor of the earth. And more difficult, he so needed support in the further challenges which were bound to disrupt the whole being of one who has a commitment to take seriously the majority of the human race – those who might envy the U.S., but don't want to buy into the whole American Way. She well knew how those challenges would threaten his sense of who he was, and further, of how he made sense of life. Her struggle with these two issues had taken much of her own resources for several years. The seeds of these challenges had been sown in Eric by his Singapore experience and his dissertation on Fulbright, but of that fact he was still not aware.

All he knew, cognitively, was that she was walking beside him, her hand in his, and that he must give this all up. Her hand felt so little, yet so significant. When it answered his squeeze, he stole a sidelong glance and found the customary smile waiting for his look. They said very little. There seemed little point in going over the same stuff. It never occurred to him that sex did not enter his mind at any time during their walk, even though it was determining the end of this valued connectedness. He did not even think about the value he placed on the customary talk between them. He knew only an empty sense in his stomach. When they parted with an acceptable public kiss she turned away quickly enough for him not to see the tear starting down her left cheek.

###

The next day he telephoned: "I can't wait three weeks. I know what . . . How can I say it?"

"You don't really have to, my love. As we were talking I knew you had already come to a decision. And I knew what it was."

### ###

Could it have played out otherwise between them? Miriam Kendall had been in a position to re-script the outcome, and she made no attempt to do so. She could have, perhaps should have helped Eric to think laterally – to brainstorm other scenarios which might be considered. But she allowed herself to be constrained by the single-track presented by the man facing her, and the limited picture he provided of the others he needed in his life.

Eric had sought her help because of his limitations: brilliant man though he was among peers, concerning Minah he was, and felt like a dumb teenager. His sensations which had been sharpened in relating to nature, became even sharper when consciously driven by testosterone. His feelings accompanying them were often visible to others, but only two kinds were known to him – sexual desires for Minah and his dream of family. He did not even realize that he had experienced a third profundity: he had been safely known by another for the first time in his life. The brilliant mind which could strategize about national politics and in the field of education was unavailable to deal with these matters of the heart. Normally skilled at getting what he wanted, he had not even recognized the deeper wants struggling to surface as he responded to his Indonesian love, see-sawing between conscious and self-conscious actions. Given all these factors, how could he have done otherwise?

Minah could not see any way she could have changed the outcome. In contrast with her lover, all her feelings were clear, known, and acknowledged, only submission to Allah taking precedence over her need to be loved. At the same time, this vitally alive woman was a neophyte to the world of sensations. She who had fantasized with co-conspirators all through girls' school, was now playing out and enjoying a range of reality and a depth of sensations beyond all prior fantasies. To these she had honestly responded with the delight of a child. But that enlarged repertoire of emotional responses had yet to fit in her thinking. While adjusting to a total new world, she had yet to figure her way out of many mazes. To date this was the most confusing of them all.

He was sure he would not have felt more bereft if he'd lost his whole family. The whole of the afternoon was spent walking the Fens - around and around, he knew not how many times. Nothing seemed real. His body moved without him knowing. He could not have told you whether the sun shone or if it drizzled. The sunshine had all gone. "But it is the only thing I can do, really," he repeated at intervals – a new mantra, very different from the old self-confident, even superior one. How ironic that those words could have been interpreted by the one he loved most as - 'submission'.

Phoning Frankie he explained that he simply HAD to go see his folks ("I'm feeling really guilty about neglecting them.") His parents accepted his wish to retire early, and a long night alone put him in the place where he felt he could hide his distress when he walked back into his own home.

That evening Eric arrived home neither irritable nor glum. Bouncing through the front door he grabbed up both girls saying: You'll never guess what I've got in my brief-case: two new puzzles! The three of them were on the floor as soon as dinner was done. Frankie could not believe how much 'out of himself' and into the children's reality he had miraculously come. When doing something like this with his daughters he usually held back for a time, and then did it for them. Tonight he asked questions such as "Now what shaped piece might fit here?" Or "What colors should we be looking for to go over in that spot?" When Jennifer or Nicole would find it there came from him a big, hearty applause, with comments like, "How did you ever find the right one so quickly?" Frankie was pleasantly puzzled. If you could have asked the man himself, he would have explained this new Eric in one word: "Minah".

Had this man known, he would have recognized that he had done what he would likely keep on doing. He had fallen back on his habitual symbol for his own fulfillment, as if it were the only mode of that realization – the family. There he felt connected to other humans. There he did feel safe, though not 'known'. 'The family' was not the only available symbol, let alone the only means to remaining safe while being deeply connected and completely known, but how is a man to know?

An hour later Frankie had to call, "Eric, it's bedtime! Put away your puzzles." He was struck by her suggestion that he was one of the three, rather than two children there on the floor. The feeling that she had caught him at play was both surprising and discomforting. For a few minutes he had lost himself, but reminded of doing so by his wife's words, something a bit like guilt surfaced for a second. But the girls' ebullience won, and it was a boy that bounded to his feet and the four traipsed off to the bedrooms. Bedtime duties done, his adult side joined his wife in the final parental duty of the day – of tucking their two little treasures safely between the sheets of their family.

# BOOK II

# Chapter Nine

Eric became very busy. It's a common way for men to deny their feelings, for how does an Eric even acknowledge grief? He spent hours every week ferreting out background material relevant to his foreign aid course proposal. He threw himself into every professional opportunity available. When not working, he spent many hours playing with the girls, taking them to the Children's Museum, and when the snow came, they slid down their first slopes atop their father's back, to the delight of their photographer mother who was determined to catch every phase of her children's development. He even edged away from his solitary style into the occasional drinking fountain conversation in the department's hallway, and sometimes had coffee after the monthly meeting of the Boston Political Science Teachers Association with one or other of its members.

Unsurprisingly then, given the vulnerability he had acknowledged to Minah, he was to be found more in the presence of attractive women than before she came into his life. Because he had moved beyond his unconscious habit of repression and had awakened sexually, he was conscious of desire much of his time. "Every three minutes" might not have been much of an exaggeration. But he was no "smooth operator"; his hunger was obvious. The woman who walked with him to the parking lot after one Association meeting knew exactly what she was doing when she said, "I've been thinking that it's time I had another affair. My husband and I both do so from time to time. It keeps our marriage fresh."

The words excited him. Maybe life wasn't so bad after all. Lately he had been dominated by a sense of entrapment – by Frankie. Repeatedly he found himself blaming her for the unhappy end to his affair with Minah. The irrationality of such blame did not occur to him. He was angry, the situation was unfair, and someone else must be to blame! Why, even Minah herself was not blameless. She *could* have met his wishes, but she *would* not. The more he had thought about it all, the more convinced he became that he was the undeserving victim in the whole situation. The last thing he was inclined to do was to test such thoughts with his friend Michael – possibly because of a fear that his pal would tell him that all these thoughts were rubbish. In silence he could blame everyone else. And now, out of the blue, appeared this woman.

Helen's rationalization fell on deaf ears because he was so excited by the first sentence: "It's time I had another affair." Little surprise that the next day he found himself on the phone proposing coffee together. She continued to be as blunt as the previous day, ending her acceptance with: "as long as we have somewhere to go afterwards." He found himself sexually more excited than he had been since ending his relationship with Minah. He puzzled long over where they could find a motel that would be safe from accidental observation.

So began a lustful experience which carried the big positive of making him less demanding of Frankie and more importantly, less irritable at home, finding fault with his wife but rarely during those weeks. He was quite aware of the improved home climate, deeming it more than sufficient justification for the logistical games he now played in order to meet his desire.

On that first occasion he was trying to undress her before the sound of their slammed door had died away. Pushing him slightly away she ordered him to "Slow down. You act as if you had been dieting for a year. We've got two full hours."

"Well I have, pretty much. And it certainly feels that way," was his lame response.

Her expression might have said to a more grown man that "I knew as much. That's why I approached you." But Helen knew exactly what she was doing. This was a nice, naïve man, a man she could handle. This was a man who looked at her as if she were special. And even though she knew she was no glamour queen, that her face would not have launched a single ship, she knew that naked she could compete with most. In that respect she was special.

Very slowly now, he was taking off her heavy coat, and hanging it up; then the belt around her skirt, coiled before meticulously laying it on one of the beds. Apparently not amused, suddenly she kicked off her shoes before tearing his coat off and taking him firmly, but gently by the shoulders, looking straight at him and saying, "But not that slow." She followed the words with a soft kiss. His mouth tried to envelop hers, and again she stepped back with, "Careful, you'll get indigestion."

At this he laughed and, overwhelmed by desire, tore off her clothes, got his own pants off, and was headed for the only thing he could think of when 'crash' he fell flat on his face at her feet while the back of her knees folded over the end of the bed and she fell back onto the bed. But Eric was in good shape, not to be hobbled either by laughter or the shorts around his calves. The would-be stallion found sufficient of her unclad and her vagina already so wet that penetration, accompanied by a great gasp of relief and ejaculation that came all too soon. To all of this she offered a sage word from experience: "The first time is never great, is it?" Not wanting to admit his inexperience he managed a nonchalant "Relatively speaking, I'd say that's right."

They now quietly removed the various garments in which both were tangled, and fell into a quiet fondling and kissing, which was what she had wanted initially. But best of all, from her perspective, was the way he now visually discovered her body. "My god, he exploded, "I never dreamed . . .," he didn't know how to say it, but she was impatient.

"You never dreamed what?"

"I can't find words. I mean, I've never tried to say . . . I mean, can't you tell?"

She wasn't letting him off: "No, I can't tell. You will have to tell me."

"I've never," he started, then hesitated, not wanting to admit his small sample of fully naked women. Changing the verb slightly he recovered and found the right words: "I would never have guessed you would be so beautiful under all those clothes which our climate requires." His eyes feasted on the 38-26-34 form which he now leaned back to appraise.

"You like?"

"More than 'like.' Sitting here, on top of you, I'm on cloud nine."

"Then be one of those male angels I've always dreamed of swooping down and carrying me off to some sylvan glade where they can ravish me for hours and hours, then returning me to a quiet sleep in my own bed."

"I make no claim to all those competencies, but maybe we can now do it . . . how would you say?"

"Ever so slowly." And, step by step, starting with her toes, nibbling one ear, then caressing a nipple, then another ear, then the inside of her thighs, he behaved as desired – without the shady glade or the unique transportation. But it was very nice, thank you.

### 

After four such weekly assignations something special occurred: Helen and Eric found themselves both bound for a regional conference in Albany. His mind, new to such games and very timid, eventually produced a plan which could satisfy the need to be available in his own room if called, while being able to spend three whole nights with this so, so sexy body. She was sure there would be some adjoining rooms.

As wild as were his fantasies about the projected time with Helen, when alone his mind always wandered back to Minah. At such times he found himself re-living the Joget, their long walks, the greatest vulnerability he had known, the closeness which also went beyond all precedents, the spirited exchanges which pushed him to excel intellectually, and above all, the warmth which pervaded him whenever in her presence, not so much for physical reasons as for a profound sense of being safe. He recalled the walk around Walden Pond, how easy it had been to disclose things he had never told a soul. What was happening with Helen was not in the same category; it was no more or less than good spontaneous sex. There was none of the deep, safely-known connected feeling he always had with Minah.

There were adjoining rooms. To him, sex had never been so good, for Helen was right there every time he became slightly awake, whether on the other side of the bed, half under him, or, to his surprised delight, totally on top of him.

The third and final evening of the conference Eric found it almost impossible to get her attention at the group table. But with his ceaseless fantasies in motion, 'No matter, later I'll have her all to myself! If she wants to talk and talk to Roger now, that's fine with me.' Two rounds later he rose announcing to the group that "This has been a demanding three days. I'm for bed. See you all later."

An hour later he heard movement next door and quietly knocked. There was silence. He knocked again. More silence answered this subtle request to enjoy their last such opportunity. Puzzled, he dialed her room number. An impatient voice answered "Room 308."

"Helen?"

"Yes."

"Why don't you open the door?"

"I have no idea what you are asking. But it's not convenient right now. I have company."

Minutes later the sound of her especially deep laughter combined with deeper tones to produce a long-lasting duet. He fumed, tossed and turned trying to shut out the sounds which occurred sporadically all night. His fury knew no bounds, knowing that some one like Roger had taken his 'reservation.'

There was little conversation between the two side-by-side passengers on the returning American flight. He seethed in silence. She seemed very amused by the cheap novel picked up at the bookstore. When she stumbled on the word "cuckold" she actually laughed out loud. Needless to say, she gave no response to his, "What?"

The drive home from Logan was just sufficient for him to regain the equilibrium necessary for him to greet his wife minimally, with the comment, "I'm bushed." But home did give him a place where, after all were asleep, he could silently utter the universal curse of his gender: "Women!?!"

### 

"Are you awake?"

79

Through the mists which precede real consciousness Frankie heard, and thought she answered. But the words came again, impatiently this time: "You're awake, aren't you?"

Surrendering to the demand for attention she rolled over hoping to receive some token of affection. He remained stiffly on his back, with a very impersonal proposition: "This is Saturday. How about we check out the sliding with the girls this morning?"

"I've got to do the grocery shopping this morning."

"Well, this afternoon, early, because it gets dark by four, and it's getting colder even by three."

"It's a great idea, and the kids would love it. But there's a problem. It's Jennifer. While you were away, in fact just yesterday I took her back for a checkup after that nasty scare we had."

"And?"

"He says it must have been rheumatic fever, and we have to take special care that she doesn't get colds or the flu this winter."

"Damn! That means no sledding. And it was such fun." With that he was up and into the girls' room. A very still, tussled head in each bed confronted his need to hug his little treasure. He just stood there. Rheumatic fever! Isn't that serious stuff? Then came another thought: What if . . .? He could have returned to share such thoughts with his wife, but he didn't. Instead he returned to demand: "Why the hell is she sleeping without a comforter? Are you crazy?"

"Darling," soothed his wife, "The thermostat is way up, there's a humidifier working, and she has her favorite blanket up around her ears. I checked them twice during the night, and they were both very cozy."

"Well, you've got to be careful," he blurted as an advance accusation, as if she had not been the responsible one since the day of the girls' birth.

Resignedly, as always, and feeling deeply unappreciated, she gave him what he wanted: "I promise."

### ###

Eric was not happy. Life was not going well. Sure, work was good, for he loved teaching and was finding his colleagues much more congenial now that he was learning to engage them without confrontation. But the dominant fact of his life was his sexuality. It would be wrong to say that he fantasized about sex all the time. Although the subject was continually central, it was not limited to the reliving of specific acts or even the imagining of others. That practice was interspersed with a good deal of cogitation. After all, he was a man whose life had meaning because he could think well. He was who he was because he had excelled in manipulating things and ideas – in his head.

Yes, there was a lot of explicit visualization. Images of Helen came to mind all too easily - as he had first enjoyed her voluptuous nakedness stretched out on that motel bed. He could imagine feeling every inch of her with his hands, gently in places, in hungry fistfuls elsewhere. His lips would moisten at the thought of her nipples. But even as he was savoring the memory of taste, touch, smell and the sense of their closely twined bodies there would intrude an unwanted feeling: "The bitch! The unprincipled, fucking, fucking" (and he said it to himself a third time, as a curse) "the fucking bitch!" While his anger at her behavior in Albany would have been understandable to most, his judgment was completely blind. Had he talked with her – an act which was quite beyond his ability at this time in his life – he would have been told very clearly that she had proposed and he had accepted, a proposition which had no strings, no attachment, and certainly no obligations. She would have laughed with gusto had he happened to use the word love. He certainly knew that lust was central. For her that was where it began and ended. That had not been so with Minah. Their closeness had almost been accentuated by the deprivation of desire. In his quietest moments he would re-live that closeness with Minah, then become angry about being deprived – not knowing whether it was her body or her total presence that he missed so much. Sadly for Eric at this stage, he lacked any ability to separate the two. Yes, he could use the word 'love' when thinking of his mother and the twins. But his real and imagined relationships with all other women? Any thoughts focused on how they satisfied his needs, the primary one of which was copulation.

Indeed, he acknowledged, almost with pride, I am a sexual being. I want sex. I love sex. I have a considerable sexual appetite. And I am able to satisfy a woman. But, he had to admit to himself, civilization does limit whatever wish I have to screw every beautiful woman I see. (Whether, one might ask, the woman wants to indulge with him or not?) The reality that extramarital sex is complicated struck him as unfair. Life should be better, easier than that.

The reality that Minah put God before sex was, to put it mildly, maddening. And what was the impediment? His being married. What do you get out of your marriage, anyhow? He found himself asking. Despite the many reasonable answers an observer would have given, he found himself repeating over and over that "she does not give me the sex I want, and she stops me from getting it from a woman who wants with all her heart to give it to me. How could I have been so stupid as to marry her? Well, I admit I wanted a big, boisterous home like the one she grew up in. Oh, I know, I was just a repressed nerd. But now I have to suffer the rest of my life because I had such a conservative Mum. Damn! Damn them all! Maybe except, no, even Minah!

If it weren't for the girls! Oh how I love them. Not in the way I loved Minah. No, more. No, differently. Oh damn. I simply don't know. But did I love Minah in any of the ways that I love Nicole and Jennifer? I did and do want to be with them, or her. That's the same. And maybe, apart from sex, I had no desire for Helen's company. And I suppose I am sorry to think that Minah is still deeply saddened by our separation; that's another kind of feeling that I have for my daughters and for Minah. And, even Frankie, I must admit, as well as the girls and Minah – but certainly not Helen – wants me to be happy. How ironic that the very presence of Frankie and that wish are so at odds.

At this point, emotion would again take over, with some anger at Frankie, lots of anger at Helen, and even some at Minah. Then he would recycle the same thoughts. A third time, they would come in a different order, with longer and longer periods of mindless anger. Finally, he would sink into a silence, as deep within as without, and surrender to a semi comatose state out of which a student or a daughter would have to rouse him by knocking twice or calling very loudly "Daddy! Daddy!"

### 

One day he received a call from his Harvard Professor Harrari asking if he would mind talking with an Iranian in their department who was very interested in Senator Fulbright. Eric jumped at the opportunity. Ever since returning from Singapore he had thirsted for friendships beyond his fellow countrymen, but his innate shyness had precluded any initiative in that direction. This was the first possibility that had been thrust upon him.

Ahad was a delight. Initially he seemed a little too slick for Eric's taste; his easy style and charming smile were reinforced by a strikingly handsome face with penetrating dark brown eyes and neatly trimmed goatee. But he was always congenial. ("We are taught we have no right to trouble others with our burdens", he explained one day.) He was always asking difficult questions, and Eric found himself constantly pushed toward places he found risky but enticing. Feeling very grateful to Dr Harrari, the relationship quickly developed beyond the reasons for the referral.

Those reasons behind Ahad's initial contact with him were soon lost in talk of such things as the carpet factory which was owned by Ahad's father, who had two wives, and Ahad's ability to combine the regimen of prayer five times daily with an easy relationship with Christians, Jews and anyone else he met. "Then polygamy is still very much a part of Islam?" Eric asked, with a momentary recollection of Minah.

"Oh, no! My father is quite an exception. He can afford it. But it is quite beyond most Iranians. Furthermore, things are in such an upheaval ever since the Shah left, that its acceptability changes every few years. For my part, I'm against it. The fact that my mother is the junior wife means more than being in second place. She is supported, but only minimally, and my father rarely visits Qum. My mother is a very unhappy woman, whose life is only bearable because she has three of us and lives near all her relatives. While I was in school in Teheran, where my father lives with his other wife, I only saw him once. He is paying for me to be here, but I suspect that is to placate my mother and to get me out of his way in Teheran."

This conversation was taking place as the two of them awaited their turn to use the nearest public tennis courts. When Eric faced Ahad across the net he discovered the latter's years at an English boarding school had refined a backhand which inevitably forced him to exclaim, "Fantastic! There's no way I can get those." But Eric was a good player, thereafter pounding powerful winning shots deep into Ahad's forehand court. With each having a basic shot which out-powered the other, it was not surprising that the first set went to Ahad 7-5, and the second to Eric by the same score. It was probably Ahad's interpersonal skill which led him to then suggest: "I have to leave in half an hour, so how about we call it a draw? We can talk for a bit until I have to go."

"OK, at least for now. The draw I mean," Eric agreed, but only postponed gratification of his need to win. Ahad's only reply was his charming smile; he had no need to win.

As they found a shaded seat under a giant oak it was Ahad who began: "There's something I would really like to discuss."

"Shoot! Whatever's on your mind," Eric responded, keen to get to know this man with whom he felt so much more comfortable than with most people.

"I'm trying to understand what's happening to me here, an Iranian in America."

"What do you mean? Your English is so good, and you seem so comfortable. What's wrong?"

"It's nothing like that. I mean no real external problem. It's how I feel about myself. I was feeling so exhausted in my first month here that I attended a lecture on culture shock. It made so much sense that I did some research on what happens to people when they move into another culture, and it was a real eye opener. I even joined an organization devoted to understanding such matters. It's called the Society for Intercultural Education, Training and Research – SIETAR. I'm going to their next national conference."

"Sounds intriguing. It makes me recall how I felt the first few weeks in Singapore."

"Well, what they say is that there is a pattern of adjustment common to everyone when they go into another culture: 'The U-curve Pattern of Adjustment', they call it."

"Why call it a 'U' curve?"

"That's a diagram for how you feel. Immediately on arrival it's all fascinating; you're up! But very quickly you find there are challenges which don't respond to your established ways of dealing with such things. Moreover, you find your talk and intentions are often misunderstood. So you feel inadequate, even despondent. That's the down stroke of the U."

"I remember that in Singapore. It hit me the second week. I began to have difficulties with almost everything."

"And how long did it last?"

"About three months."

"Then what?"

"I met a senior teacher in the high school where I was teaching who took me under her wing, had me to her home where I played tennis with her two kids much younger than me, and suddenly I no longer felt helpless."

"Exactly! That's the pattern. You had three months along the bottom of the U, then suddenly . . ."

"I was up. Yes, I was. And I felt great about Singapore, myself and the rest of my time there. I was really sad to leave."

"I looked up the research on culture contact, and there are dozens of studies which support that theory. The trouble is, I'm not going back to Iran, and I found only a few studies and articles which help me with my problems now."

"And what are those problems?"

"Well, to put it very simply: how American do I want to be? And more difficult, can I be both American and Iranian? Putting it more technically, what happens to me and my identity in this process?"

"This may surprise you Ahad, but I have been facing a similar problem."

"But you live where you were born!"

"True, but last year I became closer to a Muslim than I have ever been to anyone."

"You're kidding?"

"No. But I don't feel comfortable saying any more than that; at least, not right now."

Ahad nodded in agreement, well aware of the inappropriateness of sensitive disclosures between new acquaintances. "May I share some of what I have learned?" he continued.

"Sure. I'd be absolutely fascinated," came Eric's reply.

"From what I've read, we go through a kind of progression as we deal with other-ness."

"Otherness?"

"Yes. That's a fancy word for cultural differences I picked up. I rather like it, don't you?"

"Well," and he paused thoughtfully, "Yes. But otherness includes a lot more than different cultures. It really means any and every thing that I sense to be 'other' than me, everything that is 'different' to me."

"Exactly! That's why I like it. It even refers to the opposite gender. But let me continue. I would call these the stages through which we pass. I can see four in my life up to this date. The first was the time when we were completely untouched by differences. At this stage I was completely oriented to my own culture, my own country. The idea that there could be anything else, even as a perverse aberration, simply did not occur to me. Everything is predictable. For you in the U.S. of course freedom is a good thing, of course progress is desirable, of course the individual matters more than any group, and so on. You never even consider such things are not necessarily so; of course they are absolutely true."

"I'm sure you're talking of children, but I know some adults like that too. They seem to live in their own isolated world of thought and feeling. It must be very dull, but I suppose it is also very comfortable."

"So the next stage is to become aware that some really do think, feel and live differently."

"That happens in school, and in good stories."

"Sure does. But the differences just pass us by. We think them quaint or odd. We compare them with our own ways . . ."

"You said it. I did just that in Singapore. Even before. That was my motivation. To help them. Because they were inferior. Why! I even used Christianity as the norm by which I judged their religions to be "superstitions", and inferior. Me! And I don't believe any of that stuff. But I used the norm from my own culture."

"Growing up in Qum I certainly did that. I got nothing else from the ayotullohs. I was sure of the superiority of everything Muslim and Iranian. This is all part of the second stage. It is a time of intolerance. The writings suggest that the reason we act that way is to keep our identity secure. We know who we are. At that stage I was very much an Iranian Muslim."

"But then I got a bit more tolerant, particularly when I met a great Singaporean teacher on the same staff."

"So did I, when I got into reading the basis of the U.S. Constitution, via the Federal Papers. It was my Muslim professor in Qum who insisted I do that for my honors degree. That's the third stage: you know about otherness, tolerate it, even respect it, but you don't feel anything in you needs to change."

"Fantastic. I recall how I used to say that I had been painlessly tolerant, but now I had grown to respect them. That was my feeling on leaving Singapore. But I was really glad to get back where I belonged."

"I can understand that. You've no idea how I long for Teheran – its markets, its noise, its smell! Even the bad parts of life there. But something must happen to me here, soon, because I can't spend my life wanting to be two places."

"Maybe something will happen to you like my friendship with an Indonesian Muslim. I find myself defending her. It's almost as if I were defending myself. Would your theorists say that means my identity is changing? God! What a thought! And we didn't even have sex!"

Ahad laughed, a deep belly laugh, then looked at his watch. "Look. I'm late. I must hurry, or I'll be paying a fine on seven library books. More next time, huh?"

"I should say so. This has gotten so interesting I don't want to stop."

# Chapter Ten

"Johnson!" the department chair turned toward him during the January Department meeting. "You are interested in foreign affairs, Eric. Maybe you are the person we should put on that panel about, what's it called? 'The U.S. and The New China.' It's still six months away, but the Dean wants to put on a good show. She feels that with a new relationship developing with the Peoples Republic, we should do something special in graduation week to show we are in the current swim, as it were. She has asked Sociology, Economics, History and us in Political Science to each provide one member for the colloquium panel which will respond to a major address by the College's visiting scholar from Taiwan. Think you can do us justice, Eric?"

"I'm honored to be asked. Given this kind of lead time I think I can hold up our end. When's he coming in, the visiting scholar?"

"Not 'he', 'she'. She, Professor Wong Siok Yim can't arrive until two days prior to the event, so I guess there will be no time to get any face-to-face briefing. The Dean will just take her out for a quiet dinner the evening she arrives and do the usual nice reception the next evening. No time for real conversation about content, I guess. But we have asked if she would let us have her notes in advance. You'll have to just produce something cold, I'm afraid. But for God's sake don't make it a speech about some hobby-horse or other. Let it be something that sounds like we know the political significance of the new China."

### ###

88

It was two days before Commencement week, and Eric had indeed done his preparatory work. He had a folder of notes on every political element of the China situation which he could imagine. With that data he felt he could respond to anything this Professor Yim might say as she enlarged on the very brief notes which had come by fax only yesterday, headed by an apology that a family health crisis had prevented her fulfilling her promise as she would have wished. The four college speakers groaned, looked skeptical, and accepted what could not be changed. Eric was musing about that meeting when the phone rang.

"Eric?" came a somewhat familiar voice, which he couldn't quite place.

"Yes, this is Eric Johnson."

"Eric, this is Marcia Conner."

"Oh! Hello Dean Conner. Sorry I didn't recognize your voice."

Eric felt a pause, which told him there was something untoward in the wind, and he hoped it was not a cancellation, for this colloquium was going to be real fun, "Eric, I'm in a spot, and hope you might be willing to help me out."

"Of course! I'm at your disposal."

"Are you busy tomorrow afternoon?"

"I could be free, if that will help."

"Great. I'm so glad. Then I want you, as a member of the panel which will be up front with her, to go out to Logan Airport and meet our visiting professor when she gets in from Taiwan. I know she'll like you. She certainly does not want a whole troop to deal with. And all you need do is to see that she gets her baggage and gets to the hotel where we've booked a suite for her first few days here. After that she is to stay with a Chinese who went through college with her in the Peoples Republic but who is at a conference in Chicago until next Thursday. I'm sure all that she will want before our evening reception will be to rest. Then if you wouldn't mind . . ."

"Of course! I'll simply pick her up and get her to the 6:30 reception the next evening."

"No. I'll be able to do that. But I would like you to have a small bunch of flowers from me." Then, realizing she was asking this of a man, with a stranger, she added, "I know it's a lot, but . . ."

"No problem. I'm not that much of a chauvinist! Or whatever it is that makes men so reticent about bouquets." It had never occurred to Eric that such things carry symbolic significance out of all proportion to the effort required to procure them. He was even farther from the stage when he would make such a gift and receive one with the depth of feeling about such things which women consider to be 'normal.'

### 

As he stood at the arrival gate he did feel odd, holding a small bunch of flowers. Three times he looked at the tiny card with her name, for he wanted to get it right. As the first passengers came through the doors he had a clear picture in his mind's eye: a tiny, somewhat wizened, middle-aged, grim-faced replica of women he had seen as coolies in Singapore. As he recollected now, he had been quite blind to any of the dominant race in Singapore except his students, waiters, and those women workers on construction sites with ornate headwear and immaculate uniforms. He had heard that they were almost like nuns, belonging to and living in a kind of a commune which guaranteed their care for as long as they lived. His mind had left his responsibilities as greeter and was pursuing the line of universal health care when he realized that the flow of passengers had slowed to a few stragglers. Among them was no woman remotely resembling his imagined assignment. In fact there was only one woman, but though she was Asian she was quite tall, with just a hint of her figure curving an exquisitely tailored dress and immaculately groomed. She was now turning toward him with an inquiring look. Who else could it be? He reasoned. Taking the initiative, he ventured: "Professor Yim?"

"Well" and she had some of the same teasing smile as Minah, but gentler, "I am Wong Siok Yim."

"I'm so glad you're here. Welcome, Dr Yim."

Again the smile, which displayed a different set of curves and fullness than any he'd seen, so that its meaning quite escaped him. "Forgive my smile, but please, no one calls me Dr Yim."

He was about to blurt out some question like: But that's your name, isn't it? Then he vaguely remembered, from a decade earlier in Singapore, how Chinese family and personal names are placed differently from ours.

"Of course!. Please forgive me. Yim is your first name, isn't it?"

Possibly both of them now felt this was ridiculous, but she felt it was the time to make clear how she should be named by Americans. "My family name is Wong, and we put that first, but my personal name is Siok Yim. That's what my close friends call me. No one calls me Yim."

More than ready to let it all be behind them he now proffered the flowers and a little speech: "I am Eric Johnson. Dean Conner had an emergency and asked that I greet you with this small token of her wishes that your time with us be among the most treasured of your life."

"Thank you sir! Thank you very much. I'm sure the time will be. I've been looking forward to it for so long, even before your college contacted me. I've so wanted to see for myself what your country is really like."

As they made their way to 'Baggage', and waited interminably she took the initiative, in her immaculate grammar, to ask in a somewhat British accent about himself. Being acknowledged in this unusual way by their own little celebrity made him almost light-headed, and he opened like a flower to the warmth. Her response was similarly unexpected. She could hardly believe she was in a foreign country: far from feeling lost and in shock from a new environment, she was simply enjoying this meeting in which she was feeling so appreciated. She had only just met this man, who seemed such a boy, almost like her teenagers, as transparent in his enjoyment of their present exchange as he had been embarrassed about her names. Yet there was a strange sense that she had always known him, that he was connected to her at some deep level which transcended all the normal concepts of knowing somebody. The feeling puzzled her, even as she told herself: "This is going to be a great summer. I don't think I will even get homesick for the children and Chen Hua."

### 

"Let's go over and talk to Michael and his wife," Frankie suggested as they walked into the reception. Frankie was looking gorgeous: the occasion gave her an excuse to wear the daring dress she had bought so that her husband would be proud of her at such functions.

"What?" came an absent-minded query from her husband.

"I want to get to know them better."

"Wow! You look stunning," was Michael's first remark.

Aside to Mary, but still in her husband's hearing, Frankie allowed that "I wish Eric would take a few lessons from his buddy."

They stood around in the Alumni Center chatting, drinking and joking, with an air of anticipation. It seemed that the four hosting departments were fully represented with many spouses. Tonight, his colleagues seemed more friendly than they had been. All, that is, except Beverly Thompson, who offered a two-edged remark when they met her across the punch bowl: "We're looking forward to your performance, Professor Johnson."

Dean Conner arrived precisely at the time announced, arm in arm with the guest of honor. No one had expected a tall, stately, youthful woman who simply glowed from some unquenchable fire deep within. Her glow reached Eric, warmed even more, and caused him to respond in a way beyond his control.

"You didn't describe her looks," Frankie whispered beneath her breath, even while Michael was commenting *soto voce* that "You seem to have made a big impression at the airport." Eric's silence witnessed volubly to his confusion.

"Friends," Marcia Conner announced, "It is with great pleasure that I introduce and present to you our Visiting Professor for this summer, Dr Wong Siok Yim." There was loud applause. "With almost forty of you present, I will not play introducer but let you each meet her in your own (may I say, usually inimitable?) styles whenever it happens in the next two hours. For myself and for the College, I just want to say to you, Dr Wong, that we are indeed honored. We will do all we can to make your stay a rich and profitable one, and we hope that when the summer ends and you must leave us, that it will be with the warmest feelings." More applause followed.

When the Johnsons and Dr. Wong found each other together she began the conversation: "Mrs. Johnson, your husband was so kind to meet and greet me when I arrived yesterday. I hope I'll get to know all the Johnsons including the girls of whom he is so proud."

"Of course we will. And please call me Frankie."

"And I would be gratified if you would call me . . ." she paused, looking directly at Eric with a smile that said they had a secret, "Well, what should she call me, as a Chinese friend, Professor?"

Eric was quick to explain: "I made a real fool of myself when I addressed her at the airport. I'd completely forgotten the order between the parts of a Chinese name and called her Dr Yim. I can see I'll never live it down."

"Not if I can help it," teased the cool lady with the enchanting smile.

When she had moved on to speak with others Frankie could not resist the comment-cum-question: "What's between you and her? Anyone would think you had known each other for years. I'm not sure what to make of her."

This brought a nod of agreement from Mary, with the words, "She's not what I expected."

### 

The Memorial lecture the next evening was a great success. Dr Wong held the audience spellbound as she told of her birth in The People's Republic, of how she had joined the destructive activities of the Red Guard when in high school, and how she had become completely disaffected with Communism long before she finished university. Yet she still spent a year as a laborer before being sent to England on a government scholarship. However she never returned to the mainland, but joined her husband in Taiwan, where she had gained her doctorate and her reputation. Following a version of this personal history little longer than it has taken to write it, she embarked full steam on her announced topi: 'Two Chinas or One, Internationally'.

After a break for refreshments the audience returned to hear the colloquium part of the program. The four departmental representatives all performed well, with their guest and the audience giving more than average attention to the big issues she had raised. Only one of the four really challenged her.

"Dr. Wong," Eric began without a trace of a smile, in spite of the warm glow she directed toward him, "I cannot believe that Beijing will ever allow Taiwan to become a fully separate nation. Their formal position has always been that the Kuomintang regime was replaced by Mao, and that that is as applicable to the offshore province as it is to Quemoy, Matsu, or any other offshore islands which are Chinese."

"You are right, Professor, in your reading of their wishes. But you have not taken account of the determination of the people of Taiwan."

"But the real 'people of Taiwan', as you refer to them, are a minority of original, uneducated peasants who are now dominated by the descendants of Chiang Kai Chek's people. Those people will be obliged to bow to the enormous power of the Peoples Republic of China."

"I'm glad you have opened up that issue, Dr. Johnson. I intend to deal with it at length in my formal lecture series which begins a week from tomorrow."

At this point Dean Conner interjected with the comment: "I'm sorry that time seems to have beaten us. The lecture series will be in this hall, 7 p.m., every Monday, starting a week from tomorrow. I hope to see you all then."

Eric was frustrated. He wanted a real hearing for his perspective on the future of the people who were so determined to be separate from their blood brothers across the Straits of Formosa. So he remained until the rest had met their need to shake her hand and then asked: "When can we continue this? I want you to hear my argument."

He knew that was not what he was asking, but he could not have told you what he really wanted. He was in awe of this woman, yet she acted as if she liked him. This made no sense. The more he felt attracted by any impressive woman the less confident he always felt. The confidence was always inversely proportional to the attraction. So how come she was so positive towards him? Unfortunately but predictably such thoughtful responses soon took the form which so often becomes a man's prime activity – sexual fantasy.

In such a state her response surprised him. "Eric, I may call you that, may I? I am still getting over the big time change between home and here and noticed that the hotel offers all kinds of amenities to help travelers like me. If your schedule allows it, I wonder if you might like to join me for my first cup of coffee which I plan to follow with a swim in the hotel's pool tomorrow morning? If you can get away from here? And if you don't have other responsibilities or obligations?"

"Sounds great. I have nothing on this week except meetings, and none at all tomorrow."

"Then how about 8:30 by the hotel's pool?"

"I'll see you there."

### 

His Achilles heel again: a beautiful woman, with whom there seemed to be some special (what do they call it?) chemistry was inviting him for a swim? The politics of Taiwan was swamped by a tidal wave of feelings, most of which he could not name. But he knew he would be there, without telling Frankie where he was going, which would be easily explained as "going to clarify what is really going on between Taiwan and its parent nation."

"With whom?" Frankie thought a superfluous question, but she had to make him say:

"Dr Wong, of course."

"Of course!"

Entering the hotel lobby he felt strange. He had no idea why, it was an overall uncertainty. What would he say? How would he begin the conversation?

The lady herself was seated at a table overhung by a glorious fantail palm, a good distance back from the pool. "Hello!' she smiled at him, starting to rise.

"Please. Please don't get up," came automatically. Yet she did rise and held out her hand, which he took awkwardly and shook with even less confidence.

He soon discovered that his rehearsals had been unnecessary: Siok Yim was brimming with energy and had lots she wanted to talk about. "I'm so glad you could join me," she began. There's so much I need to know if I'm to make the most of my weeks here. So give me a brief orientation. First, just where are we in relation to downtown? But, forgive my rudeness," she hurried on before he could begin to formulate a response, "How are you this morning?"

"Great," he beamed and really meant it.

"I can see that. I'm so glad. I guess I am too. That's a surprise, because my inner clock was off for days the only other time I made a long flight."

"Maybe it was easier because you were flying east!"

"So what are your obligations this summer?" After answering that question briefly, and the one requesting some orientation to Boston, their related conversation went on until she announced: "Did you notice the time? We've been talking for nearly an hour and a half – and I've had more than enough coffee."

All thoughts about the reason for this meeting had long since left his head, but now he remembered: "Hey! We've not even started on that question of mine."

"Forgive me," was less a plea than an invitation to more relaxing activities. "We can talk about it after a swim."

Having changed in the adjacent facilities, he found Siok Yim stretched out to get some sun. They lay there in silence for several minutes, Eric having accepted the reality that she would take the conversational initiative. Then: "I've missed this in Taiwan lately, I've been so busy. I just love the feel of sun on my body. But now I'm ready for a few lengths. What about you?"

He hardly had time to answer before she simply flew into the water. With an unexpected racing dive before he realized it she was a third of the way up the pool, stroking slowly but with such efficiency the it was all he could do to catch her at the end of the second lap. "Give me a break!" he gasped. "I'm just an ordinary mortal."

"Sorry, I was so warm and so enthusiastic I guess I forgot about you for a moment."

"That's ok. Now I've got my breath back I'll happily do a few more lengths at a leisurely pace." Accordingly, they swam for twenty minutes, each surprised to find the other as competent at backstroke or breaststroke as in doing the crawl, one ahead at one style, a little behind at another.

"Nothing like it, is there?" Eric had to comment as they clambered out onto a pair of green chaises.

"I agree, completely. I've been crazy about swimming since I was very young. But what I'd now love is to get into that spa – if it's really warm."

"It is, if you can judge by the steam rising."

Soon they were seated on the edge of the spa, feet enjoying the warmth. Then both her body and his were quickly hidden as, facing each other, all but their heads disappeared under the bubbles. Do Chinese generally wear such tiny bikinis, he found himself wondering. But he said: "Now, about your assertions that there will be two Chinas."

"Really, Dr Johnson! Really! Does an American man join a woman in a spa to talk politics?"

Such directness confounded this normally articulate professor. He had no idea how to respond. This was not her country and she had just arrived so she should have been suffering culture shock. He was still conjuring up a clever retort which would make her laugh, when a foot touched his thigh. To this moment he had not realized that his sensual nature was already in high gear. He knew he was attracted to her in many ways that he could not articulate. She both excited and scared him. A tingle ran right up his leg from the place where he realized her toes were wiggling. Is she testing me? he wondered. This proper, prestigious, certainly married , real *lady* from China, of all places, cannot be coming on to me, surely? Avoiding her eyes, he reached down to touch the intruding, but most welcome foot. How wonderful that it was not withdrawn. So he held and even massaged this gift from the deep. There was a long silence.

She consciously wondered what he was thinking. Did he read her unpremeditated act as anything more than the fun tease as she now realized it had been. She always did something like that, as though it were a secret, with her kids, her sister, her brother-in-law. But how was he taking it? This was a bit stupid, being carried away by the simple pleasure of the warm swirling water and the enjoyable, brilliant, but only half-grown man who had some mysterious attraction for her. And, she secretly asked herself, half afraid to acknowledge the thought even to herself, am I exciting to an American who must surely have any number of women available to him, given his appearance and intelligence? She did not allow a further question to enter her consciousness – a question not unrelated to her oncologist's dire predictions: physically, do I still compare favorably with female grad students?

During the flight she had spent several of the long, long hours imagining what this month in the U.S. would be like – famous places, unknown landscape, explanations of its special story as a nation, answers to the puzzlement she felt about these "not quite English", as she thought of them. None of those half conscious ponderings had included an affair, but something had happened when he said "Dr. Yim?" Siok Yim was both a superstitious and an intuitional person. Before leaving she had consulted the requisite fortune teller and had been told to her great amusement, that "In America you will meet the man of your life." The memory still brought a chuckle: "Such rubbish! Especially after the operation. But who knows?" she had whispered to herself. None of that skepticism applied, however, to her intuitions. She had lived by them, they had never misled her, and by her thirty-fifth birthday she had come to trust them completely, even when, as sometimes happened, they were contrary to the messages from the left side of her exceptional brain.

He sat, bemused, enjoying, anticipating - he knew not what. But it was all very nice. He did not want it to stop. He had even gotten as far as fantasizing the sight of more than the brief glimpse offered before her bikinied body had submerged, mermaid-like. That wish was giving way to further imagined developments when he looked up. She was simply looking straight at him, almost expressionless, gazing deep into him. Never had a woman looked at him with such scrutiny. He liked it but it made him uncomfortable. He wanted her to smile, as she had done so kindly at the airport. But she just stared, it seemed deep into his very soul. He stared back. Neither could have told you how long they just looked at each other before the words came from her lips which were to haunt him for years:

"What do you want? What do you want, Eric?"

He told himself that the looks exchanged had answered that question before they were uttered. 'Sex', was the obvious first answer when you're in a hot tub and a woman reaches out to touch you. Yes, there had been sex in his mind. But how could she have read that? Do women really know what you are thinking? Does this one? How can he have even a clue what she was doing, behind those quiet, unsmiling eyes that he would have much preferred to smile. Yes, of course I want sex, he could answer. But something told him she would not settle for such a simple, such an obvious answer, that she knew he wanted sex but that she was probing much, much deeper than the obvious. Something deep within wanted to respond at an equal depth. It would have seemed trite to answer: tenure, a big rowdy home, or for the whole world to be as happy as I feel at this very moment. Something he could not articulate was asking for voice. Something in him started to say: What I want . . . and faded into silence because it refused to surface. And powerful feeling, begun deep within his very soul, and certainly not in his groin, gave way to feelings that did. He wanted to ask: "Could we go up to your room?" But Helen was the only woman with whom anything like that had ever happened, and that had been a fiasco. Here he was with a very different kind of woman, assuredly not one who made a habit of affairs, and he felt like an awkward fourteen-year-old. Still . . . and he looked into those eyes which refused to waver from his, I've got to answer. So he said it: "Could we go up to your room?" There it was, the old pattern: a man's thought processes cycled through his gonads. Meanwhile he was adding to himself 'At least that is more subtle than directly saying what was really on my mind.'

I knew I was vulnerable, she was telling herself. Life at home is so rich with the children, but so empty of the closeness I feel I deserve at thirty-five. Yet why did I touch this man with my foot? It had nothing to do with sex. He is hard to ignore, given the feeling of intensity about all of life which he exudes. But those are not the sex-oriented eyes of a lustful pick-up in a Taipei bar. There's something there which I feel is part of my world – intelligent and spiritual, yet fully, yes fully sensed, fully aware of every sensation which sight, sound, touch and feel bring to him. I can imagine walking with him in a field of English wildflowers.

Yet his question had taken Siok Yim aback. Her touching had not been meant as an invitation, it had simply happened, because she needed to express the intuition that she could be close to this man, that she wanted to connect to him in a deep way. But that he should read her foot's playfulness as a proposition! No way! Yet she was not about to give some smart comeback for she knew, in the way women do know such things, that this man's assurance was only skin deep, a façade behind which hid a very uncertain little boy, but a little boy just yearning to play, but scared to do so.. Had she been completely rational, she would have responded otherwise. Intuition triumphed over all thought. No way would she have said "Yes" to sex had she believed that was primary. Furthermore, she was pleased that he had hesitated so long before his answer.

As all that happened in at most, two minutes of silence. Then she simply rose and started toward the elevators with just the hint of an affirmative head movement. It was barely noticeable, but he had no doubt about the message.

In fact, Eric would have been quite incredulous if he could have known the complex of thoughts and feelings within the divine form he was following with new appreciation, and newer, quite unbelievable expectations. Little did he guess that he was experiencing perhaps the most critical moment in his life. Yet this man, like most of his kind, never asked himself, even for an instant, what is going on in her mind. He had heard that thoughts quite different from his own did exist; but who knows what they are? Women want what we want, don't they?

As they entered her room she silently shed the gown she had worn up from the pool, then as quietly lay back on the bed in her still damp bikini and continued to stare, without a blink, at the face and eyes of this man. He stood there, feeling quite stupid, and very defensive, not knowing what to do. This was not a Helen, another lusty woman who could and would just take it or leave it. But what was this woman, who had, after all, agreed that he might come to her room?

"You look very uncertain, Eric. I'm sorry if I am the cause. I didn't mean to make you uncomfortable. In fact, quite the opposite. I felt so comfortable with you that I simply became the playful child which is so much a part of my nature." With that she continued her stare, but now with a big smile.

He gave a big sigh. "The truth is, I'm not a Don Juan. I don't spend my spare time getting into situations like this. In fact, I think I should thank you for being so gracious – if that's the right word for the situation - and take my leave."

"Is that what you want to do?"

"To be honest, no."

"Then, to be equally honest, and very forward, what I would like is for you to stay right here, beside me, until you have to leave."

Given this much encouragement, plus her warm, welcoming smile, he suggested: "Then maybe you might want to keep the bed from getting soaked by wet bathing suits."

"I leave it to you sir," she invited, now in the playful mood which had begun in the spa. With some hesitation he removed his wet suit, helped her do the same, and laid down on the free part of the queen-sized bed.

Without the slightest self-consciousness she propped herself on one elbow, looked his body up and down quickly and surprised him with the blunt question: "You don't know much about women, do you?"

He had blurted out "No" before he could get any real thoughts together.

"Then, Professor Johnston, may I offer to teach you what little I can."

What could he have done but assent when asked so sweetly, in such a situation?

"Then let's begin this way, she said as an introduction. For a few minutes, I want you to just lie very still but allow yourself to feel as fully as you can without moving. Do you think you can do that?"

For a brief moment he felt like saying "No", not enjoying the idea of changing places with the class members who he was sometimes accused of manipulating – albeit for their own "good". Then he simply nodded and closed his eyes.

A finger touched his neck, then lightly moved gently across his chest, then to his hip, the outside of his thigh and right down to his heel. Then, just as lightly, the finger retraced its course, at the same speed. She repeated that twice, in the same way. At the end of the third course however, her fingers, then her whole hand began to explore the shape of his neck and the adjacent collar-bone. "Quiet" came a command, "don't move, don't think, just let yourself feel." And feel was what he did.

At first he was aware of being touched, in a variety of ways, every one a little different, frustrating a wish for more of the same, but then delighting in a new sensation which seemed to surpass the one it replaced. But soon the dominant sensation was a warmth over his whole body, as if someone had wrapped it with a very warm towel. Then he was awakened by a finger tracing the musculature around his left nipple. At first it moved the muscles themselves. Then, like an eagle soaring in ever decreasing circles centered on its prey, something other than the finger landed on his nipple. He shuddered at the soft wetness. Then, cooling with the air around it, his nipple was about to demand "More" when the wish was met. This time her lips savored him, taking sweet amounts of an area he had not known he owned. When wanting to cry for more, her tongue began to tease the nipple. He shuddered spontaneously, then found himself arching his back in ecstasy. A very quiet voice asked "yes?" to which he murmured the same word in reply. Time stood still. He was unsure what he sensed as her mouth came and went: his neck itself? his chest? his nipples? And then it all stopped. He felt replete, as if a great burden had gone. As if he could fly. As if nothing else in the world mattered, even existed, but his own body. He had no idea how long it was until his eyes opened and she was still there, in exactly the same position, just looking at him with what something told him was a copy of the Mona Lisa's smile.

He started to smile, then to phrase something, but was interrupted by her new command: "Now it's your turn."

He was about to answer, to correct her pronoun, then realized she was saying that it was now his turn to reciprocate. She closed her eyes, just as he had done, which gave him a chance to savor every inch of her body, appraising at first, then simply enjoying every curve, every hollow, every mound, whether of muscle or of flesh. His eyes caressed her form, with precisely the same appreciation he had for a tree or a rock. His finer senses had long been attuned to such things. The same senses now began to appreciate the beauty of this warmer expression of nature.

For reasons of which he had no clue, he found himself studying the form of the ear nearest to him. For some minutes he just looked. He had never really seen an ear before. Sure, everyone has two, but he'd not noticed the way the outer form merges into the next - not quite "concentric" - shape. Nor had he noticed how very soft the lobe even looked. He touched it, as if it were something which his fingers might damage inadvertently, marveling at the softness. Feeling a need to do so, he first kissed it then drew it into his mouth, tasting as delicious something which his head told him had no taste. But it did. It tasted of her - at least partly. He felt sure some of the taste was her perfume. Yes. He had noticed something in the air whenever they were close. It had been there the day he met her at the airport. It was her particular brand of perfume. But something else was there in his mouth, something he would always think of as "her".

A tiny murmur escaped her and spontaneously he found himself leaning over to bring his ear near her mouth, which also caused his eye to fasten on her breasts. They were quite small, and he had always thought of himself as "a breast man." As he traced the outline of the darkness around her nipple he became aware of a texture, like little peaks, surrounding the main one. Licking them all, then the mountain-top brought the same murmur as the ear lobes. He was copying her behaviors with him, and as he did so, became powerfully aware of the responses of her skin wherever he touched or kissed it.

Then her eyes were open and she was saying. "Forgive me."

"Forgive you? Whatever for?"

"For frustrating you," Siok Yim replied, glancing at his stiffness. With those words she moved as if to help him to move over her, and in seconds they were one.

While Siok Yim had been aware of the spreading moisture between her legs when he played first with her ears and then with her breasts, her mind was not on herself, but on the man himself. Did she really want to be doing this? Her body's answer was obviously affirmative. It would be, indeed is, so, so nice, she heard one of her voices report. Another was asking about Chen Hua, her husband. He would not like this, not at all. In fact, he would probably want to kill both of us. He was a terribly jealous man. But what had he ever given her? Children she adored, yes. A certain respectability, yes. A wider family who she cared for much more than for their Chen Hua. But she had three months here, then back to all that. And no one would ever know a thing about this. Besides, Eric's very boyishness and naivete is so delightful. And . . . her soliloquy was interrupted by a comment from the source of her increasing pleasure:

In a deeply relaxed state Eric had to say: "Nothing like that has ever happened to me before. The way you were touching me, I mean."

"You are a good student. You get at least an A minus for your lesson today. The way you touched me was just so wonderful. You touched me exactly as I had touched you."

"I know. It seemed so natural."

"And your own feelings, Eric? While I was touching you?"

"At the very first, I was in my head."

"Yes. I knew that. But then you let yourself feel."

"Oh yes! And yes! Yes, yes!"

They quietly smiled, wrapped arms around each other, held on for a time, as she nuzzled his neck. She felt so complete. No other word could describe it. A void had been filled. A part of her which she had sought her whole life was recovered. Or was it discovered? This was absurd. It was also true. It was something of the feeling she had in simply seeing or touching one of her children, the flesh of her flesh. But it was more. It wasn't just a great feeling, a glow over her whole body. She recognized that warmth after the sense of release had faded. Could she believe the thought that was intruding relentlessly: this is my other half?

Eric was also feeling more than the release of tension. It was something far more, far deeper. But what, he could not tell. He was very much aware that he felt he was in a new place, a place he had never been, or even imagined. Well, not quite. Just sometimes, as he lay beside Minah, deeply satisfied and frustrated at the same time, there had come hints of what might be. This inexplicable feeling here with Siok Yim was related to that . . .. That what? It is very frustrating for the highly cognitive to find themselves reaching for a thought, and finding none which begins to capture something. That was Eric's condition in these moments. Right now, he thought they were related to sex. They were. But they were also to do with something much more – a yearning, which he could not name or remember being without, but which would be with him at the very thought of this woman, from now on. It was a profound sense of connection, of connection beyond the physical, to realms beyond articulation, even beyond conception,

After a long time, they fell comfortably apart. While he could not believe how comfortably, for a long time he rested in silence on one elbow, then awkwardly clearing his throat he asked, "What about your husband, your marriage, your boy and girl, and all that?"

"Well. What about yours?"

"To tell you the truth, things aren't really very rosy between us. I don't have a clue how she feels. (Silently his Chinese lady commented that he would probably have to admit the same sad truth about every woman he had ever known, at any age.) But I am more than at the seven-year-itch stage. What we had when we married is all gone, or almost. I feel 'judged' every time I say anything. And there never were lots of what I had dreamed a marriage would involve."

"Have you worked to preserve it?"

"What?"

"Have you told her you want to work on what has been lost? Have you told her you feel 'judged'? Have you talked about your troubles to friends? I suppose here in this country it would also be appropriate to talk to a therapist. Have you?"

He did not want to be grilled like this, and she immediately realized it.

"Come," she invited, spreading her legs and smoothing back her extensive raven colored pubic hair. In his view, there could have been no better way to change the subject.

"Oh Eric, Eric," she whispered several minutes later, "How could I have found you? I believe I was meant to. This was meant to be."

Because he could think of no response he started kissing her, gently at first, then when he found her tongue in places no one else had ever explored, he did the same thing. It was a long time before they could say a thing. When their mouths separated, it was mainly so that he could ask: "Would you like me inside you again?"

Her kiss was part of the answer; its conclusion was the way their bodies seemed to flow into a oneness which he had never known.

Satisfied, very satisfied, she nudged him off her body then sat on his belly, stroking his chest, his neck, his face, tracing his jawbone, his nose, his chin, all the time looking into his very soul, or so it seemed. She was very happy. She felt whole, whole in a way without precedent. She had no recollection of ever feeling this way before. So calm, so peaceful, so full of what could not be explained. She had followed her intuition, and it had not betrayed her. But who was this other part of her, if she dared to think such a thing? A natural way for this kind of feeling to be expressed was for her to ask:

"Now tell me all. Tell me about Eric Johnson."

No one had ever asked in just that way. It puzzled him. She was a real demon at confusing him. Such simple questions: "What do you want?" and "Tell me about Eric." Well, he knew a lot about the second, he was completely relaxed and so he began: "I wonder if I'm really just a typical thirty-year-old."

"Yes?"

"They say that thirty is a crisis time. It's when you ask about the value of all the effort it has taken to reach this stage of your life."

"You mean it's a surprise that you've lived so long? And don't answer that without remembering that I'm thirty-five."

He knew she was teasing, so with a big smile he very honestly responded: "You have the body of a twenty-five-year-old."

"Thank you sir! I like to be complimented."

"And it is wonderful that you let me."

"But back to my question. You were saying that some review is going on inside you."

"Well, yes. I guess a bit more so than at other times in my life. Some of it is to do with my marriage. Some of it is to do with my relationships with people at the college. Some of it has to do with my need to change the world. Some of it has to do with other women in my life." He could not believe that the last comment had slipped out. But there it was, just asking for clarification. But her follow-up question was not what he expected.

"And am I one of what you call 'The other women in your life'?" Needing reassurance she was teasing, but he didn't realize it.

Without thinking he started, "No. You're . . ." and found himself speechless. Then he recovered enough to add, "You're different. You're different from any other human I have ever met." He could not have said how, or why. He just knew he was now in a place completely new. And he liked it. There it was again, that sensation of being in a way he had always wanted to be.

"And so are you."

"No. Seriously, you are." Words eluded him. He grasped for a way to say what had first become conscious with Minah. It was a feeling which had never existed with his wife Frankie or with that Helen. But today it had become a recognizable, even though indescribable part of his very self. That she should have made that happen meant she certainly was very different.

"And seriously, so are you," she continued the exchange, which then continued in silence.

At this point they both lay back, side by side, holding hands, basking in a level of appreciation, acceptance and comfort which neither had known at any time in adult life. To her, that was no surprise. It was unexpected, as are most of the big experiences in our lives, but even the unexpectedness of life was known to and accepted by her. It was one of the great gifts of living – that today was always a present, a gift which came out of the blue. Yet not out of the blue, but out of a complex which it was foolish to ignore or to deny. It was not for us to know in advance. And it was certainly not for us to deny something which potentially offered more of what she wanted than she had yet known. Moreover, she told herself, although that "little tumor" they removed from my breast was "nothing", life is never certain. But today I can grasp, and live fully.

Eric had no such richly complicated feelings. He simply lay there, euphoric, aware of the warm glow throughout his body and of the warm mouth and deep gaze which met his when he turned to look into her face from time to time - and aware of something wonderful just beyond cognition. He hadn't a clue why, or what, but there was simply this wonderful sensation, through his whole body.

Eric checked as he left: "So I'll pick you up here tomorrow at 1:15, and introduce you to the heart of our wonderful city."

With another warm, wet kiss she confirmed the date, adding: "Until 1:15 tomorrow, then."

As Eric went back to his daily routines, only one cloud appeared in his sky. It was very tiny, almost unnoticed, which came and went. Indeed, he looked the other way each time he caught even a hint of it in the wild blue which was so wonderful – even better than being on any mountain-top. That little cloud had nothing to do with the fact that he had just begun an extramarital affair. It had nothing to do with Frankie his wife. The cloud was, in fact, part of the wonder he had found. He could never have guessed that some day it would grow and grow until he could see nothing else.

# Chapter Eleven

Entering the lobby in his normal, purposeful walk, Eric found Siok Yim already waiting for him. A safely formal public greeting was followed by an unexpected question from her:

"So something else came before me, even on our second date?"

"What do you mean?"

"You said, and I recall it clearly, 1:15. It's now 1:25."

"Sure, but . . . ."

"I mean sir, that something important must have come up."

"Why? Why do you say that?"

"Because you said we'd meet here at 1:15."

His first annoyance towards Siok Yim was giving him trouble. He did not want to acknowledge the trouble. Truth was, he couldn't get a clear picture in his mind of what the trouble was; it just was. So move on; that's always the way to go. With the biggest smile possible, he guided her out to his car, commenting that: "We'll park at the Common. It would be easier to go by the MTA, but the car will work best for getting home later." As he easily dealt with other cars behaving in ways which would have terrified her, he explained: "I thought we'd just wander on foot around the central part of the city, and look at a couple of the main parts of the Freedom Trail."

"What's the Freedom Trail?"

"The Trail, my dear, sweet lady, is a walking route which links most of Boston's important historic sites."

"Why's it called the Freedom Trail? Why not the Liberty trail? or the Independence Trail?"

"I think you know the answer to that - because freedom is at the heart of what they did, way back then, and at the heart of our life today. Without freedom there would be no USA."

"But isn't something else, like independence, just as central? After all, freedom itself guarantees nothing. It can be, as it has been in my country through the centuries, a real danger."

"What? That's absurd."

"It certainly is not." She was not going to give in to his insistence - just because she had this "thing" about him. "We believe that order is far more basic than freedom. Freedom without order is anarchy. China has had periods of terrible chaos whenever the natural order of society has been ignored."

"Well. Say what you will about China. The U.S. was and still is based on freedom. And it has lasted nearly four hundred years."

"And say what you will, dear sir, even the U.S. is based on order. And further, it is the order which makes freedom possible. That's how we have kept a people together - not for four hundred, but for four thousand years."

He was about to point out what they were passing when she insisted on a last word: "And at a more suitable time, let me tell you about my heritage. For all your learning, I'll bet you hardly ever cracked a book about Confucius or Lao Tse."

She caught the shadow which passed quickly over his face. Unintentionally, she had hit a nerve: this professor could not acknowledge a simple, understandable deficiency in his nation's approach to education. She sympathized, knowing that the U.S. was so much broader in its education than the PRC, or even Taiwan. Siok Yim could appreciate some discomfort at her making the point the way she had. But anger! He needed her at levels he had never plumbed. But that's OK, she told herself. I'm sure we'll get there. During her split-second soliloquy Eric regained his normal sense of control, and with all the ease in the world conceded: "I'll look forward to it, very soon."

She slipped her arm into his as they walked. That was what it seemed to him, at first. But ever so slowly he realized that she was actually holding his forearm in her hand, and, in spite of the day's warmth, the extra warmth from her seemed to move from her palm and finger tips right through his body. Later he was to recall this as she just lightly touched him at every opportunity, and every time it seemed to say more than he could conceptualize. It was magic. Never in his whole life had a touch meant so much.

"This is not what I expected," SiokYim introduced a new topic. "I expected a Caucasian city. This is so cosmopolitan. A third of the people we have passed must be Asian of some type. A good ten per cent are black, as I think of black Americans. Then there seem to be lot of other blacks, without the full lips and round faces."

"They are probably Somalis. A lot have entered the northeast in the last few years."

"Then there are all these middle-eastern looking women who are so beautiful."

"I guess I'd never have said that about them. But how could I appreciate them with you at my side? I really don't want to look at them to even check out my perceptions. Now this," he lectured as they left the Commons, "is called the Old Burying Ground. Samuel Adams and many other founding fathers were buried here."

"Let's look." So for a full hour they wondered at the small sloping stones and at the primitive carving and the inscriptions on them.

"Whatever is this skull motif?" she asked.

"I believe you can tell the period very precisely by that, and other motifs. That one seems to be a warning about the possibility of death and an admonition to be virtuous, because there is no end to what follows this life. But around the year 1740," he paused to glance around, "let's look at dates on ones which don't have that skull stuff. I think we'll find flowers and angels."

"You're right. Look at this! And this! And this! How come?"

"They all date from after a great revival, a religious one. People had been convinced that their particular destiny, beyond this life, was heaven, with all kinds of goodies."

"What a contrast to our ideas. I'll have to tell you about our funerals sometimes. And about how much our lives are dominated by the need to take care of multitudes of spirits, who can both help and harm you."

They took in the Old State House, with Eric allowing her to read the inscriptions without comment. But he had to lead her to the circle of stones which memorialized what was known as The Boston Massacre."

"I've heard of it. But I've no idea what happened. Were thousands killed mercilessly, by the English?"

"Actually, it's not the killing I wanted to boast about. It was the fact that John Adams successfully defended the English who fired the shots. That's what a high principled man he was. But in The Massacre – that was the first bloodshed of the Revolution - only five were killed. They asked for it. A big crowd was taunting and jeering at a small squad of Brits. They were scared to death, and fired into the crowd. At the trial, only two were found guilty. And they are also buried in the old cemetery we just visited. I wish we had a lot more like Adams to lead our country today."

"There's that freedom again. I'll bet that crowd had no respect at all for the order which the British had established for them. I'll probably never be allowed to return for saying this, but I want both, and if I had to give up one, it would be freedom."

Just then they passed a poster/print shop. "Look!" she exclaimed, "I'd love to see what they have." After only a few minutes she was calling him over to the group which had attracted her. "Just look at this. Isn't it wonderful?" She held up a large color print of trees in autumn, by the famed Eliot Porter.

"Don't think I'm kidding," he exulted, "but that just happens to be my second favorite photographer, and that very poster hangs on the wall above my desk at home."

"It's one of the most beautiful photos I've ever seen." She was being completely honest, unsurprised at their agreement because of her deepening conviction that this man had been destined to fill the void which had always haunted her. That void was now filled; with him she could be completely herself.

"I wonder what you think, then, of my favorite nature photographer. Come and look."

The pictures were all black and white. But the contrasts were so strong, and the subject matter so arranged that each was almost like a still life painting. She couldn't say anything but: "The fact they're black and white makes them even better than if they were in color. That's amazing. Where are the places he has pictured?"

"Sadly, I've never been there. Mostly in the southwest, or the Sierras, I believe."

"Then let's go there as soon as our lectures are done."

"Great thought, but don't you have obligations in Austin and somewhere in the Northwest?"

They just stood and gazed at one photo for what seemed to the shop attendant to be forever. "It's so different from our mountains here in the east. In most of Ansel Adams' photos the vistas seem endless. Here in New England you are lucky to get a glimpse of the horizon just once or twice on a whole hike. And I don't know that I have ever stood on a mountain-top anywhere here and found a single tree like that one."

"And just look at the story it tells."

"What do you mean?"

"The tree tells the story of its whole life in the way it has grown. It tells me it's very old, that it has been buffeted around by terrible winds more than once every year, that it has bent with the wind, and so has avoided breaking. It tells me that a rough life has made it very strong."

"And," Eric now joined in the story, "It tells me it's proud of the twists and gnarls which all that has produced." Then, feeling he's contributed all he could, he did add: "I suppose the rocks are special, too. I'll have to look again by my desk at home. I'll let you know what I find."

### 

The next afternoon he knocked at the door just five minutes after the agreed time of 2 o'clock. There was no answer for a long time. Only on the third knock was the door opened and two waiting arms enfolded him. "Just thought I'd let you know there was something more important than responding to you," she almost teased. "Actually, there really was – a call from home."

"Everything OK?"

"Sure. It was so wonderful to talk to both of the children. My eldest, he's sixteen, was very interested in hearing about The Freedom Trail. He's doing US history at the moment, and knows a lot more about it than I did the day before yesterday."

"So you were not teasing me because I was five minutes late. After all," defensively, "that's better than yesterday."

"Right!" She became the lecturer. "It's time to clue you into Chinese culture a little."

He had other things right on top of his mind, but settled for holding both of her hands as she told him about the traditions which, she proudly repeated, had been a reliable foundation of their culture for twenty five hundred years.

"Tell me your impressions of Chinese before meeting me," she began.

"That won't take long. A handful of fellow grad students, plus another handful of foreign students I have taught. Oh! And of course, the kids I taught in Singapore."

"And what would you say they were like?"

"They were always respectful. They were very hard-workers. And everything they did was so organized, so ordered. That seemed to me to matter more to them than the content."

"I'm sure that few of them would have made the connection, but all those three qualities go back to Confucius."

"How so?"

"They all express what is most important to our tradition – the well-ordered life. Confucius called it LI. Li is the way things should be done. He said that it is particularly expressed in respect for age. That is certainly shown in the respect the students accorded you."

113

"You're not kidding! I wish the Americans were half as respectful. They would learn twice as much and I would enjoy my life much more. Do you know I always have a sizeable part of every class complain about their grades – as if they should make the final decision whether they have met the course requirements?"

"And," she interrupted so as to keep concepts coming, "Li is also a reason you should fulfill your obligations to them. Indeed, every relationship has a right form, and society goes wrong if those relationships aren't as they should be. Confucius spelled out what the relation should be, and that means the obligation from each side, of student/teacher, parent/child, master/slave, ruler/citizen, and so on."

"I'd be interested in whether you are following the proper order in your marriage - by being here with me?" he teased.

"A husband must be "good" and the wife must be "listening". For five, maybe eight years I worked very hard at being "listening". I tried to anticipate my husband's needs, physical and emotional, and to give him the home and family I thought he wanted. But he was never "good" to me. We may be still married, but he's never at home, even when in the country. He provided only a tiny fraction of what the children and I needed to live on, so my parents helped until I got my present level of salary. These days, when he does come home there's alcohol and . . . and he's physically as well as psychologically abusive. That's all a long, long way from Li."

His other hand squeezed hers that was on his arm. In his eyes she found all she needed to blot out the story she'd been telling about "home.' "I think you would also like to hear that one of the other ways in which right order gets expressed is by Wen. Wen are the "arts of peace". You know how we felt the same way about those photographs in downtown Boston? Well, Confucius said that art, poetry, music etc. all elicit similar emotional responses from every kind of person. As a result, these arts make for peaceful relationships between people. If only Chen Hua and I had ever been able to share some of them! But we weren't."

"One thing I don't understand, is why you are such a stickler for punctuality."

"Ah! You've noticed? I was wondering how long it would take. That's obvious, isn't it? If life is to be good, it must be really organized, structured. If it's not reliably ordered, then everything will fall apart. So it is essential that commitments are followed, that arrangements are clearly understood and agreed, and so on. Even though I am only here for six weeks, the children are writing every other Monday and they telephone me on the other Monday mornings. But you know that; I was on the phone when you came to pick me up that first Monday."

"Maybe that's enough for me to digest for the moment. But more later, please."

"On one condition: that you help me to understand why individuals and their wishes and whims are more important to you than the common good. Now, how about a swim?"

"How about some sex?"

"Whatever you say!"

So casually requested, so beyond belief, was all she could think. The first time had been surprising, an intimation of a dream she never fully believed could be realized. It had nothing to do with sex, yet it had everything. Part of it was inseparable from sex, another independent. This time the experience became clearer.

It was like attending a theatre performance you have wanted to see more than anything else. In advance you know something of what it will be like. But more than thoughts about what will be are the feelings of anticipation. You know that something great will happen, not only on stage, but in and to you because you are there. You heard about this when quite young; now you are to experience it. There have been intangible touches of its feeling, hints, even samples of what will happen to you. This all intensifies as you enter the foyer. The moments before the curtain rises seem to last forever. Yet you don't want it to happen too soon, the anticipation at this moment is beyond belief. But when the curtain rises, and you feel as if yourself is on stage, you know that for this you were born. For Siok Yim, everything before this moment had been prelude.

After such a sense of completion and the after-glow's quietness had somewhat passed she suggested, "What about that swim? Although, to tell the truth, the activity I most crave, at least after making love with you, is a game of tennis."

"Tennis? I love to play. And I can bring an extra racket tomorrow and it'll be easy to get onto the college courts early afternoon, if that's not too hot for your liking." Again came that rush of pleasure, a rush so unprecedented, yet so anticipated, if not in the person of an American.

"I like it hot. You should experience Taipei at this time of the year."

### 

Straight after a very quick sandwich while he saw the last student in his appointed summer school office hours he was off, and soon thereafter they were on the court. It was just the kind of tennis he liked. They were more evenly matched than he and Ahad had been, neither having a particular shot which overwhelmed the other. About half of their first serves went in. Occasionally a shot was simply too well-placed for the other, but most of the time rallies went to three or four returns before one made an error.

"You're quite good," SiokYim acknowledged.

"Who's talking? You look like a woman who plays competition, the way you get across to anything I hit."

He also wanted to express admiration for the way her body performed anything she demanded of it – reaching, turning, speeding, stopping – all with consummate grace, but he hadn't the words. Beauty had always been something you gave yourself to. It evoked a transcendent experience, which he would not have been able to so name, but which for him was the life experience beyond all others – except sex. If pressed he might have said that her performance was ballet on the court.

"Well, I do. And even in a week, I'm missing it."

"But you don't seem like a competitor."

"That's because I'm with you. This is just fun."

"You mean you're being easy on me?"

"Oh no! I just mean that this is for fun. I notice that you place your shots so that you hope I won't get there, but it doesn't upset you when I do."

"That's true, but why don't you try to outplay me?"

"I never do that when I'm playing for enjoyment, only when team-mates depend on me doing so."

116

"I like that. I do. In fact, I hate having to win at something you do for fun. It's the same as climbing a mountain. Getting there, and doing it, the tennis I mean, is what I enjoy."

He could not have found a more perfect tennis partner. Each time they changed ends, she touched him as they passed. It always gave the same feeling, although the actual way she touched him was different every time. It was a confirmation of the growing conviction that "something is happening between us which I have always wanted", but the thought had no sooner come than it was gone, swallowed up by the experience itself.

As they finished he had to ask: "You might think this a strange question, but do you always touch men as much as you touch me?"

"Do I? I mean, do I touch you a lot? Truthfully, I hadn't realized."

"You're kidding?"

"No I'm not. Other people have made comments that I touch a lot, but I'm never aware of it. Actually, by other people I mean other people who are important to me. It just seems the natural thing to do. Although, like most Chinese, I would hesitate to do so with anyone I did not know well."

"But we have only known each other a matter of days."

"Yes, that's objectively true. But - now don't think this is silly - our souls have been together for ages. The few days is the time that our bodies have connected, but the other stuff has been there for who knows how many aeons."

"You don't believe that kind of stuff, do you?"

"I do indeed."

He thought about arguing, then, thinking better of that possibility, said: "Well, I like it. I find the whole world seems different whenever I feel your hand on mine, or on my arm, or lightly around my waist, or pulling my arm more tightly around your waist." She simply smiled, too happy to bother formulating further comment or explanation of a behavior which was the prime physical way she expressed the deep intimacy she felt with this, so special man.

###

"You haven't told me a thing about your early years. Do you realize that?" asked Eric after they had done some sight-seeing the next day.

"I'm sure you would accuse me of repressing that part of my life. It was very painful. Of course, I do owe to it a lot of what I am. But I don't like to recall much of what happened in those years – to my parents, to relatives, to old servants, to friends."

"I can respect that. I don't want to dig in places that hurt."

"Thanks. But I think you should know all of me, and not just the way I am now. For reasons I have never understood, my parents were both enthusiastic supporters of Mao Zedong and against the Kuomintang (Chiang Kai-Shek's people) as young adults. So when the People's Republic was established in 1949 they were each given quite important administrative jobs for the party, at a regional level. They both had to work and so we kids had to be in a nursery from birth, until school began."

"No real family life?"

"Yes, there was, in a way. We had two grandparents living with us, and though they too had so-called 'work' to do, they had time for us, while my parents were still working in the evenings. I loved how my grandmother told stories, and nursery rhymes, in that sing-song way that people often parody Chinese."

"Sounds beautiful."

"Perhaps. By contrast with the rest of our life, it was beautiful. Perhaps that was the one beautiful part of my childhood and youth. It was actually a terrifying time, as the government tried to root out what they called counterrevolutionaries. Anyone accused was sacked from a good job and sent to manual labor. This happened to many of our friends. All relatives of one accused would also be under suspicion, and if one was found guilty and executed, so were many others of that extended family."

"I find it hard to imagine, but it seems very real as I hear you tell about it."

"Not that I remember a lot of detail. I was only eight when the Great Leap Forward started. That became The Great Famine. Mao was crazy about industrialization. He claimed the one essential was steel production. So everyone - yes everyone had to contribute. We had a furnace in our backyard and another in the hospital parking lot, and one at our school.

Teachers, doctors, and everyone had to gather wood, from wherever it could be found, to keep them going. Into them were placed all the little bits we kids could find, and all the metal from the kitchens of laborers and the like, who now had to eat at communal kitchens. Everywhere there were big banners saying 'Long Live The Great Leap Forward' and 'Everybody, Make Steel'."

"Was there enough to eat, if all were at work making steel?"

"There was not. Our family was well off, as high officials, but we had only sixteen eggs a month between six of us. Most of the people starved, many died."

"Was that the time of the Red Guard?"

"No. They came five years later. After that five-year-plan called the Great Leap Forward (the five-year-plan from '58 to '63) came another five-year-plan, called The Cultural Revolution. The Red Guard was part of it. I have to confess that, at sixteen, I was one of them. I hated it, but I couldn't avoid it. You see, I was already a questionable young woman, because my parents had several privileges."

"So you went around destroying things, and intimidating people?"

"The students at my school did. Ours was a very special building, very old, with lots of books in the library, and pieces of sculpture at the entrance and in a great courtyard. They destroyed all that seemed to them to have any connection with the past. The claim was that it represented a decadence which the Cultural Revolution would replace. I tried to keep out of that, and many other Red Guard activities in our city, and was not noticed. But I still felt responsible. I had believed that Mao was good for China, but my doubts were growing more every time some new thing happened – especially when people died because of our actions in the group."

"Then what?"

"The Cultural Revolution's aim was to destroy the old traditions, so it was necessary to re-educate any who had fallen under their spell. My siblings, and even my parents for a time, were sent to be farm laborers, almost as far away as possible. 'To be reformed,' was the explanation, and they expected us to be enthusiastic about leaving everything behind."

"But your parents were officials of the party?"

"No matter! Rumors were spread that my mother and father still held onto some of the old ways of thought. And the young acted like gods. Rumors were treated as truth. At eighteen I was sent to a distant province to make sure my thinking was right. We ten of us, both sexes, had a hut that kept out nothing – wind, cold, flies, bugs, dust storms, you name it. I spent four years there, as a kind of farm laborer."

"At twenty-two things changed a bit, and I was allowed to return to the city of Tianjin, to work in a factory, as an apprentice carpenter. There was no alternative, for even had I been able to gain admission, the university there (like all others) was still closed down. When it opened in '72 I was nominated by my factory for the one university place they had allotted to them. I won nomination to the competitive exams, did well in the exams in Chinese, English and mathematics, but was only finally admitted 'by the back door' as influence is called."

"When did you marry?"

"Oh, there! But secretly, to another student! Two years later I was sent to Britain, where I received my masters degree. My husband escaped to Taiwan, to which I managed to go directly from England. Oh, and then I conceived the two you have heard about, got a doctorate, and was greeted," and she smiled, "at your airport by a lovely man who called me Dr. <u>Yim</u>."

In their laughing together there seemed few remnants of her tumultuous story. Indeed, it is unlikely that Eric absorbed much more than the bare facts. But to Siok Yim, even their rehearsal had been totally exhausting.

### 

One other day she asked, out of the blue: "How do you, in this country, define what is proper?"

"I don't understand that question. Could you put it another way?"

"Maybe I should have asked how you decide what is right. We Chinese believe it is vital to follow Confucius' teachings about the way character develops and expresses itself in social life. That quality is called JEN. Jen means to feel that others are as human as oneself, and to respect both. How do you do this? The Teacher said 'you must measure the feelings of others by your own'. The result is kind of like your Golden Rule."

"You're not serious? I thought the Golden Rule came from Jesus."

"Confucius put it a bit differently. He said: 'Don't do unto others what you don't want done to yourself.' And if you possess Jen, you will to enlarge others just as you try to fulfill yourself."

"Two thousand five hundred years ago?"

"Yes, long before anyone thought of psychology or sociology."

"So shared humanness and right relationships and order are all basic for the Chinese?"

"I think so. Of course, I'm no Confucius scholar. Let me recite something which seems to sum it all up for me. This is what results if you live the poised, gracious life which Confucius taught. This is chun tzu. This kind of life, I mean.

If there is righteousness in the heart, there will be beauty in the character.

If there is beauty in the character, there will be harmony in the home.

If there is harmony in the home, there will be order in the nation.

If there be order in the nation, there will be peace in the world.

That is my dream. That is what guides my life."

### 

On another occasion, they had barely finished eating when he dove into his satchel and produced a single, typewritten page. Keeping it partly hidden, he began. "I want to share something with you. It's something I've written. I've never shared any of my non-political writing with anyone. But I would like to share this with you."

She was touched, and it showed in the smile as well as the way one hand smoothed his left while the other reached to accept the gift – a gift which he felt was a sharing, and a baring of his very soul. She silently read the page, headed "Just walking":

Last night I was just walking.

Just walking in the patchy darkness of a residential area; just walking, tired but awake, the day a vague memory, going nowhere, with time standing still.

Just walking, still going nowhere, but on a deserted road in New England's backwoods, able to see nothing but dim silhouettes, until my gaze rises to the wonder of a million points of light against the deepest of blue grounds – up there.

Just walking by quiet water, across from a lighted city, every reflection mesmerizing you into the same distanced sensation you have whenever you walk at night.

Just walking by the ocean, wet sand between your toes, waves challenging you to keep dry even while they sing you a lullaby, and lose yourself by taking the silver way across all the waves to a brilliant moon just wishing you a good night.

> Every time, every place, it's different.
> Every time, every place, it is the same
> Sometimes I walk to "work it out."
> Sometimes I am seduced by the night, moon, stars, or ocean.
> Sometimes I even go to leave physical pain behind me.
> But whenever, wherever, it always works its own magic:
> I come back smaller – and larger – but always whole,
> By just walking.

She finished and was silent, eyes down. When they lifted, they glistened. "That is so wonderful. I feel so honored that I am the first to see the work of such a poet. No. I'm not kidding. That really says so much. It says so much about what happens to me, often. And it is all the more reason I feel so sure about my love for you. There's so much more to you than you ever let anyone see. What a shame! They'd all be the richer for it."

"When I'm in such places," Eric now confided, "I have no sense of surprise at where I am, but I am always overwhelmed by such a place, inside me, as it were."

SiokYim was quite overcome. Her intuition had assured her that in this relationship was the intimation of the completeness she was meant to have, that together they made one whole which was almost too great to bear, but so wonderful. The man revealed in such words about nature was a richer, deeper being than she had sensed, would surely grow into a partner who could access and express equally deep connections with people – and particularly with her – as he did with nature. Oh what a future they had!

He basked silently in her praise for a while, then: "I did some more thinking about Ansell Adams' black and white of the tree and the boulders on top of the Sierras."

"Yes?" came eagerly.

"I found that I can just sit with that picture, for hours, and be kind of, what would you say? Fed? It's so different from what I feel when I look at Porter's color photo of Fall foliage. That delights me, and makes me want to dance off into some new pleasure search. But the Adams makes me feel very strong. If I stay with that picture, I feel confident that I can do whatever is needed, and that I will feel good about the result. To many, the contrasts and the brightness of the light parts would seem harsh; to me they make it strong."

"Would you believe? I have been thinking about it too. I don't usually like black and white, but you pushed me to look at it, and so I have thought more. It's got a lot to do with ying and yang."

"Yeah? That's wild. But from you I'm sure I'll be impressed. What I mean is, you are always fun, but never frivolous. Go on."

"It's the balance of elements that gives it such strength, which in turn are enhanced by the strong natural light and shade. It's both, and in many ways. For instance, there is both grandeur and tranquility; not the tranquility of the English countryside but of two giants, resting side by side after wrestling." She paused, quietly meeting his eyes, waiting for his next reaction.

"Another thing I found was that it contrasts the slowly growing with the slowly grinding away of the boulders, by wind and freezing. Is grinding and growing ying and yang? Then there's more about the shapes of the rocks and the trees. The trees are stocky, bent, distorted and twisted, yet strong. In fact they are miniaturized but made stronger by that very process."

"And the rocks?"

"You would ask that. Now I'm going to sound a bit sexist. Or something! They seem to have two qualities. They look male to me, because they are big, heavy, giant pebbles, almost like a giant's marbles. At the same time, they are seductively rounded, so much so that I want to run my hand over and under every inch of them."

"Now, Eric!" she teased, capturing one of his hands and helping its exploration.

Which ended that shared head trip!

### 

.The following afternoon he was delayed by Marion Halliday, his best student in this summer course, who was breaking her back trying to complete all her graduation requirements before talking a job in September. He simply had to give her the ten minutes she needed.

"Come in," was the response to his knocking beside the open door of Siok Yim's temporary office. She was just sitting there, staring into nowhere, a mixture of anger and disappointment.

Puzzled, with no clue of what was wrong, but feeling quite fearful he asked: "What's up?"

"Do you really have to be told?"

"I'm in the dark, please do."

"I thought I was at least slightly important to you."

"But you are; you are!" he insisted.

"I am not!"

"You are, you are," he repeated again, this time from his knees, as he wrapped his arms around her legs and kissed her knees, alternately. Then her hand was on his head, that same touch which was such magic. He was no longer aware of her anger any more than it still possessed her. In concert with the passion that seemed to be coming up from the depths of both he found himself rising, lifting her to her feet, and wrapping her in his arms with the same strength that was now evident in her body pressing powerfully against his.

His hands dropped to cradle her tight buns, and her hands found that special spot behind his ears. With passion rising to a crescendo, as one they stood back, then literally each tore the clothes off the other. Blouse, shirt, trousers, skirt, pants, panties, bra, flew in every direction. Naked, in a professor's office! No matter! The commercial quality carpet so rough; mo matter!

Each strove to outdo the other's initiative, forcing and being forced in turn to meet the ravenous hunger which had dismissed from the room every last glimmer of respectability and propriety. "You are such an animal!" she accused, only to be rebuffed with his "Who's talking? So different from the proper lady I met at the airport."

"My turn!" she announced as she rolled him off her. "I mean your turn, underneath. I want you to share my pain." He grimaced, then smiled in sheer pleasure as she met his every fantasy.

A little later, dressed again, he repeated his question: "I would like very, very much to know why you were so down when I arrived?"

"Because you were so late," was all the explanation she gave. Why say more? Life to him was really so matter-of-fact. There were always reasons which he found sensible. No matter that they contradicted the meaning she read into his inability to meet his obligations. Maybe, she wondered, I should teach him how to please me. "A phone call next time you are delayed would be nice," was how it came out.

###

"So what's going on with our Chinese lady?" Was Frankie's greeting one evening that week.

Somewhat defensively, Eric attacked the form of her question: "I wish you wouldn't refer to her as 'our Chinese lady'. You make her sound like a freak we have from some circus."

"Well. She certainly isn't your run-of-the-mill visiting prof, is she? But what did you learn today from her, that you didn't already know Mister Professor?"

He did not like this style of conversation. Such aggressive talk had never been Frankie's style. How come now? Especially since he did not quite know how to respond to either the general inquiry or the specific question concerning how he had spent this particular morning. Uncertainty flared out as anger:

"What's this "Mister Professor" stuff?"

"I don't have a good feeling about that woman. Why has she come to the U.S.? There's something phony about her." Such were Frankie's words, but her thoughts went more along the lines of "I think she has an interest in you that is more than academic collegiality."

"She's an outstanding scholar, and we're lucky to have her enrich the summer offerings of the College. To say nothing of how much I can benefit in my understanding of the culture which underlies the behavior of the world's most populous nation. Actually, I was thinking it might be nice of us to take her up to the lake place for the coming weekend."

"There wouldn't be room. Mum and Dad and my brother will all be there this weekend, and Amy and Terrance are coming on the Saturday."

"Well, what about the next? I'll be coming up anyhow just on weekends until my course is done by the fourth of July."

"Let's wait and see how things are going up there."

### 

"You have a Chagall over your desk! I can't believe it."

"Why?"

"He just happens to be my favorite painter." He looked at her with incredulity, then with a smile as she sat drew a chair up beside his and gazed silently at the picture.

"I have no idea why I like it so much, but I was going through a whole lot of prints, and it just caught my eye. I kept coming back to it, and to no other. So I bought it. I guess I really love the colors. And the contrasts!"

"I love what it says."

"Which is?"

"Well, remembering that he was a Jew, who wanted more than anything to be with one particular woman, that's where I begin. I have this strong, strong feeling of both joy and sadness, all mixed together."

"But why the goat? And why is he flying? Both of those always trouble me."

"I see those as the heart of the work. The goat tells me that there are forces which get in the way of this wonderful dream of being with this woman in a place and in a way where nothing can hinder their fulfillment. That's why it's a bit unreal. But he doesn't just point out the nasty side of life (like Picasso did about the cruelty of war in Guernica), he paints it as a dream."

"You mean I enjoy this picture because it avoids reality?"

"Not at all! I enjoy it because it makes me feel that life is a mix, but there is always beauty and goodness to be found. Even if the only place is in my dreams!"

"Well. Whatever your reasons and mine, isn't it amazing that we both are so attracted to it?"

"Perhaps not Eric! Perhaps not! So when will we go to the Boston Museum of Fine Arts?"

He was so enthusiastic about this newly discovered interest that they went that very afternoon, right after lectures were done. On the way she told him that her favorite artist after Chagall was Matissse, and his painting she loved best was The Dance.

"You mean that group of women, in a circle?"

"Yes. Why do you look at me like that? Don't you like it?"

"I love the human body. Always have. I find the world full of beautiful things. And I love ballet."

"You do?" she interrupted with delight.

"Yes. But let me finish about that painting. Human movement is extraordinary, and when it is accompanied by music, well, I can't say. But if someone wants to paint the body in movement, I wish they would honor its beauty – like the Greeks did."

"So you don't want to admit that most of us, both sexes, have tummies? And some have very big behinds. And many are not at all graceful?"

"I admit all of that. But why not paint the best?"

"My dear," and she laid her hand very gently on his driving arm, "I see some other wonderful things in this painting. I see five women having real fun, like children even though they have stretch marks from childbearing and sagging bellies and sagging breasts. But they are having a ball. And they are fitting together.  They aren't stumbling over each other, but going around and around, in harmony, as the human race was meant to do.  For me, that painting comes a close second to the Chagall one in your office."

"Then I must find a reproduction, and try to see it through your eyes."

They only had two hours in the gallery before it closed, but already knew that this visual sharing was one more intimacy added to what was already a very long list.  And they had only met six days ago.

# Chapter Twelve

A week after Siok Yim's arrival Eric had spent the week-end by the lake, leaving Frankie and the girls there for the next three weeks with her divorced sister Amy and her small son, Terrance. The plan was for Eric to then join them at week-ends during his six-week summer course and for the rest of the summer.

The Sunday evening he got back to town, Siok Yim had moved in with Kathy Chang. Eric delivered her to the door, but quickly excused himself from an offered drink. Their parting presented him with the dilemma of public intimacy. Not so for Siok Yim. As he drove off and they turned to enter the house Kathy inquired: "Something big is happening, isn't it?"

"How would you have guessed.?"

"I'm not dumb. I'm not blind. And I know you fairly well from the year we shared in England."

"OK!" came Siok Yim's concession. "It's like this. Even if things were OK with my husband Chen Hua, this would still be the love of my life. . . ."

"You can't be serious?" Kathy exploded.

"Completely! There are some things you just know. Eric is in some ways a very immature man. But he has depths that are rare, depths which we seem to share - almost all of them. I can't believe it." Siok Yim then regaled Kathy about the mysterious oneness which had been evident around so many different things, in just seven days. "I feel alive to a degree which I've not felt for years and years."

Kathy's response had been predictable; it was also dependable. "Well. Please know this. I am your friend, your true friend. Everything between us is completely confidential. And if you want to bring him here when I'm not at home, that's fine with me. In fact, if he wants to stay over and share your bed, that's fine too. But I don't want a couple of love birds chasing each other around my small house when I'm here trying to get things done. OK?"

"Wonderful. I don't know how to thank you."

"You don't really need to. The look in your face is enough. I've never seen you like this before."

### 

For Eric the second of her four weeks in Boston passed like a dream. As a bachelor he had twenty four hours a day when he could dream about, or be with SiokYim, without questions like "Where are you going?" Or "What are you thinking about daddy?" Each of them had a class from 9 to 10:30 and he had office hours for the following ninety minutes Tuesday and Thursday. But the rest of the time, day and night was his own. Furthermore, he soon learned that the rest of SiokYim's time was his. The arrangement could not have been better. Well, it would have been better if he had not felt he could not bring her to sleep in his own home, but otherwise . . .

For five days they met as soon as college obligations were done. Sometimes he would arrive outside her classroom with the Subway foot-long sandwich he acquired en route. Lunch then happened flat on their backs, looking up through the trees. He felt guilty about resenting her obligation to lunch with the Dean on Thursdays. For her part, his proprietary attitude pleased, rather than annoyed.

Sex could have been a frustration. But it wasn't. Her friend had made it very clear that they should "make themselves at home" any time she was not there – and that was from 8 to 6 every day of the week. The result: lunch, then love, then whatever else took their fancy. Sessions of sex now had their own 'Siok Yim format.' A "lesson" came first, always introduced with humor. Each time she would demonstrate how some new touching would bring him to awareness of strong responses in a particular area of his body. Then she would say "My turn!" Emulating her touching he began to discover the subtleties of her pleasure. He watched her closed eyes, the movements of her mouth, the slight but real tremors of her skin.

He found himself experiencing some of the feelings he knew in his deep intimacy with nature. Between such times together he found himself largely focused on two thoughts – the old one about copulation, and a new one, wondering in what new way he would learn to please her next time.

Eric did give some moments to asking what this feeling about Siok Yim really was. It was a new experience – of feeling 'lost' in another as he often felt with nature. For much of his waking life these days he could not separate his own reality from hers. He found himself wondering "Is this what women talk about as 'falling in love'?" If so, went his thoughts, I've been missing a lot; I want this to go on forever.

But there was another sensation, from somewhere down deep, which just showed its head for a second or two at any one time. It was as if a shadow had just passed across the sun, but looking up, you could no longer see it for the brightness which filled the sky so that there was room for nothing else.

By the time Kathy came home, they usually were off to some aspect of summer in Boston that he just 'had' to show her. For her part, anything and everything was "perfect" as long as they were together. This was even true of big arguments about global politics, and what she insisted (when alone with him) on labeling U.S. imperialism, always, she claimed, abetted by double standards, or its manipulations of and through such organizations as the International Monetary Fund and The World Bank.

None of these things made any difference to the dominant reality for both – they had lost their separate individuality in a larger whole which she was secretly calling "us". She revealed that "us-ness" slowly. The very thought of him stimulated the sensation, a sense which of itself brought both excitement and quietude. She was sure this blend was meant to be. The excitement came from her expectation of the lightness of being which she knew would intensify from the moment she laid eyes upon him. Their mutual pleasuring would build that combined expectation until the moment she had felt that set of spasms and the warmth pulsing from his penis. Then the door opened wide – to a whole other world, a world of completeness beyond conception, in which she would remain for the eternity before one of them broke the silence.

On the Wednesday evening they were wanting each other intensely when they reached the friend's home with a bottle of good wine. Eric invited Kathy: "How about sharing this superb Merlot and the gorgonzola which SiokYim insisted we buy."

"I'd love to." For obvious reasons, neither of the love-struck ones could hold up their end of a three-sided conversation. Socially skilled as she was, this was even true of SiokYim. After nearly an hour Kathy both embarrassed and delighted Eric by announcing, with the most caring smile: "I think you two would be pleased if you could have time alone. So I want you to feel that this room is yours for the night. That is, at least after we all make use of the facilities. I'm sure SiokYim can help you with any toothbrush problem you may have, Eric." It was all so conspiratorial, yet also so natural and empathic.

As they made up a pad on the floor and fell into each other's arms, SiokYim commented: "She's a gem. But we must not assume that we can do this again."

"Then let's make the most of it now."

In the middle of the night his heavy sleep was gently disturbed by an arm sneaking around to find his penis. He started to kiss and caress her but she simply held on tightly with the command: "No! not until you hear what I need to say."

"But it's not the time for conversation."

"Oh yes, it is. It is the time for me to say what is going on for me – with you."

"OK," came sleepily from the form beside her.

"I know just what I want. I always have. But I have learned that you have great difficulty in knowing what you want."

He had to admit the truth of that statement. She was ready, more than ready to declare her readiness to spend the rest of her life with him. She was ready to pay any price. She did not yet see how it could be accomplished, but she knew she would find a way for her children to be part of this new dominant reality of her life, rather than a barrier to it. But she was equally sure that such a declaration by her would throw him into a place where he would hide from his feelings so well that she might never hear another open word from him. So she began:

"You know, my dear, that what is going on between us is more than special. You must believe me when I say it is unique. I have never felt this way about anyone else in my whole life."

"Yes," Eric hesitantly added, "and I have never felt like this about anyone. I'm sure that's why the time we spend together is so magical. It's why the lovemaking is beyond anything I had imagined could be. I feel that way even when you just put your hand on my arm. It doesn't even require the touch you are now making."

In the light from the street lamp he saw the tears sparkling in the corner of her eyes. "What's the matter?"

She could not respond, for her only response would be more than he could cope with. Of that she was quite sure. "Nothing, my dear, sweet, wonderful love. Nothing is wrong, Everything is right. Oh, so right!" With which she did release his penis so that he could enter her. The next thing they knew was the sun coming right into the room onto this completely entwined duo.

### 

The Toyota rolled almost silently over the dried leaves from last winter to a quiet stop under the car port at the Squam Lake cottage. "Daddy! Daddy!" came the excited welcome of two small girls. "Mummy, Mummy! Daddy's here!" as they ran to announce his arrival. But no one else rushed out to greet him. Going through the house he found Frankie and sister-in-law Amy preoccupied with watching something out on the lake, far more important than him.

His mother-in law was the only adult to acknowledge him: "Much traffic?"

"No. Just the usual week-end stuff, Gran. And the Throughway north is never a problem after you leave the 495." With no one wanting to say anything more, he found a beer and joined in the silent gaze out into the glorious lake. "I can never get over what a different world it is here," was his only, and failed attempt to promote interaction. Well hell, he thought, getting up and going down to the dock, if they want to freeze me out, so be it. I'd much rather think about Siok Yim than talk to them, anyhow.

It went that way all evening, and darkness came only at ten. There was lots of fun with the girls, including cousin Terrence in the water.

Both Nicole and Jennifer were now swimming quite well, and he, as a relative stranger, was able to get their cousin to make the first real step towards water-worthiness – putting one's face comfortably under water. Eric was being "captured" by the three little ones, then escaping so that he could tickle them, until the shrieks of delight were interrupted by Frankie: "Eric, we're planning to go to a quilt show at Center Sandwich tomorrow. Probably for the whole day."

"You're taking the girls?"

"Amy's Sarah is crazy about learning to do needlework, and she has already said she wants to go. Of course we'll take Terrence, he's no trouble. Our two? Well, look at their faces right now. Get the picture?"

"I'll tell you what. The forecast is for tomorrow to be a bright, but breezy day - just right for sailing. What would you say girls, to a real adventure, discovering and exploring islands? We could even pretend we were the first people ever to land on one of them. We could build a fire to cook lunch and . . ."

"And pretend we were Indian girls. Could we? Could we?"

"Of course! And what would I be?"

"You would be the great chief who had found his lost daughters and was rescuing them."

"There you are then," said the gracious husband. "I'll take the girls off your hands for the day and you can quilt till your hearts are content." He was almost ecstatic at the thought of avoiding the chill emanating from these two younger women while getting what he most wanted for the whole day. But what was going on with Frankie and co? Women! You can never understand them!

That night he found Frankie as far away on the other side of their bed as she could get. Fact was, she wanted to imagine he was not there at all. She had no proof that anything was "happening" with "that woman", but she had a really bad feeling about Siok Yim's presence, particularly when Eric was down there alone.

### 

Too early next morning the twins were shaking him into consciousness: "Come on Daddy! Come on! It's time to go sailing!" But it was two

134

hours before they had eaten breakfast, packed the food, and shoved off from the dock, with Frankie's admonition to her husband, more as a goad than anything else. "Now you take good care of my precious daughters, Eric."

Nicole called back consolation as she waved goodbye, "Don't worry Mummy, our big chief will take good care of us."

The island he had in mind proved to have a trail right around it – hardly the uncharted territory the girls had fantasized. The walk took an hour, and there wasn't a soul in sight. Everything seemed quite unspoiled, much to Eric's pleasure and approval. There was not a single sign of human use, except the trail itself. "Leave no trace" had apparently taken hold of the public far more than he had feared it might.

Hot dogs on the end of sharpened sticks over a small fire were all the girls needed to prove that they were Indian maidens. No matter that the follow-ups were Hostess cup-cakes and Coke.

The tiny beach – up which they had pulled the boat – was a perfect spot to swim. There was just enough exposed sand for them to build castles while he swam out to a single large rock which stuck high enough above the water to provide a seat from which to luxuriate in the beauty of the White Mountains surrounding such lakes as this one. The quiet undulations of the nearby Sandwich Range gave no hint of the difficulty of some trails hidden by the complete coverage of deciduous trees. The ridges seemed almost unreal with their bluish haze. But where they spilled down into the edges of the lake a careful observer could identify well-hidden cottages, from which he imagined other Squam Lake lovers were at this very moment running out to dive off the end of their dock into this clear, pure water. "Only one thing lacking, he told himself. How I wish Siok Yim were here, on this rock, with me and the girls."

They were sailing just off the end of the island when everything happened at once. There had been a strong breeze following them from the port (left) side of the boat. This put the sail and the boom along its lower edge well out over the other side of the small boat. Accordingly, both father and small daughter were half sitting on the port gunwhale, Eric himself leaning back, the rope controlling the boom straining in his grasp. Suddenly his other daughter who was in front of the mast was screaming, he was rubbing his head from a crouched position on the other side of the boat, the sail was flapping wildly, and Nicole was in the water. The island had created a gust which came from the opposite side from where it had been propelling them, causing the phenomenon called a jibe. With great force the sail and boom had whipped across the boat almost capsizing it. Eric had automatically ducked, but not quite low enough, so that the heavy, wind-driven boom cracked him on its way as he tried to get under it. But Nicole, no seasoned sailor, had not been as lucky. Her spontaneous response had been to stand, as she would often do to get around the front of the mast. Barely vertical, she had been struck in the chest, and toppling backwards over the gunnel, found herself dazed and panicking in the water. The dazed Eric was in no state to think through the situation: he simply jumped after his daughter, not thinking that her lifejacket would keep her afloat while he sailed the boat in a circle and back to pick her up.

"You're OK sweetheart," he sputtered as he took hold of her and held her face well above the water.

"But Daddy, the boat?" for it now seemed quite out of control, the strong breeze whipping the sail and the boat itself around until it would jibe again, all the time with one terrified little girl crouching in the bow. She did not realize she was out of reach of that lethal boom, and set up a scream to waken the dead.

"Don't worry! Yelled her dad, you won't go far. Just sit still. I'll get you."

To her little mind such a promise seemed vain. There was a strong wind that had been pushing them along at a great rate, so of course the boat would continue to do just that. Because her cries continued unabated by his assurance, he explained, "The boat will just go in noisy circles, as long as you don't touch anything." It did move slightly downwind, some hundred yards before father, with a little girl clinging as if for very life to his neck, caught up with it.

"Now," he instructed his increasingly confident passenger, "You will be ok for one minute alone while I jump in the boat." One of his hands was now grabbing its stern, stopping the circular game played by it and the wind.

"That's alright, Daddy, I'm quite OK now. I was just scared back there." With one quick heave he was in the boat, under the boom, had uncleated the rope which hauls the sail to the top of the mast, and dropped the flapping monster into the boat on top of the centerboard housing. In another few seconds he had Nicole on board, and both the centerboard and the tiller had been raised.

With a great broad smile at the two of them he commented, "That really was an adventure, wasn't it?"

"I never want to come with you again," came tearfully from the bow.

While Nicole's admonition was "Let's do it again, Daddy, but tell me before it all happens."

"I don't think so. You might feel fine now. But I have a really big lump on my head, and it's going to ache for hours."

The story was considerably embellished as told to the family who greeted their belated return to the dock, for the wind had died down almost completely and the return had taken not one, but three hours.

"No time for me to eat a real dinner," announced Eric. "Sorry. But you know how much longer it will take to get back at this time." In truth, he was overjoyed that he could just change and get on the way back to Boston, with adrenaline still high from time with the girls, but without the stony looks from Frankie and company.

### 

"Eric. Is that really you?"

"Of course, who else?" recognizing his wife's voice on the telephone.

"Where the hell have you been? In fact, where the hell are you this summer? When you were here you weren't here. Everyone felt you were off in some dreamland, not like your usual pushy self at all."

This was not Frankie's language, sounded more like Amy's interrogative style, so he placated. "You've been calling without getting me?"

"Are you kidding? Four times at home at all hours, twice each afternoon at the office. This morning, now, is the first time there's been an answer. Where <u>have</u> you been? What's going on? Where have you been?"

"Nowhere! I mean I've just been here. Doing my job! That's in the mornings; afternoons at the library, mostly."

"I tried them yesterday afternoon. They said they hadn't seen you."

"Oh yesterday I played tennis."

"With whom?

"With SiokYim. She's a really good player. Gave me a real run around."

Sarcastically: "I'll bet she did."

"We had a really great game."

"And where have you been the last three evenings?"

"Look. What is this? You sound like your sister."

"Don't bring her into it."

"Why not? Every time you two spend any extended time together you get like this with me. You just tell her that I'm earning what it takes for us to enjoy the life you expect, and that part of it is to share in the hosting of an important visitor, for dinner once a week."

"And tennis. And what else?"

"You're making a mountain out of a close relationship with an interesting colleague who is only here for ten more days. And while we're talking: I'm behind with my preparation for fall teaching, and I don't want to have to come back in the middle of my month with you all at the Lake in order to use the libraries around here. So I'm going to stay here this weekend to get on top of things." In fact, he had been wondering how to make arrangements to give him a clear, uninterrupted three days with Siok Yim. Before she could respond he added what he was sure was the clincher: "I'm sure your sister won't miss me."

### 

Friday evening was spent at Tanglewood, the fabled outdoor concert venue of the Boston Symphony Orchestra in the Berkshire Hills of Western Massachusetts to which Eric had been introduced by his mom when he was only twelve. Although it failed to inspire diligence in violin practice, it made him a lifelong addict of classical music. "You've never heard Tchaikovsky until you lie on your back, gazing up at the stars, with no civilization in sight, yet with a full orchestra playing, it seems, just for you. Wow!" Siok Yim needed no persuasion to accompany him.

"I'm sold," was her immediate response. The reality was something she really had not been able to imagine. Like hundreds of others, they spread a rug, unpacked a grand meal, replete with a good wine, and watched evening fall quietly. Shadows from the thick maples, beeches and oaks lengthened quickly, colorful clouds briefly lit up the scene with a warm glow, and then it was dusk. Around and on the stage there was the beginning of action, as music stands were arranged, seats placed, and sound technicians made a final check. They had barely finished their coffee when the orchestra filed up onto the platform, and an expectant but patient hush fell on the crowd.

After a few opening bars Eric and Siok Yim did lie back, her head on his shoulder, and lo, there were stars overhead. Each was completely given to the music, but aware of the other. It was as he had promised: there seemed to be nothing but them, the stars playing for them alone. A familiar passage caused her to hum silently. She closed her eyes and in seconds was a ten-year-old again. An old-fashioned gramophone was playing this very music inside their small – but by Chinese standards of the Maoist time, quite large – house. A warm glow took over her whole body – then, and now. The notes, particularly from the string section – of that recorded performance, and this one – caused a vibration in her body which was second only to sex. Or was it?

Almost in shame she found herself taken up with that question. Was any adult emotion equal to joys experienced in childhood innocence? She recalled that was the year before all hell broke loose with the Red Guard. Her extended family had been so safe, so eternal up to that year. And this music, this feeling was/is one of pure joy. Do I want to go back to that world? Part of me does. But there I would have no Eric. But I would have untainted certainty about tomorrow. But I now know that was an illusion back then. It would be a greater illusion to make such an assumption here, with Eric, in conscious adulthood.

The finale was perfect, as the end of a composition, but it also constituted an intrusion upon the idyll they had entered for those minutes. She certainly did not need to say anything, but Eric did. She had already accepted that he always needed confirmation of his convictions, no matter how certain he had sounded. "Well! Was it what I promised, or wasn't it?"

"Even more so, my darling," was all he needed to hear. After the second half they stayed for a long time, just lying there, with an occasional kiss, but nothing more. But as they started to head back to the car with spare arms around each other's waists, he was very glad they were not about to spend two hours returning to Boston.

"It's a long ride back, isn't it? I hope you don't fall asleep," she commented.

"Not to worry, I've taken care of that."

"What do you mean?"

"I booked at a great place just a few minutes away. I've even got a spare toothbrush," he teased. "And in the morning, we can go for a hike I love not far from here. That's the advantage of having worn casual clothes."

She had some hesitation about that. A new day required new clothes. But, wanting nothing so much as to be without them, and in his arms her other thoughts found voice. "I need you. Let's get there."

### 

"Eric," she asked after the second time they had made their bodies one, "I have something to tell you." Surprising himself, he simply looked at her expectantly. "I want to spend the rest of my life with you."

"I love you, too." Was his semi-cautious response.

"I am saying that. Yes! But much more."

"You said . . ." he paused, only now realizing what she had said, and beginning to think about how big it was. Sex and being cherished in her way were all he wanted. What more could there be than being lost in this oneness they both referred to as "us". Thoughts of any implications for the future were the last that he wished to entertain. My God, it's only two and a half weeks since we met! Yet a response was being demanded, a rational response. Yes, that is what is demanded, he thought, I need to get this onto a rational basis.

"You said you wanted to spend the rest of your life with me. But you can't really mean that?" In no way was he able to consider what she was saying: she would give up everything! For him? Absurd! Moreover, he had his family. But ever the debater, he fired back: "You have such deep commitments in Taipei: your whole family, whom I understand you to love deeply, except for your husband. And you talk of what? Of coming here, permanently?"

"Not necessarily here. Anywhere! I love you so much that I will go with you anywhere you want to go, just so long as we can be together forever."

Slowly, at what was a fraction of glacial speed, his mind began to register what she had said. The ideas were more than strange; from another planet they would have seemed incomprehensible. But on this planet? Nevertheless, a glimmer of reality about Siok Yim was allowed a tiny space in the mind of this intellectual: perhaps she does mean these words literally. No, impossible! That was the only label he could put on these proclamations. At the same time as he found them incomprehensible he found something far more troubling. That small elusive cloud, of which he caught such brief glimpses in the past weeks had now shown itself again. He didn't like it; not at all. It also had a label, quite an incongruous one given the unprecedented joy this woman brought into his life. Its name was fear.

Siok Yim could see that the whole situation was far too much for Eric. She also knew that being touched all over, very gently, was the surest way of convincing him that these were her deepest wishes. So they just lay there, until first he, then, after a very long time she fell asleep.

### 

As they strolled down a Berkshires trail the next morning Siok Yim began with: "Time flies; and we have not started to touch some very important things about each of us."

"Of course," Eric responded, "But what particularly did you have in mind right now?"

"I was thinking of your need to know about the Chinese. And particularly about me."

"But I'm learning about you, all the time."

"Yes. But I'm referring to our tradition. Which, I think you know by now, I take very seriously."

"Sure. There's the idea of LI, and how that gets expressed in the ordered life."

"That, my dear, is the Confucian side of it. Then there's the Taoist side. The Tao."

"You mean The Tao of Pooh, a book I noticed the other day, with a picture of the bear, from the great kids' book, Winnie the Pooh."

"Yes, I know. And I'm glad that has been published. It's a fine way to communicate the balance between the serious and the fun aspects of the well-ordered life."

"I thought Tao was some kind of spiritualism. Something to do with what we know by intuition."

"That's quite true. One expression of the teaching of Lao Tse is by a kind of spiritualism. But for me, the main idea is expressed in the symbol of the Ying and the Yang. You know, the two tadpoles curled around each other to form a circle. A bit like us, now I come to think of it. But seriously, the idea most valuable to me is the way opposites complement each other. All values are relative. All contraries are parts of the same whole. Even what is and what is not are part of something bigger. And so are we. Taoism helps me get beyond myself."

"How?"

"By urging me to be open to what I don't like, or to people who oppose me. When I succeed in doing that, it's amazing what happens. Mostly, the problems just evaporate. And the people – they seem so much more congenial. I then find it a lot easier to be mannerly toward them. You know, the way Confucius would approve."

Not surprisingly, these two then fell into expressing *their* particular polarities in ways which each found most engrossing, even with the limitations of underbrush and the like.

Later, on the way home, he raised another matter: "What will happen to us after . . . ?"

"After I leave?" she clarified. He was quite unable to think. The issue had occurred to him, but he had always quickly replaced it with what was about to happen next. That technique seemed to work well, had done so all his life. But now there was a demand, a demand which came almost as much from within him as from her: What next?

"I guess I've been ignoring the reality that we only have five more days. And I must make it clear, I must tell you that these last twenty have been the most wonderful of my life."

"So you'll write every day?" She teased.

"At least once a month," he teased in reply, "and that would be a miracle for Eric Johnson."

"Seriously, I hope we can agree to write every week. You love me at least that much?"

"You can certainly say that." And he did mean it. At that moment he would have even promised to write daily. And would have believed himself – even though none who knew him would have believed it.

# Chapter Thirteen

Frankie and Amy were walking down the New Hampshire heavily wooded road, the girls and Sarah and Terrance having been left in "mother's" care.

"So what did you learn when you finally got him on the phone?"

"Nothing! Just a lot of excuses! You know! 'I was doing this' or 'I had to do that' etc. Of course he had to admit that some of the time out of touch he has been what he calls 'sharing the responsibilities of hosting their guest'. I'd love to hear how much time Dean Conner has been sharing that responsibility. To say nothing of all the others on the panel which we all attended for the big lecture. She's far too attractive for my liking."

"Are you sure you're not making a mountain out of a molehill?"

"Don't use that expression. That's exactly what Eric accused me of doing. And he's not coming up this weekend. Some thin excuse about fall course preparation. I'll bet it's all with her."

"Just why are you so sure about that?"

"I can tell. You could too, if you were around them. It's not only the kind of looks between them. He's so obvious. I know him, remember? After eight years of marriage you have a pretty good idea of what's going on with a man."

"I never did with James."

"Oh, James! But then he was really strange. Even you say so. I never could understand why you married him in the first place. But to get back to Eric. What I was trying to tell you is about the feel, in the atmosphere, when you see them together. I can sense it. You may call it sexual pheromones, or chemistry, or the meeting of auras, or what you will. But I know it."

"OK. He's your husband. You should know. Let's assume he is involved with her. What are you going to do about it? He won't do anything. They never do. Men will take all that they can get – sex that is. I don't think they want anything else."

"Sometimes I say that about Eric, but not always. Look at the way he took responsibility for the girls on Sunday. And they adore him, particularly Nicole. What is reasonable to expect of a marriage, after the first bloom has worn off?"

"Sometimes I think we should just use them to fertilize us, then leave us alone. And if some of our sisters want that kind of stuff, let them all have it and don't worry us."

"You forget Amy, that it costs to raise the kids you talk about conceiving without ties. Eric does provide for us. I have to admit that."

"So you will just suck it up and shut up?"

"I think so. Can you see any sense, any real sense I mean, in making a case out of these four weeks. She will be gone at the end of next week, and we'll never see or hear from her again. And good riddance! In fact, as I think about it a bit more, here in this clean beautiful place, I would be stupid to give her the power to upset our family. She would probably just love to do that, so maybe I should just act as if it had never happened."

"But what's to say it won't happen again? I mean, what's to say that there will not be another woman, a month or a year from now?"

"I've never told you, but I think there was."

"That's just what I mean."

"He was telling me for months about a grad student at Tufts that he had met on a plane. From Indonesia, as I recall. I had not thought of it in this light. But now . . . "

145

"So what are you going to do?  Why not just give him an ultimatum: No more, or I'm out of here!  And I'll take you for all you've got!"

"Maybe we should get into therapy.  It's all very well for you to counsel the gun- at-the-head approach, but we are a family.  You never were.  And that has enormous importance for the girls.  They do adore him.  And they need him.  Of course, he does treat them as toys which he takes out when he wants to play.  But that's most men.  How many do you know who are any better than he as a father?"

### 

One evening after Amy had gone back to Boston with her two children, Frankie and her Mom were seated quietly in the dusk, the twins sleeping soundly, listening to the magic sounds of night by a mountain lake.

"Mom?"  Gran heard the tentative way in which her daughter had always begun a difficult question, even as a small girl.  There had been a long hiatus between the questions of girlhood and those of early motherhood.  Truth to tell, she had missed this dependence on the part of her favorite child.  But, she told herself, she is becoming a woman in her own right, and must move beyond being my child.  Nevertheless, this 'Mom' did warm her heart.

"Yes Dear?"

"Mom.  May I ask you something, about my marriage?"

"I'm listening."

"Things aren't what I'd like them to be these days."

"That was very apparent to all of us when Eric was here at the week-end."

"Yes.  Well, right now it's the presence of a woman professor from China – I mean Taiwan.  He seems to be quite taken with her."

"And that has you worried?"

Yes.  And no!  I mean this: Our marriage was perfect for the years before the girls arrived; and for a few months after.  But these last few years it has . . . .  No, that's not the way to say it.  Eric has - that's the way it is - Eric has become more and more distant.  I find myself feeling I'm just a mother, not a wife."

"What's wrong with being a mother? I've found it to be the best part of my life, and I've had lots of great experiences besides."

"I wasn't demeaning motherhood. Sorry! It's just that Eric seems to find me of no interest except as the mother of his daughters. I did think he would feel different if I had a son. But now I think that was naïve of me. His work and his dreams about changing the world seem to be the only things that matter. Amy thinks we should get into therapy. I'd really like to know what you think."

Her mother had been watching her closely during this brief monologue. Even in the faint light Frankie's anguish had shown itself in the trembling of her bottom jaw, and her mother reached out to hold her hand in silence. They sat that way for some time, the evening's calm a marvelous salve. Eventually, feeling they were on the same wave-length Gran took the initiative, in the style inimitably hers:

"Are you *happy* in your marriage?"

"I don't understand why you're asking that. Surely it's clear I'm not."

"Sorry, my dear! I wasn't asking whether you are happy *with* your marriage. None of us is, all the time. I am asking whether you want to stay in this marriage. No! Don't answer me now. That's a big question. Take time to find your answer. Make a time, alone. Maybe all day if you want me to take the girls off for a train ride through The Notch from North Conway; whatever you want. But make a time, for yourself, and answer the question."

"I thought it would be a good time for Eric and me to see a therapist."

"No way! You first! I don't think it would be productive for you to go into counseling together until after . . ."

"After what?"

"Until after you sort out what you want for yourself and your daughters. That's the first thing you must do. You have to know who you are and what you want out of life, with or without him."

"You mean alone?"

"I mean that you must answer those questions alone, yes! Then you can talk with him about how your wants do, or do not fit with his."

In the ensuing silence she found herself with second thoughts about how they had parented Frankie. They had given her lots of love, but had it been tough enough? When Frankie wanted to avoid the socializing her father wanted, her Mom had taken her part, as often as not with the rationale: 'She'll get more out of reading a good book, anyhow!' Maybe we should have fostered socialization more; that way she would now have lots of social outlets and a large support network. She certainly has resolve, but she'll need more than determination if she's to be happy.

Her soliloquy was interrupted by: "That's clear. As you always are, Mom. But I thought couples should work these things out together."

"They can't do that until each is clear in themselves. You aren't. The basic fact is that we each make our own happiness – in a final sense. We do. Your happiness is in your hands. From time to time each of us needs help – to figure it out. But we do it alone. The key is what you feel, and what you want."

"Then what?"

"When you are clear on what you want, figure out whether that might be possible, even if he doesn't want to change. Only then would I suggest you talk to Eric. Ask him what he wants, and demand he be clear about his answer, just as you will be by then.".

"But Mom!"

"No need for but's my dear. I knew that word was coming before you said it."

Frankie looked like she might pout, or perhaps cry, so her mother jumped in quickly with: "Remember when you went to your first summer camp and phoned home in tears to say you couldn't compete with the rest of the girls?"

"Do I? That was one of the worst weeks of my life."

"And how did you feel at the end of the last week?"

"I didn't want to come home."

"Get the point?"

"Ah! Yes! You asked, back then, 'What is new to all the girls?' and when I answered 'Archery' you said 'That's it then; become better than any of them at that.' AND I DID!"

"You learned that you have potential quite beyond what you have achieved to date. Isn't that still true?"

"What do you mean?'

"Look at it this way. What proven skills of yours could be raised to new heights?"

"That's easy. I'm a born nurturer. Mothering and nursing have both taught me that."

"I can imagine you building on that natural quality in you."

"Really? How?"

"As a counselor, for starters. In fact, I'll bet there's lots of nursing slots in which you are technically a nurse, but spend most of your time counseling."

"So there is – as a school nurse," came with such a smile that Gran saw it even in the starlight. Quietly rising, she excused herself, and without turning on any lights, found her way to bed with a glow that comes only after effective parenting of kids who believe themselves too old for that kind of thing.

### 

Eric and SiokYim found Week Four very difficult. She repeated only once that she was willing to leave all, to go wherever he goes, as long as they can be together forever. He could not handle this. He was still mute when faced with the question "Eric, what do you want?" But it was in the air every time they were together. Yet this inability seemed to make no difference to their intimacy. Furthermore, the oneness was there with and without sex. The warm wonderful feeling was always there, beginning whenever their eyes touched. All separate identity had disappeared from his life.

But SiokYim received an irritated response whenever she pressed for regular correspondence after her departure. "Why?" he asked, being averse to writing anything which is not abstract, except his poetry.

"And I will telephone. Perhaps at the office would be better," Siok Yim added.

This was all too much for him to handle. It all came as a surprise. He had never had any need for letters, or frequent calls, especially if they cost a fortune. "But overseas calls cost so much."

"Costs?" she asked. "What are you talking about? What a call might cost never occurred to me. It never would. And if it is the way we can stay together, in a sense, then no cost would be too great."

At which point in these recurrent conversations he would simply enfold her and smother her with kisses, not so much for her sake as for his. He just had to have her love even while he could not respond in any of the ways of which she now spoke.

### 

The last Thursday morning she called to say: "Kathy has a gift for us. She says she will spend Friday night, my last night here, with a friend, so that we can have her place all to ourselves, for the whole night. She will then pick me up around noon and take me to the airport. Doesn't that sound wonderful?"

### 

For the rest of Thursday and much of Friday he could think of little but how they would spend that gift. Thoughts of her touching him, here, there, everywhere; thoughts of seeing her svelte body, moving around as if they were living together all the time and not just for eighteen hours, thoughts of endless caresses; all these held at bay the appalling realization that by three on Saturday she would be airborne and he en route to New Hampshire. And it would be over.

When Friday came he packed for the week-end, and then called her. She was doing the same. Tender nothings were being expressed when she announced, "Oops, there's the door. It's my cleaning being delivered. I must go." In that strange world which is anticipatory grief he tried to think through the state of his preparation for fall courses, and what he would he really need in New Hampshire. Getting nowhere, able to think of nothing, very unsure of what was going on, he simply sank into a chair. A long time later the phone rang.

"My love. Is that really you? Do you know what time it is?"

"What?"

"Yes, it's three o'clock, and you had promised to be here at two-thirty!" She didn't want to harp. This was their last night. But how could he? How could he have so little sensitivity to what it meant to be careless about obligations – not just to anyone, but to the woman he claimed to love. But, she told herself, I'll have to remember he's American, and not Chinese. Nevertheless, something deep within told her that this particular man, the love of her life, could not begin to understand symbolism, whether in Chagall or in punctuality.

He did arrive, very soon after. Their eighteen hours were all that he had hoped, and more. They were all she had hoped, and more. When Kathy arrived to be chauffer they were just inside the front door, stroking, soothing, and comforting every part of each other's bodies (which were fully clothed for the first time since ten minutes after his arrival).

### 

The airport drive was almost funereal. Kathy drove; they sat, holding hands in the back seat. "It's not as comfortable as the front passenger seat," she had suggested, but they thanked her with a smile, realizing she hadn't expected a positive response from either.

The lights through the tunnel made SiokYim think of his poem, and she smiled at him: "They're lovely, even if they have to be there for practical reasons." He smiled back his uncertainty about what she had said, his uncertainty about everything.

At the gate SiokYim first kissed Kathy, thanking her profusely. Then she turned to Eric. "It will be very soon, I promise."

To his responsive kiss he added, "I promise."

Then she turned and walked away with the same air of certainty about life and the world with which she had approached him only twenty-six days earlier.

### 

Airborne, gazing down at cloud comforters while Eric drove mindlessly toward New Hampshire barely aware of the scenery or the traffic, SiokYim pondered and reveled in what was between them. Theirs was an intimacy she had dreamed ever since puberty, but never fulfilled,

151

till now. Sure, there were moments with her family in which, for minutes, even hours, they were all taken up in a shared experience. There had been many times when Chi Nan, her boy and she had walked by the sea and suddenly both had stopped, silently, without a word, and stood, transfixed by the way the waves approached, expanded, crashed on the rocks, and then were lost in a swirl of wild conflicting waters. There were moments when her daughter Chr Hau had perfectly performed a ballet pose which had been beyond her for months, and looked up to see her mother, body as involved as the child's, her face aglow with her daughter' realization that "I did it Mom, didn't I?"

Yes, the intimacy she knew with Eric had all those qualities. Her afternoon with him in the maple and oak woods at Mount Monadnoc, when they had to walk single file on the path narrowed by a lush under-story in one place and from behind came a quiet voice ordering her to stop, and as she turned he pointed to a very large black bird with a red crest clinging to the side of a very high tree. Suddenly the silence was broken as it produced sounds as swift and powerful as a jack hammer in its determination to dig for a grub deep in that trunk. They had just looked at each other, and without knowing it, their fingers had joined and a deep sigh came in chorus.

Yes, the intimacy with Eric occurred around shared experiences which overwhelmed them both. But she could not begin to comprehend how, with this man, the sense of one-ness would persist long after the stimulus had passed. The result was apparently obvious. One day, as they stood barely touching except for stability as their MTA car swayed along the inadequate tracks she had noticed that most people in the car seemed to be staring at them. When she caught any eye it would not turn away until its owner had given just the hint of a smile, right at her, as if to say "Wow! You two really have it, don't you?" It was never a look of appreciation of two of "the beautiful people", for she realized that she was not exceptionally beautiful by American standards, and that Eric was simply a high average American. No, she told herself, it's the fact that the chemistry between us effects them in ways that they may not understand, but which they enjoy; that makes me so happy.

How natural then, she cogitated, that my body should always be ready, to speak what is beyond words, what is better done than said. How natural that I need to touch him all the time; that I am always ready to have him enter me and flow completely together. How odd he does not realize that, because I feel it all the time. I would express this intimacy physically, almost anywhere, under any conditions which did not offend others. And more, how odd that he does not understand that I would give up everything else in my life in order for this to continue forever.

# Chapter Fourteen

Eric's condition challenges description. In time, he was to write some of it to "My Love." But from the moment she disappeared onto that plane he was forlorn, confused, empty. Perhaps this was what a therapist would have called grief. Perhaps more basically it was the loss of the self which had melded with hers into oneness – at the cost of his separate individual identity. He certainly had no clue as to its name or definition. It seemed that the whole of his life had gone somewhere else. It was not simply the focus of his every waking thought. It was not simply the recollection of feelings being shared even before they were expressed. It was not simply the heightened sensitivity of every inch of his skin. It was not simply the sight of her, statuesque, proud, smiling just for him. It was not simply her naked, waiting, welcoming. It had no focus in any one of these things. It was all of them at once.

Everywhere, in every situation, she was there and not there. In bed, lying on his belly he felt her comfortable weight covering his back, his legs, his arms, even his head as she melded their bodies simply by touch. Turning over she felt as close to his chest and all the rest of him. On his side his arms wrapped around a pillow, trying for the entwinement which had become their practice, sensing it for seconds, and then it was gone. He could not walk without her, but suddenly she was not there. He felt her arm around his waist, her body pressing up against his side, her other hand pulling his arm even tighter around her waist. Then, romping through old fallen leaves he would reach out a hand, and his playmate would join it with glee - and not be there.

Her being there had been wonderful, miraculous, a time of ecstasy. But now the recollection of every such moment accentuated the void within. Every miraculous phantom presence was followed by pain through his whole body. And he cried - sometimes with sobs which wracked his body, sometimes soundlessly, as tears flowed down his cheeks. In two situations it was worst – when he received a letter from her, and when he wrote one. Even while at the lake he would structure the times of opening and the times of replying so there was no chance of interruption. How could he have answered a little girl's question: 'Why are you crying, daddy?' Why? He couldn't even answer that question himself. It just was so.

He would try to look critically at her picture, try to get perspective on the transience of their meeting, and the reality that she had come, and was now gone, forever. He would appraise the facial features, the lines of her shoulders, arms, breasts, hips and legs, telling himself they rated a seven or eight, not a ten, so why all the fuss? But to no avail. He would remind himself of his vocational objectives and achievements, of present rank, and reputation, and the plans which had always been dead center in his daydreaming time. Now that time was hers. He would remind himself of the importance to him of Jennifer and Nicole, smiling at the way their developing personalities had been so evidenced during that sailing "adventure", as they liked to call it. Now she gently intruded, and in a moment he was again all hers. The only escape, an escape he did not really desire, was to become even more intense than usual about what he was doing, whether reading, chopping wood, or playing with the girls as they arranged and rearranged the furniture in their dolls' house.

For Frankie, now they were only four, he seemed never present. Repetitions were now required if she was to get his attention, so she simply stayed in her own world. That world wasn't bad. She lived, more deeply and more fully, when here among the quiet woods, than anywhere else in her experience. Long walks alone, or with one or both of her daughters filled much of her time. She began to fill in the blanks of her thought about political activity back home – in addition to trying to answer the deep questions about her future which her mother had pushed. And not a day went by without what she called "glowtimes" concerning these two beautiful products of her own body - and his. Which brought her full circle to Eric.

Who was this distant man? Why was he so angry? It was not credible that his mind was where he always claimed: working some concepts through in my head, for Fall. One break, though: these days he made no sexual demands. She felt a bit of relief that he stayed so far over on his own side of the bed. And the two nights he had taken the girls up to a hut in the mountains she had been deliciously alone. But even on his return, from what they all three said was "a fantastic trip" he bit my head off when I asked the simple question: "How did the food work out?" Judging by the last few years, any initiative to improve the quality of domestic life would have to come from her.

"Darling" (She hadn't used that word for some time, and it got his immediate attention, not without suspicion.) " I think we ought to talk together with someone. You know. Get someone to help us get beyond this present communication barrier." It was not that she had discarded her Mom's advice, but that she *had* to do something to improve things, right now.

"Why ever would we do that?"

"Simply because there has not been a single conversation (of more than two sentences) between us in the six days since you came up to stay and the others left. I think the girls are noticing it. They really study both of us in some of those long silences at the meal-table."

The appeal to his paternal values always worked. Thus he agreed, and a week later they had left the girls with a neighbor by the lake and gone to Boston for the day to see a therapist.

"I'm always glad to see a couple working together," began the therapist. Eric winced. "Would one of you like to begin?"

A glance at Eric told Frankie, "No way!"

So she began: "I have no clear idea when it began, but Eric and I seem to talk less and less. In fact, the only conversation we have these days is about practical arrangements for our family. We have two girls, fraternal twins, and our home would have no life at all but for them."

"Mmm," murmured the lady.

"This has all become worse now we are on vacation by a lake."

"I'd like to know if you see it that way, Mr. Johnson. May I call you Eric and Frankie? I hear Frankie feels things are almost incommunicado between you. Do you share that feeling?"

"I suppose so."

"It really isn't just this time at the lake. It's been developing for at least two years. You just seem to spend more and more time at the college, Eric. I've no idea what you spend all that time doing. Why can't you spend more time at home?"

"Well, Eric?"

"Well what?"

"I'd like to hear you respond to your wife."

"I don't really have anything to say."

"Then why did you agree to come today?" demanded his angry wife.

"It seemed the easiest thing to do. I thought it would satisfy your need to do something about whatever is bugging you."

"It's *us* that is bugging me."

There was a long silence, the kind that is spent wondering which of the other two would break it. Eventually their therapist started over: "I get the impression that you had no real communication about coming here today. Right?"

"Yup," they chorused.

"Then how about we talk about the pattern of communication between you, back then, and now. Eric, I wonder if you could get us started. How would you characterize communication earlier, and these days?"

His extensive education remained quite hidden in his response: "I guess it was good a long time ago, and it's almost non-existent now."

"Any idea why?"

"Chiefly because there's nothing to say, except about the girls."

"What do you feel when you tell me that?"

"Nothing. Nothing at all. I just stated the facts."

"And what do you feel when he describes the situation that way, Frankie?"

"I feel he doesn't care at all."

"May I tell you what I hear in the way you responded when I asked for a description, Eric?"

"I guess so."

"Was I detecting a bit of anger?"

"Anger!" shouted Frankie, "That's the only emotion I ever get from him."

"That's quite ridiculous," retorted Eric, "I just state the facts, as I did when asked here. If you think I sound angry, that's just your imagination."

The session dragged on for another forty minutes, Frankie talking most of the time, comparing life now with the way it used to be. She became teary at one stage. But at no time did Eric join in the process which the therapist was trying to promote, evading all her attempts to get him to buy into the game. She did offer two suggestions – "homework for next time" she called them. The first was for Eric to say the first thing that came to mind each time he wanted to ignore his wife. The second was that Frankie should try to stick with the conversation, no matter what he said.

As they started off back to New Hampshire, all that Eric could think of was how very easy it was to express whatever he felt with Siok Yim, and how it contrasted to the inevitable situation with his wife. But, he told himself, there was no way he was about to disclose that, even if it came to mind the next time with Frankie that he shut down. He just knew she would counter with "Why can't you . . .?" or "You should . . ." As the miles sped by, all that Frankie could think was, "What am I to do? There must be something that will help me rescue our family."

# Chapter Fifteen

"What a place!" Ahad gasped. "I had no idea it would be like this up here." The two were seated atop Mount Chocorua, that volcano-shaped rocky cone which features in every second calendar depicting the glories of New England. For the lowlanders, its beauty is etched in their minds by the view of its reflection in a lake by the same name, the white trunk of a birch in the foreground, with both blue sky and blue water contrasting with the riot of Fall in New Hampshire. But at that time of the year, the peak rewards those with the energy of Ahad and Eric with a view of endless painted valleys between other mountain ranges in all four directions, the northern one being the Presidentials, climaxing in the just visible Mount Washington.

"It's more than worth the four miles and three thousand feet climb, isn't it?" Eric responded.

For a long time they just sat, recovering their wind, and allowing the place to possess them. On the way up they had shared something of what they wanted to do with their lives. At least Ahad had done so. "I want to be significant in the socio-political future of the land of my birth – even if I am a political exile," he declared, unselfconsciously and without affectation. Eric was quite certain that his friend would have influence of such dimensions. The ease with which Ahad voiced these dreams came as both a shock and a stimulus to the man who had been at a complete loss when SiokYim had asked him, "What do you want?" Then "I want sex with you" had been his immediate and honest response, albeit only a partial one. But her question had required a far deeper answer. That he knew, even though he still had not begun to formulate one.

More silence, until one active mind had to ask the other a question which was powerfully on many American minds at that time: "I've been waiting for a chance to ask, when we have time for a really extended answer: What can you tell me about this Khomeini? The Ayatollah? The guy who looks and sounds like he's the dictator of Iran?"

"That is more than a coincidental question, you know," Ahad began. "I'm beginning to think that my dissertation might eventually be something about the relationship between your William Fulbright's thinking about Iran, and how it was perceived by the Ayatollah."

"But that's a stretch," countered Eric. "The Ayatollah came to power several years after Fulbright's 25 years as Chair of the Senate Committee on Foreign Relations."

"Quite so. Five to be exact. But the Ayatollah Khomeini was an important figure from the time of my fifth birthday."

"When was that?"

"On my birthday, March 22, 1963, the anniversary of the martyrdom of the Sixth Imam (in 765), the Shah's brutal military police, the SAVAK, surrounded the school where he taught, right there in my home town Qum. They killed a lot of students and arrested Khomeini because he had been so outspoken against the cruelty and injustice of the Shah's rule."

"Quite a birthday!"

"Well, not exactly. I didn't know much about it, except that everyone was very excited and I'm told they could talk about nothing else. He was released after a week, but he again preached (I guess you would call what goes on in the schools we call madrasas), and was immediately re-arrested. His arrest led to more riots and deaths. There was no way of preventing his influence short of killing or deporting him, so he was deported a bit over a year later."

"But what kind of a man was he, and what was he saying? After all, if you can believe our media – which I can rarely do – he's just a dangerous demagogue. Are Iranians easily influenced because a guy can coin a phrase to describe the U.S. President as 'The Great Satan'?"

"Far from it. But the power of the man arose from his background, in which he was not alone. In fact, he is quite representative of the Ulema in Iran for decades."

"I think I recall what that is, but remind me."

"The clergy, I suppose you would call them. In Mediaeval Europe they would have been like the theological faculty at a university. You could call them the teachers of the faith. Anyhow, the Ulema at Qum were a bit different from elsewhere: they were both deeply mystical and deeply political."

"Sounds odd to me."

"Not so odd, when you consider that Islam is supposed to dominate all of life. The word means submission, you know."

"Yeah, I do know a bit about that. I used to know a Muslim woman quite well."

"Really?"

"Yep. But another time, perhaps."

"To get back to the fact that our clerics-cum-teachers-cum-professors at Qum were mystics and political, and the Khomeini seemed to have such guts. It's not surprising, you know!"

"That he was fearless?"

"Sure. Some one once wrote 'The mystic is invulnerable.' That's because they know for absolute certain, and the certainty is not an intellectual thing. It is really because mysticism is another way of knowing."

"I know with my head, and with my senses. How can there be any other way?"

"What does your Bible mean that 'Adam knew Eve'?"

"Physically, of course."

"And is 'physically' all there is to your knowing a woman?"

"I suppose there is something beyond my power to explain in terms of thoughts and sensations."

"There sure is. That is what mysticism is all about. It's a direct knowing. Mystics say they were, for some moments, part of the Ultimate, or whatever word you want to use for what we call Allah and Westerners usually label as God."

"How come no one ever explained anything about mysticism when I was forced to go to Sunday School in my teens? I would have been fascinated to learn about that kind of stuff. In fact, now you talk about it, maybe I will."

"Will what?"

"I will see if I can learn something about mysticism. It sounds a bit like something spiritual, and I can buy that, at least a bit. But no religion for me, thank you very much."

"Well, back to Khomeini. So he had a deeply quiet air about him which engendered respect toward him as a mystical source of knowledge, ideas, and inspiration. His works were widely read at home. While in London he wrote, extensively, about the plight of the great majority of Iranians. In '71 while there, he published Islamic Government. While the Brits and the Yanks continued during the early seventies to milk Iran, with the Shah's acquiescence, the Ulema as a whole were quiet. Then in '77 Khomeini's son died under mysterious circumstances in neighboring Iraq. Radical restrictions against mourning angered the frustrated populace. Then Carter visited the Shah on New Year's Eve and was characterized as The Great Satan. When students at Qum demanded their idol be allowed to return they were massacred. Even the middle class deserted the Shah after six more months, and in September of '78 he declared martial law. There were more massacres and a major strike of oil workers. A few months later (early in '79), the Prime Minister allowed Khomeini to return just after he had allowed the Shah to depart. The rest of that year he used much of his popularity and respect in trying to get several groups together, for the good of the nation, but without success."

"But, if I recall a tiny bit of the history, that was not the last we were to hear of Khomeini?"

"No. But you know most of what happened that November: angry students mindlessly stormed the US Embassy. What had begun spontaneously was feted by their compatriots, and fifty-two Americans began their 444 day "stay". There was some initial abuse of those prisoners, which Khomeini tried to prevent, which discredited Islamic behavior to the whole world. At the same time, it pushed this Ayatollah into the world spotlight."

"And that's the bad guy we know most about."

"That's largely true. Circumstances gave him more and more power, in a practical sense, rather than as the inspirer of a revolution. In one year, 1980, there were four attempted coups against him and his forces. He appealed against such actions as contrary to Islamic law. At the same time, with the help of the U.S., Iraq's Saddam Hussein attacked. Khomeini had to put off several critical social reforms. Clerics were now the majority in the parliament (the Majlis). More and more he and they have adopted the rhetoric of God's chosen fighting a hostile world – a jihad. They are as bad as the self- righteous fundamentalists here, if you ask me. Of course, that's four years ago, about the time I escaped with my mother and two sisters. So I don't have any more I can relate that is first hand."

"So is he a good guy or a bad guy?"

"He's in a box fighting for his life. I think he would have been different if the Iraqis had not added the extra threat. But I do believe that he really is trying to create a just society."

### 

Days later over coffee Eric found himself saying to Michael: "I had a really interesting talk with my Iranian refugee friend the other day."

"I don't understand your relationships with all these foreigners."

"What do you mean 'all'?"

"Well, there was that Indonesian, then this Iranian guy, and this summer, well, you know, it was pretty obvious."

Eric ignored the reference to Siok Yim, finding it easy and natural to enter into a real exposition of where he currently stood about "foreign-ness."

"Michael, as my best friend I have to tell you that I don't exactly feel that any of those three is what you call foreign."

"Yeah?"

"I am an American, very much so, and very proudly so. And that was not modified by my year in Singapore. But what has happened as I became very close to Minah, Siok Yim and Ahad is that I can now put myself in their shoes."

163

"OK, so can I! I don't mean with those particular foreigners, I mean with foreigners in general. I can learn about them to the point where I can imagine their lives."

"I mean more than that. I mean really identify with them. When I hear a criticism of them, of any one of those three, or their countries, or their ways, or their political orientation I feel their emotional reactions. It's as if they were inside me, part of me. It's more than getting defensive on their behalf; I feel I'm *defending me!*"

"That's heavy. How come?"

"I'm not sure. I do know that with all three I have come to know them as closely as I have ever known anyone. I also have to confess that the two women have intentionally helped me to empathize. But the important factor is that I wanted to be in their skins. And now I am, for bad as well as good. I want others to understand them, their heritage, as I now do. And I do not want us to fight them – or even interfere with them in ways they don't want. We wouldn't want them interfering with us, and I feel sufficiently in their shoes that I don't want us interfering with them."

"I think I can imagine that."

"I talk to Ahad a lot about this. He is going through big changes, as an immigrant. The challenges are not the same for him as for me, but he's been reading up on theories about it, and thinks what happens to our personalities is the same."

"And what is happening to your personality - that I don't see?"

"He says that getting serious with another culture affects your identity, your idea of who you are. More than ideas, it's your gut feeling – of who is part of you. That's what I was really saying when I said that defending Minah and Islam felt like I was defending ME."

"I have had that experience – concerning French West Africans, because I worked and lived there for two years, and became very close to several."

"Then he says that serious contact also demands a change in the way you make sense of the world, of everything. It is no longer possible to make sense of the world by thinking of 'us' and 'them'. That's a big jump. That's how we define everything – as yes or no, in or out, good and bad, you're either with us or against us. Why, that's how we do our science, by eliminating possibilities. He says this crisis of meaning (that's the label he gives this issue) is unconscious most of our time, but it bubbles up in very personal matters occasionally, and we are torn in making a decision which once would have been one of those things where you just say 'of course . . .'."

"And I avoided philosophy as much as possible."

"Oh, so do most people. But we all have to make sense out of life."

"I guess I have to concede that."

"I used to get my sense of identity clearer because of my foreign friendships. My sense of meaning too. Their values and life styles titillated me, fascinated me, gave me a real buzz, but they didn't challenge me. Not until I sought of took those friends inside me. Does that make sense?"

"Yep. It does concerning my wife and children. They are inside me, inseparable parts of me."

"Well, I don't know that experience with Frankie: but I do know it with the girls and with the three foreigners we are talking about. I would fight for anyone because I believe in justice and fairness. I would fight harder for my family, for those same reasons, and because I care about them more. That's all paternalistic. Maybe it's even patronizing."

"My expressions of caring for mine are much different from "paternalistic", as you put it."

"Yeah! That's just the point. So are mine concerning Minah and Siok Yim. Even their personal preferences which I dislike, which bug me, seem to be part of what is now "me.' It's strange. We fight like mad about some of those. I get furious, and into a real stew. But if another were to criticize those same things, I would feel personally attacked."

"Can you make sense of that?"

"No. Neither in terms of who I feel I am, or as part of the total pattern of how I fit the world together. But because these are so much part of me, this discombobulation is bound to continue."

"Wow!" was all Michael could say. "How about that question about what you want. You wanted to talk about it. Truthfully, I have a very clear idea of what I want in life. What do you want?"

"Well, beyond being promoted to a full professor and getting a bit more money, and having a healthy family. Beyond those things, what do I want?"

"Ok, beyond the usual professional ambitions, what do you want?"

"I don't have a clue, that's why I'm asking you about the issue."

"Very simply, and I know this sounds West Coastish, I want to be all that I can be."

"All that you can be?"

"Yes, in every way. I have a clear image of the ideal I want to become; and I feel sure that the more I approximate that ideal, the happier, and maybe even the richer, I will be."

"Good heavens!" was all that Eric could respond. So he changed the subject.

### 

There had been one letter from Siok Yim, mailed from Austin, collected by Eric from the General Delivery two villages away, where he knew there was absolutely no chance of Frankie knowing of its arrival. He could not have said why, but he knew she would be very upset to know they were communicating. The result had been the need for a longer walk than usual, to allow a longer cry than occurred each day without the stimulus of a letter. He also found his favorite rock, half way up the Sandwich Mountain trail, to be the perfect place to compose a reply. Its four pages described life around the mountains and the lake, but boiled down to one single thought: without you everything is empty.

### 

There was a month planned at the Lake, after which three weeks before fall semester started. Two weeks into his month at the lake, the department chair called:

"Eric, Jonathon was to represent us at that international studies meeting the first week of September, and he's really ill. They say he will not be well enough to begin teaching mid September. Could you, would you go in his place? To Stanford, I mean. We need to know what's going on, who's producing what, and what the related foundations are doing, but that doesn't require any formal report."

Eric needed no further persuasion: "I'd be delighted." This was something he could throw himself into, something to get his mind off SiokYim. Delightful though part of every Siok Yim memory was, there always came the emptiness. He knew his only way of dealing with that was action, lots of action.

###

Early the first morning back he was at the office, checking his mail box. There was indeed a letter postmarked Taipei. Tearing it open with expectation of the warm glow which he always felt at the slightest suggestion of her presence he read:

My beloved,

I have the most wonderful news to share with you! It is something I'm sure will surprise you. But it is true! We, you and I, are to have a baby. Yes, I am pregnant. I knew this in my body from the moment of conception – the second week of our time together. I always do know, for I have been pregnant so many times, but only twice have I avoided a miscarriage. I'm sure that is because I did not want any more of his children. But Oh! I do so want yours. And I know I won't lose it. So there, that's the news of the decade.

Of course, there is other news here, but nothing else seems important beside this. So I'll get it off to you immediately. This is only my second day back at teaching, and I'm only just back from confirming this with my gynecologist.

I do love you so.

Your SiokYim

Eric could not believe what he was reading! It was more than incredible. It was stupid. She must have taken leave of her senses. What to say? But no time to waste! Something must be done! Clearly he must put some sense into her head, for she had obviously taken leave of all that high-powered gray matter displayed during her month here. Within an hour he had a reply in the post. It read:

My Dear SiokYim,

I am very sensitive to the excitement and pleasure you expressed in the letter I just read. It troubles me greatly that your emotions have so obviously taken charge. Please know that what I am about to say comes solely from my concern for you and all that you treasure most.

If you keep this child, several things will suffer. First, there is the child. It will be of mixed blood. This is a problem at all ages, but terrible in a kid's teen years. I recall how Eurasians in Singapore had it tough. Do you want your child to suffer all his or her life? Second, there is you and your career. What will everyone say? Won't they shame you? Your parents - to say nothing of your husband, who will certainly do the math, and realize in weeks that it is not his? Then there is your career. A baby takes a lot of time and energy. You are becoming famous. Do you want to ditch all that you have worked so hard to achieve? Fourth, and this I hate to say, but my finances are already so stretched that I would not be much financial help. I am certain that these things will all have occurred to you by the time this reaches you, and that you will have by then decided what I am sure is the only thing to do.

I do care about you.

Sincerely, Eric

Having pushed it with certainty into the mail chute, he breathed a sigh of relief, then added that old explanation-cum-expletive: "Women!" But at least he had bitten the bullet, and he was absolutely certain the matter would now be handled as it should. Her expected reply the second Monday from now should confirm that confidence. That settled, within hours he found himself thinking and feeling about her with the same ecstasy that had filled his waking hours since two days after her arrival. Moreover, he found that thoughts of her continued to evoke tears – from the sense of a void where she had filled his life in that new way. How he longed for that warm hand on his forearm.

### 

It was now seven weeks since SiokYim had left; and they had only had twenty-six days together. But he felt that he would never, could never have any deep feelings for anyone else again. He felt he had given to her something which he had not known to be part of himself, something which only came into existence because of her, something for which he had always yearned. That part of his very self was and was not his. He had not known of its existence before he met her. There it had been every single moment of her presence. Then she left, and that part of his very self went with her. Without her that part was totally missing Yet he wished he were not possessed by her, by this woman who was so happy to be pregnant by him, who wanted to spend her whole life with him, at any price. He felt that something (could it be his very manhood?) had been carried off on that plane to Taipei.

Then followed a terrible thought: maybe he would never be able to respond to any other woman, not ever again. He felt that he had given something which was now gone, and which denied him forever the possibility of being – in a profound way - with any other person. He couldn't give any of himself to Frankie, so why expect to give, or get, with anyone else. The thought horrified him. What had become of him? Worse than some amputation, had he lost the essence of being the lusty, exciting, vibrant personality he had only seen because it had blossomed in the company of SiokYim?

As the San Francisco plane climbed through the messy stuff into the clear, a bright thought came with the brilliance: maybe I'll meet someone new at this Stanford conference, and she will help me get clear of this thing about SiokYim. Maybe I could use such a person to free me of this wonderful but distressing sense of being possessed by her so completely that most of me is no longer available, even to me, its owner. Thank God the Chair asked me to fill in for the department by going West.

# BOOK III

# Chapter Sixteen

Only two things troubled Dr. Rani Mitchell. She had come to Arizona State as an undergraduate seventeen years ago after secondary school in India, and ever since then she had felt herself to be a person without a home. She functioned with ease both in the land of her birth and her adopted country, but she could never feel free of the sense that a part of her was lacking, whether in India or the U.S. The other continuing trouble was that she and her chemical engineer husband Gustavo had less in common every year, so that now they met and talked only with or about the twelve-year-old child of their college love - Lakshmi. Yet these two "realities" had become part of her persona, not given much more thought than the raven color of the tresses which, when free, hung almost to her tiny waist.

As a mid level staff person at The Peace Foundation of Phoenix she traveled a lot, partly as the public face of her organization, partly to deal with those superficially interested in its work, but chiefly to keep in touch with what was going on in the field of international studies, and who was doing it. Every year she managed to arrange her travels so that she could visit her extensive family in Chennai (formerly Madras, India). All in all, life was almost all she could ask for. She was excited about attending a conference on the Stanford campus.

The Stanford dorms and related cafeteria turned out to be less than the institution's reputation led her to expect. They were not exactly the

Hilton-style facilities at which most of her meetings occurred. It was a lifetime since she had been sequestered in a 'girls only' dormitory with one large shower room per floor. But these were not the kind of things that worried her. She was such a tranquil personality that she would have been hard pressed to name anything which she found unbearable. The same applied to people: their peculiarities always fascinated; they never seemed to annoy. She was the perfect representative of some utopian idea of what each person could become in a world completely at peace. Couple that temperament with a pleasant shape and good features always lit by a radiant smile, and you have the inevitable nucleus of a small group engaged in spirited conversation punctuated by lots of laughter.

Eric drifted up to one such group the second day at Stanford. Present in body, trying to be part of things, his heart and mind were still watching that departing Chinese back at Logan Airport five weeks earlier, and anticipating the letter which he had requested be mailed to reach him here during these five days, confirming that the crisis (as he considered her pregnancy) was passed.

In such a state he would not have been coherent had he tried to join in, yet he found himself warmed by the mood of these seven or eight people as they joked about every holy cow in the current international scene. One person in the group seemed to create its dynamic, yet without dominating: a small, shapely Indian woman with very long straight black hair. When a joke was borderline, her expression neither condoned nor condemned; when it was really clever, she saw the point immediately and led the mirth. Eric found himself thinking: I like her. If there is any woman here who might take my mind off SiokYim, this is the woman.

With whom else to sit at the next meal? He hated to admit the fact, but he had waited unobtrusively for her to join the line along the cafeteria counter. She noted his behavior, enjoyed the fact, but played the game of surprise to his: "Well, hello! I haven't seen you before. I'm Eric."

"I'm Rani; but of course, we don't need someone to read the name tags for us, do we?" He was no good at saying nothing, but that is exactly what he did until they sought a table.

"May I join you?" he asked, almost as a duet with another man who seemed to have been waiting, tray in hand, for her to get through the line. Damn, he thought, she's already got a chaperone, or something else. But having made the request, he tagged along as she turned her smile on both of them. In minutes their table was filled by three more and the meal's gaiety ended when one of the group reminded them that "The next session begins in four minutes, we'd better hurry." As the speaker and three others rushed off, he found himself left behind – with Rani.

"I'm in no hurry," she volunteered.

"Sounds like you have no more need for that session than I?"

"No. I don't. I've been to every session so far, and I want to enjoy these beautiful grounds before the conference ends. This is such a perfect Fall day."

"Would you mind me coming along?"

"Not at all," making him feel part of her world with her big, warm smile.

He seemed to her as quiet as she was talkative, so after a couple of innocuous remarks about the program, she allowed him to take responsibility for choosing the next conversation topic. They had reached the center of the campus, and were both gazing at the imposing façade of the administrative building when, out of nowhere came his question: "Do you believe there is just one right person in the whole world for a person to marry?"

Never at a loss for words her reply came instantly: "Of course not. There are bound to be, gosh, who knows? Maybe hundreds, maybe even thousands of great potential partners." Then, when he remained silent she went on, "Why do you ask?"

Not wanting to answer openly he offered: "That's not quite what I was asking. I mean, do you think there is a soul-mate, one specially made to fit you and only you, whom you are meant to marry?"

"Eric, do you realize you are talking to a woman from a country which has a tradition of arranged marriages? Not that mine was, but my parents certainly wanted me to go back to India and marry one of about six they decided were 'suitable'."

"But if there is a perfect person, somewhere, maybe we were meant to find that person sometime in life." He wasn't even sure why he said that, and, getting uncomfortable, decided to change the subject. With a nervous cough, which she noted, he asked, "And what does the Peace Foundation do?"

"Do you want the short answer or the long one?"

"How about one between?"

"Our stated motto, or vision, is 'Peace through Education'. That's very broad, but we support a great variety of educational projects, both in this country, and in the Third World. We are particularly interested these days in curriculum development, in this country and in poor nations. That's largely because of the orientation of some new members of our Board and a new Director they hired"

"Hey! That's interesting. I have been thinking about that problem ever since I was teaching in Singapore for a year. It was absurd to find high-schoolers there memorizing English rivers when they could have been learning about the people who lived by those rivers."

"Well. I try to keep on top of what is happening in this country. I get the occasional trip abroad, mainly as a part of the deal I struck when I joined them. I take in a lot of conferences in the U.S., but my real work is with particular groups who are designing and trying out new approaches to growing kids up to be more fully a part of the big human family."

"You believe that is a possibility?"

"What?"

"The human race becoming one big family."

"Believe it? It already IS one big family. We are already totally interdependent. The problem is that we let the small differences between cultures hide our similarities."

"I guess that is true. I'd never thought of it that way."

"Then there's the wonderful fact that the world is such a big place – so rich and varied, there's something fascinating at every turn. Why deprive ourselves?"

"You want to have it all?"

"Of course! There are no limits. Why should I limit myself?"

The remainder of the walk they shared views of the practicality of working to minimize those cultural differences. As they re-entered the next plenary session both were feeling grateful they had "played hookie." He felt at ease in communicating with her: "We must do this again. We've only just started to talk."

He could not have told you what the next speaker said. As he sat beside Rani he slowly became aware of something which had transpired without him realizing it was happening: He was getting to know a woman who had completely taken his mind off Siok Yim, at least for the last forty minutes. Moreover, he had to admit, she was even a bit of a turn-on sexually. Maybe this conference was going to be more than a chore after all.

Three sessions later Eric and Rani found themselves in the same small session - with a panel of three presenters on the topic of "U.S. Foreign Relations in Social Studies Curricula." At the end of the panelists' statements they both wanted the floor: "Madame Chairperson," they began in chorus, then looked at each other, laughed, and Rani said: "I'll yield to the gentleman; go on, Eric."

Not noticing the irony in the concession he charged in: "I completely disagree with the idea of one major segment, for a whole term, about what the U.S. is doing in the world. Kids just don't have that much interest in the topic. You'd bore them to death. What they need is a brief input about a current headline, the very same day. That way you would get more interest. If I taught high school I'd hate to try to hold the interest of thirty kids concerning the whole globe, and all the ins and outs of foreign policy."

"That's almost exactly what I was going to say," chimed in Rani, as she took her turn. "In a study we funded in Oklahoma we found that foreign affairs was rated lower by sixteen-year-olds than any other topic in the local press. I know that doesn't mean we should not teach it. Quite the opposite! But it does mean that we will have to be very inventive if we are to get such kids motivated enough to listen, let alone to do some research on a topic which engages them minimally."

As they left the room together, Eric was earnestly haranguing Rani about what a tough time he had evoking any global interest among Political Science majors, and she was nodding supportively, adding more data from the work which was so central in her life.

Later that afternoon the two wandered off through several quads, eventually settling down on a concrete bench and idly watching five sparrows squabble over something quite invisible to the observers. "Crazy, aren't they?" she observed.

"Perhaps; but maybe there's a lot going on between them which we don't see."

Teasingly, with a twinkle she suggested: "That can be as true with other species, can't it?"

The remark's reference to themselves went right by him. Then, without knowing why, he leaned forward and delivered a short, gentle, kiss to her forehead.

"Doctor Johnson!" she exclaimed in mock criticism. "What do you think you're doing, here, in a public place? What will people think?"

"Whoa. One question at a time. I expressed my liking you, that's what I did. I didn't think before doing that. But now that you cause me to think, I do want to kiss the lovely lips under that funny Indian nose you have. And as for being in public? I can't see a soul. I hope you didn't mind *too* much." With which she was kissed on the lips he found so seductive. His action was met neither by withdrawal or complaint. But she was cautious.

Not to be sidetracked, she pursued her query. "When I asked 'what would people think?' I guess I was thinking about your spouse - you look married - and mine. What would they think?"

There was silence from his end of the seat. Then: "But I'd like to do it again." He did, finding her sufficiently responsive to his gentle, experimentally careful action that it seemed to him to be a first mutual kiss.

Then, settling back away from each other, Eric offered a minimal answer to her question: "I don't have a clue what my wife would think. But more importantly, I don't think I would care, no matter what she thought about it."

"That's heavy. But also very vague. Unlike my situation."

"How so?"

175

"We are almost separated. Our daughter Lakshmi doesn't know about it yet. She won't until I have an apartment lined up for the two of us. She's thirteen, and I'm sure she won't be surprised. Kids are very aware by that time in a break-up, particularly girls. But my husband and I have been through a year of trying to get clear where we should go and we have decided to separate for a bit. So I have to confess that he would probably answer in terms just like those you just used, he wouldn't care."

For reasons Eric could not explain, he dropped her hand as they returned to the part of the campus where they were most likely to meet other conferees. But after dark it was different. Long walks on the remaining two evenings were punctuated by long embraces and deepening kisses. For Rani, this was all simply enjoyable – an outlet in a not-to-be-repeated situation. For Eric, it was both confusing, and extremely intentional. He had come with the idea of experimenting with the question: Can I ever respond to any other woman as long as I live? Within the limits of the situation, he had a tentative answer: maybe. But intention went further than that. Unless they made love, how would he know whether or not SiokYim would be there, in whatever body seemed to be attracting, stimulating, welcoming, and satisfying him? He thought it almost certain, even if he was somewhat turned on by this woman, that the power of SiokYim would keep him in its hold. For whatever reason, that scared him. He must know. Somehow he disregarded that miraculous "extra" with Siok Yim which was quite beyond sexuality. Such was the basis of his intentional use of this new friend, who in her own right was a delightful addition to his life.

They had first spoken four days earlier. It was now the last night of the conference, and in a dark corner of a small courtyard they sat necking. Small as she was, the most comfortable arrangement was for her to be on his lap, his right arm around her back, the left on her hip. A few long kisses and his left hand was exploring, first her breasts, then inside the waist band of her skirt, under her panties, and as she gave an enormous sigh, between her legs. It was very wet. "I want to take you to bed" was a hardly needed and very safe comment for him to make.

"But we're in segregated dorms. That's impossible." She said with a tone that implied acquiescence.

Like two kids, the professor and the foundation executive waited outside the men's building until it appeared all had retired, then quickly ran up the stairs and into his room.. In seconds they were naked together, under the sheets, both feeling awkward, and slightly stupid. "Do you really want to do this? She ventured. With the SiokYim phantom in mind his automatic answer was a definite "Yes!"

Neither would have raved about the experience. After a brief time he took her back to her building, agreeing they would breakfast together at 8:30, giving them both the time needed to catch their returning flights. On parting he felt that, after all, there could be alternatives to domination by the very thought of SiokYim. At the same time, she decided that even though the sex was mediocre, she and this man had a lot in common, and he was "a very nice person", with an unusual passion for life in all its dimensions. Neither had any doubt that it was more than a formality when she said, "I'll see you again, soon." And he replied: "You certainly will." And with a brief embrace and a real kiss, they turned and went their respective ways.

### 

"Daddy, we can have new dresses for Easter, can't we?" Was the confident chorus which greeted him as he walked in from the airport. The girls rushed upon him, hugging his knees, and soon were both held high, one in each of Eric's arms. Again came the cry, "Can't we Daddy?"

Eric looked to his wife for the prompt. When none seemed forthcoming he asked, "Frankie, what's this new dresses thing?"

"It's Easter in three weeks, and the main topic in their Sunday School class seems to have nothing to do with Jesus and everything to do with what the other girls will wear. On our way home last Sunday they gave me no peace until I agreed we could stop in at one place in the mall 'just to see' as they put it."

"OK. They want new dresses. What's another ten bucks each?"

"Where have you been, sir? Fifty would be nearer the mark."

"What! That's absurd."

"No it isn't. We're not just talking about one piece each, you know. A dress requires matching shoes, and hat!"

"And purses to match too! Please Daddy, can we?"

"But you've got many beautiful dresses. You both looked so lovely going off to church the day I left. You'll look like young princesses, the way you always do."

"We will not. We'll be laughed at by Monica and Sarah. They're getting new dresses at Easter."

"That doesn't matter. It's just not in our budget. We still have doctors' bills owing. Isn't that right, Frankie?" He looked pleadingly at his wife, hoping to be rescued from an onslaught he did not understand, but knew he could not win alone. She said nothing.

Again came the argument: "But all the others will have new dresses. They'll say, why don't we?" With this Jennifer dissolved in tears, clinging to her mother's skirt, while Nicole stomped away and pretended to find something fascinating outside the window. Frankie now added her ten cents worth.

"It's true, Eric, this peer pressure thing, I mean. It is ridiculous, but it is real. We should find the money, somehow. I'm sure the dentist can wait a bit longer."

Eric glared at her. This was a no-win situation, a set-up. She knew they would attack as soon as he appeared, but she had done nothing to prevent that greeting! Now, in their hearing, she was saying the cash flow was no problem.

"I don't know why you give in to their every whim. Sure, I want my girls to look beautiful, but . . ."

"But nothing!" now Frankie was a full-blown antagonist. "The issue is not money, Eric, and you know it. Do you think that expense is the cause of Jennifer's tears and Nicole's pout? It's all about peer pressure. When they were two, you could get away with denying them some things. But at five it's another story."

"Alright, do what you damned well please. But they have to learn some day to go against the crowd!" With that he stamped off to the bedroom to unpack his bag, after which there were things he had to do in his study before supper, during which he sat in stolid silence, looking at neither the girls or his wife.

###

"There's a regional meeting Friday through Sunday at New Haven, three weeks from now. Are you going?" came the slightly Indian voice when he picked up the receiver in his campus office.

Delighted to hear Rani's voice, which, no matter how badly he felt he had performed this last hour in class, simply made him feel good, he asked, "Are you?"

"Yes."

Then, checking to be sure he wasn't overheard, he found himself saying, "I am too. I wonder what you think of the idea of us sharing."

"I think it would work best if we each had separate rooms. But we don't have to use both, do we?" So it was arranged, and accepted by all involved at home, with some slight distortions.

Rani was ecstatic. The doubts which had surrounded the Stanford encounter had now been quite swept away. She wanted real companionship, plus sex, plus affirmation that she was still an interesting and desirable woman. The apparent relief with which her husband welcomed their separation had left her with more than a few doubts about her desirability. Now that another man , supposedly safely married, but very fancy free, was clearly appreciative of her in all ways, she felt on top of the world again. That was not surprising. Her total approach to life was a positive one, and only the female part of her identity had been challenged in the separation agreement. Her femininity reassured, she was her energetic, bouncy self once again. With the old spring back in her step she included in her carry-on one extra object which took very little space – her tiniest bikini, for they had, in jest, agreed to meet "in the pool" (which was covered and heated) as soon as possible after four on Friday.

Eric's feelings were, as usual, available to him only in sexual form; the others were completely unfocussed. The excitement was partly explained by the memory of their first kiss, and not the night in the dorm. At the same time, he was feeling some discomfort about SiokYim. There were now two reasons for this. First was the fact that in a whole month he had not had a letter from her: he still did not know whether she had aborted the pregnancy. But of course she would have, on realizing the wisdom so clearly expounded in his letter responding to her news. But the real point was that he still felt as he had the day she left – bereft, forlorn, lost – as if a central part of him had been excised and carried off to a far country. Being attracted to Rani and acting on that attraction had not mitigated 'the

SiokYim sensation'. He still wanted her presence, craved it every day to the point of tears, and looked daily for the letters she had been so adamant about exchanging with lock-step regularity.

But the very next day there was a letter. His heart leaped as he noted the stamp: Taiwan. Pocketing it until after class, he then found a quiet spot under a tree and read:

My love,

All is well here now.

Sorry I have been quite unwell and have been unable to correspond these last few weeks. But I did get your letters, infrequent as they are.

I should be able to write you a real letter next time.

As ever,

Your SY.

The brevity frustrated even while it puzzled him. Why so short? Why nothing about his careful letter to her? And about the two other letters he had written, even though they had been two weeks apart rather than weekly as he had promised? Yet there was still *the SiokYim effect*. He felt a warm glow over his whole body, found himself walking more lightly, even inadvertently smiling at Beverly Thompson, that ogre of a colleague who seemed to hate him.

# Chapter Seventeen

Yes, he uncertainly told himself; that looks like her, there in the shallow end. But gee, I didn't realize she had quite such a body. It's not the curves, nice as they are, it's the movement. When she looks up or down, or reaches for that ball, or grabs that youngster it's like I was watching a ballet. And that suit, there's nothing of it. Yet it's the movements I could watch all day. So he stood silently feasting on this delight. Thank God this is not the hotel where the conferees are supposed to stay. She seemed involved with two small children playing near, so he slipped into the pool and swam underwater until he touched her legs. She squealed: "You imp! But who else would attack me like that?" He liked her calling him an imp; maybe he was one at heart. They kissed, as conservatively as the pool required, then found they could get closer in the deeper water without attracting undue attention. In a few lengths of the pool, to his surprise she kept pace with him. "You're very good," he complimented her.

"Time to get dressed?" she asked, with that mischievous smile.

"In a manner of speaking," he cracked back.

In comfortable clothes he soon found himself knocking at her door. "Come in, Sir," welcomed a bare-footed, long-robed woman, the garb making her look much taller than her sixty three inches. She latched the door, advanced in front of him into the center of the room and turned. It might have seemed like forever, but actually it was only for a few seconds that they looked at each other, enjoying the other's visible appraisal.

Rani's look nearly always contained the hint of a mischievous child. Life actually was like a game to her, with the acceptance of surprises

181

and the creation of them for others. While that might have indicated immaturity in another, it manifested her considered approach to the whole of human existence: life contains endless wonderful possibilities for both fun and growth, if you embrace them. Eric was full of intriguing potential. Let it take her wherever it leads.

Eric was simply turned on, wordless.

Slowly he put his arms around her as his mouth found hers. It was like no kiss he had ever known. It was like none she had known herself to give. Quietly, softly, very slowly one tongue explored the other's mouth, then rested while the other did the same thing. Then their tongues danced. Time no longer existed for her, for this could only be called "the melting"; she felt that was what had happened to her. She was quite unable to distinguish her own tongue from his, his mouth from her own. Their very beings seemed to be joined in this kiss. It went on and on. Neither wanted the experience to end. He was aware of nothing but their mouths, but she was suffused with a glow which might have started there, but now made her whole body feel hot.

Drawing away from the embrace, she waited while he undressed, then allowed him to untie her sash and slip off her robe. It was all she wore, and it slipped silently to the floor as they moved with the certainty of long-time lovers to the bed and, without a second's hesitation, became one body. Eric could not believe what had happened. Nothing in his past, and certainly not their time in Stanford had prepared him for this. Copulation at Stanford had been (dare he use such a word?) perfunctory. This union was physically and emotionally beyond anything he had known.

Some time later he exclaimed: "Did you see the time? It's 8:30! We've been making love for three hours. I can't believe it." Nor could he believe the positions, and the activities, of which he had never heard, or dreamed.

"You really are a physical person, aren't you, Eric?"

"Yes and no. I don't know. I've always liked athletic activities, but if you're asking whether I'm sexually more physical than the norm, I really don't know. I don't have a clue. But I do know that the human body is like a temple to me. It is a holy thing, to be treated with reverence. I guess when I say it's holy I'm trying to say that what happens to my body, when I'm not directing it, is somehow more than me, greater than me. I don't know. That doesn't say it. I have never tried to put this stuff into words."

"Is that what you have been thinking about these last two hours?"

"NO. Certainly not! It's been much more elemental – just your body, and mine, and what has been happening between us. between our bodies, that is. I haven't been thinking at all."

"I'm delighted to hear that. I wasn't either. But the feelings - they have been so delicious."

"What really amazes me is just how sensitive I am in so many parts of my body. You know, parts you always thought were not erogenous. So much of me is just beginning to wake up."

"That's what I mean. Didn't you know that about yourself?" as she ran her finger from the tip of his nose all the way down to his toes, pausing for a few seconds at - he seemed to remember – six places on the way.

"Well, I am extremely sensual –with nature. I love to see smell and hear what goes on whenever I'm out of doors."

"I'd guessed that, the day you commented on the sparrows at Stanford."

"But my own body's reactions to all that, and to your body. That's' obvious. But don't ask me to put it into words."

"Why not?"

"Well, I guess I'm like all men in my approach to sex. Or at least I was."

"You changed?"

"With someone's help."

"I'm glad for that. What changed you?"

"I've thought about that a bit."

"Yes?"

"Well it happened like this. A really wonderful woman helped me to imagine what would please her, by giving me pleasure."

"I don't quite understand."

"She demanded that when she touched me I should stay quite still and enjoy the feelings which came. Then I would touch her in the same way, and I could guess her feelings. And if I watched her expressions, I could tell when to continue, to change what I was doing, and so on."

"So she used your reactions to help you understand hers?"

"I guess so."

"With what result?"

"I think you know the answer to that. Already, by what has just happened. Before her I would have never pleased you. I probably would have just made you mad that first time I even kissed you. We would not be here, now."

"Then I am profoundly thankful to that lady."

There was a long smile between them before she asked: "Can you tell me what pleases you? And how?"

"I don't think I understand."

"I'm asking about what gives you great sensual pleasure."

"You know the answer to that."

"No I don't. I want to know the many things that bring sensations in your body that are worth dwelling on, for moments, or even hours."

"I've never tried to do that, except to make Siok Yim as happy as I wanted her to be."

"Then use my weakness: I love to touch. I love to be touched. I think I've had a deficit of touch since childhood, and I don't think I'll ever make up for it, but I need to try. You apparently like touching me, and so wonderfully. How about you just linger over my touching you, and enjoy it to the full."

"Sounds like a great proposition to me."

A long time later he whispered in a hushed voice: "I think we've blown the evening session. Thank you. I could not have imagined anything I'd rather have done, or had done to me - or with anyone else."

"I feel exactly the same."

So off they went, found a fast food place handy, brought it back and spent five more hours very much awake, alternating between giving each other pleasure, and learning about each other. She knew a great deal about her own body; that night she had the joy of giving him more than the ABCs about his own sensual pleasures.

### 

"How come you're more globally oriented than I would have expected? Is there an underlying global commitment at your college?"

"No way, almost the opposite. We do have a dean who acknowledges that the rest of the world matters. And my department has a chair and one other who share such concerns. But for the most part, it's an uphill battle. That's why . . ." and he paused.

"Why what?"

There was silence for a long time. Then, with a sigh, he said one sentence: "That's why the dean asked me to help in hosting a visiting professor from Taiwan this summer."

Another silence was more than Rani could resist. Gently, she inquired: "And something happened between you? Between you and that Taiwanese professor? What was the name you mentioned, Siok something?"

How could she have guessed that? He asked himself. But having no answer, and not wishing to look completely stupid, he waded in, soon finding himself telling about the wonderful aura about her and the way it made him feel completely bewitched.

"Did you say bewitched?"

"Well, maybe that's the wrong word. I feel she owns me. I feel, except when I'm with you Rani (at which she gave him a skeptical look), I feel empty all the time. I don't have a clue what happened between us, but I feel my life started the moment I met her at the airport, and it seems to be in pause all the time we are not in contact, physically or by letter."

He had watched her in his intense way through this last statement, straining to catch any hint of distaste, or resentment. There was none. How amazing, he thought. It's almost as if she is happy to know about the

185

most important woman in my life, and it's no skin off her nose. This is an unusual woman. How lucky can you get!

"Ah! Now I see why you asked me about soul-mates. That's what you feel you have found."

"Yes. And given the fact that I'm married, and . . . Well, you know."

But Rani did not "know." How could she? She liked Eric very much. Perhaps more than she had intended. But they had shared almost nothing about his marriage. She did realize that there was no way he would ever leave his daughters, for every time they were mentioned she received a lengthy appreciation, as if nobody else had ever fathered a girl. He seemed to have no clues concerning what matters to women. Even his daughters' pleasures and sense of fun were largely a mystery to him – except for the shared tickles and cuddles, of which he quickly tired.

Now she responded: "No Eric, I don't know what you will do. But I do know you have to give it some real attention, and not just let things take their course. There are endless possibilities." At this point she was thinking that she would soon be 'available'. At the same time, she felt that this lover was also a friend, who she would want to help if he asked, and support, even if he didn't. "But if we don't take care of ourselves, we may not like the outcome. But tell me more about SiokYim."

He did so, quite surprised that such a conversation should be accompanied by kisses all over his chest. Other pleasures also mixed with his undefended outpouring of the confusion which had dominated him for three months. He told Rani everything – or almost. He revealed nothing about the pregnancy, or the way her need for order and meticulous commitments irritated him. In this silence he felt himself defending her, with no clue that SiokYim would have loved him for his openness about their relationship, but not for keeping silent about what was basic to her identity as a Chinese.

### 

One day toward Christmas Michael suggested he and Eric take a long walk together. "I wanted to get your feedback and support on something," his red-headed buddy began. "It's this Apartheid business. You know that I went there (to South Africa I mean) as an AFS (American Field Service) exchange student. I stayed with some wonderful Afrikaans people. I think of Hans as more my father than the one I lost when I was 23. That's the way it often happens when exchange host families make you part of their family for a long time. And we always write, and so on."

"OK. So what is it that we need to plot?"

"I wouldn't say 'plot'. Well, maybe I would. I'm proposing a course. . ."

"You must be kidding! Look at the beating I took when I proposed that course on foreign aid."

"Forgive me putting it this way, buddy, but the South African situation is acute, and urgent. We have to teach the campus about it."

"I agree. But I have come to realize that those of us who have lived in another culture are different. I don't think a course can make up for that difference. That year in Singapore was much more than a head trip year. I'll never be the same again."

"I agree. The overseas living changed me too. Now I bleed every time I think of poverty. I don't even have to close my eyes to see deformed beggars, or the prematurely aged spitting blood as they wait in a stinking emergency waiting room at a tragically understaffed and under-equipped hospital. Those people are part of me. Maybe there are situations just as sad here. But I saw and felt those. And I felt so guilty at not giving to beggars. To say nothing of how I felt that I often spent on a meal, right there, an amount which my waiter had to feed his family of six for a week."

"And what the numbers look like, when you compare our income and theirs - that my wife and I consume more in a day than the maker of my pants gets in a year. Or that each Norwegian gives to other nations *seventeen times as much* as I do, as a citizen of the U.S."

"But the South African situation is about freedom, more than about economics. I am confident this nation will eventually see that. It's such an obvious parallel to our own civil rights problem."

"OK. Fair enough. It does have more immediate appeal than my foreign aid concern. So why this secret strategizing?"

"Simply this: the course is a ploy. It's a way to form a nucleus who will work politically, here on campus. You must realize that much of our college's endowment is invested in South Africa, and just as New England firms are also abetting that terrible system by letting them - the Afrikaans that is - use their cash, so is our college. If that cash weren't available, there would be a chance for the blacks. But not so long as we continue to give tacit, and financial support to their abuse of eighty per cent of the population - to say nothing of the imprisonment of many like Nelson Mandela on Robbins Island, for years."

"No wonder we're friends. You're even worse than I. Each of us is a real and present danger to the status quo around here. But I share your passion abut the injustices visited on the poor of the earth – nearly all to our advantage. That's what I was really getting at about foreign aid, and why I wanted to teach that. I want things to change so there'll be more justice around this globe. If we don't help, how will the poor ever get what they have every right to enjoy?"

The mention of this conversation to Frankie that night brought a surprising response. "I'm part of a group of women that is into this issue – of divestment from South Africa. We are picketing Harvard on Saturday – if you can care for the girls."

He looked at her in wonder and appreciation. Not without a tinge of irony he responded: "I knew there must have been something which brought us together." She did not appreciate that – not one little bit.

### 

Two weeks later the department meeting took place. The proposal was argued vociferously, particularly by Beverly Thompson and Michael. Michael seemed to get along no better than Eric did with Beverly. Again, the argument which won the day was staff time.

"Does goodness never win?" was Michael's bitter under-the-breath comment as they left.

"I've decided we must fight for this, and my course."

"Isn't that what we just spent two hours doing?"

"Yes. But there is the next battle of this war. That's what I'm thinking about. And here's an idea. What if I volunteered to take one of your sections of intro, as well as my own two, so that you were freed up to teach that course. The department would be better off, with more FTE's, and I could manage it. Teaching another section of the same course means that many more student conferences, and lots of papers. But using scantrons for mid-terms and finals makes it very easy once you have the questions – which would be the same for all three of my sections."

"That's all very noble of you, Eric, but . . ."

"But nothing! I'm determined we are going to move this place off dead center, globally, I mean. Maybe next year you could do the same thing to persuade these bean counters that it would be no loss to allow me to teach the course I proposed on aid."

"Ah! I see that you are not suddenly all altruism," Michael teased.

"Yes and no. I'm altruistic about the big goal. I'm selfish about wanting an ally, especially one who'll share some of the burden."

They agreed. The Chair was hesitant, arguing that quality might suffer with the extra load, but eventually agreed to take Michael's proposal back to the department meeting, without reference to Eric's other course proposal. Moreover, he assured them that he would talk it up with one or two in advance, and would back it when they all met.

### 

"Well, sometimes dreamers win," smiled Michael over their celebratory beers five weeks later.

"Welcome, world, to at least *this* political science department!" was Eric's toast.

### 

Letters now came every Thursday to the department mail boxes, and Eric found himself counting the hours until the next one. Not that their receipt was all pleasure. Almost every one contained some comment like – "And what kept my love so occupied that he could not find five minutes to send a Valentine card to the woman he calls 'the most important person in my life'?" Nowhere was mention made of her health or abortion. This in spite of his indirect asking by way of inquiries and wishes about her physical well-being.

A January letter announced that Siok Yim would be visiting the U.S. the following August. "I have some money saved up, and there is nothing matters so much as seeing you, my Eric." He loved reading

189

such endearments, finding in them the nourishment which made him feel whole. She ended: "Any ideas?"

His mind went into high gear. How to get away from everyone, to some other part of the country, without rocking the boat? For two weeks he searched the journals for likely conferences in an exciting part of the country, eventually settling on one in LA. He had frequently dreamed out loud about wanting to visit the headquarters of the John Birch Society in Pasadena "to demonstrate my perversity, as well as learning what really motivates such people" he would explain. They could see some sights and share the conference, with no one the wiser. Two letters later, the dates were set, the tickets bought, and both were feeling: But I have six whole months to wait!

By the time the detail program of the conference was out, Eric's name was there, as a member of a panel discussing the long-term effects of Fulbright–related programs of student and faculty exchange. Because of his related dissertation, and the fact that he was working on a book for which the tentative title was The Fulbright Legacy, it had been easy for him to persuade the panel's convenor that he should be included. This helped publicize the college which, because of that benefit, paid transportation. He would be somewhat out of pocket. But time with SiokYim! He would have stolen from his mother if need be.

### 

Mount Monadnoc was little more than an hour's drive away, and with just Ahad for company, the perfect hike on which to get another perspective on the world –right away from academia, its politics, and other stresses. This peak had no connection to any range of hills or mountains. Alone, it simply rose two thousand feet above all the surrounding countryside. It could have been a small Mount Fuji, but it wasn't volcanic. But, as in all New Hampshire hikes, 'being on top, in the clear' was only to be experienced after climbing three fourths of its elevation. The dense, richly hued woods, however, were just what both needed.

"I really can't believe how different the world seems once you get into a forest like this. How does it feel to an Iranian?" Eric inquired.

"Very strange, but quite wonderful. It is so gentle. If you want me to compare? I guess the shade is the most obvious difference. A few trees right beside a stream is the best I could hope for around my city. Heat, lots of it, and none of this strenuous walking in mid summer. It'd be far too hot." A pause. "But may I change the subject, Eric?"

"Of course."

"What are your honest feelings about Iranians?"

"Wow! You put me on a bit of a spot."

"How?"

"It's like this. I think of the occupation of the U.S. Embassy in Teheran and some of the stories about torture, or at least abuse, of those Americans. That all gives me a bad feeling about your countrymen. But then there's you. Except in some small ways, I see and feel you to be just like me. In fact, I feel you are more my brother than my blood brothers! Why? Especially when you so often tell me I'm wrong."

"And I have to agree, in feeling we're like brothers!" came back instantly from Ahad.

"It really makes you wonder how real the differences are between cultures. Maybe those dreamy-eyed co-eds are not so naïve when they claim that we are all the same, in all countries, and there are wonderful and evil people spread all over."

"I share that conjecture."

"What a word! I can't remember how long it is since I heard someone use the word conjecture. You foreigners put us to shame, the way you master our tongue."

"But seriously, you, personally, have no antipathy toward Iranians?"

"Heck no!"

"But you're not typical?"

"That is only too true."

###

"Eric!" He didn't want to acknowledge the command. Particularly in the middle of a paragraph which was demanding all his attention to understand. Why can't people write clearly?

"Yes dear."

"I've been thinking. There's a shortage of nurses at the moment. You know how it goes up and down. Well, it occurs to me that this might be a good time for me to get back into it. I hear they are still looking for one at the girls' school."

"But what about the girls? Who will take care of them?"

"I beg your pardon. The same one who gets them up, gets them dressed for school, takes them there or to the bus, feeds them when they get home . . .You know very well who will take care of the girls."

"No need to get into a tizz. It was just my first thought. The money would certainly be nice. Specially when I do not have any assurance about my job. You realize that their decision not to give me tenure means that I will have to find somewhere else a year from now? I was simply appointed on a three year contract. Anyhow, I must get a tenured job, and the fact that they turned me down here means they are unlikely to give me another short-term commitment. But anyhow, what do you want me to say about you going back to work again? As long as it works with the rest of your stuff, it's OK with me."

"That's nice to hear," came back, sarcastically. "You mean as long as it doesn't affect you in any way at all. That's what you mean, isn't it?"

"Of course! I am the main breadwinner. I take care of what's outside the house; you take care of what's inside. Right?"

"Wrong. You take care of what suits you, and you scream bloody murder if I don't take care of every other thing, small or large. Who arranges baby-sitters? Who plans the food and other stuff when we go up to the Lake? Who lines up all the details of the girls' activities, and coaches their kick-ball team, and arranges for their check-ups, and sends Christmas cards, and even buys their gifts for me?"

"You are in a tizz!"

"Me? It's you who are in a tizz!"

"Whatever. I have reading I want to do. So just go and nurse, as long as you don't bother me."

"Thank you. Thank you very much Eric. I knew I could count on an angry response. That's all I ever get these days. I think it's about time we talked to a counselor, or my minister, or someone."

"What? We're fine. We don't need anyone prying into our lives, telling us what to do."

"You are absurd. You know as well as I that no counseling professional tells people what to do." There was no answer from the man who gave every effort to focus on the page and end this conversation.

"Well? Can I make an appointment with someone?"

"If you insist! But I think it's a waste of time and money."

"Well I think it might just be of benefit to the girls, even if not to us."

# Chapter Eighteen

If the plane is due at 7:40 Eric reasoned: That means she will clear customs sometime after eight. It will take me thirty minutes to drive out and park. If I leave for the airport at seven I'll be a good thirty minutes early; that will show her that I am not always as casual about such matters as she believes. He had called at six about the expected arrival, but the arrivals board now showed 8:40. What a waste of my good time, he found himself muttering.

But when she walked through the Customs door all such thoughts melted away. Enfolded in each other's arms he whispered: "Oh my love, my love, how wonderful to feel you in my arms. Welcome back to my world." Her response was a long, warm kiss, accompanied by hands caressing his neck and ears, then his scalp, and then, after she stood back to look at him from head to toe, his face received the same treatment. The only thing he noticed but euphoria was a slight hesitation of her appraisal over his feet, but that awareness was gone as fast as it came.

An hour later the room service arrived with the light but restoring food and beverage she needed. "Thank you for the thought, darling," she responded, "but no wine for me just now. I find I get less jet-lag if I completely avoid alcohol during and just after the long trip. And you don't want me collapsing prematurely, now do you?" Her eating was slow, for she had to touch some part of him constantly, but eventually he was able to say:

"Now . . ."

"You have been wonderfully patient, my love," was all she said before they kissed again. This time the sequence was predictable. Each was undressed by the other in what amounted to slow motion, savoring each additional glimpse of the other's body. If either went as if to remove a second garments of the other there was a chastisement: "Uh Uh! It's my turn," followed by shared giggling. "I want it to be just like the first time," she said, lying back, spreading her legs only a little, so that he had to help their position some.

"How can you always be so wet? No matter when, where, or how often?"

"How come you don't know? It's because of what you are to me. Our bodies and our spirits are joined, even at a distance of five thousand miles. How could it be otherwise now when I can see, hear, and touch you?" Whereupon she did all the touching possible with his penis thrusting as far into her as he could get.

They were relaxed, stroking each other in every available place, as she began, "Now about these habits of yours."

"These habits?" he parroted.

"Yes. Like correspondence and footwear."

"What! I don't believe this."

She could sense the irritation change his body, and while her hands continued to caress him she whispered "Oh my love, my dearest love. I should not be so Chinese. I'm sorry. But I also need you to know me, through and through."

He could not suppress a retort: "I can't believe you are saying any such things now, here, within two hours of arrival."

"We'll talk about it later."

"No. We've started now. What was that strange way you looked at my feet at the airport?"

"Alright. You really want to understand me? Very briefly, propriety is of the essence, as your colloquialism goes. So wearing a dirty old pair of sneakers when you are meeting the most important person in your life for the first time in a year is . . ."

"Fourteen months," he interrupted, in more anger than affection.

"And, as I have said in every second letter, your failure to keep your promise to write at the beginning of every second week has really hurt me. It really has." She was near to tears in her attempt to make him understand. For it must be his lack of understanding which makes him so careless of what matters to me. The only other explanation is that he doesn't really love me, that his protestations are in fact contradicted by his behavior. But that she could not bear, and it was the pain that she had known every second week since they last parted. How could he not understand?

Although he was far from understanding her distress, the fact of it was now obvious to him, so he tried to jolly her out of it: "Come on, now. You're exaggerating!"

"I am not. Promises are sacred to me, made by anyone, or made to anyone. And to the woman of your life, as you claim I am . . . " She lapsed into silent frustration.

Eric also lapsed into silence. It continued until he had to use the bathroom. She followed him, and sat astride his thighs as he sat on the toilet seat, her hands fondling the back of his head and neck. "Oh my love, my dearest love, I'll be waiting when you come back to me."

And she was. How could she be otherwise? Why was he so silent? So removed? As if a wall had been built between them? Yes, he's now inside where he belongs. He is about to ejaculate. "Oh! That's so-o-o-o-."

The night was mostly sleep, with two pleasant, if silent interruptions. Breakfast, by a pool, should have been idyllic. It would have been if she had dictated how it went.

But he would have none of her excited talk of her son, of the way the family had found it difficult to see her leave. She wanted to tell him that her mother seemed to sense - immediately on hearing her daughter's description of her U.S. visit - that SiokYim might well be leaving permanently for the States. Indeed, she was ready to do so, down to the point of having acquired a resident visa for this trip, which would allow her to remain in the U.S. permanently and bring the children. She wanted to talk in those terms. But what was she to do? He had withdrawn – into some shell, behind some wall, which she was powerless to penetrate.

"I can see, darling, that you're in a pensive mood. I'm going back to brush my teeth then look around some of the boutiques. I'll be back at the room by ten. OK?"

"OK" was all she got back, not even a smile.

Twenty minutes later Eric was back in their room, to brush his teeth. There on the counter lay his toothbrush, with a piece of paper wrapped around it. Flattened, it revealed a very rough drawing with a stick figure trying to climb a wall. Underneath were the words: "Please help me climb this wall!" How could he help her climb the wall behind which his feelings hid? They were hidden even from himself. It was difficult to say which was the stronger – his feelings of regret, or his feelings of helplessness, not knowing what to do, or say. All of which seemed to jell into a sense of anger – at being "made" to feel so uncomfortable.

She entered the room at ten, precisely, with the words: "How are things at home, Eric? The girls, I mean?"

"OK," came a barely audible mutter.

"And how is Frankie? Does she have any clue of what is between us?"

"She's OK too. And no, with your letters coming to me at the college and me having a valid excuse to be here in LA, she has no hint."

Again a long silence, for Eric was making it quite clear he was not in a conversational mood.

"Are you always like this for whole mornings?"

"No."

"Then why now?"

"Because you got my back up."

"What does that expression mean: got your back up?"

"It means you're angry at me."

"I did say something critical last night. But that was then. This is now. I love you, you crazy man. And I am hurt when you leave me forlorn at my mail box because Monday or Tuesday or even Wednesday is OK for the busy professor."

Eric did not have an answer to those words. They made no sense to him. That was then; this is now. But they are the same. If she's angry at me, she's angry. That means she doesn't love me. What came out was: "I don't think you love me."

"What an absurd statement! I have just spent three year's savings to be here with you. It's our first morning, and you don't think I love you?"

"How can you, if you are angry with me – all the time in fact – about letter writing, and being punctual, and dressing appropriately, and so on, and so on?"

She arose, came around and stretched her arms right around him, smothering his head with kisses while she said, tearfully, "Oh my love, my love. My crazy love! You are not perfect. I know that. I accept that fact. Well, more or less, except when it hurts too much. But whatever you do, and whatever I say about things I dislike, I love you. That is that. Understand?"

His bowed head nodded, just slightly. It was the minimum response he could make. But he did not understand. He felt lost. Her hands, her body gave him one message, but the words seemed to contradict it. He was very confused.

For Siok Yim', the day was a dead loss. She wondered at his silence. The energetic style with which he did everything had disappeared. Even occasional teasing did not rouse the sulking boy, as she saw him at this moment. But by the time they had driven out to see the Santa Monica/ Malibu area, walked on the beach for an hour or so, then found a super Thai restaurant, he was warming up again. Over dinner he did not withdraw his hand, and afterwards, under the palms, he initiated a kiss, followed by the suggestion that there were more congenial places for what was on his mind. So passed the day, a disappointment, and a mood.

### 

"What the bloody hell did you think you were doing?" As that accusation began, Eric turned to face an obviously irate colleague, Beverly, who was attending the same conference on her own dollar, and had been in his session.

"What do you mean, what was I doing?, As part of a panel, I was giving my take on 'the politics of student exchanges'."

"And sounding about as un-American as anyone could be. How could you represent our college and argue that foreign students are just pawns which our government uses to help win the Cold War?"

"Well, I believe they are."

"That's not the point, you stupid man."

"Then what is?"

"How we come across, as a college. Your personal opinions reflect badly on us. You can be sure that the Credentials Committee will hear the full story when we get to discussing your tenure application."

Eric could not believe his ears. That this woman, (and no woman should be chairing the committee which held his future in their hands) would bad-mouth him because of an honest debate at a professional meeting. How could anything said here have any effect on the future of his college? And how outrageous that she should use such a thing in her fight to keep him from getting tenure. And as he turned, the old curse came to his lips: "Women!"

### ###

"No one will listen to that at your campus, or any other," consoled SiokYim that evening. She then helped him see how threatening he might have been to some. "Those who are applying for grants and using this organization in support of their applications are going to feel threatened, for one. The fact that you said critical things here would probably not be taken seriously by such people, but insecure people fear everything, and I'm sure there would be some in your audience. Sure, she'll carry on, but the other members of your department will not be swayed. They'll judge you by all the other ways they know you. You mark my words."

His apprehension melted away in the warm glow of her words and he asked. "What was it that you proposed doing tomorrow afternoon, when the conference will be over?"

"It's a contact I've made from Taiwan. We've corresponded for years. I told her I'd be here very briefly. When I called on the day after I arrived

I promised to suggest to you that we join the picnic she has on tomorrow afternoon."

"That's fine with me, if it's what you'd like."

"I'd very much like. And thanks for being so understanding."

### 

The picnic turned out to be at a famous place pictured in many movies, Doheny Beach, at San Juan Capistrano. The long, long beach is backed by palms which gives the feeling of a tropical isle. It was her friend's youth group from a Chinese church. For the two hours before the barbecue they played games - not competitive games, but games which Eric felt he had "left behind in kindergarten", like "drop the hanky." Some involved passing a ball between people around the circle and one in the center, who stayed there until he or she dropped the ball. Then individuals made up verses to a very simple parody tune, always involving one of the group by name. The words were never critical, always just good fun.

Eric had never seen any group of Caucasian teens behave like this. Every moment was spent as a complete group, laughing with, never at any member. Far from any pairing off among these sixteen-to-eighteen-year-olds they stayed together like a flock of migrating birds. He couldn't help thinking of the ubiquitous Japanese tour groups you fear will trample you to death unnoticed in their rush to stay close together. Eric was astonished that none seemed to find this group-orientation to be inhibiting or their group decision-making to be a source of friction.

"Well, what's your reaction to a group of youth from my culture, Eric?" asked Siok Yim as soon as they left the group.

"Wow! So un-American. It was almost as if no one wanted to stand out. And I couldn't get who was dating who."

"They didn't stand out. That's our way. None of us does. Standing out has the effect of spoiling the enjoyment of others. No one has a right to do that. In fact, the opposite: Everyone has an obligation to do what is most appropriate in the situation, which means, what makes for greatest comfort. As for dating, that would have the same bad effect. Moreover, it could lead to other things which must be postponed until marriage."

"You don't mean it?"

"I do."

"What impressed me was that they seemed so happy. They were really having a ball."

"Could that be because no individual egos were ever at stake? Ever on the line?"

"What do you mean?"

"Well, your games pit one against another. Ours didn't. You argue towards a decision, each trying to dominate. These kids were jointly seeking what worked best for the whole group."

"I grant you that. In fact, it had never occurred to me how very self-oriented we are even in our fun. Now I think about it, that's crazy – a formula for stress and distancing from each other. I don't know what I'll do with what I've learned being with them, but I won't forget it. Thanks so much for setting it up. If you'd warned me of the format I would have found a way to talk you out of it. Now I'm so glad you just let me discover that some Chinese ways might even be better than some of ours. Not of course that you'd ever find me giving up my freedom for some 'good of the group' concept."

She let the implied superiority go, loving him far too much to allow such a small thing to cloud their evening.

### 

"So where's the closest real mountain?" Eric found himself asking the first day in LA. He badly needed nature. And he so wanted to share a real experience of nature with Siok Yim, especially when her response was "I could not imagine any way I would prefer to spend a day." It had occurred to him to ask about her pregnancy, but given her complete silence about the matter, here as in her letters, he decided not to mar their reunion any further. For her part, Siok Yim felt her approach of silence about the whole painful issue was the best. There seemed no way she could begin to share the feelings she experienced upon receiving his "wise advice" to have their child aborted. He could never understand that his letter had absolutely shattered her, not only on its arrival, but for weeks! So now, without discussion, there was agreed avoidance of this major topic.

Given the visibility of the mountains around LA when the smog allowed he was appalled at the need to drive more than two hours in order to have the "good walk" he promised. They approached one range, crossed it, and saw their destination Mount San Jacinto still an hour away.

From the trailhead in Strawberry Valley the climb to Saddle Junction was both demanding and rewarding. There camping spots abounded, with San Jacinto's peak standing guard three thousand feet higher. Do you want that grand western view when you poke your head out in the cold early sunlight? Do you prefer a glade between giant granite boulders, hosting a doe or two both early and late in the day? Do you want to simply wander among and wonder at the girth of trees widely spaced as if by a gardener so that their two-to-three hundred feet of grandeur can be fully admired – and allowed to humble any of your kind who has made it up Devil's Slide. Or would you prefer the spot they chose to picnic, then made love for two hours, secluded by dense thorn bushes with one clean, juvenile Jeffrey Pine with its enormous heavy cones, and two boulders perfectly placed so that they could combine both the hundred-mile western view of ridge upon purpled ridge and a clear view of the summit itself.

What a reward for two and a half miles and two hours! Even if it did demand the ascent of two thousand feet! Only as Eric and Siok Yim started back down did they realize what had been going on with them these last hours, for every yard of the tough two and a half miles of "up" and in the two hours there "on Top." Almost wordlessly they had found that each had been losing themselves and all self consciousness – in nature. For both of them, the physical self-awareness at the bottom had quickly given way to being lost in the trail. Perhaps we should say, lost *to* the trail. Harder breathing had become a part of that one-ness - rather than "good for my health" or a price of enjoying the views. Who knows that perhaps the increased blood flow had stimulated all their senses, so that this "hard work" had become the vehicle of a heightened sensuality? They did know this had to be expressed sexually, but in no hurry. They did know that they had never felt more alive – or more one.

At this moment Siok Yim knew that nothing could touch her. She knew that the downers of life were as far from her as if she were the red-tailed hawk flying high above her. She felt as strong, feeling the power to swoop and enjoy whatever she wanted, free. Light as a feather, strong as a lioness were her feelings; as vulnerable as a baby, yet completely safe. All that had ever worried seemed clear, confusion had given way to inspiration. She knew she could do anything, no matter how difficult. She knew every signal sent forth by this man, with or without intention, yet now without fear, though as sensitive as a rabbit emerging from its covey.

Time stood still. Moments lasted forever. The whole of the past seemed all part of the now.

### 

Two more days and the departure scene of a year ago was repeated. They did not want to release each other - to do so felt like giving up life itself. But it had to happen. His hand tried to extend the parting; her determined turn away clinched it.

For Siok Yim, like the time together the parting was completely realistic. This was her man. He would always be. These seven days together had done nothing to reduce that certainty. She would still go anywhere, do anything, live in any way needed, in order for them to be together forever. But she was a stern realist, acknowledging that his need for his daughters would keep him close to them for some time, maybe for another decade. But that's life. It does not give us endless sunshine. One must live with both the ying and the yang, and gracefully, learning from the combination without complaint. But his writing habits! That was a frequent source of disappointment. She could go seven days without the nurture of words and paper which he had touched but last week. But when the wait stretched – she had to admit to hunger, then sorrow, then hurt, then annoyance. Thus she would begin the next letter with some reference to her disappointment, even going so far (perhaps out of her basic academic habit of skepticism) as to question his love for her.

And why not question his love? What proclamations had he made which were in the same order as hers? None! There had been endless proclamations of love, of its uniqueness, of how he missed her. These were genuine, and they fed her. But intentions? Intentions with even a hint of the clarity with which she knew her own? Despite her wisdom, she repeatedly found herself unbelieving that he was so much a boy. In this respect his boyishness came near to being unforgivable.

For Eric the parting was in every way a repeat of the previous year's. For these seven days he too had felt complete. The few hours away from her at conference sessions seemed as unreal as they were brief. In all the hours together, at least after the first night and next morning when they had felt so estranged over the correspondence difference he had again felt his 'real self' returned.

As he found himself thinking about it, the assurance that her body would always be waiting to receive him, wet, warm, and so tenderly wonderful, was quite beyond his understanding. But it was not beyond his notice. She does love me. And she does criticize me. And she finds the two in no way mutually exclusive. How can that possibly be?

The parting was the same as the previous year for him in another way. While she may have been able to accept the separation, falling as it did into a total lifetime orientation, for Eric there was only one real feeling after she turned. It was a feeling he knew would go on haunting his every day. He was emptied of that which had made him feel complete; he was forlorn, suddenly devoid of the vitality which made him feel really real, really alive. In grief, he cried. Not only then at the airport, but during some solitary private moments of every day – until he saw her again. He thought he was crying for her. In fact he was bereft for his own self.

One other emotion added to his confusion – at least when he allowed it, which was as rarely as possible. It was that little cloud. It felt a bit like his anger, but not quite the same. It was unpleasant. It came from nowhere. The more he tried to think it away, the more it stayed. So he just did what he did with all unwanted emotions: he drowned them in activity, mainly work. What else is a man to do?

# Chapter Nineteen

The routine of school-days was a complete joy for Frankie that Fall. Now in her seventh week as school nurse she was finding there were more benefits than the money. There was real satisfaction in salving worries, treating scratches and catching the occasional infectious patient "in time". An unexpected benefit was the clutch of friends who welcomed her as one of themselves. In less than two months she felt she had known them all her life.

"But aren't all men just big boys?" came as a question by one of the group which caused her to disclose more than she had done to date.

"Let me answer that! My husband Eric seemed surprised that he was not given tenure last month. We were both terribly disappointed. But he was surprised; I wasn't. He had alienated the chair of the committee which makes recommendations about tenure and promotions. I mean really angered her, in all sorts of ways. And until I suggested it he never spent any time just relaxing together with the rest of his department, like we do every day after school. I think that's the way boys are – surprised at the consequences of their behavior."

"Are you disappointed?"

"Disappointment would be an understatement. This means he'll have to find a tenure-track appointment somewhere else. God knows where. We might even have to move out of the Boston area, which would break my heart. And think of taking the girls out of this school and dumping them into some strange place. I've lived here all my life and I don't want to move now. Or any time."

As the group wandered off Cheryl, the one to whom she felt closest, asked: "How are you both doing with this news?"

"Doing!" Frankie exploded. "It means I have even more glum silences to live with. And can you believe - even more anger? He's even angry with the girls at the smallest things - like books left on the dining table. For God's sake!!!"

The year went on that way – down hill. It was a busy time for the four of them in that little world. If the girls felt any of the tension between their parents their behavior remained unaffected for the first few months. They grew like weeds, and there seemed to be something new every day. Yet a perceptive observer would have noticed the shy one was a little shyer, and her outgoing sister just slightly more hesitant in taking the initiative, even with the father who doted upon her. You just didn't know what you would get – from one day to the next.

### 

In the following summer of '87 it would have been hard to imagine a more perfect conference setting than Asilomar. Pacific Grove is at the southern headland which ends the partly enclosed piece of Californian coastline made famous by the once-sardine-town-now-up-scale recreational destination town of Monterey. For golfing fanatics, the government-owned retreat center is close by the world-famous Pebble Beach course. And to share it with Rani, albeit in separate rooms – as far as the front desk was concerned! What could have been more perfect?

Rani's committee on Guidelines for Globalizing Social Studies was significant to Eric in three ways. He was aware of and overjoyed by two of them. First, the meetings facilitated time with Rani, which was reliably wonderful. Second, it gave him a sense of seriously contributing to world peace and understanding, goals he had affirmed in depth by his doctoral work on Senator Fulbright. The third significance was the challenge posed both by the total committee and each of its members to that basis of personality – his identity as an American. Of this he was largely unaware.

Eric's cultural identity had started out, way back when, completely oriented to his own culture and country, ignorant of all otherness. "Of course" he would have said as a boy, "everything is as it's supposed to be." At that time the very concept of a culture was quite beyond him. Exposure to other traditions had later combined with a noblesse oblige

206

indoctrination to modify his early absolute ethnocentrism into an idealistic paternalism. The base of that paternalism was an assumed supremacy of "his own", and this had fueled his overseas voluntarism in Singapore. His time there, subsequently augmented by his intimate friendships with Minah, Ahad, and Siok Yim had slowly led him to a place where he found himself automatically identifying with them, their concerns, their reputations, their well-being. This identification did not take away the fact that he was still proud to be American, nor had he lost the assumption that the West is best, particularly the U.S. But more and more often he found himself being an apologist for another culture, championing them and their interests in any argument because he felt strongly the need to see that "they got a fair deal". Had you asked him, he would have told you that he was a very cosmopolitan guy, who had little to learn in that area. This Peace Foundation group was to teach him just how wrong he was in that assumption. Kicking and screaming, he was about to change even further from his original identity as "a good Massachusetts boy".

Rani had recruited this group from seven different countries. All except herself and Eric were candidates for doctoral degrees in education who were about to start work on their dissertations. They had been eager to commit to three annual meetings each connected to this annual conference.

Meeting the morning before that conference began she laid out her agenda: "I envisage us spending this morning getting to know each other, and this afternoon hearing from each the specific ways in which our country's teaching of social studies is culturally biased," she began. "Next year I hope we can each report on the hurdles we would face in our respective countries in order to make social studies teaching more global. On that basis, I would hope we can then identify the problems we have in common as we strive to get our systems out of their ethnocentrism." Affirmative nods and knowing smiles were apparent all around the group. "In the third, final, and I hope climactic year of our work I hope we will be able to delineate general principles which could be used all over the world. That will help our Foundation to make grants which really count. And I can assure you that our top brass is really behind this work we begin today."

They all applauded. There was a strong feeling of camaraderie in the comfortable, wood-paneled Lloyd Wright style suite in which they both slept and worked. Its six bedrooms meant that the group would get to know each other very well in the coming five days, and would be able to

207

interact in many ways which no convener could plan, out of which would come a product to exceed her expectations. For now, she wanted them to get some of the potentially disruptive agendas out of the way. First they went around the room each recounting one vivid memory from childhood. Then each was asked to share a dream which had brought them to this place in their life.

When it came to Francois' turn she surprised everyone: "I'm not prepared to do this. I'm very sorry, and I apologize, but may I please pass on this one."

The others' attention was now riveted upon this French Canadian, at the same time glancing sideways to see what Rani would do. She had paid for Francois to attend, and now that young woman was refusing to cooperate.

"Thanks for your directness and honesty," their leader responded. "Would it be OK to tell me a bit more about your reaction to this activity?"

"It's too personal. That's really all." But seeing the incredulity on all their faces, she added, "We French treat the internal personal lives of others with great respect. We never demand disclosure of what is deep. And for me, the answer would get into that kind of stuff. Does that make sense?"

"Perfect sense," came supportively from Rani.

"Well not to me," chimed in Eric, at which all turned to look more carefully at this person who would trouble the waters of congeniality so early in the meeting.

The arrogantly sophisticated Thomas from Brazil jumped right in with: "Would it be best if we made sure that each one's orientation is accepted without question, at least for now, until we know each other better?" This easy out met with smiles of relief and acquiescence all around, and Nat, from Ghana, continued the process which Rani had instigated..

Eric was not happy at being silenced, particularly by one who had so much more polish. When it came to Thomas' turn, that annoyance surfaced in Eric's challenge: "It sounds to me that you are really here to stay and find a good job." Turning to Rani he asaked: "Isn't the aim to get us to go back and work for globalization at home?"

Rani's group skills showed instantly: "As you said earlier Thomas, we appreciate the honesty of your statement. Anyhow, who is to know how much the dissertation activity will change the directions of all our lives? Mine certainly did. And look at me now!" This slightly self-deprecatory ending elicited a chuckle all around, and the meeting flowed on.

Later however, Eric again found himself unexpectedly in conflict with Francois. He had taken very seriously the prospectus mailed to them a month earlier, and had dreamed up a very useful suggestion. Following the mid-afternoon coffee break Eric began the session, "I want to propose that each of us gets a study done in the next months, to fill out our own intuitions about how narrow was our nation's teaching of social studies."

"I wondered how soon we would start to sound all-American in our approach, even here," challenged the tall blonde Mimi, from Denmark. "Not that I have any problems with studies, Eric, but it is always the way Americans think."

It did not seem peculiarly American to him. He said so. "Just plain good sense, that's what I'd call it. If I analyze my own experience, that's not any guide to the experience of all Americans, is it? Anyhow, please hear me out. I propose each of us takes this questionnaire which I have created, modifies it, and then gets as many students from his or her country to fill it out. That way we'll have much more reliable data to move from when we are doing next year's work."

"Let me be clear," Francois began, but was interrupted by Eric

"Here - look at this! The questions fit the US practices, but slightly different wording might improve it for each of you so that it fits your situations."

Francois took a quick glance at the sheet, and was back to the attack: "You want to ask all these very personal questions?"

"Of course. How else can we help people if we don't know what really goes on inside them?"

"But you've no right to know. It's their personal lives you're getting at here. Madame Chairperson, Rani, we must not do this kind of thing. The only outcome will be to annoy people and create hostility toward your wonderful Foundation. They helped me come here. If we are to decide about Eric's suggestion, I move we do not adopt it. If you are to decide, please respect the position of those who treat the individual differently from this proposal."

Eric looked around the room, at every face. He did not like what he saw. How could his sense of minoritization be so overwhelming? That sensation was the only thing in his whole world which was real at this moment? Eric felt he was shrinking. Or rather, he felt he was being shrunk. Already he was so little as to be of no account to the other seven in the room. Soon he would be almost forgotten, but not quite. He would end up crushed by one, perhaps by all of them, trampled under foot as they went on their way.

He looked from face to face, from one frightening presence to the next. The Dane seemed even more beautiful in her disregard for everything about him. The French woman was infinitely superior, but particularly toward him. The arrogant Brazilian had endless better things to do, a glance would be over-generous. The Vietnamese was more inscrutable than the Asian stereotype. Ghana projected a look to shackle and restrain this insignificant, tiny slave. Costa Rica offered not aid, but complete ignore, already moving on. Last, in desperation he sought solace in Rani's countenance, but found none. She was one of them – who held him less than of no account, a bug for riddance.

He knew only one thing. There was only one thing he wanted - to be home. His whole being yearned for home. It yearned to be home. His essence told him that home was where he would be safe, OK again, back to full size, certainly noticed, likely respected, maybe even admired. But what is home? Where is home? How can I feel I know it, without ever having seen it? Was it a place? A person? A condition? How can I yearn for that which I have never experienced.? But if it did not exist, how could I have imagined it, been so sure it was there for me, somewhere? Why can't I re-live the reality of home I knew when I was naturally little? Why does home elude me now that I am little again?

Right now I can do nothing, say nothing, be nothing which will change these implacable faces They do not so much wish me ill as ignore my right to exist; so they will soon go on without me. I am as nothing. But a nothing that wants, with all that is left of it, to be 'home', and safe.

### 

After dinner that evening Eric and Rani went out across the brief section of dunes to gaze at the ocean. There were kisses, then quiet. More kisses, some frustrated stimulation, partially expressed, then suppressed by Rani's "Not now!" She was thinking about her project. She had put all her marbles in this basket when asked by the director if she had a dream that she would like to work on. She was profoundly distressed by the universal ignorance of Americans, even those professors like Eric, concerning the land of her birth. She understood that India's neutral stance in the Cold war had been a thorn in the side for the U.S., particularly as it was the world's largest democracy, but how could they allow Americans to know NOTHING about India? These thoughts were recurring when Eric asked:

"Can you believe that Francois?"

"Can I believe what?"

"That she should be so obstructionist! Just because we don't hit it off. I knew the moment she took a long look at me that we would tangle."

"Hold on. Her argument was not about you! The importance of individual privacy to a French woman is an objective fact. That it ran counter to the work into which you had invested so much was a coincidence having nothing to do with whether she likes or dislikes you."

"It certainly felt like she was getting at me."

"I know. I could see that was how it felt to you - but not to the rest of us." While saying this she had tucked her shoulder under his arm and circled both of her arms right around his body. Giving an extra squeeze she continued: "It's so common for people to see things as either/or, as black and white, as right versus wrong."

"Don't you?"

"To be perfectly frank, no! I don't see things that way. It goes with my genes. Indians are different from you in that way. I am too."

"You're saying that you're easy to get along with because you don't distinguish right from wrong?"

"Is that your opinion of me? Have I given the impression that I don't really care what way things go?"

"OK. No you don't come across that way. Sorry if I offended you."

"You didn't, but you were a long way short of being fair to me, so I said something."

"Of course."

"About respect! I know you respect the differences between cultures. But it gets hard when the other culture is in your face, as it was with Francois."

"Yeah, go on."

"I've come to the conclusion that the only way to show respect when you feel you want to fight is just to be silent."

"Really? To me that would mean you agreed."

"Well, respect is always a way of saying 'I'm sure you're right, where you're coming from'. If you contradict, or argue emotionally, it comes across as if you are saying the person is wrong. In that exchange with Francois you were both saying valid things. Yes, it is dangerous for us to generalize from one person's perspective on their social studies background. But also yes, it is unacceptable to ask very personal questions of a Frenchman, or woman. Especially if it's Francois!" and she chuckled very quietly, sneaked one hand inside his waist-band and reported: "He says it's time."

"That may be what 'he' as you call my penis says, but now I'm thinking. I'm into what she said and what you have said about it. I have to admit that I do always assume that our way is best. I thought I was more tolerant than that."

"Oh, I'm sure you are," she teased, "but only when it doesn't matter very much to you. You have done a lot of work in preparation. It's great. I'm sure it will eventually be useful. In the meantime, you will learn about yourself, from Francois if you're ready to do so."

That night in bed was even better than the two previous times they had been able to spend several nights together. On the very first weekend together she had challenged him about the level of his own sensuality: "Do you really enjoy being a sensual being?" His answer had been that he was sensually very much aware, that he saw more than most people when in the woods, and that his other four senses were pretty well developed. She had not accepted that definition of sensuality: "To live fully every sensation" were her words. Now, with this woman who so enjoyed touching, and who wanted the same from him, he was more in control. That did not mean more restrained, except concerning the urgency of copulation. Now he was finding it possible to "be" in any moment completely, without any preoccupation with the future, even ten minutes away!

Rani had never been loved by a man who would spend half an hour just watching her reactions to touches. She luxuriated in her responses: "I'm an unrepentant hedonist," she proudly announced whenever he teased about her indulgence. He loved to watch the almost "stupid" grin that stretched her face during such moments, a grin which remained unchanged for minutes at a time, and which was the outer sign of an inner, invisible sensation she thought must surely what the religious call "grace." Between the times they found to be together she often found herself smiling that same smile, and feeling good "all over."

### 

"Good heavens! I expect Yoda just around the next cypress!" This comment came from Rani, but was also near to Eric's lips as they stole tip-toe through the cypresses at Point Lobos. It was so mysterious, so quiet, so unusual, with a complete canopy above, supported by twisted branches which seem to be exuded from hoary, ancient, gnarled trunks. All the branches moved away from the ocean, whose fierce winds allowed no other development. Yet they were enormous.

"You quite expect to meet Luke Skywalker as well, don't you?"

"Sure do." Then, after just standing reverently for who knows how long, Eric launched into a new topic. "But it also makes me wonder what is real. This feels more real than most places I have ever been. Yet it is unlike anything I've seen. Which all makes me wonder about the things which I take for granted, every day. I almost feel I belong here, more than in any of those other places."

"You're talking about my whole life, now."

"Really?"

"Yes. I feel like that everywhere. What I mean is this: Everywhere I feel pretty much at home, as if I belong. That is really great. It's the same warm comfortable sense of belonging that we are feeling here. Right?"

He did agree, so responded, "Right."

"But there is nowhere I can feel complete. It's as if I have left part of me behind, in every country I have been. Anywhere, I can find some of me. But nowhere can I find all of me."

"To use a fancy term, it sounds like you have an inclusive identity. But not an integrated one."

"Do you? I mean, do you have an integrated identity?"

"Sure. I'm American. I could never feel at home, really at home, anywhere else. I certainly do appreciate lots of other places, and other cultures and people, but I'm not, as you put it, really at home in any other situation. It's like the Thanksgiving I remember in Singapore: It was so good to be just with Americans, to be, for a few hours one hundred percent, unapologetically, American."

They both lapsed into silence, walking hand–in–hand, very slowly. Then through the first break in the dense umbrella covering and enclosing their path came a glimpse of a deepwater cove, complete with an otter and several sea lions. "What a place!" was all they could say until, driving back to Asilomar he commented, "Can you believe that Point Lobos is not billed as one of the great destinations in this country?"

### 

At this time in his development Eric had much in common with a cat. Cats express an insatiable desire for tactile attention. When in the presence of any potential source of caresses they give that source no peace until fondled, stroked, or tickled under the chin. Ignored, their voice is harsh, demanding, critical, and eventually, dismissive. But the giver's attention once caught, they will throw themselves on their backs and squirm until the observer reaches down to stroke the softest underbelly fur. If that giver tires too soon they will follow, nudging the legs harder and harder until you again reach down, at which time the purring deepens and swells so that you vibrate with the contact. But if you desist too soon, the other lap in the room becomes the new object of seduction, where the satisfaction of this insatiable hunger will be accepted with equal pleasure. Eric's needs for physical sensuality were met almost as easily, and as promiscuously. The one difference was his acute need to feel psychologically safe in his exploitation of Minah, then Siok Yim, and at the same time, Rani. Yet each of those relationships also contained elements he distinguished but vaguely, and certainly could not name. Both cats and boys have their limitations.

At the same time, he had to admit to the occasional introspective thoughts – about these three wonderful women who had entered his life. They had awakened more than his sexuality. They had done more than heighten his sensuality, unbelievable as those new heights were. Apart from that awakening sensuality, what had been going on with Minah? You felt sorry for her? Yep, a bit. And you felt sorry for yourself, what you'd been missing? Sure did. Anything else? Nope, that's about it. But it was great! Now what about SiokYim? That's an altogether different story. How so? She's what someone has said about relationships: she's both a bright mirror, and a dark one, to me.

At that thought he became lost in a reverie about the bright mirror she held up to him - art particularly. Discovering her joy in Matisse and Chagall had shown him that these things were more than mere space-fillers in his walls; they evoked deep sensations, and complex feelings, which he enjoyed the more because she shared them. His appreciation of music had always been acknowledged, but that too was deeper than he had realized. He did not want to leave the bright mirror idea – he was quickly lost in recollections of their dazzling joys together.

But SiokYim had also been the other kind of mirror – a dark one. That mirror had shown him things about himself he would rather not have acknowledged. He had to admit he was casual about punctuality and propriety. But hell, why worry about such little things? Surely he was not that unusual? These things must just be her quirks, or maybe just Chinese ones. Her disapproval of these habits was surely of no consequence? And surely he wasn't being unreasonable largely to ignore her complaints about such things? Then there's the way she laughs at me and says "Lighten up, Eric!" That's inconsistent on her part, with her own compulsions. The admonition to lighten up annoys me, although I have never said so. She also says, "You are so like most Americans, only more so – so earnest." Am I? Do Michael and I ever laugh at the seriousness with which we treat every issue in faculty meetings? Do I act as if the world will stop turning if my dream is not realized? Well, I suppose I do. Maybe she's right on that one.

SiokYim had also given him some feedback about his conversations with Kathy which he did not like. "You listen to gain advantage, not to hear what she wants you to hear." Was that true? He was an excellent listener. He had become unusually skilful at paraphrasing back whatever a speaker said; it always impressed the speaker that he listened so carefully. "Just so you can catch them with their guard down," Siok Yim had suggested. He had bristled at that, it was such a dark interpretation of a skill in which he took great pride. And it came through to the love of his life that it was all a suave style of manipulation? I don't believe it!

His mind was quiet for a time, then suggested: That's more than enough of the dark mirror stuff for now; I'm going back to the nice things about me, and us, which I see reflected in her as my <u>bright</u> mirror. His face relaxed, eventually into a slight smile, as more pleasant memories obliterated all else.

### 

Frankie could have predicted the way the session would go. After she had answered the therapist's question: "What brings you folks here?" Eric's anger dominated the session. If it had any product, it was an increased distance between them, so that their only communication was about the essentials of family organization. Frankie went back to nursing, in the girls' school, finding new sources for support and a sense of usefulness. She consoled herself that at least her husband had some sense of fiscal responsibility, that he spent real time with his kids if not with his wife, and that he wasn't running around chasing some of those gorgeous younger women who gravitated toward him for their graduate work.

This was quite true, objectively. But subjective reality is frequently the more powerful variety. Most of his non-work thought and feeling concerned his emotional highs and lows. The highs came from Siok Yim's letters, the warm sensation which followed their reading, and the widely separated times with Rani. The lows came from job insecurity, the tearful moments in every day when he ached for Siok Yim, and the awake time in bed when his ache was for Rani's body.

### 

Eric's next letter to Siok Yim was a real whine. He sought pity – both for his marital and his vocational situations. What he received did not meet his definitions of loving support. She wrote:

Oh, My Love, My dearest Love,

What can I say to you? If I give you my spontaneous reactions concerning Frankie and your job you will be both disappointed and angry. You probably won't reply for weeks and weeks. Yet what else can I do?

First, I have to say that your reactions are from the Eric who I so love. Your frustrations come from your deep desires to be of real use in the world. They also come from the very high standards you set for yourself, as a father and as a political scientist who wants the whole world to be a better place. You know that I have similar values and standards. You know that's part of what attracts me to you. And you know, from the long conversations between us, that these noble ambitions are cemented by the union of our bodies. All that is where the following remarks come from.

So, about Frankie. You must admit that you easily get defensive. With me, you quickly feel that any criticism from me means that I do not love you. You then get very angry, but keep it bottled up. In fact, when in LA you shut yourself up from me for a whole 24 hours, immediately on my arrival. I don't know when you started being so angry, but please, please consider doing something about it, for my sake, for our sake.

Then about tenure. At this point I wish I could give you some of my Taoism. If you could just BE, and let things happen in their own time, life would feel so different. When it is time, and when the people are right, your professional life will be what it needs to be. The outcome will never be the simple product of your own striving. You want too strongly. I'm sure you then push too strongly. You probably enter those faculty meetings gritting your teeth. Relax, my love, knowing my arms are always around you. You are a very gifted man, who will certainly find the right slot. It could even be there in Boston, or it might be on the other side of the world. Just be who you are, with all of your energy. And IT, whatever it is, will certainly happen.

You must never doubt that I am all yours, and am certain your life will be far, far above even your dreams, if you will just learn to BE.

Your Siok Yim

Eric's response was anger. He had been unable to control his anticipation of the reply to his plaintive cry for support. And what he got was a lecture – the last thing he needed! That was his view. It would have profited him nothing to be told that what he "wanted" might have been a far remove from what he really "needed." He could not, at this time in life, in this set of circumstances, have been able to hear such words. The one concrete change in his life was that his crying every single day for two years for the presence of Siok Yim now suddenly ceased. The letters still came, and went, but the tears ceased to flow.

217

But the end of this physical phenomenon brought no increased feeling of control. Until Minah, and then Siok Yim, everything in his life had been under control. His intellectual life was a controlled manipulation of ideas. Classrooms were a controlled manipulation of learners, so that they would change. His tennis and soccer outlets were also exercises in control. Only one activity had hitherto pushed him beyond the sphere of his control – his times in nature. With nature he had relinquished that habit which characterized the rest of his life, and it was a special dimension, pushing him to write about his experience of "being with nature", as he put it. Now the dominant aspects of his life were not things he could control (like games and ideas and students) he felt bedeviled by people. Not only were the people uncontrollable, they also created feelings which were out of his control.

### 

Halfway through the Fall semester, "Got a minute?" came the greeting as Michael entered his office.

"Of course. You look pleased with yourself."

"I am. And so will you be when you hear my news."

"I need something to brighten my day. I was just looking at the ads for tenure track positions. There's nothing going in the Boston area, so I'll have to move to get something. And then it's a long shot, given the glut of cheaper new Ph D's in Poli Sci."

"Worry no more, my friend!" as he closed the door. "I am here, with the blessing of the Chair, to let you know that he is asking the Dean to grant you tenure, based on the unanimous recommendation of the Credentials Committee."

"You're kidding! They filled all the available slots last year, and there are no new ones."

"True. But one of the two awarded last year has been diagnosed with a terminal illness, can't work beyond this summer, and is thus leaving the department with a vacancy. The Chair brought the matter to my committee (Aren't you glad I replaced that Thompson woman when she got an admin spot at Smith?). We were more than happy to go along with his wish to grant the position to our third choice last year – which was you.

So my wife and I will be over with the champagne as soon as all our kids are tucked in tonight."

Eric didn't know what to say - or what to do - except to stand and offer his hand and an almost tearful "Thank you!"

"Thanks be damned! You were better than the two who they appointed last year. You deserve it. And I can't afford to lose a pal, can I?" With which he embraced Eric in an enormous bear hug. Although that embarrassed Eric, it did seem kind of nice. Certainly there were no sexual overtones in their relationship, and what the hell! Men seemed to be doing this kind of thing when they were happy these days – even though men my father's age would die before they would do so.

### 

Eric rested on the rake. The lawn's deep green was the perfect ground for the large piles of yellow leaves which had taken him three hours to produce. Before bagging them, he thought, I'll let the girls have a ball jumping in them, just like I did all my childhood. And what a pity I can't burn them. The smell is so wonderful. It doesn't quite seem like fall without that smell.

Raking up the remnants at the curb he stopped, looked at the other houses and at his own, and found himself wondering whether the interior of the other houses were like his. Not the layout, the walls and the furnishings, but the dynamics between the occupants. Take mine for example. If you knew it housed a couple and two eight-year-old girls you would have little difficulty imagining what went on with the children. There was lots of TV. Maybe piano practice. Some play together. Some sitting around, imagining life when older. Some school projects. And lots of logistics talk with Mother about social, athletic, school and church activities.

But how would anyone have a clue about what was really happening inside the adults? More difficult: What was happening inside us? Frankie and me? Why, she doesn't know what occupies most of my energies. And I don't have a clue about hers. How would the neighbor guess that we have these long silences every night after the kids are asleep? That we have a technique, now very refined, by which the essential decisions are not so much made as that they occur by default, she deciding and doing whatever is needed with the home and the girls, me doing the stuff in the yard and the cars and the house maintenance. There'd be a longer talk with a handyman than the brief words that come from her now and then, such as "The dishwasher, Eric!" or "Eric, my car's 'service' light is on." Consequent upon such 'notice' each can expect the other to 'perform' the requisite actions, and we do. I guess that's what a long-term marriage has to be like.

At the same time, he told himself, the man in this house has two wonderful women in his present life. There's the woman with whom I feel more profoundly than I have ever done. She loves me more than life itself, which is quite overwhelming, but is such a turn-on. Then there's Rani, not only a co-worker for a better world, and a great lover who doesn't seem upset that Siok Yim is the love of my life, but also a real friend. She had sent him details of several significant meetings which intrigued him, and they had already fallen into the habit of bouncing ideas off each other on the phone. How could he be so lucky?

Yet visit the kitchen sink mid afternoon when back from school, and get inside Frankie, and you'll find anything but quiet acceptance of the inevitability of it all. "A life of quiet desperation" would be an understatement. What is wrong? was her continual question. Or, what is wrong with him? Or, what is wrong with me? We had such a great relationship. And Eric was so pleased we began a family. He still rejoices in his daughters. In fact, that's the only positive aspect of his behavior around here these days. I'm so glad I have a job now. I'd go quite crazy if I had to rely on him for stimulus and friendship. We were such good friends. We even had a good relationship in bed, but that seems to have gone too. He used to be demanding, sometimes angry when I said NO! Even those occurrences are now rare.

But there's not much point in dwelling on the past, or even the bad parts of the present. How to make tomorrow a better day? That is the question. Maybe also, how to plan for the worst, so that we don't suddenly find ourselves, the girls and I, like Beatrice with her minimum support or Dorothy having to raise her three alone on the little she can keep after paying baby-sitters. Well, thank God I am a registered nurse and that I'm back earning again.

### 

"Eric!" Again that tone of voice he hated. "Eric, could we talk about finances some time?" Eric found an excuse to postpone the request, but the day came when they talked around and around until the issue could no longer be avoided, by Frankie's declaration: "I'd like to bank most of what I bring home."

"Why?" he asked.

"For a rainy day. We have no contingency account, and that's crazy."

"I assumed that with you earning we'd be able to make that trip to Europe and India we have promised ourselves since before the girls came."

"Are you saying you want us to spend all that we earn combined?"

"More or less, yes."

"That's ridiculous. I am prepared to put half of it into our common pot, but I want to put the other half in my account, where I can use it when, where, and how I choose. Including of course, such uses as a catastrophic accident or something else unexpected."

"Have it your own way. But don't expect me to start doing the laundry, or delivering the dry cleaning, or picking up baby sitters. And don't expect me to give up summer conferences because you have some nursing conference or other."

"You don't have to be so cross about it. You'll awaken the girls if you're not a bit quieter. And," warming to the one consideration she knew would get his attention, "I wish you'd try, for the girls sake, to be a little more pleasant toward me. Have you noticed how they notice? Particularly Jennifer? She seems the more sensitive to hurtful vibes between us."

"I think you're projecting. You want her to share any negative feelings you have about me. But the point could be important. I'll watch it. Although I don't really know what you are talking about. We're a normal couple. And kids need to grow up knowing that marriage takes determination, as well as all that nice stuff up front."

# Chapter Twenty

At the same time, Eric was being challenged from another direction, as Siok Yim wrote:

My Dearest Love

I am sending you a one-subject letter.  Why?  To say, as clearly as I can, some things about what gets in our way each time we meet.  Please don't be too offended – at least not for more than a day or two – but it's about your feelings.  More precisely, it's about what you do with your feelings.

Now that your day of being offended has passed (that's a tease) I am going to speak about "men", but please apply it to yourself after you have understood the following.  Then, when we are together next time, we'll talk about it all.  OK?

What do men do, after any experience?  Any experience – work, domestic, social, romantic – you name it, after absolutely any experience?

Answer:  They go straight on to the next thing.  Yes, no matter how engrossing, disruptive, satisfying or annoying the experience, you can be sure a man has something which demands his attention immediately thereafter.  So he focuses on the next thing, and largely, forgets the experience which just occurred.

Maybe not all men!  Maybe some women!  But my present interest is to understand this kind of behavior in a man.  It's as if a man has to be on a straight track. He sticks to it until he thinks it's time to go off at the next junction. Then he's as set on the new track as he was on the old one.

I first thought this behavior to be a product of your socialization: You men were taught, early on, to manipulate things, to get out there and win, gaining the attendant rewards. You were told, as you grew and by seeing your celebrity examples, that the U.S., and its more gorgeous women reward accomplishment, particularly by the male.

Further consideration of male "getting-on-with-it"-ness leads me to the matter of how you then deal with feelings. The truth is that every experience, regardless of its peculiar quality, produces <u>some</u> feelings. If there's something else awaiting a man's attention, the feelings are readily overlooked, put aside "till later." If the feelings demand lots of energy, except in the case of sex you males will also put those aside, until later. If the feelings should demand thought, the urge to procrastinate reaches its heights. Even in the case of sex, I suspect you are more likely to dwell on future recurrences (or escalations) than on the past. How come? It's not what I do.

I believe men's deepest problem lies in the phrase: dealing with feelings. Dealing with involves thoughts about what has happened. It also involves more feelings –about those feelings. Both these activities give men a lot of trouble.

First, the area of feeling looks quite unproductive. It is a leisure-time activity, even a luxury. Then second, the feelings about any feeling are always a mixed bag. If the feeling was great, all of us hate to imagine it might not recur, or that we were kidding ourselves. If it was bad, we are even more likely to have fears. Third come the thoughts about the original feeling, and, if you really want to get into a mire, the thoughts about the feeling about the feeling. Stupid as that all sounds, the attendant feeling is even less desirable, so let's forget it all! That's what this recurrent trouble looks like. So what to do about it?

Experience has shown me two places where something is done about dealing with feelings: women's conversation and psychotherapy. Unsurprisingly, the methods of dealing with feelings are very much alike in these two instances. We women tell and re-tell, then talk and talk about every single aspect, real and imagined, of all important interactions. Therapists have the client tell about the experience, re-live it, and talk about it, "until they are done", the saying goes. Each of these practices

223

suggests to me the truth of Gestalt Therapy's claim that any emotion must be lived out to its conclusion, or it will remain, hidden, only to return disguised at a future time (which might not be convenient or welcome).

So this is what I believe men should do about all of this (which sometimes reaches a level when we think all men are completely stupid). First, men should spend much more time with others, at minimum rehearsing your feelings by telling about the situations in which they arose, or in an atmosphere of trust, also sharing the feelings about the feelings. Second, and at the same time, men should spend enough time alone for the feelings (and the feelings about them) to run their course. Sometimes a game of golf or tennis helps, but that too easily comes to be a further escape from doing what most of us women do all the time – the real work of dealing with our own feelings.

Maybe that all means you will be doing less. Then do less.

Just in case you've forgotten, all this comes because I love you so deeply,

Siok Yim

At first he was annoyed at this lecture. But in the following days his recurrent images of Siok Yim seemed unavoidably colored by the substance of that most recent letter. He knew he would not be capable of doing those kinds of 'processing' alone. He would avoid his feelings rather than host unpleasantness. Who would be a good listener? It could be either Ahad, Michael or Rani. In spite of the openness between them, he was not yet comfortable with the last in matters which showed his dark side, so he determined to take the first opportunity with either of his close male friends.

"Got a few spare minutes?" he asked Michael, "And mind if I close the door?"

"You arrived at the perfect moment. I need something to take my mind off these tests."

I had a letter from Siok Yim the other day. She devoted the whole thing to a challenge."

"Yes?" His friend was his usual, caring self, but more so. Michael knew that the Siok Yim influence in his pal's life was pushing Eric very hard. He hoped Eric would benefit.

"She challenged me to experience my feelings more fully. I've decided I want your help."

"You have it. So what feelings will we work on, here, now?"

"God! You're as bad as she is!"

"We both love ya, buddy. That's why."

"OK. I felt pissed when I read that letter. Then I asked why I was angry at her. I got a big surprise in that conversation I had with my feeling self."

"Go on."

I realized she was trying to control me. That made me even angrier. But this escalation of negative feeling made me see her point – that I avoid ever going on to the next feelings. So here I am, talking to you about it."

"I wonder what your feelings are about feeling she is trying to control you?"

Eric was silent for a minute, an unusual behavior on his part. "Well," he began thoughtfully and slowly, "my first feeling was anger at that, too. But then I got scared - something in my gut - you know? It's hard to define."

"Don't try. Just stick with that feeling. Let it be, without trying to do anything with it."

"That's all very well for you to say. You're not the one whose gut is rumbling." There was another long silence. "It just gets intense. I don't like it. And I wish it would go away. This is crazy stuff. There's no good reason for it"

"Feelings don't have to justified. They exist in their own right. Remember that, buddy. OK? Maybe that's enough self-torture for now. But I do want you to know that you are moving. Really! Before that letter you would have immediately gone off onto something new, rather than experience the feeling. In time, I suspect you'll get sufficiently in touch with such a sensation that you'll want to get a therapist to help you. When you get there, and you will, use someone who is a pro. But I'm always here when you want to vent – or whatever they call it."

###

The summer of '88 brought time, back to back, with both Rani and Siok Yim. Both times were in the southwest, in Austin and Albuquerque, with ten days between. Rani had sent an agenda for this year's pre-conference meeting of her Globalizing the Social Studies Curriculum project. She was the instigator and chair, with her foundation providing travel expenses so that the seven members could gather annually. The date was a perfect fit. He would spend most of a week in Austin with Rani, then, after a few days alone he would spend a week with Siok Yim in Albuquerque and another five days with her at the conference where she was to be one of its four plenary speakers. "Isn't it wonderful," she had written, "they're making it possible for us to be together again this year?"

###

The first night in Austin with Rani (before the arrival of the others) went predictably. But its predictability in no way lessened its delectability. As always, the 'dessert' which followed that feast was usually an intellectual treat. At such times, senses satisfied, either or both of them would voice a topic that had been on their minds of late. On this occasion, after a brief rest Rani positioned herself astride him and asked: "What do you think about the indictments of North and Poindexter?"

"You would raise that," he smirked.

"I am conducting a gender comparison of your multi-tasking ability and mine," she chuckled, astride him.

"It's not multi-tasking for me. I'm single-mindedly thinking about the Iran/Contra scandal."

"Then it's no test unless I do this, is it?" she teased, tightening one set of well- toned muscles.

"That's not fair. Though it's so-o-o wonderful. Now what was it you were asking?"

"I have my answer," she responded, continuing to assist his focus in just the way he really wanted her to do.

Sometime later she again raised the first question: "Well! What DO you think about the Ollie North stuff at the moment?"

"Well!" Eric began, "I'm glad they're nailing North and Poindexter over the Iran/Contra scandal."

226

"You are? I'm not so sure it's a scandal. I find the whole thing just very sad."

"Sad. Those bastards have no principles."

"What are you saying?"

"That this whole Iran/Contra thing is a matter of principles. This country is great because it has very clear principles. We may no longer be as religious as we were, but we still have the same values – the individual, democracy, freedom, and of course, opportunity in a free market."

"But back to the topic Mr. Professor. You are glad that two heads of the National Security Council McFarlane and Poindexter and their key staffer, Colonel Oliver North have been indicted."

"Yeah. I'm glad that McFarlane pleaded guilty, albeit to misdemeanor counts of withholding information from a Congressional committee, but that made it possible to indict North on sixteen and Poindexter on seven felony counts. Those guys did what the President was not allowed to do. But I'll bet Reagan knew what they were doing."

"I'm still not clear what upsets you so?"

"Well first, not long after he got in Reagan asked for money to help the Contras fight the Sandanistas, who had taken over Nicaragua. Congress said 'no'. That should have been the end of it. But over these last three years the truth has been slowly coming out. Against the wishes of our representatives we have been funding the Contras by making money from completely illegal arms sales to Iran. I happen to think the Iranians aren't as bad as most people say, but we have had in place a formally ratified embargo on all dealings with them, including armament sales. So we have two wrongs here. And you don't 'understand' that it's a matter of principles.

"What I do understand, dear Eric, my wonderful lover Eric, is that you see things in black and white. I think your eyes would be telling you something different if Reagan were a Democrat. After all, Kennedy's action to place an embargo around Cuba to stop the Russians landing missiles there was also without approval by Congress. How come you all praise that action and lambaste President Reagan for a similar action?"

"A similar action?"

"Of course it was. He went to Congress back in '83, asking for money to help counter a clear and present danger to our (my adopted) nation. He saw the Sandinistas as a Communist regime which would stop at nothing, just to embarrass the U.S., who they claimed had exploited all of Central America for decades. In two days driving they could have conducted all kinds of terrorist acts right here, on our soil. He believed and said that it was his sacred duty to do all in his power to prevent such a catastrophe. What was he to do when they refused to fund it?"

"He should have conformed to the wishes of those who represent the people."

"But he does. He was elected, just like they were. And he, not they, has the final responsibility for our safety. Anyhow, it was not him personally, but the National Security Council, who are not beholden to Congress, who got the arms to Iran, thus funding the Contras, helping to free the hostages taken in Beirut, and probably did other things we both think are desirable."

"I still say it's a matter of principle," but he was now enjoying the curve where her waist became the pretty rump which he was finding more and more irresistible.

"I thought it wouldn't be long before you found something more important than principles," she teased as she turned over so that she could manually reciprocate. "Such a need to compensate for supposed prior sensory deprivation!"

### 

After lunch the next day the eight members of the Committee divided into two parts to begin discussion of the question, What problem is common to all our countries as we try to globalize our social studies courses? On the first day together this year, they had shared their perceptions of what happened in their own countries. Now they were to identify commonalities. Eric's group included Nat from Ghana, and two women, Maria from Costa Rica and Anh from Viet Nam. Almost immediately they got into the issue of how the media does or does not provide viewers, particularly students, with a global background.

"Our TV is absurd," began Maria. "Fully half of it is in English, just soaps from the U.S. which have been dubbed in Spanish."

228

Anh chimed in with: "Half! With us it's three quarters. And, like yours, it's mostly the kind of stuff that I try to avoid in the TV here."

"I guess we are at an advantage then," suggested Nat, "for our TV in Ghana is so limited that most rely on newspapers. They cover mostly the really local stuff."

"Obviously you all know about our U.S. media; it is almost entirely us. In local papers you are lucky to get any global news; TV rarely gets material that was not produced by Americans, and even when it's about other countries it has an American slant. A handful of national papers are better with their coverage, but I can't remember when I last saw an opinion piece by a foreign writer from any country which is antagonistic to us."

The other three listened in mannered silence as Eric continued: "But the statistics about viewing makes that situation with newspapers pretty irrelevant. How many university students ever read them? You should see the statistics among my students of government. You'd think there was no such thing as government anywhere else in the world - except perhaps, dictatorships. As for high-schoolers, and those poor elementary school kids, they are given the impression that the whole world is either just like us, and likes us, or is backward, uneducated, and hates us."

"But," Nat suggested, "You must at least agree that other nations should know about the most powerful nation in the world, or how will they have the right perspective when it comes to understanding power plays?"

"It's not the facts which worry me!" It was Maria talking now. "It's the values in all of it. Our country hates violence. For that reason we have no army. Yet every popular show in Costa Rica features killings, often several brutal ones in the same one-hour episode. I don't want my baby nephew to grow up believing that is good. Neither do most Costa Ricans."

"Imagine what we VietNamese who remember the war think about that! Such things on TV can't be counteracted by what a teacher says in her classroom."

"So," began Eric, becoming the one responsible for group productivity, "the barrier we all agree upon, even from different situations, is that in order to globalize social studies we will have to fight whatever the local media can sell to advertisers."

"But," Nat offered, "how do we help kids to see that many different values have their place, at least in countries with a heritage different from their own?"

"Frankly," confessed Eric, "how do I even accept such a proposition? I mean by that, why should our kids even bother to listen to perspectives they don't experience? I would never have agreed to come on this committee without . . .," he hesitated (They all wondered why he was here, "good" American that he was), then faded off with the words "without having been exposed to other values when I went overseas." He saw their disbelief, and continued in a more disclosing vein.

"Actually, Rani's request to be part of this work would have fallen on deaf ears but for two close relationships I've had. One was Indonesian, the other Chinese. Both were wonderful, so I was predisposed to widen my exposure to other cultures. But some of the values held by those two women bugged me. I no longer see the Indonesian."

"You mean," asked Anh, "that you ended a good friendship because there were values which were contrary to yours?"

"But I did really appreciate most of the differences." Eric defended himself. "That's what I was saying about my life being richer because of those friendships. But when differences are too deep, well, it just gets to be too much of a strain. After all," quite defensively now, "You couldn't expect me to become a Muslim, could you?"

"Well, why not, if the relationship was deeply important?"

"I guess it wasn't <u>that</u> important."

The others left the matter at that point, sensing it the kindest thing to do. Eric found himself admitting that while he wanted lots of foreign and exotic stimulus, there was no way in which he was about to let go of any part of his identity as an American. "So that's that!"

### 

That evening Eric and Rani escaped graciously by ten, and had indulged deliciously in each other's bodies for more than an hour before Eric felt compelled to continue the conversation of the afternoon:

"I got really uncomfortable at one point in our working group this afternoon."

"Yeah?" As her fascination continued with one particular part of his body.

"Stop that for just one minute so that I can tell you about it."

"OK."

"No, don't stop completely."

"Is this better?"

"Perfect. What happened was that we started to talk about how each culture inculcates its values. But Made In and For American TV pushes American values where thoughtful teachers wish otherwise."

"Right. So what worried you?"

"I shared a little of how my relationship with Minah ended. You know, the Muslim. They even suggested that I should have considered becoming Moslem."

"So?"

"So as I analyzed my actions I now see that I still have the same attitude: I see that I want the stimulus of other cultures and their values which run against mine. I can accept them, with their values. I really respect them. I can just keep quiet when my disagreement is very strong. But no way in the world could I consider adopting their values. Not for a moment. What's your response to that?"

"It sounds very honest. It's you. Of course, it's not me, but that's not the issue. So just accept that as being who you are. I'll accept you that way too. As far as you can go."

So the night continued, with the self-analysis postponed till a little later.

"Eric," she said in a rest between lovemaking times, "may I make a comment about the way I see your behavior in the Committee this year?"

"Sure. How do you see it?"

"You seem quite different in the way you accord respect to views which are in direct opposition to your own. Really! It just shows. You aren't at all fussed. You don't look like you're ready to explode. It's more than the fact that you just sit quietly in the face of such things. You seem different."

"I am different. Respect is a matter of feeling now. I feel comfortable with the reality that they disagree, even violently, with what I think. The first time I noticed that was in a couple of conversations with Ahad. The differences were still real, but they didn't fuss me. I used to believe that respect was a matter of thinking. Now I am sure that 'respect' is a meaningless word unless you also feel it."

"Sounds great to me."

"And while we're on the topic . . ."

"Yes?" She wanted to say that her mind was moving onto other agenda, but Eric obviously had more to say. Furthermore, she rightly suspected that only she could fill his need for a listener about this topic. "Go on."

"I'm feeling deeply challenged these days, especially here in this group, about whether I see things as they are. Or, to put it another way, I find I have to admit that often it seems that they have it right and we Americans are seeing things wrong."

"For example?"

"Well you really started this kind of insight."

"Moi? Never!" She teased in the way which never failed to excite him, then repeated the question: "Moi?"

"Yes, you! You accuse me of being obsessed with doing, with getting things done, with what you call 'being useful', of needing to be 'Mr. fix-it'."

"True, I do see you as very goal-oriented, often to the exclusion of what I think is much more important."

"Then there's the kind of thing Francois said, about my study suggestion – that we have no right to ask some questions. Maybe she's right."

"M-mm."

232

"But I guess the toughest thing is when people say (as Nat has done to me privately), that the US is involved in a new imperialism, trying to export what it wants others to do and be. He says that's the main motive behind our foreign aid. That hits a tender spot with a person who almost worships the memory of Fulbright."

"I can see it does."

"Sometimes I think this internationalism is too disruptive. I am so glad it's led me to be here with you. But it's more than an intellectual trip, taking others really seriously. When you ask the hard question: 'What do you really think?' and they give you an honest answer . . . Well, I guess I'm glad. Maybe even honored. Maybe!"

"Wonderful!" Was all she needed to say, at last feeling that they could return to other activities for which she used the same adjective. They also involved feelings much deeper than those demanded by respect. If the truth had been demanded of her, she would have confessed that this man was infinitely more than her marvelous 'occasional lover'. In the time they had been apart, she spent a lot of time imagining 'the next time' and a great deal treasuring 'the last time'.

Now, with Eric asleep in her arms, she wondered at the change that she had seen in him these three years. Little of this change had to do with their professional lives, although this evening's conversation was relevant to such matters. The important changes were in his sensitivity. Concerning her sensual needs she had to give him an A plus. Concerning her feelings, he seemed to have moved from a barely passing grade to a solid B. Concerning others in their work group he had made less progress. And in sensitivity to himself, outside the sensual area, he was still in the doldrums, not yet passing. How could a man so bright be so unaware of the most important things within himself? Sleep overtook her as she started to ask why this was the case.

# Chapter Twenty-One

Terrorism! As his plane took off from Austin, Texas headed west Eric found himself thinking about terrorism. There had been the two-hundred fifty-six marines killed in Beirut, the downing of an Air India flight laden with mothers and children going 'home' at the end of their school year in Canada, and now Pan Am Flight 103 downed over Lockerbee, Scotland. All of this, he told himself, in the same world where Rani's culturally diverse Committee had wrestled with their differences in a civilized way. Nobody would claim the Committee's interaction was peaceful. But it was certainly not destructive: 'creatively connected' would be an fair description. On the other hand, acts of terrorism were calculated expressions of hatred of some who are different. Terrorists advertised their motives; their deeds were done to proclaim their complaints. Their style also made it very clear that the ends were more important than their own lives. All of this, developing in the same world where he had come to love a devout follower of the religion proclaimed by such terrorists- Islam!

He found himself asking: what was his vocation? Far, far more than to teach about politics! Maybe, he thought, I should be able to make the world safer, less destructive. But the Fulbright Program had now been in operation forty-three years, together with myriads of look-alike programs for every age. Had they made the world more peaceful? Who could know? Further, it seemed that Islamic fundamentalism could not be ignored, that it was a mighty force to be reckoned with. But Ahad and Minah had both claimed that The Prophet taught that killing innocents was contrary to the Will of Allah! Then how are we to understand the anger of Muslim terrorists?

With such questions –about the world and his place in it as a political scientist – Eric spent two quiet days in Albuquerque, awaiting the arrival of a very important person who would fly in from Taipei, via San Francisco.

### ###

"If I'm in your arms on landing, this must be August in Albuquerque," whispered the tall, willowy Chinese figure who felt she was near to being crushed to death. But what better way to die, came quickly to her mind. They had a week, seven whole days before she had to 'work' at a conference here, and they were both determined to make it the perfect week.

Nevertheless, the first hours were predictable, to Eric. And the next day was equally predictable to her, so much so that she had brought a little gift to help the next day.

Installed, sexually as well as luggage-wise in their room, it was just a little under two hours until the subject of correspondence again arose. She had decided to make it short, so it was she who raised the topic:

"I don't want to waste our precious time on this, my love, so let's not do so. But I have to tell you that the most difficult part of the last year without you has been the number of days when I had counted on your written presence, and found myself all alone, wondering if you did love me at all."

"How ridiculous!" He was trying to make a joke of it, but quickly realized his error. "The timing of a letter never means I don't think of you, yearn for you, would give anything to be with you, every day of my life."

"But you know, Eric, what dependability and punctuality mean to me. Maybe I'm extreme in what my culture gives me, but that's me. You know. You do know. That's why we talked about the importance of order to make sense of life and to provide harmony between people. That order is the most important part of my tradition, it keeps my life together. I thought you really listened when I explained that. I thought I felt respect coming from you. But I was wrong. So I have decided I will just accept your unreliability, and suffer without writing back some of those sarcastic things I have said in the past. I am now apologizing for them, and promise they will not be repeated. OK?"

He wanted to blurt out something, but repetitions seemed pointless as a means of release, so he fell into silence. After all, he had foreseen this lecture – about what he saw as only a very 'insignificant weakness'. He simply did not know what to do with this habit of hers – she would never let him off!

The next morning unfolded precisely as she had predicted, but that fact made it no easier for her. This was the man of her life. She lived for him. She always would. For her, love was unending, not only in time, but in its dimensions. Because she knew they belonged together and that she realized and affirmed this reality, she would never let him down, she would never let him go. But it also meant that she would never let him off. Had his mother not taught him that? NO! obviously not. Had he not learned that from the wife who had been so faithful and helpful all these years? Again NO! Obviously not. His definition of love was indulgence. He indulges me, and I love it. I indulge him and he loves it. But , he takes any response to him that is non-indulgent as more than criticism; he always takes criticism as rejection. Then his response to such perceived rejection is this mix of anger and retirement into his own world. Oh my love, my love, she said to herself.

Our time together is so precious, he was telling himself. We both spend so much energy anticipating it, and now look at what we're doing. She should have more sense. She says she has, then she launches into all this criticism. If she cared half as much as she says she does she would exercise more control. Well, if that's the way she wants it . . .

"What did you say?" He asked, looking up from the piece of fruit which he had been dissecting with a meticulousness which would have outdone that of a brain surgeon.

"I didn't say anything."

"I was sure you had."

"Well, I was thinking, but no matter, later."

Breakfast stretched out for another hour, in silence. Twice she tried to raise the question of his plans for their time together, but received no answer at all. This wall he built against her was unbearable. She loved him so much she had come all this way to get, not even a glance this morning, as Eric seemed continuously fascinated by objects in the distance behind her. Heading back to their room he led, she trailing like some servant. Opening the door, but still careless of her, he marched across to the window where a stool provided the base from which he gave every appearance of being the guard of the watch, on the lookout for anything ominous which might approach their small world. There was something ominous, but not in his sight, for it was Eric himself, the present greatest danger to her world, or so it seemed to her.

The odious, yet undefined haze of his present universe was penetrated only with difficulty by soft but firm hands on his deltoids which began rhythmically to squeeze and release them. "Ahhh" escaped him, then silence. He did not know what he felt, except that the hands were a relief – from something, of something. He wanted to say: "Don't stop," but feared to do so. When they did stop it was only so that they could progress down his spine, finding every vertebra, thumbs working their ins and outs, top to bottom, then back up again, over and over. Her switching to his upper arms came as a surprise. At first she seemed to just hold them and they felt warm to her touch. Then she traced the form of both biceps and triceps, somehow stimulating them simultaneously. Even as she did so he noticed his whole body coming to life, as from a deep slumber or even a trance. It was as if her touch had hit some master switch, turning on every light in his bodily city. Thereafter the movement of those hands was like all the times she had touched him combined, as he wondered what it could have been that had held him in misery these many hours. Shrugging her hands off he turned so he could wrap her in the arms that now ached for her.

They found each other. They found themselves. They found the "us" that meant everything to Siok Yim, and in which he ached to lose his very self. They fought to be first to kiss and kiss the returned one, whichever. They found the words "I love you" and could find no others. The words were drowned in kisses. He cried; so did she. And they kissed each other's tears away, leaving the beloved to blink away new wetness. Then ever so quietly, she whispered "Come." His penis was himself; it was also hers. The warmth and oneness seemed to be the whole universe, all perfect stillness. The stillness was all consuming: where there had been tension and tumult, now there was this holy stillness. How long they lay there, unmoving, neither knew, or cared. Eventually she found herself giving him an involuntary squeeze. Awakened, he lunged deeper, over and over, deeper and deeper, as if his life depended on it. She felt as if the tensions could grow no more, yet they did so, on and on. The cry "my love" came with her climax, like none she had ever known before. "I am" came with his. Release in both of them brought back the stillness, the stillness of completeness, in one.

At this moment Siok Yim felt that nothing could touch her. The perturbations of life were as far from her as if she were that hawk she had seen above the Southern California mountain. Time stood still. Moments lasted forever. Nothing could touch them.

Heightened emotions finally gave way to thoughts about this love of her life. How forgiveness suffused her whole body as she gazed at him. She saw him as a little boy, like her own children when they were much younger, hiding in a safe place, refusing to emerge until it was safe. But the wait cost so much. The pain which had extended and expressed itself in every part of her body was gone, completely gone. No explanations necessary. When your love is temporarily rejected it hurts all over. That was a law of the universe. Now all was new, as every morning. Eric interrupted to tell her of his dream itinerary.

### ###

Early the next morning they were on their way west, "to take in a bit of the beauty, the wonder, and the archaeology of the Southwest," was the way he put it.

With her most affirming smile she responded: "Sounds great to me."

Stopping just off the main drag at Second Mesa they learned that the annual night dance at corn harvest time was scheduled three nights away up on First Mesa.

"What's that?" she asked.

"No idea, except what they've just mentioned, but the lady said we might be really fascinated. Let's go straight on to the Arizona places and plan on being in the back country here in three days. All day tomorrow at Sedona."

"Then tell me about Sedona."

"It's the center of the Red Rock Country. I get the impression from photos that there are endless shapes eroded out of red rock, quite high.

It's a mecca for artists, tourists and woo-woo types. But it's the beauty which made me think we should go there. Maybe we'll find it is the most beautiful place in the world, as some claim."

### 

"This is heaven," she whispered, pulling his arms tighter around as he stood behind her. The view possessed them. Four eyes took in the total scene, its every detail. Two bodies felt the vision in every cell, that it was shared. One spirit enfolded all – eyes, bodies, souls and the glory of nature – in a oneness of awe, of peace. He would always remember the scene, every detail. But only she would remember the feelings, his as well as hers.

At their feet Oak Creek sang softly as it played over a thousand small stones, becoming a dazzling pathway enticing them to look further, and upwards. The nearby grassy verges were backed by such lush riparian growth as occurs but rarely in the Southwest, where it is the more appreciated because it is such a contrast to the harsh, dry, brown desert. Overhead, the cleanest of blue skies was dappled with playful little clouds, its fading horizon blue the perfect background to Cathedral Rock. Really a group of rocks, but together quite reminiscent of a cathedral, atop a steeply sloping pedestal they rise vertically several hundred feet, every inch the brilliant collection from the red part of the spectrum which gives the region its name, Red Rock Country. Between those distant peaks and the place where the stream turned out of sight rose a mass of trees, colored, as if by some artist wanting to complete the palette, a rich, bright yellow.

"If someone painted that, you wouldn't believe the colors, would you?" Her nod was all the answer he needed.

They stayed there for a long time, unmoving, transported into a oneness which she (but not he) would have claimed was greater than sex. He was first to break what was a half-hour spell: "What do you say we see if it's possible to climb up those pinnacles – or at least to their feet?"

With the help of guidebooks and uncertain signs they eventually found a parking lot indicating a trail-head. To their surprise, a fifteen minute walk brought them up to the scree which formed the pedestal they had noted from afar. The path was easy, and soon they were up against the walls. These towered above, were more numerous than expected, and provided many intriguing nooks and small caves. But the greatest marvel was their stratification. The whole consisted of thousands of layers of

239

sand, compressed over the ages, each a slightly different color, the easy prey to strong winds and the abrasive action of the small particles being constantly dislodged. "Isn't it wonderful?" was all the comment needed to again express a shared delight too deep for any more words.

### 

The convenient next stop: "Oak Canyon itself," announced Eric. "All the guide books rave about it." Wandering up that stream, new marvels awaited them. They were obliged much of the time to wade through the shallow water, inevitably shadowed by fancifully shaped rock faces a few feet overhead. The waters at flood time had eroded these into shapes which any sculptor would have envied. At every bend the couple had to stop to take in a new view, holding each other's hand, breathing very deeply, smelling the soft fragrance, and sensing the cool gentle movement of the air over whatever skin was exposed.

Around one particular bend she called from just behind him, "Eric!"

"Yes."

"Stop! Just look at the strands of color in those rocks above you, the way they curve, almost like a river in motion. Oh! Thank you. Thank you for bringing me here."

He looked up at the stone canopy overhead, then at her, his face showing how much he meant every word as her replied: "No. Thank you for helping us *find* this." In those words he wanted her to know that the way this was for him, right now, could not have happened with any other.

Reaching out her hand to his she whispered, almost like a prayer of gratitude: "Yes! I know."

### 

Back at the car an excited Siok Yim was studying a guidebook. "Look at this Bell Rock. Isn't it beautiful? All those steps make it look easy to climb. Do we have time to try?"

His "Of course" soon brought them to its base. The first fifteen minutes were fun, and easy. Occasionally one would help the other to clamber up a rock which was a bit big for a single, long stretch. But then the risers became higher, and the flat ledges between them narrower. They looked across at the Cathedral Rocks against the azure sky and down at other rocky eminences which rose up from a floor of red dirt and the dark olive growth which characterizes the Sonoran Desert – scrub oak, manzanitas, and creosote bushes. Siok Yim exulted: "Look. That's where we were on the Cathedral's rocks. And look where we are on this one. We're half-way up."

"But look," he teased. "There are lots of people below us, and the only ones above look as if they have technical climbing gear, ropes and stuff." It was true, they did. So Eric and Siok Yim settled for half-way, found a spot where the rocks created a perfect love-seat, took out their cokes, and just sat. In every direction, smaller groups of rocks poked up temptingly.

"Do you know about vortices?" SiokYim asked.

"What?"

"I just read in the guidebook that many people believe there are unique spiritual powers in this area. Whenever lines of spiritual power converge, they create a vortex. People come from all over the world just because of that claim."

"I have no clue. What do you think of that stuff?"

"That sounds a bit like an adaptation of Lao Tse's concept of Feng Shui. It's the idea that the rays of energy in any place may either support or undermine anything placed or built there. I've seen Western books suggesting how to design rooms taking that into account. Maybe what they call a vortex here has something to do with that."

"Maybe," murmured a very uncertain Eric. "But what do you think about all this woo-woo stuff? You know - spiritual forces and all that."

"A lot! I think about it a lot. Confucius taught about relationships, with no hint of religion. But our other great teacher, from about the same time, taught about realizing yourself. The key to that, I think he said, was how you relate to the forces all around and within you. Many Chinese think of those forces as spirits, a bit like gremlins or fairies, but he used the word energies. I think that way. It all makes sense to me."

"Are you saying you don't believe in any god?"

"I guess you could say that, but I wouldn't put it that way."

"Why not?"

"Simply because dualism is a big trap! Lao Tse taught that the oneness of all things is what really matters, and is where it all begins. The whole of reality does not begin in some superhuman-but-still-made-in-our-image creature; it begins in the oneness. That is also where it ends, if it is accurate to talk of beginnings and endings. He taught that there will always be strife between and within each of us until we realize this truth with our minds and live it with our lives."

"That's heavy, but very interesting. Maybe I could go for that more easily than for this big-guy-in-the-sky idea."

"Lao Tse taught that we don't need special places, special things, special rituals to be holy, to be at one with the Way (he called that the Tao, and that is why one Chinese religion is called Taoism.) He said we just need to live fully a simple life. So I guess I think that what people are more open to here in this Red Rock Country can happen to them anywhere, if they are open to it happening. And when you are more open, it is to energy that you are open, so you are, and feel . . . ".

"Yes, let me finish. You are and feel *more alive.*"

"Quite."

"And, this just stuck me. That happens when I am with you. Not the first day, I admit, but every moment since then."

"Would you say that is because the energy lines are flowing more freely than at other times?"

"That's not a bad idea. Let's think about it as we descend. Or we'll get lost when the light has gone."

### 

The next morning found them en route to Tuzigoot National Monument. Although without any idea what to expect, they were still surprised to find themselves in a dull, flat, sandy wasteland, with just the hint of a stream somewhere in the distance, with something like the banks of a major stream farther off. "It looks," surmised Eric, "as if this was once a stream several miles wide." The road took two sharp bends, and then, out of nowhere was a small hill straight ahead, with the Fourteenth Century remains of a small city on top of that hill.

"It's as if they built in the middle of a river," commented Siok Yim.

"And look," suggested Eric, "this side drops off so steeply that no attackers could ever have approached from that direction."

A walk around the remaining walls, which had weathered seven centuries of the elements without completely disappearing, convinced them that it had been a relatively secure place, with extensive fields of cultivation on the alluvial plains below. But who were the inhabitants? And why were there no traces, as of other earlier inhabitants of the Americas?

Montezuma's Castle and Well, an hour's drive away, complicated those questions without solving them. Both bespoke a very widespread group who had formed a considerable civilization between the twelfth and fifteenth centuries, but left no clue to their complete disappearance. The "Castle", of seven stories, was built into and out from a cliff, all rooms accessible only by ladder. "A really safe place, I'd say," was Eric's assessment

"And well defended from enemies," Siok Yim added. "I'll bet that's why they built in such places."

Strangely, the last element of Hohoman culture they visited delighted them the most. It was called a "well." Really a sink hole, created by the last ice age, they came upon it "by accident". From the parking place there was no hint of water in any direction. But there was a sign, and walking five minutes and rising imperceptibly, they came upon a sudden drop – into this massive hole, full of water, right out here where water seemed quite non-existent. A steep path led them down fifty feet to the water itself where they found themselves in a fairy grotto. Rocks overhung the path, ferns grew at their feet, water trickled out of multiple springs in the hard surfaces around them, and a perfect canal had been excavated out of the solid rock on and beside which they walked. The water in it was delicious, and so cool. Follow its course, and you find yourself out of the "hole" and amid the area which had been irrigated and farmed so long ago – still growing lush grasses and cottonwood trees today.

"How absolutely wonderful! I'm so glad we decided to bring a picnic when we read that was possible here, comfortably, in spite of the heat," Siok Yim enthused.

"You know," Eric waxed speculative, "I can't help putting together the disappearance of the Hohoman, who created these things in such a desolate place, and the ideas from your religion."

"How so?"

"Well, you speak about the Way, the Tao. You tell me that what happens is according to an order, with creation and destruction going on all the time. Would you even say the creation and destruction of societies?"

"Maybe."

"That seems very different from our view of progress. And it makes more sense of this."

"How?"

"In our view, my view, the Western view, things continue, and for good reasons. If they do not, then there is also a reason for that. At first, I thought about the disappearance of the Hohoman in that way. Something must have destroyed them and their culture, or they must have left for some powerful reason."

"I see now what you're getting at. They just came to a natural end, as all things do - without any explanation. So you are asking if that is what Lao Tse would say. I don't know. I don't think he believed what you Westerners believe – that all events lead somewhere. I certainly don't. That's how I live with the frustration of not spending my whole life with the man who means as much to me as life itself."

"Really? You mean that such a belief helps you. I guess I have to admit that the world is not put together nearly as clearly as I was taught. I have to admit that we really don't know nearly as much as we pretend to have learned."

"Except that I love you! Of which there is absolutely no doubt."

Both sat in silence for a long time. Siok Yim was first to speak: "I remember part of Lao Tse's teaching: Those who wish to embody the Tao should embrace all things."

"What does that mean?"

"I think it went something like this: To embrace all things means also that one rids oneself of any concept of separation: male and female, self and other, life and death. Division is contrary to the nature of the Tao. Foregoing antagonism and separation, one enters into the harmonious oneness of all things."

"That's really hard for me to grasp. But I like it."

### 

No one could miss the Hopi Cultural Center at Second Mesa. It was right near the highway as they drove east again toward Albuquerque. But the road to Walpi was another matter. Their map did not even list such a place; fortunately a small road sign told them this dirt track was the right way to go in search of the Hopi festival dance at First Mesa. Additionally, no sign anywhere said that name, nor did their map. In faith they drove off, soon finding themselves in what Siok Yim described as "nowhere". Almost ready to give up, they spotted mesas in the distance. "Those tall, flat topped mountains seem to have been produced like mushrooms. Are they mesas?" Siok Yim asked.

"I've never seen a mesa, but that is what their photographs look like."

Which one was called 'First' soon became apparent. Bumping over a small rise there, right in front of them stood a wall of rock rising a couple of hundred feet above them. A hovel or two and they came to a divergent track with a broken board labeled 'First Mesa'. The road, such as it was, veered away from the mesa for a bit, with enough impoverished domiciles to be worthy of a village name, then turned abruptly and began a precipitous climb.

"Do we want to go up there?" asked the now uncertain passenger.

"Where else? If we're going to see this."

Loose dirt giving way on both sides to nothing did not make for a pleasant Sunday drive, but they soon found the road went no farther. They were confronted by a large group of vehicles, some fairly new, most very dilapidated. They left theirs and continued a short distance on foot. Now they spied the summit, probably thirty yards across, ahead of them. A considerable group of adobe buildings was crowded onto the table top, itself on the far side of a natural causeway just two paces wide, with the valley floor immediately two hundred feet below on both sides. Timidly, looking neither to right or left, they walked the ten paces, onto and into what felt like a tiny village square

There were very few people about, and every one was Indian. "Should we be here at all?" Siok Yim wondered aloud.

"Well, they told us it was OK to come and watch."

Fortunately, a curious child made the first overture, and soon they were engaged in talk with three mothers, all the time marveling at the spectacular sunset which brightened one side of each mesa while shadowing the other. The couple inquired, and were reassured that it was perfectly acceptable for them to watch. "But how did you know? How did you find us?" were questions which caused the outlanders to smile. Then, almost by magic, the place was overflowing, except for a small space intended for the dancers. The couple found themselves squeezed among Hopi seated on the roof of one of the cliff-edge dwellings, watching a full moon just peeping above the horizon as if to check whether all the audience was ready.

Then the dancers came. In procession, from across the causeway they appeared without warning. Their costumes took the two foreigners back to western movies, but these dancers were flesh and blood. Eric and Siok Yim still felt themselves to be awkward, tolerated intruders. But the rhythm of clap sticks and a droning kind if noise from the audience wrapped them up as one with the kids, the dogs, the old and the young, for the next hour. They understood not a word. There were no explanations, no guide-book; but they felt part of the ceremony. And when it was over quietly, albeit trembling, Eric and Siok Yim felt their way by moonlight across the causeway to their car, and following other tail-lights, eventually found their way back to Second Mesa.

"What are we going to do now?" Siok Yim exclaimed on realizing they had nothing to eat and nowhere to stay the night, out here four hours from Albuquerque.

They had nothing to worry about. The Hopi Cultural Center was more than a museum and information center. It boasted a four-star restaurant and a first class, Hopi-style, adobe hotel. Its sand-textured, sand colored walls, quite devoid of sharp edges or corners, seemed such a perfect fit with the wind-blown desert. Even the interiors and their personal fireplace had the same integrated feeling.

"What a perfect climax to these days!" was one of the few comments to break a silence between them which was too rich for any more words. They held hands across the table, relished a great meal with good wine, and tumbled under clean-smelling sheets in air-conditioned comfort to share the most perfect benediction to their time together – until her next visit.

### 

Getting together with his Iranian friend that September Eric was asked, "How was your summer? I know that's a strange question to be asking such a close friend, but we haven't seen each other for so long. How has it been?"

"Wonderful, Ahad, absolutely wonderful. And I'll tell you more about why some time. But right now, in the hour or so we've got, would you mind if we talked about the one part which wasn't so wonderful."

"What was that?"

"My dealing with other cultures. Michael laughs when I talk about them discombobulating me. I don't think he has experienced the upheaval I seem to. But I had a really tough time in that respect, and I hope you can help me sort it out."

"I'm no expert. I'm just learning from my own experiences. But I got a lot from that SIETAR conference which I attended last month."

"Great. May I start?"

"Go right ahead."

"Rani's committee was where it all developed. Afterwards she and I talked at length. But I'm still very unsure of what's going on inside me. You know, inside both my head and my gut."

"I know the experience. It's mine every couple of days, sometimes all day."

"How can you stand it?"

"What option do I have? As a migrant?"

"True. I guess I put myself into this situation occasionally, but you have bought into it full-time."

247

"It wouldn't be that way for me if I were like most migrants. They seem to just go native, and without qualms. I suppose my serious faith makes it worse for me. But back to you - what happened?"

"I think I told you about the first time Rani's Globalizing Social Studies group met. My hard work developing an instrument went down the drain because French people are more private than us."

"I do remember. You were really pissed, particularly at that French Canadian woman."

"You remember! Wow! I must have been on a rant. This time I felt they were *all* against me. Even Rani on one occasion, when she moved the whole conversation onto something else when two of us were getting into it." Ahad's quiet smile signified understanding more sympathetic with her action than with Eric's. But Eric didn't seem to read it that way; he took it as support.

"I don't know how it came up. but the first of our two days I mentioned a little of my sad ending with Minah. They couldn't believe that I ended a good friendship because she held values which were contrary to mine. Of course, I didn't tell them it involved sex, or that I was already married. But I felt they were saying I had no right to stick by my own heritage as an American."

"How? If they didn't know the details?"

"I don't know. It just felt that way."

"But maybe they weren't, as you felt, rejecting you for your actions."

"Maybe! Maybe not! I certainly want the stimulus of other cultures, and of confronting values which are contrary to my own. But when I'm in the middle of that interchange it sometimes turns from pleasant to unpleasant."

"So it wasn't all bad?"

"Rani said not. She congratulated me on being very different this year. She said I was not as fussed by contrary values as in the previous year. When she said that I realized that respect for otherness now has become (at least sometimes) the way I *feel*, and not merely a head trip. I love being with foreigners when I can do that."

"I guess I no longer get into that place concerning American values which run against my upbringing – at least most of the time."

"How do you explain that? And my greater comfort some of the time?"

"I think it has little to do with identity, and lots to do with meaning. If others believe they are right . . ."

Eric couldn't keep from interrupting: "I often feel others are right and we Americans have got it wrong. If you believe others have it right, and you respect them, how do we make sense of such a world?"

"I see two ways. The first is that it is 'right' for their situation. The second is that "rightness" is really psychological; it's how the individual experiences, or sees something."

"So you can make sense of it in either way, all the time respecting the other person?"

"Sure."

"What about the possibility that both are right? I mean, what about the possibility that two absolutes which seem in contradiction, should both be right?"

"That's too much for me, unless you've got a good example. But please go on about my changing some time, but not all the time."

"I said it was about you changing your way of making sense of the world. You are honestly seeing things in more than one way, and sometimes you can reject neither of two ways. I think you are on the edge of becoming a relativist."

"But a relativist holds that there are no absolutes! That's not Eric Johnson."

"No. And I think that's why all this troubles you at this time in your life. What you are, and the way you make sense of things are not fitting together."

"Wow! You might have hit it. I wish we had more time. What about the day after tomorrow? I'll give you my response then."

"Let's meet for a hit of tennis, then talk over lunch."

"You're on."

# Chapter Twenty-Two

With better than average eye-hand coordination Eric had played almost every sport, representing his high school in water polo, tennis and soccer. When Frankie suggested he help the girls, now eight, to get involved in soccer through AYSO he jumped at the thought. "What a great idea," he began, "and I could offer to help with coaching their team also. I'll bet they have real needs there. That's certainly the picture Michael gives me about AYSO in Medford. It'll be the same here in Needham." She smiled. This was the impulsive, intense man she'd met and married. Thank God for the girls, she thought, they keep alive the best things in him.

Eric threw himself into the girls' soccer. He set aside Saturday mornings at the park to help them, and encouraged simple drills in their back yard. Well ahead of the playing season they could both dribble the ball with good control, in addition to being able to block a ball rolling at them. Nicole could also then kick it a considerable distance, with some control of its direction. But poor Jennifer! Try as she would, her toe never connected quite right. One time her foot would go clear over the top even of a stationary ball; the next it would be at the right height but her foot would just glance off the side, causing the ball to wobble drunkenly away to the other side, a result of no use when the aim was to pass it to another player.

When the season started, their team the Jays proved to be about Jennifer's level. The result was that Nicole soon became its star. For the first time in years Eric and Frankie found themselves emoting strongly at the same time and in the same way. Like the rest of the parents they would scream encouragement as their side dominated and share subdued groans when their offspring could get nothing right. They were both highly sensitive to the problem confronting all parents of children's teams – of taking it more seriously than their kids. What did it really matter if two opposing players on the wing were too busy catching up on each other's news to notice the ball coming right to their feet, followed by a swarm of players all trying to kick what should have long since been kicked by one of them?

By mid-season, varying abilities on the field had repercussions beyond it. Jennifer had started to decry her sister's achievements and her astronomical number of goals while excusing her own performance as the result of "sore legs." Eric humored her. After every game he would call: Time for the massage, Jen! Whereupon he would remove her boots and socks, produce some oil, and spend the next half hour at work from her thighs to her toes, to the accompaniment of orders: "Not so hard" or "a bit harder there" or "Oh yes, more please, that's wonderful" It became an important ritual between them. He loved doing it, and she delighted in the complete attention from the one who she called, in that situation, "my slave." Having heard about Egyptians and their lower classes, she claimed to be an Egyptian princess. Eric found that such slavery produced a feeling of intimacy which surpassed anything he had known with her before this time. Long before the season was out he took to calling her Princess, a name which he was to use thenceforth instead of the name they had given her at birth. Furthermore, to his great satisfaction, she would allow no other to use it. That name became a deep bond between them.

On the other hand, Nicole's response to her success on the field was to ask, then to demand more and more of the same. "Come on Dad. You can't be tired just because you've been cheering for us to win. Let's practice." The two would do the same drill for an hour, or more, with her repeated self-encouragement: "I'll get it next time." And she usually did. In a different way she had found the same pearl as her sister: something she did alone with her father, the two excluding all others, which produced a mutual glow which neither could have verbalized, but which to each was worth more than any word could have expressed. At such times Frankie's private observation was always: Where could I have found a better father?

### 

In those same months, following the profoundly rich time with Siok Yim in the Southwest, Eric's moments "with" Siok Yim were different.

The sequel to each previous time together had felt like he was on a board far from land. He experienced elation as he rode up to the top of a wave, recalling their moments of union, with and without sex, then, faced with a trough the joy suddenly disappeared. For two years he would find himself crying at that stage, even sobbing for her presence. Then, in the next year the tears dried up: he still missed her, longed for the touch which was like no other, but he no longer sought secret places where he could cry in private. Now in the months following their Southwest explorations he still rode the surfboard up peaks of richest memories, but the troughs were different.

Two feelings now awaited him in those troughs. The first was quickly repressed: what man will bother about a mere suspicion of a sensation, particularly a sensation which is unpleasant and vague? Even if it was the call to a much better life than you have ever known? The other set of feelings was more accessible, more tangible, and more immediately demanding of his attention. Every letter from her filled him with as much guilt as joy. Hers came every Tuesday; his became ever less predictable so that every hour of "overdue" writing tainted his feelings about this woman who was so wonderful, so much the love of his life, as he was of hers. The troughs were becoming unbearable.

Both sets of "down" feelings were really part of one larger set. To any woman that larger set would have been obvious. But he was blind to them, as he was to much in his deeper self. To put it in practical terms: he simply could not handle her love. He wanted and feared it. For a long time his married state gave him an excuse for not responding to the combination of an overpowering feeling in himself and the unconditional commitment constantly expressed by Siok Yim. But it was wearing, deep within.

Unable to confront the real challenge, in the trough times he found himself focused on more superficial aspects of their relationship. To such an intellectual, even the superficial could be made into a convincing case against continuing the guilt and anxiety as his everyday lot.

This wen and li stuff is ridiculous, he would tell himself. How can order and appropriateness be all that important? I don't understand it. Sure, it may have been the basis of her society for three thousand years. So what? Individual freedom is the basis of mine. And I'm damned if I should feel guilty for days on end, every Tuesday, just over this letter business. And she doesn't like my shoes. They don't show respect! To hell with respect; they're comfortable! I suppose she'd have me binding my feet if that were "appropriate". So the mix of frustration, anger, deprivation, rationalization, and muddled, very non-professorial thinking interrupted the continual sense of her presence and their oneness. He did not know a replacement was happening. And if he had, he certainly would not have so analyzed it. Rani was giving much of what Siok Yim had heaped upon him, and asking nothing in return. The love which had possessed him for three years, which without question was all he had ever yearned for, was meeting its first test. But Eric did not see that.

In such a state, he asked himself how he could end this combination of pain and frustration with Siok Yim. It never occurred to him that another's perspective might help. Like an animal in pain, he saw nothing but his own resources to struggle free of the trap. Had he thought in such a metaphor, it might have occurred to him that such an animal achievement of independence usually comes at the price of a leg. But nor is that outcome anticipated by the animal.

Eric was an inveterate problem solver, proud of the fact, good at it, and willing to do whatever had to be done to solve a problem. "What else would you expect, from a real man?" would have been his justification for such behavior. So first, what could end the distress permanently? And second, what would cause her least pain? The principle which should guide the decision was that the ending would be not only his doing, it would arise from something which was completely his. There! That's it! What ends things must be so much mine that she cannot get around it with her loving acceptance. In addition, it will be something she cannot even understand. Therefore it must come out of the depths of me. What?

Thus, feeling he had almost solved the biggest problem in his life, the customary correspondence continued through the academic year, with Siok Yim all unaware that her lover was coming closer and closer to "the perfect way to end all this frustration" – even if it meant the loss of what he was ready to acknowledge as the greatest love either had known. For him there was the real consolation that what he believed he wanted above all else – really great sex – was available elsewhere, at least annually, and maybe more often if he was reading Rani correctly.

In fact, he was to see both of them in August, in The Bay Area. Rani's annual conference with its meeting of her Curriculum Committee was in San Francisco. Siok Yim had written saying that she was speaking at a Berkeley colloquium on The New China two weeks later, and they could meet up 'in the city by the bay' before she returned to Taiwan.

### ###

As Eric's best friend, Michael could have been of great help to this man who was so confused that he could see nothing but destructive options. Eric had ruled out any direct confrontation with Siok Yim about his anger at her values and habits. He was sure that such confrontation would be devastating to her; so be silent about that stuff. Michael would have shown him how wrong that assumption was. But Eric was acting the independent male. He would have been the last to admit that he was also acting the total coward.

The very week that Eric decided "what I must do" the two men spent a whole day hiking. During lunch Michael asked: "Eric, do you ever stop, really stop, and ask what has been happening in your life?"

Because it struck him as a silly question Eric only mumbled, "Of course," as if to dismiss it as of little consequence.

But Michael's concern had been growing over the weeks of early fall, and his idea of friendship was to be there for each other, even when the other doesn't even know he needs you. "It might seem uncomfortable at first," his wife had taught him, "But our worst enemy is so often ourselves that we all need others' perspectives on the biggest (often very private) issues we face. You men have this stupid thing about self-sufficiency. That's crazy!" Now Michael was determined to be - by his own, as well as his wife's definition - a real friend.

"Let me explain what I started to ask, Eric. I get the impression that you never stop, really stop, and ask what has been happening in your life. You're always on to the next thing, the next relationship."

"Oh, but I do reflect. I do that all the time. Like when I was mowing the lawn the other day. I was thinking about what's good and not so good in my life."

"Specifically, I'm thinking about relationships. Sometimes it takes an effort to get clear what is going on. You seem in such a rush to live the next thing that you never process the last thing."

"Alright! Specifically?"

"How does your relationship with Minah look, six years later? How does your relationship with Siok Yim look, three years after it began?

Where is your relationship with Rani going? And what about Frankie and the girls who mean so much to you?"

"I'm not sure I want to answer some of that."

"Ok. I'm not probing for some voyeuristic reason. To put it in less intrusive terms: What have you been seeking with other women? If you don't know what you're looking for, you're hardly likely to recognize it when you stumble on it, are you?"

"What does any man want from a woman?" was the friendly, half jest with which Eric tried to deflect this even harder question.

"Alright! You asked for it." Michael was really pushing now: "What, my dear, dear friend, what the hell do you want in your relations with women?"

"Apart from the obvious," a now suitably humbled friend replied, "I haven't a clue." Simultaneously with the answer came the thought: That's the question Siok Yim asked that day in the spa. I couldn't answer it then, and I still can't.

"I was afraid you'd say that," came an accepting response. "But let's talk about it again, sometime. Huh?"

### 

Nine months later he watched the small Indian figure approaching, her smile widening with each step. Then, arms clutching small bags and each other, they shared what must have been the longest, most exploratory kiss the shoe-shine man had ever witnessed during his dull days.

"How wonderful to be with you again," were Eric's first words.

"Mm! Mm!" constituted an affirmative, promising much, much more just as soon as they were somewhere private.

It was four hours before he, with her mouth and hands still busy but not overwhelming this tiring male, started the kind of conversation which always punctuated their nearly endless love-making.

"It's now two months, but everybody in Boston is still talking about the Tiannamen Square massacre on the fourth of June. What are your Foundation people saying about China now?"

"That it had to be. At least if the old guard is to keep power."

"But the whole world saw it. I just loved that picture of the young man confronting the massive tank with a flower in his hand. And I'll bet that very picture got back into campuses all over China."

"My own view is that the young Chinese users of the internet will become more and more a factor which cannot be suppressed. It may take time, but they will be heard, more and more. And further, if China's economy is to grow as they hope, they will be obliged to encourage this new communication. The genie is out of the bottle."

"So you think democracy is just around the corner?"

"No way! Not if what I get from Siok Yim is a true picture of Chinese values. No older Chinese is likely to give up the predictability of an ordered life."

"Are you sure?"

"Not completely. But I am sure about one thing."

"And that is?" But she hadn't needed to ask, for his actions said it all. Thus the heavy conversation ended.

### 

It was the third year that her Committee had met for this project. Rani had been in communication with all seven of her members. She had asked all of them about the universal problem of getting beyond the archaic, even "evil" practice of limiting the teaching of social studies to one's own culture and inculcating its values. She would lecture at any who would listen that "They are trying to fit students into a world which has almost completely disappeared. How stupid can you get?" But she knew the forces of conservation and tradition were arrayed against her dream of globally relevant curricula. In that year Eric had given most of his free thinking time to the question: What guidelines can be applied in all countries? This thinking led him to develop a table of topics for coverage at elementary, secondary and college levels. He had circulated this to the other seven and could not wait to get their refinements when they met at Berkeley.

But a wonderful night of love was quite forgotten when five of the seven could not wait for the first formal session to attack him. "It's so damned American," was the verdict pronounced by Thomas. All but Maria and Rani added their condemnation of his beautiful creation. He was so disturbed that Rani's quiet smile went unnoticed.

"What do you mean, 'American'? It is very broad in its coverage."

"That's just it," came from Anh. "You are so sure that everything can be objectively stated - that some listing will meet the problems, that coverage is what counts. That's what is so American – not its content but its approach."

",After all our sessions, don't you see that it isn't so much what we do in a classroom, but how we do it?" Maria joined the attack.

"What? I don't understand."

"Obviously! So I guess that will be the first thing we will have to do when breakfast is done. We'll jointly conduct a class for Professor Johnson. Subject: What matters when you are trying to get beyond your own culture."

The sarcasm was too much for Eric, so he hid his annoyance with: "I'll be a good boy, and come early to class, Teach!"

Sadly, in Rani's eyes, the gulf between Western and others' thinking in the group was too great for them to produce the universally useful guidelines she had dreamed. It's not time yet, was her philosophical way of accepting the outcome to this point. She knew that Eric was far more than an obstructionist to her dream. He represented a more open Western mentality than would be found among most teachers of social studies in the U.S. and therefore, until a means was found to convince such as him, there would be no success in one major audience she had in mind.

"Next time," was her promise as she and Eric parted. "I'll phone you real soon - to see how we can continue." It delighted him that she meant this in two ways.

# Chapter Twenty-Three

There was a full week between the end of what he had come to think of as Rani's conference and that which had invited Siok Yim as a speaker. He spent it with an old graduate school buddy, now teaching at San Francisco State. With no other agenda than its enjoyment, his first exposure to 'the city by the bay' won his heart. "If only they attracted less fruitcakes and nuts" he commented to himself, just like the Bostonian he was. Then came Siok Yim's arrival. He had thought long and hard about this time, and how it would best be structured, and decided that he should treat it "normally" until after her speech. So the plan was to enjoy the sights with her for the first four days of the week she was to be in the Bay Area before flying back 'home'.

In spite of himself, he could not wait to see her elegant form once more, could not wait to be touched, non-stop, in a thousand ways. This visit they kissed as always, and her hands never left some part of him as they cleared the baggage, found the car, and drove to the hotel in Berkeley where her conference was paying the bill. Predictably, they made love as soon as the door was shut. It was not until they were quietly lying side by side, staring blissfully at the ceiling that it occurred to him that she had made no mention of his past year's record as a regular correspondent.

"I can't believe you have gone four hours without razzing me about writing," was his thought, aloud.

"It tells you something, doesn't it, that I love you so much that I kept it to myself this year. And I have to confess that as soon as I saw you, and felt your arms around me at the airport, I knew that you do love me. So I suppose you just swept me off my feet, and swept away all my doubts."

"But why do you doubt? I just don't get it."

"Perhaps you never will. Let me put it this way. If I were to call the shots in all we do together, you would not only think I did not believe in the right to freedom, you would think I did not love you. That's what it would mean to you, if I tried to put you in a box. Right?"

"I suppose so."

"Well that's the way your behavior concerning predictability and order comes across to me. It feels like I'm being forced into such a place."

"I see."

"Maybe. It's very hard for me to tell whether you do when you put on that face."

"What do you mean?"

"Just a moment! I've brought you a little gift. No! I don't want you to open it until I'm off at some formal function and you have time to fill. But here is the package, and I'll tell you this. It's a clever, funny book about the way people hide their true feelings from others. It's called 'Facades'. You have several. I love the real you. But sometimes that person is not with me. Like now - I don't know where you are. I don't know what the real you is doing at this moment. The touch of your hands and the smile are a wall behind which you are hiding. Won't you come out and be with me? Please?"

This was all a bit much for Eric. He saw the truth in her claim – that he was hiding a lot at this moment. But all that he was withholding was not even evident to himself. Under the circumstances stroking her breasts and smiling seemed the best he could do. But after she fell asleep in his arms he found he was even more certain that he must do what had to be done. Fortunately, he could put aside that moment for the next three days and make sure that the hours between now and then would be as any had been.

For her part, Siok Yim was puzzled. Something new was going on with Eric. That she knew from the moment their eyes met. The way his body responded, and the way his skin felt were somehow different. But how? These differences in sensation had restrained what she wanted to express about his highly unpredictable writing this last year. This had been the third year that she had been filled with uncertainty as the plane came closer and closer to the man of her life. On all three occasions she had told herself: He won't be there. This love of mine never happened. It was too wonderful to be real. But each time he was there. And each time she felt exactly the same – except, if it were possible, more so. No love story, even one like that of Dante and Beatrice, could compare with the intensity and totality of this. He was her life, and – how could I have doubted? There he is, waiting with open arms. Oh Eric! My Eric! My love! How I love you, miss you, need you, want you forever.

He was still hers, but his angularities were so different from the smooth limbs and torso which so molded around, under and over hers whenever they lay together. Yet that's the way it is so often in life, she told herself. Oh how I wish it were otherwise! Such things she whispered to herself, alone, in silence, their deeper significance below her level of consciousness but bubbling up, not as anger or even as disappointment, but as pain. The excruciating pain triggered childhood memories of how all her treasured surroundings had been reduced to dust by her Red Guard peers – mindless of the treasures of love, learning and cultivation which they represented. To her that had meant the loss of everything that had made childhood warm and wonderful in spite of revolution – a place and a time of solace and safety.

When this happened to her now her limbs were reduced to jelly, her stomach to helpless churning. She would recall those old feelings, reliving them through images which were then completely obliterated by this purely physical torture. The experience would recur between letters, sometimes for days at a time, then would be forgotten at the sight of a new envelope from the U.S. But the next delay caused the same build-up of pain, followed by another delayed release. However, she would remind herself, the torture caused by the ravaging of her girlhood 'home' had been imposed - this situation with Eric was of her own choosing..

The passage of weeks, even the whole of this last year had done nothing to reduce that pain. Its origin was not memory – which does fade – but regular reminders of his limited response to her total giving. Yet not only would she not turn away; she could not. It was only to Kathy Chang that she had been able to turn, share, and find support; never from the man at the center of it all.

They spent the next day at and around Fisherman's Wharf. The sea lions surprised and delighted her. Siok Yim imagined them having been hired just for her entertainment. She was sure they were grateful for her appreciation of their smoothly sculpted forms draped over groups of pilings and anywhere else that none but they could have adorned. She and Eric talked of Tiannamen Square. He almost screamed with anger about "oppressive regimes which deny people freedom". She tried to argue that freedom is not even possible without order, and its creation and preservation is thus more important. "There could be no democracy without it!" was her conclusion. The talk ended. Or rather, it fizzled at that point. He could not grant any validity to her argument, even though he had virtually done so in a similar debate with Rani.

The reality - and he could not believe that at such a moment with Siok Yim he was thinking about such things at all - was that he was feeling profoundly challenged. The Globalizing Committee had thoroughly disconcerted him about what had been the secure foundations of his life. Truth be told, he had to agree with Siok Yim's argument that you can't have freedom without first having order. And truth be told, he had to admit that he was at the same time much more in the camp of "My country, right or wrong" than he had ever thought himself to be. And all of this was tangled into a time - days of it - with a woman who had transformed his life more than anyone he had ever known, but who also caused him feelings that he could no longer tolerate.

While she was at a closed-circle dinner that evening he opened the book she had given him. He had to admit it was right on. Yes, he did peep out at the world with extreme caution from behind a very safe wall. Certainly he was a showman in classes, but never in one-on-one student conferences. Yes, he was even proud that he could hide the disdain he often felt for pretentious people. But, the suggestion that I hide from myself, tell myself I'm great when I feel like shit! And pretend the same thing to all others, including my daughters, when I'm really down concerning Siok Yim! My God, he told himself, I hope I don't look quite as absurd, and as obvious, as the artist has drawn the man on this page. When she returned he had to ask: "I'm not like that most of the time, am I? Just occasionally?"

"What would Frankie say?"

"That's not fair."

"Oh yes it is. And what would your colleagues say? What about your students? Do they see *you* in class, or some image you have manufactured?

I don't know. But given how often I have to come around and drag you out from behind your facades I do wonder."

He was silent, with the hint of a pout, like a chastised little boy caught out. He was currently hiding a lot. But it was the only thing he knew how to do. He was in a spot, which he had chosen, and engineered. So of course he had to see it through. The anger starting to surface was quickly changed into determination – that's what a man does, isn't it? Somewhat wryly he emerged as the figure depicted on many later pages in the book – with a mask of controlling charm. She saw it for what it was, wanted to snatch it away, but agreed to go off and find somewhere for a drink where they could also dance.

The next day found him at a loose end while she attended some of the sessions, he joining her only for the meals, always with many of the acolytes she always collected so quickly. The university together with the surrounding galleries and shops more than filled the remaining hours. That evening she gave her address, and he remained on the fringes of the group of scholars who captured her for the next three hours, when he pleaded a need for sleep and excused himself. He was still uncomfortably awake when she came in. With pretended enthusiasm he talked of where they might go the next day. He was into describing the delights of Sausalito when he realized she was sound asleep.

The next morning fog lay heavily over all. The ferry finally peeped through it when almost within touching distance. In passing where Alcatraz still stood they tried to imagine its outline, but no sooner did it look like one thing than its supposed form changed dramatically.

"Well, we did see an imaginary Alcatraz," Siok Yim laughed with him.

But as the ferry approached Sausalito the fog suddenly lifted. "What a place! It's fairyland. No, it's the height of elegance." And, "Can we come and live here?" were the excited cries of a Siok Yim who at this moment was in her most natural child-persona. How could he do other than kiss, first her nose, then her forehead, and then her lips?

"You are wonderful," he found himself saying.

On the return trip the sun was setting directly behind the Golden Gate Bridge. Standing with his arms around her he just caught her whisper, "How perfect!" There were many such moments when she was with him.

He was not a grown man, but he was a wonderful one. And he was hers. But such was not the reality. Turning, she saw a look that first puzzled, then frightened her. "What is it, my love?" she wanted to know.

"Nothing! I'll tell you later, after we have eaten."

They ate very little, neither wanting all that came on their plates. The silence was oppressive, so unlike any time except each first day when they came together. There seemed to be nothing either could do about it.

At long, long last, after what seemed to both of them like eternity since she had asked, 'What is it?' they closed the door and stood facing each other. She, the one with all the courage, who knew that love often hurts, repeated her question: "It is later, my love. What is it that you want to say?"

Eric could not have known how he then placed between them his best mask of gentlemanly rationality and began: "There is something I have to tell you. I have thought and thought about what is between us. For two years I missed you so terribly that I cried every day for your presence, for your touch. In this third year since we met I have asked myself how can this be, what is going on."

"Yes?" she encouraged, in what was barely a whisper, for fear was already near to paralyzing her.

"And I came to a conclusion. What has been going on inside me - what I have labeled as the love of my life, just as you called it - has been for me," and he paused, not for effect, but from fear, "it has all been a fantasy." Because he could not tell from her face of stone that she had heard, he repeated: "I have concluded that what I have felt for you has all been a fantasy, which I apparently needed for some reason or other. It's as simple as that."

She turned away, too anguished for tears, for a few minutes as still as stone. Then something akin to pain shook her whole being, the equivalent of an earthquake within the human form. She did not know what was happening to her, just that it was completely unbearable. As in all charged situations, Eric was as surprised as he was helpless. What he had said made sense. It also placed all the blame on him. So why is she so upset? This urbane, highly educated thirty-seven year old father of two nine-year-olds did not have a clue!

For the next hour the only verbal communication was her repeated question: "A fantasy?" Each question brought the one-word answer, "Yes." Otherwise there was complete silence, she stunned, both seeking something to look at rather than the other. Overcome with embarrassment, he sensed he was in the presence of something quite beyond explanation. The expected satisfaction eluded him. He had no idea what to say and so, perhaps for the first time in his life, he was deeply silent. The awe grew in him, at being in the presence of something quite beyond his ken, involving both surprise and fear, and something else, bigger than both.

Eventually she moved toward the bathroom, from which she soon emerged, ready for bed, where she quietly laid down without a word. Unsure whether to settle down in one of the chairs for the night, his urge toward comfort won out, and he joined her, staying as far on the outside of the mattress as possible. His face away from her, the gentle touch of her hand on his back came as a complete surprise. While under the circumstances it was in character for her, this act too was beyond his experience, or comprehension, to say nothing of his expectation. Had she screamed and yelled, he would have found that explicable. Had she demanded he go and find some other room, that too! Had she attacked him, beating out her feelings physically upon his head - that too he would have understood. But her hand was moving over his back. Now it was around the place he liked best, behind his ears. And a voice was saying, "Come."

What else could she have done? As bereft of understanding as he, yet still as certain as on her first American visit that they were meant for each other, wet as ever, as if nothing had come between them, she welcomed him into her body.

Then she cried.

### 

There were three more days until her departure. He had waited until after her address to make his shattering announcement, with three days of the conference still to run and their separate departures planned for its last day. The next morning she had quietly slipped out of bed and gone to breakfast. When he found her, with three friends, he sat with them rather sheepishly, not at all his exuberant self. The behavior did not go unnoticed by the three women. Later in private Susan asked Siok Yim what was wrong. "We just had a bit of an argument last night, that's all," Siok Yim explained.

At lunch, spotting Siok Yim seated alone, Susan joined her. "Where's Eric?" she asked, having grown accustomed to his presence beside Siok Yim every moment.

"I don't know," was the quiet reply. Susan had marveled at the aura which seemed to surround these two. Indeed, she had been more attracted to the aura than to the fact that Siok Yim was the honored visitor from Taipei. At breakfast she had felt a shadow seemed to blot out the aura. Instead of scintillation what she saw in Siok Yim was something nearer to deflation, as if all of something had been lost, leaving a sadly sagging envelope. She chose to be silent, sure that further probing was not the kindest way to treat her new friend right now.

For her part, Siok Yim could not have told you what was going on. She was in shock. None of her intellect was any use at this time. Her world had fallen apart. Her relationship with Eric had become the integrating center of her life. Her letters and his were the regular reinforcement of that conviction, the times in the U.S. were the catalysts for new dimensions and new heights. Even the continued reality of family in Taiwan was now placed securely on the periphery of the way life's circles traveled – the Eric relationship was their center too. They had all been placed in an order which had made sense, even with the uncertainty of when their relationship would be fully, publicly consummated; for she had known, in every cell of her body, that such was their destiny. Every act, every waking moment had fit into that framework. Now its very center - that around which it all held together, good and bad, satisfactions and frustrations – had evaporated in one instant.

### 

There was no program offering distraction for the last morning. Indeed they had until four that afternoon when first hers, then his plane would depart.

They stood awkwardly in the waiting area outside the departure gate for American Airlines Flight 78, to Taipei. Minutes passed between each of those mundane comments with which we fill our airport waits, such as the flight's duration, required connections, and details concerning arrival at the final destination. Then: "There's my boarding call!" She put down her carry-on, took both his hands in hers, looked straight into his eyes, and asked, "Do you mind if I write you from time to time? I doubt whether we will ever see each other again."

"That's fine," was all he could get out before she had dropped his hands, lifted her bag, and with that now familiar determined step, was walking down the walkway into the plane.

Long after her graceful back had disappeared he was still standing stock still, deep in a troubled, incoherent condition. What have I done? At least the worry and annoying part of that has ended. So why do I feel like my world has ended?

He could not begin to imagine how much his entire life would be influenced by what had happened with this woman. But because such feelings were beyond him, he simply *did* something. He turned, as resolutely as she, and strode toward the gate for Boston.

# BOOK IV

# Chapter Twenty-Four

With SiokYim "out of his hair," as he phrased it to Michael, Eric increasingly found himself deeply into the question with which she had so disturbed him. He had never begun to answer her question: "What do you want?" It still filled most of his non-working hours. What, Eric, do you really want? Well, he told himself, I will come up with a few answers, evaluate them, then see where to go from there. But why am I bugged by the fact that there is some doubt? Although he could find no explanation for that discomfort, now he did find himself able to admit that the question made him uncomfortable. Now, feeling he had emerged into a new kind of world - where things were different, even more manageable – maybe he could deal with such philosophical questions. Why should this - and many other things in life- not be more clear?

After getting back from San Francisco Eric's life became intensely busy. Classes were to begin in two weeks, Nicole and Jennifer were bubbling with excitement about going into fifth grade, and Frankie was obliged to ask more of Eric in order to keep the home front functioning smoothly. For some reason beyond his comprehension, probably a combination of guilt and relief, he did so efficiently and with exceeding good grace, at least for such a male chauvinist who had the gender roles so clearly in mind. "I guess I have to help her a bit" was how he explained his own "generous" behavior.

Frankie was relieved, and went into high gear at school. There her first year as nurse had confirmed good relationships all around, close relationships with a handful of women, and an excellent rapport with the vice principal. He, Gregory, was obviously of Greek origin, with all the charm of a Zorba. He always made her feel that he had spent the previous six hours in his office just waiting for her to drop by. She well knew this was not so, but she glowed at the thought, to say nothing of its reality as she would comfortably ask "May I come in?" and find him rising to usher her into the one spare chair in his cramped, messy office. She could not remember when Eric had been so attentive, even at formal college dinners.

### ###

"So what's the urgency?" Eric asked Ahad as they settled down in a quiet corner with their steaming cups of coffee.

Ahad had called saying he wanted to talk. When Eric had suggested a hike two weeks hence, Ahad had replied, "Yes, of course, but I need to talk as soon as possible. Two weeks is a long time!"

Now he launched into the story: "It's like this. You know I've been seeing a lot of Angeline, who is a grad student in Social Relations at Harvard. I made a point of meeting her because she was always just leaving a room where I was about to have a class and, well, you've met her once. I couldn't just ignore such a gorgeous woman, could I? It wouldn't have been good manners, would it?"

Being of similar mind, Eric just chuckled supportively, while Ahad pressed on: "We've been dating for three months, and I really like her. In fact, you would probably say that we have a good thing going."

"Wonderful. I'm glad for you. What more could you ask?"

"Not much. The trouble is that I've been offered it - the 'more' that I could ask - that's what I mean. She has asked me to move in with her. She has an apartment which has more living space than the one I share with two guys. She has lots of money, and proposed I simply contribute the same as I've been out of pocket in my present situation. Who could ask for more?"

"So why are we here, with some urgency?"

"Eric, this isn't just great sex, with a woman beyond any of my fantasies. I think I love her. She's in my mind all the time. And I don't think it is limited to lust. I so want to take her to Detroit next vacation to meet my Mom. You knew she migrated from Iran , didn't you? And Angeline's mentioned the same thing, from her side."

"So?"

"But she's a good Catholic and I'm Muslim."

"Ooh!"

"I just cannot imagine our marrying!"

"Why not? Mixed marriages are as common as twins, maybe more so."

"But Catholic and Muslim? My parents would have a fit. And it almost certainly would not work for the two of us. And what about kids?"

"Now wait a moment. I hear three issues here. Let's take them in order of importance. Start with what is between you two, and how that could be made to work."

"No! Let's start with our parents."

"But you are first; that's where you need to start."

"Look! You said to start with the most important of the three issues?"

"Yes?"

"The most important is my family – mother, sisters, brothers – and how they deal with this son and his wife and children. That comes before my wants, or Angeline's."

"Really?"

"Yep!"

"You surprise me. I thought that for a Muslim it was the will of Allah which came first."

"That is true. But it is more true for some Muslims than others. It is for my family. For me, it's the matter of The Family, with capitals. I

270

am certain that socially they would fall in love with Angeline. But as the mother of their grandchildren? That's another matter. And I don't think it will matter how long they live in this country."

"All right! Let's leave the most important issue, your parents, for a moment, and go on to whether it is good for both of you, as individuals."

"Wouldn't I have to convert?

Not from what I have heard. For her sake, I think you would need to be married by a priest, but priests do mixed marriages all the time, as long as you agree to rear the children as Catholics."

"Guess I could live with that. And she has such respect for me that she would have no problem with my occasional visit to the mosque and a very nominal kind of fasting over the period of Ramadan. But . . ."

"But what?"

"But nothing."

"Ahad, I don't believe you would frown like that if it was 'nothing'."

"Well! Alright! I wasn't going to tell you this. And for the sake of Allah, never let Angeline know that I told you. It's all too stupid. She was a virgin when we got together. She had no intention of having a relationship, as you people refer to it. But it happened. I mean we couldn't resist. Well, it was all very complicated, and very much out of our control, and, and . . ."

"I can guess."

"So now that she's learned she is pregnant, we really have four problems, rather than just the three you enumerated."

"I know which of the four I would call most important."

"So do I! But it's more complicated than you think. She is sufficiently Catholic that there is no way in the world she would have an abortion. She says it is already a person, with an immortal soul. She claims it got that soul the moment of conception. And when I try to talk sense to her, all I get is tears."

That last sentence set off an alarm, not in Eric's head, but in his chest. A big lump arose where there should have been air. Had he not written

271

three years ago to a just-pregnant woman who was all the world to him – about being sensible? And had she ever responded? She may have taken his 'sensible' advice, but he had never been given the satisfaction of knowing so. Ahad had to deal with this same problem face-to-face; all the more difficult! After a long silence, he took the fifth, saying, "Let me think over it, and I'll call tomorrow, at a time when you'll have privacy, from my office."

What did I really want? What do I really want, now? The old SiokYim question drove home with him, flavored his dinner, and sent him into the world of nod. What was I asking for that day when I first played with her feet? What did I really want when I married? When I took on a doctorate? Is my life made up of separate, small decisions driven by specific wants? Or is it made of small upheavals from some underlying matter, so that meeting the immediate demand is like putting salve on a stomach growling with hunger? Thank God sleep finally overtook me, Eric said quietly, as he picked up the phone to call as promised.

"Ahad! it's Eric. Your crisis set me onto a long journey last night. It put the whole thing in a bigger context."

"And what was that? What could be bigger, at least for Angeline, right now?"

"I'm talking about the big picture of what you want in your whole life. I think you ought to be asking yourself those four questions on the basis of the way you see your whole life."

"I guess I just want to be happy."

"Is that all? I've heard talk of your mother's happiness. You speak of Angeline's happiness as if it is vital to your own. I know how passionate you are about getting your doctorate, not just for prestige or a job, but as preparation for doing something major concerning the Muslim/Western interface. You've got a lot of wants beyond being happy."

"Yes. But all of those will help to make me happy."

Eric had reached the end of his own insights – into himself as well as into his friend's life – so he moved onto safer ground. But as he did so it occurred to him for the first time that the following option had never really occurred to him concerning SiokYim's pregnancy. "Have you looked at the pros and cons of marrying her?" he now asked.

"I had imagined no marriage until well after my degree is finished and I have a good job."

"Well, I suggest you make two lists, then let me add a few considerations, then you go off alone for a day and come up with an answer to the question: to marry now, or not? Just give me a yell if you want to talk it over in any way at all."

He felt quite good as he hung up. Ahad was more to him than his own brothers; he would do all he could to be a real friend. He might even be a little wiser for his own loves – first of a Muslim, then of a woman he impregnated. He felt good, really good about his relation with Ahad: there was a deep connection, and it was creative. Like it was with Rani! And for that matter, with his daughter Nicole! And Michael! What about with Siok Yim? Connection? Yes. Creative? No, often destructive of his own comfort and . . . and of my wife? There is some kind of connecting, but it causes more pain than pleasure.

### 

The next evening Frankie took the initiative, asking after the girls were in bed: "You look particularly pensive tonight. What's happened?"

"What do you mean, what has happened? Just another day at school!"

"OK, whatever you say."

"Alright, I might as well tell you. A really good guy I know has gotten a girl pregnant, and asked my advice."

"What did you say?"

"I suggested he write down all the pros and cons of marrying her."

"Whatever for? Given your lack of religious convictions, I thought you would have just said something like: 'Tell her to get an abortion and move on.'"

"That's hardly fair to me, Frankie. I do have some principles."

"Such as? Sorry, that just slipped out."

"Of course it did. You would never be guilty of being nasty, would you.? Look! You asked me a question. If you want to talk about it, OK. If you just want to take shots at me, well, I've got something else to do."

"You always have. I feel like less than an unwanted guest around you. Why can't we have a real conversation about something that matters beyond our daughters?"

"Because you always make it personal, about us I mean."

"That's because your tone is always one of two kinds; it's either sullen, or it's belligerent. Either way, I feel put down. And I have to . . .. Oh go and read your so and so book! I'm going to bed."

### 

The third week of classes, at a time he knew she would be at her desk rather than in a meeting, he called Rani, for she had seemed the obvious one in his life to ask about "woman stuff". It never entered his mind to ask either of his two buddies about anything related to the emotions.

"How nice to hear your voice, Eric. It's almost as if you cared!" was her tease.

"I do. You know that. I really cherish the great relationship between us. And I'm so grateful for all the Globalizing Committee work has meant for me. But I'm calling for something very personal. You know me pretty well. In fact, you know me far better, and know more about me than any person I'm not . . ."

Because his silence betrayed the fact that he couldn't find the right expression, she ended the sentence for him: "committed to. You know me far better than any other person you're not committed to."

"I guess that's right," he mumbled uncertainly, disliking the overtones of that word commitment. "Well, this may seem odd, but can I ask your advice about a woman?"

"Go ahead. I feel it's a privilege."

"There is a Russian graduate student in one of my courses who really turns me on. And I can't believe that a woman who must surely belong in a James Bond movie seems interested in me. Given my level of sexual frustration at home and my ending with Siok Yim such a temptation is almost irresistible. I know you don't mind me saying that, do you?"

"I feel privileged that you should feel able to do so, Eric, my very special man. But whence the uncertainty I detect in your voice?"

"A few things. She's separated from a husband I think she married for the sake of a U.S. green card. He's a shady character, with connections in Russia which sound iffy. She clams up when I push any questions about him. Then there's his verbal abuse of her for all the three years they were together. And it's become physical in the last months. At least until she moved in with another Russian family."

"Quite a story! You do like them exotic, don't you?"

"That's not fair," he countered defensively. "But, seriously, what is your off-the-cuff reaction to this scene?"

"Suspicious, would be my immediate word. Dangerous comes quickly to mind also." There was a long silence, while he contemplated her two words and she wrestled with her feelings, then added, "Please, Eric, please be careful."

"Thanks. I will. And thanks for making clear what should have been obvious to me. I've never had a friend like you."

Hanging up, he found himself smiling, wondered why for a few moments, then wrote it off to a new clarity about how to deal with Natasha – as a formal student/teacher relationship, carefully controlled.

### ###

"Eric," Frankie began carefully, using the one approach likely to evoke a creative response from her husband, "I'm concerned about the girls."

"Yeah?"

"I'm wondering how much they feel constrained by the traditional gender restraints that our parents grew up with. And there's also the way we behave toward each other. I'm sure the girls notice things, of which we might be unaware."

"Such as?"

"Such as the way we communicate. Sometimes we are so abrupt with each other. I really want them to grow up with an ideal in mind about how rich marriage can be. That couples enrich each other. Does that make sense?"

"Sure. And I agree."

"Then why don't we try? Why don't we really try," she hurried on, "to talk more?"

"About what?"

"About all the things we used to talk about. For starters, what goes on at the college, and at my school. I'm sure there's as much in one as in the other that would interest us."

"I don't feel any need to do that. That's my life, and my business." With this he lapsed into silence, angry at the impossibility of separating objective facts about his work from his emotional life - which he thought of as very private and too personal to discuss with his wife, of all people. The reality was that he had developed an emotional life quite separate from his wife, a life to which he found himself giving all his attention, except when the girls were actually in his presence.

"Well, if you don't want to talk about us, maybe we could have a conversation about gender roles."

"What? A conversation about gender roles? Whatever for?"

'For starters, because what is going on in our society about that is a vital matter. We talk about it all the time at school. And with a woman running for governor who is also pregnant, the issue is on the lips of lots of people in Massachusetts these days. Then there's the matter of how our responsibilities here have changed. And I thank you for that. But at the same time I get the impression that your expectations are still about the same as your father's."

"That's almost certainly true. That our fathers would think we should just do what each of us was born to do."

"Do you think that?"

"With some modifications, yes."

"What modifications?"

276

"Well, I'm doing the laundry these days to help you out because you are bringing in a second income."

"I'm grateful. But also a bit angry."

"At what?"

"I don't like your words about helping me out. They sound like the same old song - that the laundry is my responsibility. Why can't it just become *your* responsibility?"

"But it's not."

"What do you mean it's not? It has become yours. To call it mine rests on the assumption that laundry is 'women's work'. You have agreed to be responsible for it. Now it's your responsibility, no matter what your father would call it."

"Maybe."

"And so, when you do the laundry you are not helping me, you're fulfilling a responsibility which you now own. That's how I think of it. You don't say you help me put the girls to bed; you just do it, as part of what it means to be part of this family. So my dear, next time we have friends here would you please refrain from saying you will help me with the dishes."

"What the heck am I to say?"

"Simply that you will do the dishes. That avoids all this male stuff that I hate."

"You didn't hate it before you went back to work!"

"Oh yes. I did. It's just that I wasn't able to say what I have just said to you. I am me. That is first. Second, I am your wife. But being myself comes first. And always will from now on."

"I don't know that I can buy all that. I mean, I agree with the basic thesis, that sex roles are changing, and I'm OK with doing my share around the house, but," and he paused.

"But what?"

"I dunno."

277

"Look at it this way. Mother has changed. She simply told Dad that it is not her responsibility to take care of all personal matters in their lives now that he has retired. She has insisted that they split it right down the middle. Especially since she loves to garden and he can't say that is his domain, his share. I think Dad even enjoys taking over the check book."

"She does? Gran? I can't believe it. She's always seemed so traditional."

"And so was I, until I woke up, just this last year, with Mum's help. And another thing, Eric: we are raising girls. I don't want them confined by gender restraints which I have left behind. Given the right models they can be saved a lot of anguish a few years down the road."

"That's a point," he acknowledged.

For the sake of peace – and the girls – he never again talked about 'helping' with domestic responsibilities. Alone, he found that this conversation rang bells related to Rani. She had shared with him her convictions about the equality of the sexes, and how it had been a major issue in the breakup of her marriage. But at the time it had seemed unimportant. Now he called and ran past her the conversation with Frankie. She repeated what she had previously shared. He listened attentively while she expressed her feelings about "slights" by her former husband, finding himself nodding at the phone in empathy. When he hung up he had the feeling that independently he had made the right decision about what a woman should do and be. Frankie would have been delighted at the outcome. But she would have been furious about whose support had moved her husband towards agreement.

Frankie felt wonderful about her conversation with Eric. It was the most real talk they'd had in months, maybe even years. Perhaps it was the strength she got from related conversations with Greg. But she wasn't about to mention him to Eric. That relationship with Greg was so different from what went on between her and her husband. She couldn't quite figure out how, but it was. "Greg always makes me feel understood, and important," was the way she explained it to Christine.

"Sounds like a real friend. That's what I am to you, and you to me. Why expect it to be different because the friend is male?"

"But it's never happened before. That's what's so odd. Why hasn't it, if it's so natural for a man and a woman to have a close friendship which remains platonic?"

"Because they never remain platonic, that's why."

"This will. You will see that it will."

"So it's just intellectual, is it?"

"Of course not! Don't be silly. You know better than that. I have lots of good feelings towards Greg – but not sexual ones."

"Tell me this," and Christine 's tone changed, signaling Frankie that she was getting into another level of talk, "Just how broad is the subject matter of your conversations?"

"With the exception of sex, almost as broad as ours, yours and mine."

"Do you mean two-way? Does he disclose as much as you, about very personal matters?"

"Oh yes. His life is pretty tough. Both his wife and one of his three kids have a congenital disease which is bound to shorten their lives. It also makes them much less energetic, so that Greg does an enormous amount at home. And every few weeks she'll have a flair-up of one of the symptoms, and . . ."

"I get the picture. You are an important support to him, emotionally."

"I've never thought of it that way. But yes, I guess that's so."

"Is that reciprocated? I mean, is he a support to you?"

"I hadn't thought of it that way. But now you push me to acknowledge that I support him by listening to his stresses etc, I have to admit that he listens to mine. In fact, that's the most wonderful thing about him. I will be feeling really strongly about what most would call "some little thing" with a stress on the little. When he looks at me and asks 'What's troubling that happy face today?' I always find that he appreciates that it is not "little" but very important, just like you do."

"And Eric never does?"

"That is absolutely true - even though he's much less chauvinistic than he used to be."

### 

Several weeks later Eric dragged in at the end of a very heavy day to be greeted by: "Thank God you're home at last. Where have you been? I've been waiting for you to get here."

"What do you mean, 'Where have I been?' At school, of course, in a damned meeting that went on and on. I thought when Beverly left that we would have peaceful faculty meetings, but was I wrong! Today was devoted to the whole faculty discussing the procedures for new hires. As chair of the Committee I assumed it would be straightforward and . . ."

"Eric! You didn't hear me! I have been waiting, so I could leave the girls with you."

"What? But it's nearly dinner time!"

"Yes, and that's the issue. I promised to take a dinner over to a family where the mother has been seriously ill and in bed for a week now. I cooked two casseroles the same. Ours is there, and you and the girls can eat as soon as you're ready. I'll have mine when I get back. I shouldn't be more than forty five minutes, 'cause the traffic will be slowing down by now."

"But where? Who? Who's sick? And why you?"

"It's a long story. But the short version is this: When I learned that my boss has both his wife and a son sick at the moment my generosity bubbled over and I blurted out that I'd bring a good solid meal over today. They seem to have been existing on fast food for nearly a week. That's terrible, isn't it?"

Eric wanted to say a lot of things, but simply clammed up with an "OK." He did admire this quality in his wife. It's just that her generosity towards others did often come, as he saw it, at his expense. He rounded up the girls by helping them with the tail-end of homework, washed up, and the three of them sat down – for a meal which bubbled with laughter, perhaps because he was so unrestrained that Jennifer asked, "Daddy, why aren't you always like this?"

# Chapter Twenty-Five

Eighteen months later, on December 2, Eric had a call from Anh, the Vietnamese woman who had been part of the "Globalizing Committee. "Eric," she began after the usual pleasantries, "Could I see you for a couple of hours during my Christmas visit to Boston?"

"It's amazing that you should be calling. I've been really frustrated that we've always been so rushed when the group meets for business. There never is enough time to really talk." He reflected her wishes.

"Exactly! So when and where?"

"Given the uncertainty of the weather, let me buy you dinner one evening before I go off to New Hampshire immediately after I finish my exam stuff. How would Friday, the 21st suit you? I have to get my grades in that afternoon, so I'll be ready to kick back over dinner."

"Sure. I can make that."

"The next day my family all goes up to the lake, so that would be perfect. Call me a soon as you get in, and we'll settle on where to meet."

### 

On the agreed evening Anh began, "The longer I stay here, the more I feel like a kind of missionary."

"You? I've heard you say some quite anti-Christian things during our work on the Committee. You really surprise me."

"No! Not a Christian missionary! Indeed, not a proselytizer for Buddhism, although that's my religion. No! What I mean is that I find myself giving more and more talks, and more and more mini speeches to help Americans understand how we Vietnamese relate to the world."

"That's the kind of thing I've been wanting to talk about with you."

"It usually arises in conversation about Vietnam. You know. People are all talking about creating a memorial in DC. They seem to feel free to ask me about what was going on for me, a native. You know, during the fighting, when I was in the middle of it all?"

"What do you say?"

"I start by telling them how ignorant this country was concerning mine. Not a single professor of Vietnamese studies in the whole country when the US got into that conflict. Then I tell them about my brothers."

"What about your brothers?"

"They fought on opposite sides. Brothers! It was not a war against the Chinese. It was a war amongst ourselves – even between brothers."

"What happened to them?"

"They were both killed."

"I'm sorry."

"But what I really try to explain is how we think."

"And how do you explain that?"

"I tell them that you all, all you Americans like to believe you know. But you don't. You know *about*. And that's not the same thing as knowing."

"Isn't that what academia is for? To learn about a field, or a topic?"

"Sadly, yes."

"It's not sad to me. It's great fun – the learning I mean. I'd happily be a student all my life, if someone would pay me for it."

"What I have tried to explain is that when we, we Buddhists talk about knowing we mean a lot more than knowing facts. You think you know when you know the chemistry of something, or its story, or its relationships. You define and explain – forever. You create concepts, and use endless words."

"Yes. We do. We try to be precise. What do you mean when you say you know something?"

"Let's be specific. Take a flower. When I say I know a flower I mean I have become the flower."

He just looked, respectfully, puzzled, waiting for her to continue. Which she did with her characteristic intensity: "To know a flower is to become the flower. To know the Vietnamese required you Americans to become the Vietnamese. But you've never lived that way. To become something takes work. It takes time. It requires you to be with the thing, or the person. When you can just *be* with them the knowing can start to happen."

"Yeah! It's good to hike together, or work in the garden, or on a committee which is constructive, like ours. I always feel I know people so much better if I actually work with them on something, or do something together."

"But those times are not BE-ing with each other."

"I'm lost."

"Maybe that's the basic problem you have, you Americans. You are lost because you are always so focused on doing. There's all the world of difference in being. When you do something, it's always for a purpose. Our Committee is doing things to create a new approach to teaching social studies."

"Yes."

"And how much time have you and I spent at those meetings just DOING nothing."

"But that would be such a waste of time."

"The perfect American answer! That is exactly how you all see it."

"No, not all! I have heard the occasional person talk about visiting gurus and popular books by, who is it, Thich Nat Than?"

"But you haven't read them?"

"No."

"Then you must. He talks about how to be one hundred percent in the moment, without any intentions or planned outcome."

"How do you do that?"

"Well I focus all my senses upon it - the flower, the person, whatever."

"Focus?"

"Yes. I do not see, smell, taste, touch or feel anything but what I want to BE with. I empty my head of thoughts about it. This is very important for you, who are so brilliantly analytical that you never stop *doing*."

"Then what?"

"Ah, second problem. Then for as long as necessary, you must DO nothing. At least nothing but lose yourself in that other thing, or person, or situation."

"I think maybe I have done that sometimes with classical music."

"Great. You do know how. Why not try now? Why not try, here at this table, to BE me?"

"That's ridiculous."

"No! Try! You might be surprised."

It would have seemed stupid, had his mind not wondered off to times of love making, with Minah first, then Siok Yim, and now, from time to time, with Rani. As Anh gave him time to ponder her challenge, he recollected moments with each of those women, and then found himself wondering about his compulsive achievement orientation. How busy he always was! Were there really that many things which urgently demanded his attention? Had they not all disappeared each time he made love? But was not the love-making aimed at a particular goal?

"You're wondering, and feeling a bit self critical?" she queried.

"How did you know that? It's a very good guess."

"No guess. I just focused all my attention on you. I mimicked your expressions. When I did so, I felt stupid, well maybe not stupid, maybe unsure that what you automatically do is what you really want to do."

"That's awful close," Eric confessed. "I was realizing I probably keep busy to avoid something else. Sometimes, no, often it's to avoid thinking about uncomfortable stuff that I can't change. You know. When you want to do something about something, but you can't. Then it's a great solution to have something useful to do. Like Mom always said," he finished lamely.

"Eric," she now challenged, "Are you going to try just *being* with me right here, or not?"

"OK!" he surrendered, and gave himself to the experiment. "Did you say you not only watched intently, but also mimicked my facial expressions?"

"Yes. And the ways you held the other parts of your body, and moved them. The gurus call it mirroring."

"Now it's coming to me. This is what I do with nature. I feel one with trees, clouds, trails, you name it. Yes. It's what I enjoy most. Or almost 'most'!"

"That's great! But right now, you are procrastinating."

### 

He wrote to Rani while Frankie and the girls were at the Christmas eve service in Center Harbor:

My Love,

"I have to tell you about Anh's visit to Boston. I took her out to dinner the evening before we drove up here for the Christmas break, and we had the most wonderful conversation – about the difference between being and doing, and about her way of knowing. The reason I have to talk to you about it is that it ties in so much with what happens between us, when we are together.

She forced me to attempt to just BE, with her, across the table, in the restaurant. At first it was hard. I was self-conscious. What would people say about the way I was just staring at her, but not a word between us.

285

Then I forgot where I was. I let my mouth open slightly, the way hers did. Then I copied, mirrored is what she would say, the general position of her head - eyes looking down at the cloth with head bent the same direction. I noticed her face seemed to sag a bit; that was hard to copy. But her shoulders were easy, and her arms, with one hand on the table, just moving occasionally. Every so often I came back to her face. Then I seemed to stop trying. I just was. I suppose I was looking intently at her face when I realized there was a tear slowly edging its way down my cheek. I let it go for a while. Then as I brushed it away she looked at me, almost as if surprised that she was here, in this restaurant.

I found myself saying to her: "You are very sad."

"How did you know?" She asked.

I felt a bit foolish when I gave the true answer: "A tear rolled down my cheek."

"I was thinking about my brothers. When I last saw them I was nine."

Can you believe that? I was completely focused on her, and without a single word I felt, in my own body, what was happening in hers, as she remembered her dead brothers.

She also told me about Thich Nhat Han, who I must now read.

### 

He should not have been surprised by Rani's reply which awaited his return to campus ten days later.

My dear, dear Eric,

I do know Thich Nhat Hahn. He's wonderful. Do read him. And have you read The Unbearable Lightness of Being, by the Czech Milan Kundera?. It's the most wonderful love story – about a man quite like you. It's been made into a movie. I'd love to see it again, with you if we could. Why? Well, because I so identified with Juliette Binoche, who plays the love of this man's life. And because I really understood it because of what has happened between me and you. I'll try to explain that the next time I'm sitting in my favorite spot, on top of you. In all seriousness, that's where I have felt a sense of being rather than doing. Really!

My fantasies are overwhelming. So good-night.

No. There's something else that's important. Thich Nhat Han talks about "washing the dishes to wash the dishes." That sounds stupid, until you list the reasons each of us has for doing such a thing. We do things for some end. He says to do things for no end, just focus totally on doing them. It's a bit like your focussing on Anh. He has another book with a title that has the same message: Chop Wood, Carry Water. Again, if you'll forgive me for explaining, the idea is that these things, which are usually thought of as a chore, can be moments when you lose yourself in something else, moments of pure BE-ing.

So now I'm telling you: good night, my love.

### 

Almost two years after their parting Eric received a letter from Siok Yim. It read:

My Dear, Dear Eric,

You said I may write, and today I felt the need to do so. I hope you don't mind too much.

My life this past year has been very rich, even wonderful, because it has contained the full range of human experience. There have been profound depths – illness, even death. There have been great heights – my daughter's national acclaim as a cellist, at the age of twelve! My academic life goes well, with more invites than I can honor, I guess because of my several presentations in the U.S. Funny that should make me an authority, isn't it? My husband I separated, and are now divorced –for reasons I do not need to spell out; you have heard them.

I think often of your little family. I hope Frankie and the girls are well. Tell (no, I guess you can't tell Nicole) but I hope her soccer is still going well. Are you still the great coach?

My sincerest best wishes, Siok Yim.

This letter confused Eric. The passing of time had not dimmed his recollection of the feelings he had known with her, or the way he had ended the relationship. As he read these words all the old feelings seemed written on every line. He was certain that the verbiage camouflaged her abiding love for him, and that made him feel rotten. When he rehearsed his lie that it had all been a fantasy there was even more confusion. "But you had to end it!" came a voice from somewhere within, and with it a senseless depression for the rest of that day. The "real" self-justification – that he could not stand her "rigidities" – seemed equally empty for the next few days. The knot in his belly persisted, defying explanation and resisting all attempts to alleviate it. Eventually busy-ness won out, but only as a means of repression. The resolution would have to wait until the pain became either uncontrollable or incapacitating.

### 

Frankie had driven the girls home from their first Fall day of school – Jennifer silent all the way, in a world of her own, Nicole bubbling over about two new boys in her sixth grade class who made her laugh and laugh, Frankie herself glowing, inexplicably. Somber-faced Eric dragged in at suppertime to find Frankie and Nicole busy in the kitchen, the former humming to herself, Nicole excited about her last hour's success at dribbling the soccer ball, and Jennifer nowhere to be seen.

"Hi, darling!" Frankie greeted her husband. "Don't start doing anything. Supper's only ten minutes away. And it's your favorite."

"You should see my ball control today, Daddy. It's much better than last year. I get better every day. Do you think I might make the regional team?"

Eric caught some of Nicole's enthusiasm: "Great, sweetheart. Where's Jennifer, Nicole?'

"I think she's still in her room, Dad. She just flopped down on the bed when we came in, and she was still just lying there after I changed and was going out to play."

"Darling", came Frankie's request, "She's in one of her 'I want to be alone' moods. Perhaps she'll respond to you more positively than she did to me. The only words I got out of her all afternoon were 'Why do you have to be so happy? It depresses me.' Would you see if you can get her down to eat with a smile on her face?"

After knocking gently a second time a small voice invited him in. He approached the form lying face down on her bed with: "Hi Princess, got a hug for your slave?"

A curt "No!" gave him the clue to what he must do next. Sitting on the edge of the bed and scrunching her over a little, he had been rubbing her back for a couple of minutes before he realized she was crying. A gentle inquiry elicited the response, "I've got Mrs Tomlinson this year. The other sixth grade, the one Nicole's in, has Mr Tomlinson, and he's great. But his wife is a cow! She already hates me. And I hate her." Then the tears began to flow in earnest. His response was to raise her to a position in which he could take her in his arms, and holding her to him with one hand, gently stroke her hair with the other. After several minutes the tears stopped, she gave him a wan smile, received a kiss on the forehead, and then relapsed into self-pity: "But it's not fair."

"I think it will seem a lot better tomorrow."

"No it won't. It'll be worse. She hates me already. She asked me how to spell 'receive' and when I got it wrong she asked how I came to be in sixth grade."

"That does sound hard," Eric consoled her, "But maybe she was a bit nervous on her first day with you all. I'll bet she'll be more patient once you all get to know each other. I'm that way my first day with a new class. I'm sure you can be patient with her."

"I want her to be patient with me. That's her job, not mine."

"How about coming down to supper? Mom's made Shepherd's Pie. That's your favorite, as well as mine. I won't even notice if you put half the bottle of ketchup on it." With this incentive and bribe, she led her dad downstairs and gave a grunt to her mother's welcome as they all sat down.

"You should hear Nicole mimic one of the boys in her class," Frankie proclaimed to her husband, who barely had time to respond before Nicole was on her feet walking around the table in the most peculiar gait. Eric couldn't help laughing, albeit in a manner restrained by the new unhappiness he caught on his other daughter's face as she watched her sister.

Nevertheless he couldn't restrain his predictable applause: "I think you'll be on the stage when you're not on the soccer field." But the enthusiasm disappeared as quickly as it had arisen, and they all settled into their food. Eric found himself drained, his responses to the girls having taken more than all he had to give to anyone tonight. Nicole , brimming with energy, restrained her desire to carry on about her wonderful first day at school and her excitement at having a man teacher for a change. Jennifer poured a mountain of ketchup, took two mouthfuls of the pie, then fell into a reverie only interrupted by the occasional poke at her plate.

Frankie looked at each of them in turn, considering whether to promote further conversation. Except with Nicole the prospect looked like a lot of work, and realizing that alternative might further depress Jennifer, she opted for a few minutes of silence. What a pity, she was feeling, because I feel great! It had been a beautiful first day at school. The advance week's review of new students' medical records had left her free to respond to all of the day's immediate demands, which she had done with patience and satisfaction, consoling newly-deprived mothers and several scraped knees. Everything around her had felt like "home'. She found it hard to say why, but it had. The place itself was part of this feeling – she liked the colors of the walls, the pictures in the halls, even the auditorium with its old-fashioned stage. Then there were the people, particularly the people in administration. There was never enough time to talk, there was always so much to say; but then it was fun, even when they had to go through routine stuff, as was the case every day with Greg, the vice principal. He was great, really great. "Well," she found herself saying here at the table, "on with the evening!"

"How was your day?" she now asked Eric.

"Normal pre-semester conversations, meetings, and other stuff," came the brief answer, in the flattest of tones, with the underlying message in his facial expression: "and that's all I'm going to say".

"We had lots of excitement, particularly with five new staff," offered Frankie, in the hope of beginning a conversation with her husband.

"Oh." Was all she got.

The girls' silence was now broken with the accusation from Jennifer: "She kicked me! Under the table! She kicked me!"

"I did no such thing," countered Nicole. "I simply moved my foot, and it brushed hers. Why do you have to be such a . . .?"

The words had not been expressed before her sister was in tears. Eric's response was to gentle the one while mildly 'correcting' the other. Frankie persevered with conversation, asking how Michael's summer had been, and about his wife's health, which had been in some serious question when they had barbecued at their home four weeks ago. One question she found Eric had not heard, and to all of her questions she received little more than a grunt or an OK. Maybe the desert surprise would evoke more response.

"Jennifer," Frankie began, "What do you think I made for desert tonight?"

"Mom! You didn't. Blueberry pie?"

"I thought that might change your expression. Actually, I made it to celebrate the beginning of the new school year. But I guess we should all treat it as a way to say we treasure Jennifer."

"Because," injected her sister, "Jennifer is good excuse for you to make what we all love. Can I cut it?"

Suddenly Jennifer was all energy: "No way. Mom made it for me so I'll cut it. That way the pieces will all be the same size."

"With enough left for seconds for the two growing ones in the family," suggested Nicole.

"That's fine, do it that way," Frankie agreed, and was soon getting the token of gratitude which mothers must often accept as a substitute for a verbal expression. In the middle of their enjoyment she injected: "What would you all say to spending next Sunday at Gran's. She says it's been months since we were at Marblehead!"

"But she was with us for a week at the lake," an again unhappy Jennifer complained. "Gran's is such a bore!"

"Do we have to go? I don't want to miss Sunday School the first day," Nicole added to the discouragement.

"I know why that is!" Jennifer now countered her sister. "It's because you realize that one of those new boys in your sixth grade class will be there on Sunday."

"What's your reaction, Eric?" came Frankie's re-direction of the way things were shaping up.

"I couldn't care less."

"What? You always love to go to Gran's," came Frankie's puzzled response.

"Whatever!" in the same listless tone.

"Sounds like I'd best call and take a rain-check," concluded the would-be family coordinator. Eric soon rose to join Nicole in clearing the dishes, as he did every night with one of the girls, while his wife went off to her one sit-com. Jennifer stayed in the family room, idly thumbing through the latest women's magazines. Later, there being no homework tonight, she knew she would have no trouble in getting her dad to meet her challenge to a game of rummy.

Her sit-com over, Frankie showered and hopped into bed with the novel she was half-through. Her reading came to a halt, not momentarily, but for the night when she happened upon a description of the hero's declaration of love to his counterpart. She savored the words he used. They made her feel so good. Somehow, she imagined Greg had probably said just that when he proposed to his wife. And then, try as she would, she could not remember what Eric had said when he proposed. Or had it been she who made the suggestion? Yes, that was it: it seemed such a good idea. Not long afterwards she fell asleep and dreamed that she was being proposed to by a strange man; but though she had no idea who he was, his words were wonderful.

### 

During one of her fleeting visits to New England Rani suggested Eric "play hookie" in order to join her to attend an Indian wedding in Worcester. He agreed primarily because of the chance to see her. In Singapore he had met individuals and gone to ceremonies and temples whenever an important date in any one faith occurred; many of the latter being recognized by the Government of Singapore as public holidays. Inevitably he came away with one or both of the following assessments: First he had compared their beliefs and judged them lacking, and/or he had looked at their lives, and judged them inferior. Of course, both judgements were by his own standards, and not by any really objective criteria.

There must have been fifty non-Indians at the wedding in Worcester. To Westerners that might seem like a total guest list, but not for an Indian wedding! The crowd probably totaled five hundred! They came, in typical Indian fashion to be a part, not just of the ceremony, but of the life-long union of two persons.

For the first time in his life Eric felt self-conscious about his attire – the 'best' turtle-neck et cetera. Even the "Sunday best" of the other Westerners seemed 'ordinary' in the presence of hundreds of saris, mostly red with gold thread, and more gold and diamond jewelry than he had ever seen in one place. Coifed and made up to perfection, every woman moved with the poise of one of their poorer sisters back home carrying a huge water jar balanced on her head.

By contrast of movement as well as attire, he felt the Westerners just slouched into that huge hotel space - which had been quite transformed by the erection of an elevated, garlanded booth with steps up three sides, which was to accommodate the Hindu priest, the marrying couple, and four parents for the next ninety minutes. While waiting they were treated to songs about marriage and English explanations of them and of the ceremony they were about to share

Ninety minutes! All of it in Sanscrit except for the occasional translation! Yet all to whom Eric spoke later reported being spellbound and delighted! Never bored! Later he was to recount to Michael a few of his main impressions:

"The very length – several times that of a basic western wedding – told how very, very important this ceremony and this union were.

"Then there was the centrality of the four parents for ninety percent of that time, who had numerous spoken and action parts in the ceremony and, at the end, gave their final blessings while the couple knelt at their feet. Those parents did not ritually 'give away'; the new marriage was part of them, and they of it, as long as they live. This was no send-off!

"The beauty and profundity of the poetry about what makes a good marriage quite outclassed the sum total of what we have heard by westerners on the same subject. Throughout there was much use made of sharing and offering two symbols of the "life force", namely rice and fruit - fitting images for what is arguably the major "passage" during our lives. And for the holy – much use was made of fire and water, symbols found in all religions.

"My strongest reaction to this whole experience was profound respect. Fifteen years ago, when I attended a Hindu wedding in Singapore I experienced no such emotion. Here, in a Worcester hotel, I was again a bystander, but *this time I was moved to tears.*

"I was struck by the India/US contrast between the place of parents (and friends) in the new family unit. We Christians wish a couple well and honor their independence; those Indian parents and their whole network of friends will permanently be integral to this Indian couple's life together. This was all so vividly symbolized by the length of the ceremony (days not hours in India) and the size of the gathering - (the whole village in India and) as many as the bride's father can afford.

"Later I found myself recalling how clear India is about religion and culture being inextricably connected. What we did and shared that afternoon, what it was OK and not OK to do, to wear, the relation between making a family and worshipping that which is beyond yet within – all are Indian culture, and all are seen as part of their religion. So their great religious works are great sagas. We Westerners often forget that ours are too, whether we believe them or not.

"I must say one more thing. The very foreignness of this deeply spiritual experience reminded me how limited are the words for and about whatever is ultimate. We can learn a lot from the Indian notion that a thousand images still cannot capture what is ultimate. Whenever I feel forced to be very quiet because I am awestruck, then I am in the presence of that which is beyond all naming. Previously that has really only happened to me with nature. But I was there during that Indian wedding."

# Chapter Twenty-Six

Two years went by. Two years went by as they do in all our lives - years characterized by nothing in particular, everything in general, as the girls grew while parental responsibilities and two full-time jobs kept Eric and Frankie more than 'busy'.

For Frankie they were two very good years. Warm, supportive friends of her own gender, usefulness as the school nurse, in which role she found herself doing more and more counseling, the girls doing well academically and in other activities, and a constantly growing ease in her daily interaction with Greg, who she helped with his wife's crises and to whom she gave more support than she realized. While Eric seemed to have settled down into a routine where they did few social things together, he did share several routines responsibilities at home. It was a convenient set-up, which stretched her less than her marriage ever had done.

For Eric life was also rewarding, in a comfortable if not-very-exciting way. His career established, he acceded to the vote of his colleagues which made him Chair of the Department's Personnel Committee. At first he found this hard to believe, recalling the stress over tenure which had filled his life so recently. Now as a matter of course, he found himself talking at professional meetings about, as well interviewing potential additions to what he now thought of as "my staff". Life in the classroom was endlessly rewarding: he would tell you that "I never teach the same course; the students are always different, and it is the stimulation of change in every one of them that turns me on." His sex life was no better at home, a situation which was made bearable by two factors. First was the lightness which Nicole and Jennifer gave to home-life, together with involvement in their soccer and music. But most important was the ongoing relation with the Projects Director of The Peace Foundation - Rani. Their letters were never more than two weeks apart, their phone contacts at least monthly (except when organizing a rendez-vous) and "meetings" at least three times a year. It was not "all" that he wanted but, he consoled himself, it was better than many had to accept. When sexually frustrated, he found private opportunities to masturbate, and told himself that "one day . . ." But he still could not answer, in fact he avoided the SiokYim question: 'Eric. What do you want?'

While Eric would have sworn that his life was under control, depression was more and more a part of his general condition. How many hours were spent gazing at a page without a hint of comprehension? How much of his gym or hiking time was spent suppressing a sense of dissatisfaction? How many more hours did he need to sleep? How many more beers until he relaxed? How much determination to continue to be the good father, the responsible academic?

For Rani herself, life was full, rewarding, and included frequent phone conversations with her lover/friend between the times they spent at the same professional meetings. She never ceased to be grateful for that Stanford encounter. Most of her peers seemed hell-bent on finding the right man - for the first, second, or even the third time. They thought about Mr. Right as one with whom they would build a nest etc. etc. She had done that – mainly, she recalled, in blind obedience to pressures around her. But whatever the reasons, that was done and over with, except for a wonderful daughter who seemed very happy as a college freshman. The Stanford encounter with Eric had produced a relationship which few younger women understood – in its undefined future, albeit five years after they met.

But the relationship was a perfect fit with her whole approach to life. Rani lived open to all possibilities. Her life was no arrow to be directed to the bull's eye; it was more like a bird, finding unexpected fruit after alighting on each new tree. She opened herself to the fresh kind of being evoked by such moments. Always on the look-out, assuming she would only know the precious moment when she gave herself to it, her vitality and joie de vivre attracted all who caught even a glimpse of this bird of paradise. She lived by no fantasy of what might be, with a man, probing new depths of what was between them, and their ways of meeting. She knew such miraculous meeting, such new depths, in her meetings with Eric, recognized, welcomed, and gave herself to them. But every meeting had its own qualities, its own birth, its own life span, and its death as they parted. The only future with Eric lay in a single, clear (and secure) assumption - that there would always be a next time. When hearing of the movie "Same Time Next Year", they laughed together that someone in their professional organization had immortalized their relationship. The only distortion, they claimed, was that their "times" occurred more than yearly.

She claimed not to be a romantic. Such people she said, are intoxicated by a non-life which is beyond life, which never happens. To Rani "happily ever after" expectations are a formula for missing what was still to come, and which you can never foresee. So why limit my future, she would ask, to settling for half a glass of something you have dreamed when you could allow the unknown future to overflow it? Eric had told her how Siok Yim felt her glass was full (of her dreams) because Eric had come into her life. Rani could not comprehend that. She continued to hold out her glass, drank to the full what was always poured to overflowing, and then (between such times) went about the rest of life until another time.

Not one moment was spent trying for replication. She spent only rare times dwelling on them. She allowed their ethereal quality to remain a complete mystery, beyond description, except on the occasion when she penned one of her rare poems, which she called "Erewhon", (which is almost, but intentionally not quite, the reversed spelling of "nowhere"):

The dimension when we were together
Can be known by no other.
It was a particular time, a specific place:
As tangible as the look between us,
As hugs for dear life,
As shared secrets.

Symbols? Meanings?
They ever fall short of reality itself.
As we met, "God" was.
Often sharing did become
The idol clay –
But not always.

297

I seek no explanation of what's beyond:
"Is" happened
does happen
will happen.

There is a sense beyond the five.
You ask me how I know.
Witches told me so.

There is a place - which takes no space
A time – beyond define.
And I have been there – with you.

# Chapter Twenty-Seven

In 1990 the whole family went to Europe for a month, at Gran's expense. On their last day in Florence Eric found himself wandering along the murky River Arno with Gran while Frankie and the girls did some last-minute shopping. He felt very comfortable with this matriarch, whose total style produced the "family" environment he so admired and yearned to have in his own home. He was thus quite accepting of her request: "Now we have a few minutes alone, Eric, may I make a comment about your method of getting what you want?"

Under other circumstances, his automatic association of such a remark with SiokYim would have brought a quick negative response, but with Gran: "Sure! Fire away. I'd like to get your feedback after spending two weeks with us, tripping around - and I guess, seeing the worst as well as the best of all of us."

"I wouldn't go as far as that, Eric. What I have noticed is that you allow others to see you as the good guy, always ready to accommodate their wishes."

"Well, I do try to be considerate."

"Yes, and we all appreciate that. But it seems to me that you do so more for your own wishes than you let on."

"Go on."

"Take the decision yesterday, in which you ended up taking the girls to San Giminano while Frankie and I went back to the Ufizzi for the second time."

"Yeah, that was a good compromise."

"Between what?"

"Between what Frankie wanted and what the girls wanted."

"What about what you wanted?"

"I didn't think about that."

"You didn't? Are you sure?"

"Yeah! I just acted as a mediator between them."

"OK. Forgive my bluntness, but I felt you were primarily getting what you wanted, using the girls as a cover. Does that make any sense?"

Eric frowned in silence. She's saying what SiokYim said, about facades. She's saying that I don't disclose what I want, what my feelings are, but hide the real 'me' behind a Mr.Nice Guy mask. He gave a hesitant, "Maybe."

But Gran was not about to let it go at that: "What did YOU want, Eric?"

Again a hesitation before he responded: "I guess I preferred to go the see the towers. But that's what the girls wanted anyhow."

"And what was your feeling about seeing the Ufizzi for the second time? Honestly?"

He did not like that 'honestly'. It made him dig. He was also feeling more defensive than when this 'innocuous' conversation began. They had walked another block, with Gran enjoying the environment but Eric oblivious to everything but the simple question of what he wanted. Suddenly he almost exploded with: "There's no way in the world I could have stood another day of looking at paintings. I'd had it up to here with all this Renaissance stuff. It's marvelous in small doses. But there's no way I'm gonna stand in line to see another Botticelli. I don't care how great he was."

Gran gave a long, gentle smile, then went on: "You did want to go to San Giminano and you did not want to look at the Ufizzi any more." It was a re-statement, to communicate that she had heard his strong feelings.

His feelings burbled on: "You can say that again." Then, looking sideways at his walking companion, he asked: "What?"

"I guess two things, and then some comments about their consequences."

"Wow! How about we sit right here at this table on the pavement and order coffee?"

As they waited for their order she continued: "The two comments are both about showing up. First, you did not show up to the rest of us."

"Right. I confess to having kept my wishes to myself. So what's the second?"

"Perhaps you could not show up to us because you had not shown up to yourself?"

"What do you mean?" He feared he knew the answer, but needed to hear it from her.

"I suspect that you are so in the habit of being Mr. Nice Guy that often you are not even conscious of what you want for yourself. You are not even aware of your own feelings and wishes; they are smothered by 'oughts' and 'shoulds'."

"I don't know about that. Ask my colleagues at College. They'll tell you I always speak out."

"I guess I'm talking about personal matters, when it's a matter of what you want for your own satisfaction or comfort?"

"No. You're right there. I am guilty of not sharing. Maybe you might have a point – I don't even show up to my own inner desires. I don't even become aware of what I want. It's not that I hide it from myself; what I want is hidden even from me."

"So, to pursue the matter of consequences." He watched her attentively, amazed that she was getting so far into this issue. "The consequence of not showing up to yourself is obvious: if you don't know what you are feeling, or wanting, you certainly cannot share that with others."

"Sure. That is obvious."

"But the second consequence is the reason for my raising this issue. It is this. Your relationships with all of us suffered yesterday – with me, Frankie, Jennifer and Nicole. He looked at her incredulously. "Yes, all of us felt uncomfortable, not for ourselves, but we simply caught your discomfort."

"That's ridiculous. Everyone was pleased with the outcome."

"Yes. But not with the discussion which led up to that plan. Maybe it's mostly a woman thing, but we all felt your discomfort, even if you were not aware of it. I also think most *men* are made uncomfortable by others' discomfort. If one party in any conversation is uncomfortable, all feel a bit that way, even if they don't know why. Yesterday I thought I knew why. That's why I've shared these thoughts with you."

They drank in silence, she enjoying the passersby, he in another world. This rang a lot of bells with what Siok Yim had said about facades. Yet the troublesome part was not the challenge to be less manipulative, by not sharing his feelings. The real trouble was that he hid so many feelings from himself, so that they were simply not available for sharing. On processing the façade conversations he had realized that the behavior was often unconscious. He acknowledged the validity of Gran's comment about the effects of that upon others. He could, and would try to correct that. But what could be done about not showing up to himself. That was a problem. It had always been so. Moreover, the very suspicion of an unacknowledged feeling brought that old familiar constriction in his chest. "Damn!"

### 

Rani was not as foolish as she might have seemed to some. An attractive woman by any standards, dates were always available, so long as the man accepted the strict limitations she placed upon physical intimacy. Over time, one closer relationship developed in Phoenix, and another bloomed spontaneously while she was vacationing in Europe. She wrote to Eric about him:

I simply have to share what happened in Europe. I met this most engaging Dane. He was so like you: Also a professor; also married; also very physical; also great fun, and as intellectually stimulating. We met at the chalet I stayed in Switzerland, and then traveled together for a week. (His wife and kids were off to Disney, and there was no way he wanted that experience.) I guess I'm telling you this for a number of reasons. I want to get your reactions. I mean to get your reactions as to whether I ought to allow him to see me when he comes over next summer. I also felt a need to be open about this. So please respond specifically.

Eric responded as best he could, given what he felt, namely jealousy, about which he also had a feeling of guilt:

Sounds reasonable to me, he wrote. I wish I could just say "No way. I want to leave my family and marry you", but that's not where I am. Moreover, I have shared with you *my* other romances – both the good and the bad ones. I invited and you have given your reactions to those relationships. So your telling me about your Dane seems to be one of the qualities of our relationship.

On another track altogether, I want to share something I wrote during a camping trip to Mount Lassen last summer. I called it: PRESERVING ME

In wildness – is the preservation of the essential "me."

Unlike the other slopes of Mount Lassen
these are entirely scree:  harsh, dull-colored, an impossibly sharp footing,
yet surprising host to new spruce, flourishing amid the rubble.
Imagining the destructive power of those few minutes of volcanism decades ago
obliges thinking: "New life after all that death!"
What was it I was worried about?

Further along dense fir woods replace the spruced scree.
There open grassy interludes are dappled with sunlight
so that even a remnant of the Emigrant Trail
looks like a perfect picnic place.
I could easily escape forever into this haven of nature in a kinder mood.

A German with a red filter
(consciously emulating Ansel Adams)
joins my meander around Manzanita Lake.
An islet crowned by nesting geese almost denies my glimpse of a loon
just surfaced from grazing in the depths.

Every turn brings seductive glimpses of water and peaks through trees
I am stealing and he recording,
fleeting images of another world –
Of mystery.

An open field with a distant rocky outcrop beckons.
Underfoot gravel just freed of snow is greening with tiny new shoots.
My crunching startles a yearling doe.
An instinctive jump and she pauses, then trots off
so lightly that I am flying with her, weightless.
Then at my feet I join a million fire-ants
awakened yesterday from a long winter's nap
building a yard-wide, new summer home
for their mistress and her countless progeny,
quite unaware of me.

Cliffs looming over the road
challenge the mountain goat in me.
Age and stiffness is no excuse.
I want to sit atop that rock,
feel the spine of this ridge in my buttocks.
I want to sit there, lord of at least a small panorama,
sharing that rock's millennial view.
I want to get up there, several hundred feet higher,
testing my ingenuity and my physical strength
Just so that I can tell me: I did it.

Buoyed by this high nothing seems ordinary.
Wherever I look lies a new wonder,
a perfect composition – if untouched by human hand.

This morning on Mount Lassen takes me out of myself,
then returns a bigger me
that cannot help feeling good about all things,
untouchable for a few moments,
one with ungulates and universe.
The essential Me?

But as he dropped the letter into the mail slot he found himself almost cursing: "Why can't I keep my family AND have Rani rather than risking the loss of the one person who makes me feel good?" Life seemed stacked against him. And that made him deeply angry – even as he smiled a greeting to a passing student.

###

With the words, "Hey, Eric, I've just had a brainwave!" a very excited Michael burst into Eric's office. The latter was thus dragged away from the other world into which the reading had taken him. But rather than be annoyed, the sight of his friend's face so alive caused him to smile and begin formulating an appropriate response when Michael began to explain the idea which had just hit him.

"You know, Eric, how horrified we were to learn that Kennedy almost put his foot in it with Castro over the Cuban missile Crisis?"

"Yeah, and how he supposedly made that threat against the landing of Russian missiles without knowing they had already installed a whole batch, aimed and ready to launch at us. I sure do. When I heard that my first thought was: Why don't enemies talk to each other? It could save enormous mistakes, made in ignorance."

"You know the answer to that as well as I, Eric. In diplomatic conversation a pair of nations is frank one day, and lies the next."

"That's so tragically true. And we almost got World War III started because we were not talking to our enemies!"

"Aha! That's the phrase, that's my great idea: talking to our enemies. My idea is this. We could start a program which enables concerned American individuals to talk to persons who are labeled by our government as enemies."

"You mean a bit like the first time you and Ahad were to get together. Gee, I remember you seemed to expect some dangerous Muslim fanatic."

"And what I got was a charmingly open new colleague, who sets me right about Iran and Islam. Well, that's what set me thinking, why don't we structure a way to help people make friends with people who seem to be our enemies?"

"And just how, may I ask?"

"Easy. If what I hear about web-sites is true. We would set up a web-site headed, for instance, 'Libyan/American Friends'. We would explain

305

our purpose: to help ordinary citizens from two conflicting countries to get to know each other. We would ask them to add their names (whether they were American or Libyan, to our list,) and we would assign two such names to each, as potential "pen pals". We would suggest they communicate via the Internet, beginning with 'what *our* information sources tell us about *you*'."

"I can just imagine the shocks that will produce. But it is a great idea. I'm sure there are lots of people who don't like the way we relate to Kadaffi, officially. And what a difference we might be making, in time. Fantastic, Michael. I'll share the cost of paying for the first couple of web pages."

"Would you say Libya is one of our 'enemies'?"

"Yeah! And I suppose Iran is also an obvious one for this purpose. Can't you imagine someone with my preconceptions finding themselves in touch with another Ahad, who has not been able to leave the country?"

"And can't you imagine how such a person will open the eyes of some interested student in Nebraska, or Arizona, or somewhere else around this country?"

"What would we call this?"

"I think a name on the top would be a bad idea. But somewhere would be important. What about FAD, standing for Friends Across Differences."

"I'll buy that."

### 

It was two months before this simple idea was operational, but within two days the site had over two hundred hits and nearly twenty registrations, mostly for Libya.

"That's understandable," commented Michael. "The recent belligerence of Kaddafi would have been uppermost in people's minds, together with the memory of Clinton bombing them."

"And of course, the destruction of that Pan Am flight over Scotland blamed on Libyans. I am going to send an E-Mail to two of the Libyans, reporting to them what we are told here. It will be wonderful to know just what they are told."

"And what they think about what they are told."

The excitement grew as the numbers swelled – into the hundreds. The partners had become concerned about the time it was taking to create the desired links between Friends Across Differences when they were summoned jointly to the Dean's office. As if they were old chums, Eric led the way into Dean Conner's office with: "Marcia, it's nice to see you; I hope there's nothing wrong!"

"As a matter of fact there is. And I wish this were just a pleasant personal call. But I had to call you in because I have heard criticisms from up top – about your web-site."

"What!" The two exploded indignantly.

"Seriously, yes. The president's office asked me to talk with you."

"We'd love to tell you all about it."

Michael's boyish enthusiasm faded quickly as he realized the seriousness of her expression. "The simple problem is this: it is bringing disrepute on the college. It even makes us look like a political organization. The President has expressed concern that we might be in trouble about our 'solely for educational purposes' status with the government."

"But that's ridiculous. Our intention is completely educational."

"You consider facilitating friends among enemy nations to be 'solely educational'?"

"I guess when you put it that way, it's not 'solely', at least not in some eyes."

"That's just the point. And it only takes one person to bring a legal action on those grounds and we have a lot of publicity we do not want."

The two friends looked at each other and nodded. Eric voiced their response. "I can certainly see why they would have that concern. It makes good sense from a P/R perspective. And the more so if you have a very limited view of the purpose of an institution of higher education."

"We don't need to get into educational philosophy. I think there is a simple solution. Your names are both on the Web-page, right? There's no problem with that, if you delete the identification as professors in this institution."

"But that gives us a certain credibility. It shows we're not just a couple of wild-cards. It tells people this is no rip off!"

"I see your concern. But you have made it clear that you see the College's. So I have to ask you to make that modification. You could say something like you are both 'Ph D professors at American institutions of higher education whose names are withheld for obvious reasons'. People can read whatever they like into that without identifying you with us."

"Well," said the aggrieved Michael, "That might work. We'll see. But we will omit the name of the college."

"I thank you gentlemen, very much. And good luck. I think it's a grand idea. But if you get so big that you have a secretary, please house that person off-campus. I'd much prefer our meetings to be over a pleasant cup of coffee.

# Chapter Twenty-Eight

The girls' mid-term reports in Fall '92 brought consternation to the household. "Look at this!" Frankie demanded of Eric after the girls were in bed. "Nicole is doing great, but Jennifer is close to failing in every subject. You know what I think? Ever since her infancy problem with rheumatic fever we have coddled her. We've seen her work going downhill, and have just smiled at her. Now look where that's gotten us."

"Let me see," was his immediate response as he took the form from her. "This is awful! It must be changed," he added with no small amount of anger in his tone, at which she gave him a surprised glance.

"So?"

"So tomorrow evening we will sit down and talk to her, together."

When they did so Eric began: "Jennifer, your Mom and I are very unhappy about your report." Jennifer looked down, ready to burst into tears. "Now don't cry until you have heard us out. When I read that report I felt angry. This is our daughter, I told myself, and she can do better that D's. Then I felt disappointed and sad. I am sure I felt disappointed for myself and your Mom, but I felt sad for you. I am still angry. I am disappointed. But most of all I am sad for you. I'm sure you feel worse than we do." At this she did burst into tears, finding refuge in her mother's arms. After they had cried together for some minutes the trio got to work on basic causes of and potential aids to improvement.

"We can't work on everything at once," observed Frankie. "Which subject do you like best. Let's work on getting that one up to a B level. Then we can go on with another subject."

"That's easy. I love reading. You know that. It's just that teachers test you on what you remember about your reading, and I don't seem to be much good at that."

"Well," said Eric, I'll spend an hour with you each evening for the next two weeks, and I'll bet I can teach you how to ace any of the tests you get on reading comprehension. First we'll find out if you do understand what you read. Then, when we're sure about that, I'll teach you how to get good grades on multiple choice tests."

"You can do that?" she asked incredulously.

Moralistic Frankie now entered the conversation once more: "Yes, he can. So can I. It's disgusting. But it is very useful. But, Eric," and she gave him a demanding look, "no short cuts until we are sure she reads well."

"OK. And will you take over for the next subject, every night for the following two weeks?"

"Will do."

Later, Eric stayed up long after his wife had retired, reviewing what had happened. He felt really good about himself, quite proud that he had become aware of his own anger, and had let it show to others. He wanted to tell Gran, and even SiokYim. Neither being available, he simply re-told the conversation with Jennifer to himself, over and over. Two facts slowly dawned upon him: the world had not ended when he acknowledged to himself that he was angry, and second, no one had been hurt by his sharing that feeling. In fact, the sharing had been followed by more constructive conversation with his 'other' daughter than he had ever had. "If I could always be aware of my gut reactions!" he lamented silently as he fell asleep.

### 

"You're not serious!" the department chair exploded, tossing the resume down on the desk in front of Eric. "As department chair I can't let you take this applicant to the Committee."

"I don't know that your position as Chair gives you veto of what my Committee considers."

"Well, no. It doesn't. But I sure as hell am the funnel through which your recommendations pass on their way to the Dean. She would never go outright against me. She would first send it back to the Committee with her comments and a request that you reconsider your recommendation. That's the way it goes."

"Ken I respect you, you know that. But on this we disagree profoundly. I want a Communist among us. God knows, four years after The Wall came down in Berlin he's going to have a tough time arguing for what in his resume he calls 'Democratic Socialism'. I hope he's way out, and doesn't fold. In fact, if he gives a hint of conversion during our interview, I'll use all my influence as chair to see that his application ends right there. But his credentials are extraordinary."

"I grant that a Russian senior professor who continues to preach communism would be a cut above most of the others. Great for a place like Harvard, which can afford to take risks, but not for us."

"That's just the point. In political science, of all places, we need real diversity."

"Even when it upsets everyone and puts our department in the doghouse with every member of the Trustees and administration. You know I will be called up, with you, to defend any such proposal. They would all say that we were un-American."

"Are you saying that we should only have on our staff persons who buy our values, our political philosophy? That's a denial of what education is about."

"I'm not arguing about education, I'm arguing about the politics of this institution."

"Well, they need to wake up. There are a lot of other perspectives in the world besides ours, and it is a disservice to our students not to expose them to uncomfortable alternatives."

"I'm sure you do that, in all your teaching. I try to in mine. And so do at least half of our department. We're not as parochial as I think you are accusing us of being."

"I acknowledge the range of experience and learning we represent, as a faculty, but that's only learning ABOUT. You get a different impression when listening to someone who doesn't just know about communism, but is a communist."

"I'm sure you do. But why should we put ourselves through such discomfort?"

"I had hoped we'd get to this. It's a matter of how we relate to all the diversity in the world. We have talked about tolerance – until I'm sick and tired of the word. It makes me want to puke."

"Such academic language!"

"We say we're tolerant. But what do we mean by that? That you may have your own opinions, even your own lifestyle, as long as it doesn't discomfort us very much. And the sub-text is 'We know you'll become just like us, given time. Why? Because you'll see the light'."

"I have to admit that's what US style toleration means. I think it is toleration of their actions in their place, but not in ours, until they come around'."

"The point for me is this. I have become profoundly convinced that others' beliefs and values are as valid as my own."

"You mean they're all equally valid? Surely not?"

"No I mean relatively."

"Ah. So you've surrendered to the cult of moral grayness. What was the line from that musical group in the UK? 'Black is gray, and yellow white, and you decide which is right, and which is an illusion.' You're not serious?"

"No! And yes! I do not believe that all ethics are a matter of opinion. That is stupid, making the word meaningless. What I do believe is that political and social philosophies are relative. Each one has its own integrity, its own validity, in its particular situation."

"That relieves me. To hear that relieves me; but only a bit."

"For example, our cult of individualistic freedom did not really arise because the founding fathers went off to a retreat to decide what values were most important. They *might* have cogitated together, but they were

312

*radically influenced* by the Puritans' experience of rejection, and by the subsequent relations between their descendents and British interests in the New World. And by what they wanted, as individuals who shared this situation. No English philosopher would have settled on 'life, liberty and the pursuit of happiness' even though some had pushed for just one of those. The passion for freedom was nurtured far more by our history than by some think-tank."

"Not the way I'd put it; but yes, that's pretty much true."

"What I am saying is that such a political philosophy is as tied to its roots as say that of China or that of a Muslim nation. Or, in reference to our hiring issue, as that of a Communist nation."

"I've got five more minutes. Explain that."

"Siok Yim taught me that order is central to the Chinese way of thinking, and to the way they live together, as a culture. Of course, order is basic to the free exercise of our individualism, but it doesn't feel as important to us as it does to them. So when there's conflict between giving individuals freedom and inviting chaos, well – look at Tiananmen Square. Their history has always been a choice between chaos and order. Who wouldn't choose order rather than a life of total insecurity?"

"So where does that lead you?"

"To the proposition that order ought to be the dominant value in Chinese life, as much as individual freedom ought to be, as it is, the dominant value in ours."

"And the Muslims?"

"Their religion, and their consequent social philosophy, grew out of their situation."

"Yes?"

"For as long as any could remember, and I mean many centuries, with no 'golden age' back in their pre-history, the peoples of the Arabian Peninsula had lived a terrifying life. Tribes provided the only security against other tribes and against gangs of marauding tribal rejects. The weak – children, the pregnant, and the aged – were fair game, unless they exchanged what they had for protection by some powerful male. Patriarchy solved enough social problems that it had become the norm.

But it produced gross inequities and abuses, without completely removing the absolute uncertainty of life itself."

"OK. So what has Islam to do with that?"

"It provided a comprehensive solution. That's what! We make a big mistake if we think it's 'just a religion'. It's a total way of life, providing a map for the ways of men, as well as the way to eternal bliss. There is no separation of the sacred and the secular."

"Yes?"

"Its basis was the only answer – to their situation. Its basis is complete submission, to a power greater than any sheik's. Even the sheik had to submit to Allah. Without that primacy, that core value, there would be none of their great cultural heritage – literature, art, and of course, the basis of our mathematics and science."

"But why do you grant that tradition, or the Chinese original tradition, equality with our own, which I am convinced is superior? We *grew* from our origins, they seem stuck in theirs."

"All I'm saying is that theirs makes absolute sense to them, just as ours does to us."

"But ours is more evolved. May I even say, more enlightened."

"You may. But I don't agree."

"So let's leave it there for now. I guess you'll be arguing about where this Russian falls when you rate the candidates."

"We will. And I at least hope he'll be one of the three we bring in for an interview. There's a long way to go yet, before we face the prospects that have you worried."

### 

Eric had to check out with his Muslim friend the way he had presented Islam to his boss, so later that week he commented to Ahad: "You sound like a very tolerant Muslim, whenever we get onto anything that's religiously sensitive."

"I am, but I'm no exception. Islam is a tolerant religion, in spite of the bad press from a few angry ayatollahs."

"But for you, a real believer, to be tolerant is quite different from say me, as a completely nominal Christian?"

"It doesn't feel like a stretch at all, for me. In fact, my desire to do the will of Allah requires me to be open towards all persons. That's not the same as giving up my beliefs, you know."

"I guess that's what's on my mind. These days my openness towards those of different beliefs seem to mean that theirs are every bit as good, in their own way, as my own."

"I may respect others' beliefs, may accept that they hold them, but that doesn't affect my own."

"It does for me. As a dyed-in-the-wool Westerner in Singapore I really believed *they* were wrong. I've come through several phases – head trip toleration, then trying other ideas out, then trying to walk in their shoes."

"Yes?"

"And now I find myself honestly rejecting any assumption that one view or pattern is better than others – as I used to do. Isn't that different from your tolerance?"

"I suppose it is. But how come? What has brought you to rejecting your very heritage? I know it's politically correct, especially in matters of sex in this country. But you can't be saying that no values really matter?"

"Of course not! I'm becoming convinced that values are situational, or relative. When it's a personal matter, it depends on the circumstances. When it's a total perspective on how a group or nation lives, it's relative to their life-style, and the story which produced what they are today."

"Give me an example of the latter."

"That's easy. I have two, right on the top of my mind. Siok Yim, for starters."

"Of course, I'd forgotten. I've always wondered how it went so well for you with a Chinese."

"*Apart* from that! For the Chinese society, to this very day, the core value, without which everything would collapse, is order. They simply must preserve it - even at the expense of human rights. Otherwise they

315

could not even attempt to provide any rights. So order is more basic there, just as individualism is more basic with us. And I think they have as much right to preserve that value as we to preserve our core value."

"That is certainly relativism."

"Yes. And similarly with Minah. And probably with you, for you share her faith."

"What do you mean?"

"I mean that her life makes no sense unless she puts the will of Allah before personal (that means individual) desires."

Ahad looked carefully at his friend before deciding that he could safely end the other's statement with the words: "and before the pursuit of happiness." But the sudden change of expression on Eric's face caused him to regret the intentioned tease.

### ###

When Nicole asked: "Mother, I love you so much that I feel I have to ask you a very personal question?" Frankie wondered what was coming, but nodded in agreement. "What I'd like to ask is whether you know Jesus as your personal savior."

"Of course, Dear. What a strange question! I've been going to church all my life, and I've taken the two of you all of your lives."

"It's not church attendance that I'm talking about, Mom. That's not what I mean. What I care about is whether Jesus is your Lord, whether you've given yourself to him."

"I don't know about that. I believe in him. And I live the best life I can."

"But he doesn't live in your heart, does he?"

"I just said, I believe in him and try to live the way he taught."

"But if he lived in your heart you would know. It's because he lives in mine that I am so happy. Can you honestly say that?"

Frankie was getting annoyed. This was ridiculous. She was about to tell Nicole how inappropriate it was to be so pushy about such personal matters when her daughter delivered the fatal blow: "Don't deny it Mom! It's obvious with Dad! And with you! It's obvious you're *not* happy!"

"You're being quite ridiculous, my girl. Now what about getting on with all that homework?" With this maternal directive Frankie felt she had escaped.

A desperate Frankie pleaded with her husband later that evening. "Would you talk to her? She'll listen to you!" She had just described the awkward confrontation with Nicole which had sent her into a state of shock. Questioning Jennifer she learned that Nicole had been "saved" at a so-called music fest five weeks previously. Preoccupied as usual and oozing his normal anger at Frankie, Eric had barely noted the humming and occasional words of new songs, plus Nicole's deep concentration on Bible reading over recent days.

"Sure," was his immediate response.

After supper the following evening, alone with Nicole, he began, "Tell me about this Bible reading I see you doing these days, sweetheart."

"I've been wondering how long it would take you to notice and to ask, Dad. The Rev Koh says we should not push those we love to listen to us but wait until they notice the evidences of our faith. You must have seen my new patience with Jennifer, and my changed attitude to whoever is my opposition winger at soccer in the last few weeks. I've been giving my anger to Jesus, and he just takes it and puts love in its place."

Eric saw the contradiction between Rev Koh's instructions and Nicole's approach to Frankie but let that go. "How did this begin? I'm really curious."

"For ages, since my fourteenth birthday, I've been noticing the contrast between the kids I'd labeled The Jesus Freaks and the rest of the school. They just seemed so different. They never joined in the wild, loud stuff with the rest of us. And they always left a group when its talk became catty. They were different; but they were always happy. When I asked Mary Ann why, she told me that it was because Jesus was always with them, filling them with love and guiding their actions."

"Ok. You kind of envied them, and you became curious about them."

317

"I sure did. You and Mom always push kindness and tolerance, but it's never easy for anybody, is it? It seemed natural for these kids."

"Did you ask them to explain?"

"Yes, and they did, especially Mary-Ann. She told me about Jesus, about the song- fests at their church, about the Rev Koh and how wonderful he is. So I went along with her. He spoke about the power of Jesus to make the whole world one happy family. But, he said that it depended on each one of us giving ourselves to him, completely and without reservation. That seemed scary at first, but the more he talked, and the more we sang, the more it made sense. Near the end he gave an invitation, saying that Jesus was waiting to embrace each one of us, if we would come down and give our lives to him. I did that night. Since then, my life has been changed. It's been wonderful, and every day I'm so happy with those very people I used to say nasty words about – the Jesus Freaks. I'm so happy I'm one of them. There was a pause. Eric nodded in a quiet, accepting, but somewhat uncertain way, so she asked: Do you believe in Christ, Dad?"

"Of course! I believe he was one of a very small number of people with great spiritual power and insight. Like Buddha, Confucius, Mohammed, and a few others."

"You're saying that Jesus is no better than those other religious teachers?"

Not wanting to come through as too dogmatic about his deep relativism, Eric couched his reply as: "I guess I am."

He was not surprised that she came back at him in his own argumentative style: "Then why do you push on us, your daughters, such things as consideration and caring and giving and helping and all that?"

"I think life works better that way."

"Better than in other ways?"

"I suppose I do."

"And don't you want the whole world to be the way that works better?"

"No. It works better that way because that's the way our civilization is put together. But other cultures, other whole civilizations think differently, feel differently and act differently from us."

"But wouldn't they be better off if they followed Jesus' way, and knew him?"

"No."

"But then why do you act as if the Christian way is better if you don't really believe the whole world needs Christ?"

"My darling, I think each of us has to find his own way. You are finding yours, and I'm very glad for you. I'm still working on mine. That's why I wanted to hear about where you are - not only because I love you and want your happiness. But also because, well, if sometimes I learn from my students, why shouldn't I learn from my daughter?"

### 

The conversation had petered out soon thereafter, but Eric had been deeply stimulated by the person who meant more to him than anyone else in the world. Several questions came to mind: What does my relativism mean? Is it just a mind game that I play? If I chose, could I fully adopt another value system, like Rani's, for instance? Would it mean as much to me as it does to her? Is it a matter of how you are brought up? Is it a matter of how you were reared? Of what they taught you and how they taught you in schools? And what do you get from being brought up with a specific (does that equal narrow) set of values?

I guess the answer to that is enormous emotional drive – the values which came with your mother's milk provide the drive to conform without even thinking about doing so. For instance, say I were to adopt all the things which mean most to Siok Yim, would I get the same drive for my living that she does? Or if I were to become just like Rani in the way I thought and the values I espoused, would I get the same emotional support for such living as Rani does, simply because that is her "native" cultural and value system?

Next morning, en route to the college the thoughts continued: What is it to be the child of a culture? Can anyone ever avoid being the child of one culture or another? What does it mean for an agnostic like me to be a child of the Western civilization? They do call it Christendom. How

Christian is our civilization? And what does my lack of being "saved" have to do with what values support and inspire me to do what I do, even at some cost? What is a mature attitude to one's birth culture? What is it to be "grown-up" in one's own culture? How much does my sense of worth, my idea of being fulfilled, and my own strength to get up every morning come from my own, Western Culture? Does it in fact, in some unconscious way, come from being part of Christendom? How I hate that word? But maybe it's a valid description of the so-called West, even if most of us never darken a church door?

### ###

Such thoughts and questions arose in several family conversations over the next two years, but never in a serious way. Yet underneath, a sea change was occurring in Eric's view of differences – between behaviors, between values, between cultures. He would have sworn, until this time, that he was a thoroughgoing relativist. But a woman who was not a lover, his very own daughter had sown seeds which would suddenly enliven everything in a new way when he was to read a book which was already in press – The Clash of Civilizations. He was not to realize this, however, until after the hardest work of his life. With the help of a new therapist he was about to work on what that therapist dubbed as "his problem with women."

In one telephone conversation with Rani, on a day when Nicole's faith had been vividly in evidence, he asked: "Do you believe in God? I know that's not something we ever talk about. Not my thing usually, but sometimes Nicole makes me think. Do you?"

"Senor!" Just the tone, without the Spanish mode of address, told him to expect either a tease, or sarcasm. "Yes and no, is the simple answer. I do not believe in your Western idea of one being that you can call your father. That's too simple to explain the things in life we don't like. It also seems crazy to say that such an all powerful and good god would put some of the hurt and evil in the world."

"But what do you believe?"

"In something which cannot be defined, and which shows itself in many ways. It's those many manifestations which Hindus have sculpted so wonderfully. The three best known ones are the manifestations of the power which is behind and in all, as creator, preserver, and destroyer. They are all part of The One. And so are all the other aspects of human

320

experience. Even, my dear man, the part you enjoy so much. Go look in your Museum of Fine Arts, in Boston, just near your college. It had an Indian curator at one time, and they have a great collection of Indian art and sculpture."

Eric took her advice and was awed. She warned me, he recalled, not to view some of these as pornography, but as realistic expressions of one aspect of life which is part of whatever you call The Ultimate. "All things are expressions of some aspects of what cannot be called anything less than The All" had been her exact words.

The first object by which he lingered was about three feet high. Shiva, the Preserver was seated, the image of male strength, beautifully muscled. Seated on his knee, less than half his size, was his consort Pavarti, as voluptuous as she was naked. OK, said Eric to himself, it does take male and female to preserve life.

But Yakshi the goddess of fertility was another matter. Yes, admitted Eric, fertility is part of earth's self preservation, so I suppose it can be represented by a statue. And I must say I respond to it. Her ripe body displayed unabashed femininity. The vulva on this four feet figure was not only complete with a slit, but emphasized by a richly ornamented belt below her waist so arranged as to draw attention to that part, thus emphasizing her role as an aid to fertility. Apparently many of these exist in popular mythology, who, with their male counterparts (yakshas) are semi-divine spirits believed to bring good luck, wealth and other blessings such as the birth of children.

All of this seemed to Eric to be a very base popularization of an abstract truth. The female figures depicting the destroyer aspect of The All included Durga. She may be the slayer of demons, but her portrayal seemed to be as sexual as that of Pavarti or Yakshi, he thought. Seems like Indian religion had to express itself in the vernacular, just like we do, he concluded.

Because the Stewart Gardner Museum is adjacent and he had a membership, he wandered in to sit down and recover from this excess of sexual stimulus without any opportunity for its expression. What a stretch of the senses between the open expression of Indian art and this dark interior with its classical Renaissance paintings and the internalized music from a fiddle nearby. Here you just had to sit, listen, look and contain within yourself all of your responses. He found himself comparing the environment of Lakshi and Durga with that which had produced illuminated manuscripts and paintings of Christ with a bloodied forehead and a virgin suckling him as a babe. No wonder the Indians and the West are so different, was his dominant thought. I have never realized how different, and not just on the outside. How can we ever understand each other, really, beyond superficial head knowledge?

# Chapter Twenty-Nine

The perspective of depression: Horny but no sex, or only a nominal release every two weeks with his wife, and no chance of being with Rani for another seven months! Life at home so grim, only the sounds of silence with Frankie, the girls looking cautiously from one to the other! Walking endlessly in circles around his back yard Eric asked himself: Why do I feel this way? Why does life seem so pointless? Do I care whether I live or die? The answers all came back negative.

At school, life had been dragging on: Five sections, two of one course, two of another, and the fifth an advanced-level course which should have been fun. Eric was a "good" professor: he was on top of the subject matter, with students' personal growth the chief object of his interaction with them in class and outside it. Although the students came now as always, in every shape and orientation, they bored him almost as much as the material they were to master. Committee work seemed even duller than ever. But alone, none of the above would have produced the unprecedented sense that "nothing matters, absolutely nothing". Inquiries from Michael were fielded with a brusque phrase. Smiles from lesser associates went unnoticed.

He had passed the point of being angry most of the time he was in the presence of his wife. They had talked about the quality – or lack of quality – in their marriage. Their only commonality seemed to be the welfare of their girls. They had tried innocuous one-day workshops – on 'Marriage Enrichment', 'Saving a Sick Marriage', 'A Taste of Conjoint Family Therapy', 'A Jungian Approach to Dreams' and even one entitled 'Dealing with Jealousy'. They had sought out a therapist known for his 'Couples

Workshop', and found in the latter the first tiny glimmer of brightness they could recall. Yet Eric was more angry than ever.

But these last few weeks things had changed – for the worse. The anger was gone. In its place there was . . . what word can say it? There was just nothing. A void! Alone he would try to dredge up what was going on, always with the same answer: nothing! His innards felt about as human as a computer. He was aware that a brain was still available to process information, to get things done. He knew that his autonomic nervous system was functioning as well as ever, for all bodily functions seemed unchanged. But when he tried to visualize the Rani who turned him on, he saw a blank screen. When he read copies of love-letters he had sent her, he felt unmoved, even critical of "the goon who wrote this stuff." A long walk around The Fens, with ducks galore, evoked no appreciation, no feeling of any kind. For the first time in his life he found himself asking whether it mattered in any way whether he lived or died. And the answer was the one thing in his life which did seem clear: it did not matter.

In this condition he told himself, you need help. But who? Two tries at therapy, each with a highly-reputed M.D. psychotherapist, had been of little help. Sure, they had kept him functioning a bit better than before, but the debilitating anger persisted in one case, and arose within a month of ending the other therapy. He had seen through their manipulation, anyhow. So why go to another? If there is someone who is more than a match for me intellectually, who I cannot outfox, then maybe? In this mood he was guided to a person who turned out to exercise what he came to think of as "ridicule therapy".

Ekaterina Thompson was generally known as Tina. This large, bright, arrogant woman, born in Russia, had married an American psychiatrist while doing her own graduate work in the profession. Eric approached her for help because she had been described as skeptical about Freud, very eclectic in her approach to therapy, and "the ablest her supervisor had ever seen." Maybe a few weeks with her might help, but he doubted it. But, rationality told him, only a fool does nothing when suicide seems a good alternative.

After asking his permission to tape their sessions and explaining that he could then take the tape home each time, the first session began predictably in its delineation of his reasons for being there: baseless anger, depression which verged on feeling suicidal ("if it were worth the effort"), and a need "to do something about a lousy marriage without losing the daughters who mean the world to me." Then in his usual style Eric took control for a while, asking about her reasons for being in the profession. To this she responded openly, with some self-deprecation and a wry humor to which he warmed, even as the thought occurred to him that "I could never be interested in a woman this size."

In response to her question: "What would you like to tell me about yourself?" he was surprised to find himself ending with the statement: "I have a big need to be dependant." When she asked: "How would it feel to be taken care of completely?" he answered: "I'm above that; I don't need that."

"Is it a humiliating idea?"

"My self-esteem would be lowered."

"What would it mean about you?"

"Having to stay home from school, as a kid, when I was sick."

The session ended with two assignments: To do some drawing about staying home from school and to review the tape. He left feeling that he trusted her, even after such a short time. He also felt a deep respect. And most important, he liked her.

That afternoon he wrote to Rani:

My Love,

Now you know how to get correspondence from Eric: obtain an explicit commitment. Here is the report. Pronto!

It was a good session of getting to know you – about my thought processes, especially about relationships and sexuality. Also about Frankie and me, via the magic marker drawings I've been doing. "Where's the playmate, the co-worker, the friend, the fun?" She asked me to indicate in the drawings I had already done.

The second thing about the session was her affirmation of my current anger. "That's your life, for now. You have a right to it." And "'Why?' is not the right question from you; your wife should be demanding that." She also affirmed my right to seek support from whom I will, but was clear that it should involve "no wife-beating" to others but "sharing what is happening inside me."

325

There was no digging. The two of us were bubbling all the time. Yet I was exhausted afterwards. Most of all, I guess I feel I have a <u>paid</u> friend. That's largely what therapy is, anyhow.

Your letter with photos arrived yesterday. . . . .

Bravo on the deal with the house . . . .

Deeply sorry for the two weeks of non-contact by me! I'll do better on maintaining the erection – no, the connection.

I love ya, LADY!

P.S. When I say 'love' I mean appreciate, feel connected to, enjoy, admire, respect, care about, care for, wish well, want, etc. etc. etc. – in addition to affirming my need to share our bodies!

### 

A week later, at the second session, Eric shared his drawings, with some explanations of what each meant, and then asked: "Do you believe that we create our own reality by the way we think about or respond to anything?"

In her characteristic way she moved the discussion on, by a comment rather than the answer he had requested: "Psychological things can be hurting or not hurting. We can influence the way we experience reality by our decisions. Yet sometimes it rains, and we have nothing to do with it. You are more in charge as you are more aware of your own impulses. If you say 'I'll only respond positively', then you're going to have a problem."

"I've been thinking about intimacy."

"Yes?"

"I made a list of things about intimacy."

"Go ahead. I'd like to hear them."

"Intimacy involves as many barriers down as possible. It means you're aware of nothing else. It involves an odd combination of control and non control – you control the other but have no control of yourself. It is accompanied by all kinds of nice physical sensations, the most important of which is being touched, in a very sacred way. Intimacy is both an enormous gift and a privilege to give. And finally, in intimacy I feel completely safe."

"That's not in your drawings, the ones about staying home from school when you were little. There's no safety there."

"Yes it is. When I did this one, of me being sick and my mother walking out of the room (that's what that scribble is in the corner). That's the safety. I realized that intimacy leads to dependency. That's why there's all that angry scribble, too."

"So for you dependency was paired with being sick. When you were dependent you felt intimate with your mother. Then, when you got better you lost closeness."

"I wonder what I've done with my dependency all my adult years."

"It isn't desirable or safe. It's constraining?"

"At this point in my life, being in a wheelchair would be unbearable. The thought contains fear. Not the desire not to be a burden."

"If you have to be that sick to get intimacy, and then it's gonna be followed by a loss, then – you'd be foolish to get into a dependent situation. And if you did get into such a situation, you'd be foolish to get better." There was a long pause. "Do any of these drawings give clues about how intimacy has gone with Frankie? Does she distance from you when you're OK, not needy?"

"For her to feel close I have to be needy. Like if I have the flu, badly."

"I suspect that it would be very frightening and difficult to show need to anybody over time, because that picture with your mother is a set-up. And if in another relationship you're gonna lose, that dependency would be unwise."

"I want to tack on the love/anger problem. That FEELS related to this dependency/intimacy thing. I guess I'm more inclined to associate love with dependency than with intimacy."

"Sometimes they're so together and sometimes so separate, but love and intimacy are close."

327

"I think of love as a direction of the will; intimacy is non-volitional, gut-related, spontaneous.    Love is permanent; intimacy can be instantaneous."

"How about the intimacy which comes from and is part of a forever love?"

"I have no experience of what you're talking about.  But the intimacy of an older couple?  That was certainly there between my parents."

"I wonder how often they experienced immediate intimacy with a stranger?"

"I've said to myself:  I have the highs of intimacy these days with Rani, maybe I shouldn't ask for the tranquil kind.  But now I'm thinking that it would be real self-denial for the sake of those pay-off's if they were only available by profound, exclusive involvement."

After a silence he changed the subject: "Why am I so angry?  Am I angry because of what I don't have in my marriage?  Or am I angry because of something bigger than my marriage?  What's important about that question is the time I spend being angry."

"If I were living that paradigm I'd be pissed.  That's a real rip-off."

"Guess I've always accepted it. (A long silence) I'm feeling sorry for myself. (More silence)  I've never let myself say that I had a right to anything. (More silence)  In the love affairs I've had I've often said to myself: 'How do I deserve this?' (More silence)  I've never been angry at life."

"How could you, as a grateful son, get angry when she leaves if she's taken such good care of you when you're sick?"

More silence, then: "I'm feeling a pain in my chest."

"Even your body feels this: and remembers."

More silence, his eyes closed, discomfort visible on his face.

"It must have been very painful."

"Very.  Can you help?" (His eyes are still closed)

"Focus on the sensations in your chest, the feelings around these sensations, and let those sensations and feelings take on a substance or color, like a ribbon or a beam of light. Notice how aware you are of your choice about following that ribbon - how fast, and what direction, what part of it - until you're free to stand right there, as long as you like. You can experiment. When you feel the sensation, let the feelings come back, and experience fully the choices about staying with them, or following the ribbon to its source – in some safe space-time interception with your own story. No pushing or pulling or making or breaking. Just experience yourself with the colors. Let yourself be fully aware of everything you're experiencing. It's comfortable to know you can come back to this state at your option, always a bit different, and always safe."

He sat there very still. She added: "When you feel you've fully experienced it enough so that you can continue to process it, maybe even becoming aware of it in dreams, between now and when we meet again, open your eyes, and tell me one thing that happened."

"The hurt's worse when I've blocked the image."

### 

My Love,

Yes, it's me again, not 24 hours after your call. I'm writing, just out of bed, alone, because I've been fantasizing about "doing" or "being" and certainly "enjoying" "69" with you.

I recall the first time. We seemed to spend most of the twelve hours after your arrival lying on our sides, each one's head comfortably on the inside of the other's thigh, doing what some say comes "unnaturally." To me, the wonder as we continue such enjoyment is in the flow, the loss of separateness, and the sense of shared possession. The thought of looking, fingering, palpitating, licking, kissing, biting gently and sucking these parts of another's body so close to the waste elimination system is really quite amazing. With any less love and desire, it would be repulsive; with what we feel together, it is heaven:

I nuzzle the fuzz. I so gently explore under it to find your labia. They are small and dry, so I just touch lightly. Then I put my finger inside to find a pool – and you shudder. I search for your clitoris with my finger, stroke its tiny wetness. But I must use my mouth and tongue. What's that feeling in my balls? You/I (I can't tell which) must use my/your mouth

329

and tongue. And the flow of sensation between your mouth and tongue and mine is so fast that all are one. In brief moments of sucking your labia, then your clitoris (now big enough to feel in my mouth) I feel this, these, you, are mine. And I have this wonderful feeling that I am taken, am possessed by another, and so, so wonderfully safe. My darling, believe it or not, though I sense all of that in you, I still need to be told that you love it all as I do.

I suddenly realize that statement is very close to my fear of losing intimacy if I'm dependent. It's as if I must be reassured of the same dependence by you if I'm to feel safe in my dependence. Oh, to simply trust your love even if I knew you disliked it all!!!

And there's more to this. It is most in sex that I'm slowly coming to feel OK being dependent. How can I ever say 'Thank you' for that? And what a wonderful way to learn! I can't say any more now. The thoughts stop.

Later – after reviewing the tapes of two sessions – I want to share three comments.

1.  I have years of anger stored up. Have never let myself feel I have a right to be angry.

2.  I currently feel very strongly that I have very little control of my life.

3.  Whenever I feed back to Tina (who is a woman) it is always in a critical format, even when what she has said has been descriptive rather than critical.

So that's what I'm working on, my love. You see how profoundly I need your love. Not the love of a woman, but of the one I also like to fuck best of all.

I'm still laughing, at the thought of you, when I imagine you. More and more, as we talk, this way and by phone, I belly-laugh with you!

I love you. Eric

### 

Two therapy sessions later Ekaterina asked: "What would you like to do today?"

"I feel brave enough to visit the forest again, where I was so scared last time."

"Then close your eyes and go to that place near the river where you feel safe. Can you describe it?"

"It's a big hole in the river bank. When I first saw it I thought some animal must live there. But it is just a kind of cave. But when I'm there, I'm safe. I can't slip into the dark, still water. And nobody can see me, 'cause there's a deep shadow."

"So you are very safe, and comfortable, and nothing can hurt you. You can always go back into that safe place if you need to."

"I'm glad. But today I want to visit the forest where I was so frightened last time that I ran back here."

"There's something else you can do too – you can be invisible if you want."

"There's something there, in the forest; my legs are trembling."

"But you won't be seen, because you're invisible."

"But it's going to hurt me."

"How do you know?"

"I feel it. There's something very big behind that tree. It is almost as big as the tree. My chest hurts. It feels it's going to burst."

"But you'll be able to see it without it seeing you."

"If I cover my eyes I can see it coming out from behind the tree. It's very tall. Much bigger than the tree. It's looking everywhere for me. Even though it can't see me, it knows I am here. And it is so big and strong. It has great big thighs and very strong arms. And I want to go back where I'm safe, cause I don't want to look at it."

"Perhaps you could just get behind one of the trees and take a better look."

"Yes. I can see it better now. But I'm so frightened. But I know it wants to hurt me.

It's my mother. She's so strong – those powerful arms could crush me." He breaks down, whimpering for a time, then reports: "I'm back in my cave now, safe from her."

"Then stay until you feel ready to come out and talk to me about it."

### 

Only a week, but two sessions later, Eric reported four dreams in one night, all involving people trying to kill him. He then added: "Until puberty I feared the dark intensely,. I was afraid there was some one there."

"These are all thematically the same - a fear of being killed, not necessarily a fear of death."

"It is the same fear I felt at seeing my mother in that trance."

"More trance work could bring relief from that, or it could bring more pain."

"I've never been afraid of pain."

"I think you're saying: Please put me back together right. Even thinking that IS stressful. This material potentially can set you free. I think you've been bound by it. But this is no longer psychotherapeutic recreation – for self-enhancement."

"I'm hunching it's useful to look at the main things in those dreams that all came together - the path, a brown cat, and a bed."

"When I used to have dreams I was a sort of a James Bond. I always spent some time hidden, and picked my time to triumph over the evil ones."

"So you have mastery practice. So you know that whatever you find in trance-work you can re-do in a way you wish it would have happened. You have the capacity to get mastery over whatever we find. So close your eyes (they were already closed) and trace the path to the bed, and see what's happening there."

"OK. There's a bed; the same one as in my dream. But there's nothing else."

"Go deeper into the trance so that all parts of you are there – all your senses, and all your responses, so that you can, after the session, remember all and only what is therapeutic for you to remember, and forget all and only what is therapeutic for you to forget. Feel confident that you will be able to do the explanation with company, or alone because you need to do this for yourself. You have a safe person, your Dad, about whom you have had happy dreams, and you have a safe place, by the river, where you can be alone. Go search for information about the path, and the brown cat, and the bed, and any other features of these days you would like to explain. One gets in touch with one's own internal wisdom and feels that to be perhaps part of the wisdom of the universe."

"I know I'm sure of this place, and of being able to go back to Dad." There is silence for a time.

"I'm going to be invisible. I just see her head and arms, those big, strong arms . She's doing something. And she's looking at it. And I have no reason now to fear her because she looks happy and is smiling. She is putting something into the chamber-pot, under the bed. . . ."

There was a long pause, then a scream of utter terror shook the walls, not only of that room, but of all the adjacent ones. Tenants of adjacent suites later asked of Tina, "What's going on? Sounded like someone was being tortured, dentally or something."

When the terror had subsided a little Tina asked: "What did you see?"

"It was full of blood!"

"Now it is time to return to that safe place, where you know you will be safe."

Several minutes later, face wet with tears and distorted with anguish, he slowly looked up and said: "Thank you. I'll see you next time." And he was gone.

### ###

In the following session Eric initiated a return to that scene, with the following expressions during the trance

"It's very upsetting to be entering Mom's bedroom. The wooden bed has a brown cover. There's a cat on it. It's difficult to breathe."

"Then take enough time to get your breath back."

"I'm beside the bed now. There's no one else. There's a bucket with bloody cloths and bloody water. I'm about five. Why would she want to kill me? It feels very confusing and frightening. I believe she might. Maybe these cloths are because someone got killed or hurt. That's very frightening."

"Talking about the worst kinds of fears is a way to outgrow them."

"But I shouldn't talk about it."

"Only with certain people. Not with most, probably."

"Dad said I shouldn't talk about that bucket."

"They thought it should be private, without being ashamed. Nobody dies, or gets hurt. It's just part of nature. But you were certainly scared."

"I'm seeing Ophelia, dead in the water. No blood, but clothing the same way, swirling slowly in the water."

"Would she hurt you by putting you under the water, where you couldn't see yourself? She didn't want you to look into that bucket. But if you really thought she was trying to kill you, then the usual reaction is to hate. And that makes them really mad. If you could seem strong and tough, you'd be safe, and then she'd know she couldn't hurt you, even though you were so small. You were really brave to risk making her mad; she's so strong she could have picked you up, and thrown you off the bridge, into that water."

"I'm thinking about my blood, which has always caused me to faint. I'm seeing the cemetery near our house. I used to wonder whether the water from the coffins soaked into our garden."

"Did you think it would bring death to your house?"

"I remember when my Mom came home after having all her teeth out at the hospital, and I didn't want to go into her room because it smelled so strong of chloroform. And there was that tiny morgue outside our country hospital." A long silence ensues.

"And I remember when my smallest brother was born."

"And what did you feel?"

"I don't want a new baby." He is very upset for several minutes. "Then he had rheumatic fever at a year, and ever after I had to care for him."

"Even though you didn't want him in the first place."

After a long pause: "I don't feel frightened at the moment, just terribly sad."

"I feel some sadness for that little boy who is so frightened that some of his childhood he couldn't enjoy. He had to keep it all secret. He must have felt very alone. What would you like to say to him that might help him feel a bit better?"

"I'll teach you how to play the games that other boys play."

"So he can do it himself. Can you tell him how you feel about him, cause I think he's been pretty scared."

"About being hurt or killed?"

"I think at some point when it's right you can tell him what a valuable, special, unique person he is to be loved, cared for, protected, and have things explained to. In a way that can help him feel a lot better."

Eric opened his eyes as if from a long sleep, and when focused on and awaiting her input, she says: "That's a rich bit of work, Eric. Given the intensity there, you really have done remarkably in your life. Whatever neurological patterns were set then are still firing."

"I suspect I worked very hard at mastering this stuff."

"At this point in your life you were ready to explore vulnerability. Frankie has walked right into this, and she's gotten testy. She has unknowingly triggered the same fears, confusion and anger."

"Why would she want to do that, when I'm being so good?"

"That's one to work on until next time, eh?"

# Chapter Thirty

Eric had escaped – from all the pressures of his domestic and work lives - with merely the belligerent explanation: "I'm going to spend the week-end camping in the mountains with Ahad." Here in the mountains with Rani, he even felt completely removed from the unprecedented demands of his therapy. As they lay together but a foot apart, naked, sated, and comfortably warm, gazing at the intricate pattern of leaves silhouetted against a clear azure sky, she whispered: "This is so wonderful!"

And it was. The entire stolen week-end was wonderful for both of them. It had been easy to fit into her travel schedule, and there was so little communication between him and his wife that the one-sentence explanation had been sufficient. Indeed, to Frankie it had come as a relief because the girls were to be on a scout project all day Saturday and she dearly wanted to attend an afternoon concert. She felt no need to explain to Eric that she was doing so with Greg and his wife, whose health seemed enough improved to make this outing a possibility. But it just felt better that his week-end away made even that explanation unnecessary. She felt a real love for this sad woman and felt so good when she could join Greg's efforts in making more pleasant whatever life remained to her.

Things are unchanged, was the refrain in Rani's mind as her attention on the view outside waxed and waned. Before he met her at the airport she had been filled with uncertainty. What will he be like, really, now that he is dealing with this very heavy therapy? Will the magic between us still be there? Am I stupid to be seeing him and risking some unpredictable mess? You never know when people start to work with professional help through things that have been troubling all their lives. But this could be the breakthrough: it could empower him to do what we both want, so passionately – to spend the rest of our lives together. He hasn't said as much, but I know. We can work out the girls issue. I have with my former husband and daughter. Eric and his family can come to some agreement - but not until he changes. He's so stuck. Yet I am powerless to help him change. The best I can do is to continue to reassure him that my love, our love, is unchanging. God knows, it's no effort to do that. He is so wonderful, and when we're communicating, at whatever distance, my whole being feels so good. This, this interplay of tenderness and wild passion is us. And it is unchanged.

Eric simply felt great. He was not going to think – at least about his life – for the whole week-end, simply enjoy it. He was very unsure that would be possible, but his need for Rani had become unbearable. The intensity of life in therapy seemed not to distract him from such fantasies, but to increase them. Here, in such a place, far from Boston and all it involved, with nothing to do but to joy with and enjoy Rani, he was suddenly in heaven. This had come as a surprise, for the therapy sessions had been taking every ounce of his energy. Yet one melting kiss of Rani's, and nothing else existed.

The two days were spent as had become their habit: out of doors, doing whatever the weather allowed, joying together in nature. Sometimes it was the exhilaration of a peak; at other times, the gentleness of a meandering brook. At still other times it was like this: warmed against the chill of late fall, the deep carpet of beech leaves hid and muted the impact of the rocky trail underfoot so that all attention could be given to the maze of silver tracery through which the view opened up for a hundred times the distance visible in summer. The occasional pause for a passionate kiss seemed to occur without prior thought or word – it would just happen. Then off again, sometimes hand in hand, sometimes, when the trail widened, arm in arm, and sometimes, in precarious climbing spots, with each strongly, independently straining to clamber up small granite outcrops, at the top of which, both puffing, they would look at each other and laugh.

###

Two months into therapy Eric wrote:

My Dear Rani,

I'm barely functioning. This annoys me enormously. Tina's comment yesterday: "There's something very big going on, and it seems to be causing a lot of mourning."

A few insights from reviewing my tapes of these last sessions:

1. I see that what I did with my anger at 14 (and all my feelings) was wonderfully functional to my super-achievement for the following ten years, but it's been shitty-messy for the last ten!

2. What restricts my freedom to choose whom I want to be is still a mystery.

3. I have had to be father to all women in my life except Siok Yim. Thank God that I'm being *less* that with you these days, and that I can admit *some* dependence on you.

4. I've had enough of some patterns in my life: I want to change, *and especially to enjoy an egalitarian relationship with a competent, strong woman.*

5. I must be patient with myself when I am awkward about my feelings. If I let myself 'be' the inner core *will* change.

6. I don't have to be, any longer, everything my father was (including being *awkward* about *his* angry feelings.)

Too much! This comes from your very dependent lover – Eric.

### ###

"Today I'd like to work on my conflicts about students liking me and the matter of having to give them grades. I know what I ought to say when a student comes in all worried about the term's final grade. Something like: You've goofed off, and now you'll have to pay, unless you can pull off a straight A in the final."

"Why don't you see what a trance will bring up?" He closes his eyes and is very still. She suggests: "I seem to remember the small boy filled with fear of blood and death."

Now in a trance, Eric's response is "I mainly recall the giant mother."

"And so you set about trying to be a very good boy – to avoid death, and a graveyard. And who also acted up with tantrums and defiance – as a way to gain mastery over that which terrified you. You may even have said to her , like to that colleague Beverley: 'I don't care what you do. So kill me. So there.' Now we're in a situation where we've caught it before you've got to prove you're in control of your fear, and so you're not afraid."

"I feel more ready to face that fear than I ever have before."

"Now we can just face that fear without fear of annihilation. You feel this student stuff triggers that stuff? Does that **feel** right to you? I do not **know**."

"That rings a bell with me. The quality of feeling when several students came at me this week was just like the feeling when I saw my giant mother. But how does all that tie into wanting to be the perfect professor?"

"Perfection prevents any prompting of the danger. If you're afraid you're going to get it you don't want to make any mistakes, do you?"

"I can't believe what I've been doing all these years. I've had lots of love, and still have this great need to be perfect."

"Love is optional. Survival isn't."

There is silence, except for deepened breathing from Eric as he goes deeper into the trance. A long silence as Tina waits, yet still nothing from the figure now visibly in distress.

"What are you experiencing?"

"A great deal of fear. I'm gritting my teeth. Pressure in my solar plexus. I'm seeing those woods again. And feeling fear there. The place of safety, the hole in the river bank: that's frightening now. I can't be found here in the dark, there are other things here which might hurt me. (A long pause) I'm going to get out into the clearing, where I can see safely in every direction. The trees, big and old, go right up to the sky. They feel good. The hole probably has snakes and lice and furries. It made me scratch. Here in the open under the sun is better."

"Something scared you, so bad you were unwilling to go into that yukkie hole. Something scared you very badly. What can you tell me about it?"

"I'm no longer so little. I'm ten. My mother has come home from her teeth surgery. And there's the smell of chloroform. And the image of the little morgue building outside the hospital. I remember how terrified I was if I ever had to visit the hospital, for the smell made me think of death. I was afraid **I** would die. I guess I was terribly frightened by the sight of my mother without any teeth and all those bleeding gums. And she smelled."

"She might have been in pain, too."

"I know she wanted to touch me, and I didn't want her to. I can see where my Dad is standing, but I can't remember what he said."

"Sometimes those messages come with thoughts – like being scared to death. Fear, or going away, or leaving, doing the wrong thing, making a mistake, being sent away."

"I feel it has to do with what I felt when she was leaving for the hospital to have all her teeth out. I remember several people in my town died when they went for an operation. Maybe Mom would. And she still died without . . . (his body is wracked with sobs, and tears stream down his cheeks before he can finish) . . .without putting her arms around me. And I can't forgive her for that. It wasn't much (to ask)."

"Maybe she didn't know how to do that. And you needed it a lot. It would have helped you a lot."

"I am so unforgiving – of her."

"She's gone now. She didn't hug you. She didn't put her arms around you."

"I guess I just find myself making excuses for her now."

"But that's not necessary. How you feared her and how you yearned for her love. Your experiences did not seem optional at all."

"NO. NOT AT ALL" Eric shouts.

"But rather desperately related to survival."

Still in the trance Eric now speaks to his mother: "If you'd really known what it was doing to me you'd have been different."

"She'd have done her best to be there for you when you needed it: even when you behaved in a fearful way and avoided her. And when you were staying away. Even when you were acting up, and annoying her. If she'd known how much you needed her."

"But it would have been hard for her to get through."

"Sometimes it is just very hard for adults to understand children. Even when we now know they've been very clear. We know they couldn't hear. And if she'd known she couldn't give you this loving that you needed so desperately to reassure you in your fear, and to support your life, perhaps she would have arranged it that you could get that loving from someone else – that you could get the reassurance, that feeling of connection and sensitivity in other ways."

"No she wouldn't. I got that from my Nan, my father's mom, and my Mom resented Nan. And put her down all the time. I never heard her say a nice thing about Nan. Nan was just a very simple lady, and we just had a beautiful time together."

"And yet you always knew your mother disapproved of Nan. She couldn't give you the love you wanted, and it was as if you weren't supposed to get it from anyone else either. What would you like to say to your mother about that now? Whether you believe that was a correct message?"

There was along silence, then, with eyes still closed: "Maybe I was screwed up, and wasn't hearing what you were saying, Mom. Maybe I was just seeing you through the eyes of that fear when I was four. Those nice times we had in my teenage years – I guess we tried to make them strong enough to get rid of the bad times."

"Even when times were nicer it was hard for them to blot out the other more fearful stuff."

"It must have been."

"That fearful stuff about whether it's OK for you to be loved the way you need to be loved by someone else, by anyone you choose, in any way that serves you well – now."

"That's what I've done with other women."

"Sometimes it's real helpful to tell your mother you're not going to abide by her rules. That you are old enough now that you will make your own rules, that serve you well, in your best interests, and in the interests of the relationships in your life, and that you'll take charge of that, getting the loving that you need, and that she can't restrict that."

"And that's what I was doing when I married Frankie, but I wasn't prepared to take the responsibility that it wasn't her choice."

"Maybe you can tell your mother that not only will you get loving when you need it, but you will take charge, and responsibility for getting loving where it serves you in the largest sense."

"I will do that."

"So that rebelling against her isn't even relevant any more."

"No. It's not."

"You're an adult now, and you can make those decisions."

"I think I've made them compulsively, up to now. I can now really make them."

"Sometimes you might have made them rebelliously."

"That's what I meant by compulsively."

"And because impulsively, not using all of your good judgement."

"And notice how tall you are, now you're no longer in a hole."

"Now I notice mainly that my mother is a normal woman, and not this giant like the Statue of Liberty. Because when I was returning to being a little boy I was not seeing that pail, but the confronting Amazon woman."

"Who would not, could not, did not love you as you desperately needed."

"The image I had could not imagine wanting her to love me at all. But of course that was a nice way to handle it, saying it wasn't available."

"And it was certainly consonant with your fear of her, as well. And there must have been hundreds of interactions which fed right into that.

Because as you would defy her, and try to gain mastery over your fear, she would be annoyed, and would become an amazon, and wouldn't feel like hugging you."

"I know about that. I've been a father."

"So your interaction with her confirmed your less realistic fears – the blood and the pail didn't mean that you were going to die, but it was a perfectly reasonable sort of conclusion to come to at age four – and confirmed what was probably real, that what you needed was not there. It may not have been withheld; it may have exceeded her capacity."

"She had no model; as far as I can see."

"And sometimes folks get to a spot where they can say, 'I wish it had been otherwise, but that's the way it was. I'm grateful I know how to get it better.' And walk off."

Sobbing, Eric says: "I'm so grateful I know now how to give it better. It's amazing how my great need to parent seems to come from what I didn't get."

"And to heal yourself, as well – while you point others the way you wish you had been pointed. You get to participate in the process, which may be closer to it than you have ever been. The only guideline is that you keep your own stuff separate from your daughters', or your parents' or your students'. It's being aware each is a bit different from you. So you weave back and forth between giving Nicole what she needs and also being aware that she's a different person from you. So she might need a fine nuance here which would have been irrelevant to you, or a little less of this where you had needed more. Conceivably she and Jennifer are not as fearful as you. Certainly not for the same reasons. The individualizing of it is what matters."

Eric smiled his gratitude as she concluded the session: "It looks like you've got some fine processing to work on for the week until we meet again. Write, draw. Spend time alone – not doing anything else."

###

My Dearest Rani,

The fifteen sessions (sometimes twice a week) with Dr Ekaterina (Tina) have been different from anything I expected: much more

343

demanding: much more disturbing: much more promising. And so full of explanation of those parts of me I've wanted to be without. My greatest expectation was that I would cease to be screwed up about women, and become a feeling man who would live comfortably the total range of human experience. Now, my stated goal in the most recent session is to grow in connectedness from the place where I left off at four years of age.

So now I see a lot of things. Back then I found a way to feel more powerful against the mother I feared; that little guy turned on fearful temper tantrums which would last for hours. He also became very important to people by always being the best – in school, boy scouts, swimming competition, at college; indeed everywhere. He learned to feel good about himself not by accepting the love which was all around him at home, but by achieving. He produced lots of great things out of a combination of fear, anger, and a yearning for connection.

I think I have treated Frankie as more mother than wife. I began marriage with the sense of closeness I had wanted with my Mom. Then when the girls came, she could not give me as much, and I became the displaced four-year-old again. My little boy fear started to push, and I took to irritating her as a way to reinforce my need not to fear her. I did not understand my feelings, especially the anger which had no rationale. I even tried to be the good boy, helping in all kinds of ways with my daughters, but having no warmth toward the one who never seemed to please me.

At the same time, I think I started to look for another "mother". You know how, with all of my heart I indulged myself, with no sense of guilt, and with a feeling of being wonderfully alive, first with Minah and then with Siok Yim. Perhaps the lack of guilt was because I knew those affairs would horrify her. Were they to spite her? You were different; what began and grew between us has always been a much more intentional thing. But more of that when we are together next.

It was Siok Yim who really roused the sleeping volcano. She asked, What do you want? I did not know, but she pushed the question, for three years, and forced me to question what went on in my feelings, not why. She gave me a sense of acceptance I'd never felt before, communicated mainly by touch (more basic than any words) and I was able to tell her the very worst things I had ever thought or felt – they made no difference to the connection between us. And so I was freed to feel for the first time in my life.

When she was not in this country, I have continually sought another 'accepting mother', and so came the other women you know about, with whom my inner child could play, without a care. I was even excited by the very real physical danger involved with that married Russian student. In these, and I fear, to a degree with you, I expected the same unconditional caring and giving which a four-year-old gets in a good relationship with his mother. And then when any woman responded to me as an adult who had her own agendas, my reactions were what you'd expect of a four-year-old.

Worst of all, the anger then had to go somewhere, and so it got directed first at my wife, then at myself. And, I fear, at the girls too, although not consciously. That was a perfect set-up for the level of uselessness and suicidal depression which pushed me to begin this therapy.

Those are insights about the past, and how I come to be where I am. They free me to think about my feelings, and so (as Tina would say) to establish neural pathways which will not be so destructive of myself. They free me to see women as themselves, rather than as that four-year-old's feared and so-strong but so-desired mother. They free me to see work in a different way. They free me to distinguish good anger from extraneous anger, and to cherish the first while letting the other go. They open the possibility of simply being, to the fullness of my intellectual, emotional, interpersonal and spiritual potential. I know those potentials are extraordinary, else why would so many have given me so much? I can now nurture that child within me, giving it all it needs, and being kept young till I die because it will never grow old.

My dear, I believe all that had to happen before I could be at this wonderful beginning.

Your Eric.

### 

Frankie took great pains to respect the 'space' that her quietened husband seemed to need these days. They took turns in being at home when the girls clattered and chattered in from school each day – sharing the conviction that a present parent after school can be a significant factor in the growth, joys and troubles of each day. Their respective schedules

345

made this discipline no great burden, and every so often one of the two girls would need, and ask for just the support which these two caring parents wanted to provide.

This particular evening, the girls having gone to their own rooms, as he cleared the dishes and she was about to join Jennifer's efforts to understand chemistry, Frankie took the initiative to ask, "How's the therapy going?"

Eric looked up with some surprise, hesitated, then answered, "Profoundly. Quite beyond my expectations."

"Beyond your expectations?"

"Yes. You know. All the counseling you and I have attempted together were superficial. They didn't get below the surface, so we went nowhere."

"I wouldn't quite say that!"

"What I mean is that our agendas seemed to control how the therapist dealt with us. Tina is tough. She bullies me. She laughs at me. She makes demands. And I experience things I don't want, never intended, but am deeply grateful for."

"Wow! Sound heavy, but useful."

"I'm not ready to share how, not yet, but I feel sure it's going to make me a different person."

"Wonderful!" was how she left, to give whatever hours were needed by the two upstairs.

Later, as they both finished in the bathroom, she asked, "Maybe we could see her together?" His silence told the answer. Eric could not have explained it, but he could not bear the thought of allowing Frankie into the world of his self-discovery which Tina was facilitating. He could talk about his relation with Frankie, but he was not about to share with her these basic parts of himself. Why? The gulf seemed so wide. Thoughts about the world and issues about the girls, yes; at this level they did communicate. But to share these feelings, his lifelong fears and yearnings? No way.

###

My love,

These last two sessions Tina has pushed me very hard to hold together both my spontaneous feeling response in any situation and my desire to be considerate and caring. Wow! What a job! It's absolutely exhausting me. In the last year I've become conscious of your success in doing both of these things most of the time. I have thus found the profoundest appreciation of you to date..

Yesterday Frankie suggested we needed to either see someone jointly, or to separate. I'm seriously girding my loins for aloneness.

Your much more real – Eric.

###

"Well, where are you today, Eric?"

"I've been thinking a lot about how I've been dominated by the need for security."

"Yes?"

"Well, security and predictability seem to go together, and I've been wondering why I have felt it so important, first to get on a tenure track, and then to get promoted to Associate status."

"Why not? Everyone else has that orientation, or so it seems to me in my contacts both as a student and as a visiting lecturer."

"But it's sick! Oh, there's nothing wrong with it, it's just that it seems to me to be a commitment to a set of two rails on which you will travel, come what may, the rest of your life."

"A lot of things are like that, including partnering, whether it includes marriage or not."

"But there's commitment and insecurity."

"How so?"

"Well, I guess I'm distinguishing the act from the motive. If I commit just to get security, that's not worth much, at least in my book. You know that I have wanted off-the-tracks with women – I mean to have extra-marital relationships – but I have stayed with Frankie."

"So you are wondering why you have kept your marriage alive, even when you loved another?"

"Yes. Exactly. And I can tell you it was not because of any kind of commitment. I used to tell myself, and I told Frankie in our joint therapy that it was for the girls' sake. But I now think that was bullshit."

"You're saying that your telling Frankie you wanted to stay together for the girls sake was a lie?"

"No. It was sincere. At the time, I really believed that was why. That's what is so upsetting about this therapy stuff: it makes you wonder how far you have gone, or will go, to convince yourself."

"You reckon therapy pushes you to deeper honesty with yourself? That it has done that in your life?"

"Absolutely. I was scared, terribly, of what life would be like if I did not have the girls. I couldn't imagine life alone, without Frankie or them. I never seriously tried to imagine having the girls some of the time, like other fathers I know who are divorced. My emotions only saw two possibilities: having my daughters, or not having them."

"And that made you feel very insecure?"

"No. It made me afraid. Insecurity was the cause, not the result."

"And being apart from Frankie?"

"I never thought of it in those terms. I simply thought of being all on my own."

"Having no mother? Leaving Frankie would have meant giving up every last hint of being loved by your mother. It would have put you back to being the deprived boy of four, or eight."

"If that's what insecurity is in my history, yes, it would."

"And today? You started out saying that something has changed."

"Yes and no. I now know that I have come on so confidently in so many places because I wanted to feel secure."

"But knowing that does not yet bring the security you sought through those things."

"No. I don't feel ready to take on a new family structure. Or a new job."

"But you know you would find what it takes, if that is what you decide is best for you."

"I hope I'm not kidding myself when I say 'yes' to that question."

# Chapter Thirty-One

During their joint rooming at a conference Eric and Rani had come to that first quiet conversational time and a long, blissful, tender togetherness of bodies and spirits bathed in silence. It was suddenly broken by the sound of TV from the adjacent room. The mention of one name jolted Eric out of his séance: "O.J."

"What the hell is going on *now*?" he exploded.

A half sleepy response came from the head on his belly: "Did you say something?"

"It's about that O.J. Simpson so-and-so, and his acquittal. I just can't believe it. He murders his wife Nicole and her friend Ron Goldman. All the evidence is there. But a detective was careless. And Simpson's money bought the best legal help in the country. And he gets off!"

"My love," came the gentle voice from the person who was now stroking his chest, and nibbling one nipple so that he demanded that she "Stop that!"

"All right, my love. I hear you. The acquittal pisses you off."

"You're not kidding. There's got to be justice, or the system is a sham. Everyone knows he is guilty. But he's getting off. It's not just this case. It's all criminal cases. If the guilty verdict only goes to those who can't afford the best lawyers, then every criminal who is already alienated will feel all the more alienated."

"Yes?"

"And further, the whole of this nation's social fabric – its norms and the sanctions which push conformity to them – will fall apart. I'm no law and order freak, but .." and he spluttered into silence.

"My dear Eric," she began, "There is another way of looking at this."

"Oh yeah! Then I'd like to hear it."

"There will be reactions against this – by whites who feel this was a racially influenced judgement, first. There's to be a civil suit against him, that's probably what they are talking about in the adjacent room's TV. You'll see."

"But that's not the point!"

"Au contraire, my love. It is the point. The 'not guilty' verdict for OJ is just one tiny part of the whole. Things work together, as they should, and wrongs will be righted, in time. But they will only be truly what you would call 'right' when all of the ifs and buts have been worked into the whole."

"Whatever are you talking about?"

"I'm saying that your preoccupation with right and wrong is way off base. The world is a whole –what we see as good and bad, what we see as nice and nasty, are all part of the reality which is ultimate. It is quite beyond us to see how the apparent opposites fit together, but they do. That is why I don't get upset about this OJ kind of stuff the way you do."

"But it's wrong. It's a miscarriage of justice."

"I know that's how you see it. I'm just saying I see it differently. I think you would have just one god, who is all sweetness and light, and maybe all life and no death."

"Maybe I would, if I were a believer."

"But Hindus see death and creation and preservation as all essential parts of what is the All. And what happens to you, or me, or OJ, or his wife, is all part of a bigger picture, which we cannot understand, or know. But it will work out, in time. So what's the fuss?"

Having no answer, he lapsed into silence. Let it go, he found himself saying. Yet you can't let it go. You have to stand up for what you believe. But she doesn't believe. Not in any absolutes. Except in what she calls

The Absolute. And she says that cannot be comprehended, and is certainly beyond human description.

"We really disagree on this. don't we?" he recommenced the discussion.

"Maybe. But I doubt it. I agree with all your concerns, and values. It's just that I know their opposites have to exist, and that the very existence of those opposites helps everything to get better."

"You can't be serious. We have to stand for something or, as someone must have said, we are nothing. I thought you wanted what I want for the world, for it to be a better, happier place."

"I do. But I'm sure of two things. First, we can't even create a complete, final specification for such a world. And second, we lack the power to do the creating, even if we could specify it."

"Then why have you been working on the Foundation for so long? And why the Social Studies Curriculum project we have both spent so much energy on?"

"Given who I am, and who you are, I believe we were both internally forced to work for such ends. But," and she paused to make the point stronger, "They are not final ends, just more additions to the pot, to make a better stew, as it were."

"Well I'm a real New England Yankee. I value what I call my heritage, and my life makes no sense without such a perspective."

"I grant that. It would not. I have always seen that, even when you, my wonderful man, could not. I'm so glad your therapy has helped you come to the place where you can say that. But I use similar words about my Hindu heritage. I thought you respected that fact."

"I do. But I used to think the differences didn't matter. Now I think they do. I'm coming to think that everything is not relative, after all. You seem to say: Let things play themselves out. I am saying: Let's change them."

In the following forty-eight hours the issue continued to fester in Eric's mind. Twice he brought it up, but each time her total acceptance, even his passion about making the world better, reduced him to impotent silence.

### 

My Dear Rani,

Three days with you inevitably leaves me both satisfied and stimulated. And both terms refer to things physical and mental. Thanks for everything.

Recently a new conundrum has come up for me: how do I keep the little boy part of me alive while growing up? I want the playful part of me to continue, but I don't want to be misled by it.

I am now thinking about us in this way: I was certainly giving full rein to the spontaneous fun kid part of me when I met you at Stanford, all those years ago. There was never a thought in my mind about where it might lead. It has led to the richest relationship I have ever had, but without my thinking about it. As I look back, I think it has been you who has carried the load when needed. I certainly wanted the great stuff between us to continue, but I never figured out what I wanted or where I wanted things to go, long term.

As I now see my life, that has been the story in all places except my professional career. I have not lived the rest of my days intentionally, just spontaneously. If I'm to really mature, I must balance the two. Any thoughts?

Luv ya, Eric.

### 

"Tina, I'm so confused."

"Go on."

"Well, it's about Frankie. It's about her expectations of me, and mine of her. There is a real conflict between paying attention to her, and being true to what I honestly want."

"You're finding yourself in tune with what is going on with her, and it conflicts with what's going on in you. And they seem to war with each other."

"Yes. They do. The worst scene is in bed. It's clear she wants me to hold her - with me initiating that. This is most true when she is depressed about something in her work scene. I feel pleased that I now sense when that is so. So I cuddle her. But when I do, I start to get horny."

"And she doesn't want anything but to be held."

"Right on."

"Are you clear to her about your expectations? Not just on specific occasions, but overall, in the marriage bed particularly?"

"I guess I'm not."

"Well, what are you complaining to me for?"

"Fair enough. If I don't say what I want, how can anyone, even my wife, be able to decide whether to meet my needs?"

"Exactly. So?"

"So in the very near future we will talk about all of her expectations and all of mine. I wonder how that will go."

"But you are now able to discuss those important things without fear. Right?"

### 

Dearest Rani,

Let me first explain why I am writing this apology. I've been working on what Frankie expects of me. I have to admit that question had never even come to mind, in all these years of marriage. It's always been a matter of my expectations. I have never thought about, or asked what were hers. Not until two weeks ago.

Now the apology: what you expect of and from me has never come to my mind either, in all these years, and all these wonderful times together. So will you please, please believe that I wish I had been different. I wish I had been less self-absorbed, less into what I wanted, every moment we were together, even on the phone.

I would like a reply in just one way. Not 'Apologies accepted'. What I would like to hear is a lot about what you expect of me, now. And what do you hope from me, in the future.

Onto another subject, which is really the same one. Frankie and I really leveled with each other about sexual expectations. That was fairly predictable, and leaves me in the spot I have long talked about openly with you. The one new thing is this: I now feel differently about masturbation. You recall laughing when I recounted how my father had warned against what he referred to as "self abuse"? You might also remember I was sheepish about it, and told you it still felt somehow wrong. Well, the practical change because of my talk with Frankie is that I am now realistic about the potential sources of sexual satisfaction. I think of you even more often now.

Your humble, Eric.

### ###

"I can't believe, Tina, that I've been seeing you for eleven months."

"That first day you said you were only willing to get into this work for a few months, six max!"

"That was then. Now I'm grateful it has gone on, and to such depth."

"What are you particularly thinking of?"

"Two things: What I want, and what Frankie wants."

"Let's talk about them separately."

"The easy one is what do I want. I don't have any final answer, but the question no longer throws me. You know, the way it did when Siok Yim asked me 'What do you want, Eric?'"

"And what do you want, now?"

"When I said that's the easier one to talk about I did not mean I have THE answer. I meant that I know myself so much better."

"What do you know about yourself that you didn't know eleven months ago?"

"I have always known what my senses told me, but what I did with my sensations was always on automatic pilot. I had no clue about how to steer the controls, or even where I was going."

"You were like a pilot who sees a storm up ahead, feels the plane tossing around, but goes into a trance state in which he does react, almost without knowing why, or how, or even whether he wants to survive."

"Well, that's a bit far-fetched, but something like that. I didn't used to have any honest idea of what my emotional reactions were to stuff that happened. You know, all that fear stuff about my mother, and how it fouled up my feelings toward all women."

"We've certainly seen how you hid from lots of feelings, positive as well as negative ones."

"Then there's the matter of awareness of my actions, When I think back to that summer at Stanford with Rani I can't believe I was so unaware of what I was doing, with Rani."

"Yes?"

"And not only doing, but where I was going, where I was taking the two of us. I had absolutely no idea of my intentions. In fact I had none, except to temporarily forget Siok Yim."

"And what about Siok Yim? Did you have any clear intentions there?"

"Well she sure did. She made them quite clear."

"But you? What were your intentions?"

"You know the answer to that. I didn't have a clue what I wanted. Not really."

"Go on."

"Then there's the whole business of how I have been accustomed to think – or rather, not to think. I have always taken thinking for granted. I guess I always trusted my head to report objectively, and thoroughly. What bullshit! My head, when women were concerned, was between my legs –or (with a chuckle) – between hers."

"Is that how you feel?" (Referring to his chuckle)

"Sorry. No. It's not funny. It's tragic. But now, after the work with you, I know I'd better distrust my brain, at least to the point of asking how other aspects of me screw up its shape, and the way I interpret things."

356

"That's quite a dissertation: the whole picture of what you want and how to discern it."

"Thanks."

"Now what's on the Frankie front?"

"It's a matter of what Frankie wants."

"How do you know what she wants?"

"Well, first of all I watch and listen, then I ask, then I watch and listen some more."

"Sounds like a good formula to me. How does it work, for you, I mean?"

"The most useful thing two weeks ago was getting into the open her expectations and mine. That was a good basis for what I've done since."

"Which has been?"

"Well, I watch her. You know. How she walks: less upright, faster, or what. Then there's the expression in her eyes. They tell me what's up with her soul. No not specifics, but its general state. Sometimes they are far away, even when she's talking and looking directly at me. Sometimes they look very sad. I couldn't explain either."

"What did happen on those two occasions when you noticed the look in her eyes?"

"I felt sad. Both times. The more I looked, the sadder I became."

"We call that empathy. You don't have to put words on it.""

"I know. It's what my Vietnamese friend called 'being a flower'."

"So when you watched carefully you shared her feelings, without knowing their cause, or their details."

"Maybe. Anyhow, that was important. Because when I asked her what she wanted to do that weekend she told me honestly. I didn't want to go to that concert. She knew I wouldn't, because I hate that stuff, but she was somehow able to say what she wanted."

"And?"

"And we went. It wasn't the end of the world. In fact I hated it even more then I expected. But as I looked at her when she said thanks over a cup of coffee afterwards I felt really good."

"More empathy, huh? And perhaps other things besides."

### 

My Dearest Rani

For a long time I have been 'going to' write this letter re my feelings for you. Actually, my wishes and my feelings remain largely as they have been. The big difference is that I am now able to decide consciously, rather than being driven by unknown wants. The result is a decision to invest primarily in Frankie, for now. This makes obvious sense for the girls' sakes. It makes sense for the sake of my immediate needs for a 'nest'. At the same time, it comes at a serious cost in sexual satisfaction. (Oh, for one of our marathons!) But perhaps most important, it makes sense in terms of my emotional growth.

This latter has been the push into my present reality. I vacillate between four and forty. At times I am wanting the world to be my oyster in a very childish way: I only tolerate anything contrary to my wishes with considerable anger. At the same time, being unrealistically idealistic, I'm then unforgiving of myself. Or again, 'belonging' seems to mean no more than 'belonging to Eric'. The idea of Eric 'belonging' to another gives me real conflict. And again, accepting the 'goodies' at home is hard for me to do. That would be the case if you and I were living together. Tina (my therapist) says that "The machine is re-built; we just have to fine-tune it. However, it is a Maserati, not a Colt, so it will take careful attention." She has been surprised by some of my sensitivities, but they often lead me into a wallow. Yet she encourages me by saying that what I report here in this home these days is very "normal" for a family of four who love each other. The bottom line here is that it is never (as it used to be) grim.

I'm also working on a very difficult transition from the quantity and initiation – which has been my professional achievement approach since graduation – toward a focus on quality. This demands a style different from my adrenaline-stimulated busy-ness. Above all, it requires a patience with myself which is unimaginable to the fourteen-year-old in me. Clearly this means a depth of professional work which I have often avoided. I've thrown into the arena of thought about five or six seminal concepts, but never developed any one of them. I've started others in activities, then have left them to it and moved on. Then I am disappointed that the others don't develop the ideas I gave them.

I'm also back into philosophy some, for the first time since undergrad days. But I won't bore you with that.

All the foregoing stems from a profound belief that there should be a special use for my own specialness – not the least of which is my attempt to become more androgenous. And that something will not just come to me; I myself will have to reach out rather than waiting for the world to seek me out so it can applaud me.

All this about me! What I hope for in a reply will be all about you.

In case you are in any doubt, I DO love you, profoundly,

Eric

### 

"I think you have probably felt how much I admire you, Ahad." Eric's companion smiled across their mugs of coffee, steaming into the chill air at the foot of the ski slope where they had just finished their sandwiches in the surprising warmth of the low winter sun..

"Yeah, I do feel appreciated by you."

"That's true in many ways. But right now, these days, of this year, I feel it intensely. We don't need to get back on the slopes for another half hour, so let me tell you about a major change that has been developing, in me, ever since my Nicole got religion."

"Go Ahead. I'm all ears."

"Well, it's like this. You know that for twenty years now I have been doing things with persons of other cultures, other countries, other convictions. You and I have talked many times about the challenges that has involved, and the ways I have been pushed to change, because I was involved with them, and of, course, with you."

"And you've been in love with an equally diverse trio of women," Ahad could not resist the opportunity to tease his close friend.

"Very true! And also very relevant to what I want to run by you. You know that Rani has been a constant in my life for something like twelve years. One of the great things about her is that we never fight, even though we talk about every topic under the sun."

"I got that impression."

"Lately I've realized that the reason we never fight is because she's such a relativist."

"Would you explain that?"

"She's very Hindu, acknowledging the value, both obvious and hidden, in any and every position. She does that easily, because of her background. It makes for delightful times together."

"So she's the reason you've sounded that way these last couple of years?"

"No. I came to that position independently. I came to see that every culture is based on a set of values which has worked very well for them. I also became convinced that what is right for one person, or what is right in one situation might not be right for a different person, or in a different situation."

"I almost agree, but not quite. I do believe Allah has given us guidance, in the Koran."

"My present position is this. The relativism which says that is wrong but . . . and so allows no distinction between possibilities reduces everything to gray. AND it takes the iron out of everyone's spine. I am glad I was born in this country. I am really glad I have the values it gave me with my mothers' milk."

"So how does all this thinking affect the way you will act from here on?"

"I'm not sure. I certainly will bend over backward to understand where another is coming from. I will bend over to empathize with their position. And I will take into account all of those considerations as I make up my mind on something. But I will not demean or downplay my own convictions. Above all, I will be true to them."

"Bravo, Mr. America!"

"No! Seriously! I will not be wishy-washy. But neither will I respect any other who is wishy-washy. In fact, sometimes I feel Rani is so accepting that she stands for nothing specific. I find it hard to imagine being with that attitude all the time. From now on I will most respect those who acknowledge that they are the children of a particular tradition, which gave them birth, and because it is part of their essence it continues to enliven them and give them whatever vitality they possess. That's where I stand. That's how my new stance will work. You will no longer hear me saying that you've simply got to take them on their own terms or that we just need to make peace with it, even though we disagree radically."

"Sounds pretty good to me! I guess I have that kind of respect for those who differ from me, too. By the way, when do you two next get time together?"

"The week after next, as a matter of fact! The Society's regional meeting is at Yale."

### 

In the days before that meeting his anticipation gave way to reflection about Siok Yim, who had never been far from his consciousness in all these twelve years. She had written every twelve or eighteen months, just "updates", and he had always replied, with similar innocuous chit chat. For him, her love continued to be the norm by which all others were measured, his feelings never as overwhelming with anyone as they had been with her, for she had set the ultimate standard - both for acceptance and for holding him accountable. Yet therapy had put all that in a new light.

No longer did he weep; no longer did he suppress the unrecognizable lump in his chest at the thought of her, which he now knew to be fear. And no longer did he see her valuation of order and propriety to be the mountain between them. What had it been?

He could now admit that her commitment had not just scared him; it had literally terrified him. Moreover, the terror was more than a reliving of his fear of The Big Mother. Deep within he was simply unable to respond to a love as big as hers. Now he felt he must make some amends. He would write her a brief but honest apology.

After many drafts he sent a version which read:

My Dear Siok Yim,

I have come to the realization that you have been the greatest gift in my whole life. That is the plain, simple truth, and there is no way I can fully express the depth of that realization. Nor is there any adequate way to say thank you.

This letter is also a poor and even cowardly substitute for the personal apology which could never make up for what I did to you years ago. My words about fantasy in 1986 were unforgivable, and the cruelest thing I have ever done. They were also a fabrication.

I have only just realized these truths by spending most of my energies this last year in therapy. The main product has been an ability to see myself, and those facades it now seems I had to use with you. I hope that news of this understanding on my part will bring a smile to your life.

This letter also comes with my wish that your family, specially your son and daughter, are as well and as 'together' as are mine.

I am sending copies of this to each of the two addresses I had for you.

Very sincerely,

Eric

# Chapter Thirty-Two

"Do you really want to do this?"

"Do you?"

Given the clarity of each one's wordless responses, Eric and Rani wrapped themselves together, as if nothing had changed. What followed was as wonderful, as all engrossing, as tender as at any previous time. Afterwards, she sat on top of him, his penis still strong within her, and gazed into his face for what seemed like forever – except that there was no awareness of time. It was Eric who took the initiative to move beyond this enchantment.

"My darling!"

"You've never called me that."

"Maybe it just happened, because I want to say something different. In fact I want to talk about one thing, getting your input. Then I want to tell you something that I'm at last getting clear about."

"Go right ahead sir. You have my complete attention."

"I've been thinking a lot about sex."

"Me too. But I have known that – about both of us - for a long time."

He smiled, raised himself so that he could kiss her slowly, then leaned back and began: "I've been asking whether sex is not really a sacrament.

What happens during our physical intimacy is more than special, or wonderful."

"It is both those. And much, much more."

"That is exactly what I'm trying to understand, to find words for."

"And have you?"

"Well, I just used the word sacrament. I guess I was trying to say it brings a feeling of awe, as if I am in touch with something in me which is beyond me, and with something through you which is more than you or us. Does that make any sense at all?"

"Not much. But an awful lot. I suspect the thought of it being a sacrament was a way of saying that what we do is holy."

"You're right. That is what I was getting at. But isn't it a bit outrageous – to say that carnal desire and its satisfaction are holy. What would priests say?"

"Depends whose priests. If they were Hindu, they would probably say something like: So you have realized, at last."

"You're kidding?"

"Not at all. Just as you asked about those erotic sculptures, so the acts themselves are seen as part of The All, as I've expressed what you think of as 'god'."

"Wow!" Eric reacted. "Does that make my sex-filled letters a form of theologizing?"

After a long silence, she asked, "There was a second agenda item you said was very important? I'm ready when you want to tell me about that."

"OK. It has become quite a joke between me and Tina, my therapist, at first, then with Ahad and Michael, to talk about 'Eric's women problem'.

"I seem to remember, my beloved man, that I have been guilty of using the phrase myself."

"Well, you know, from my written and telephone communications about my therapy that the number one woman in my life is unchanged. Yes, since birth. It is my mother."

"I'm not surprised. Not in the least."

"I am, a bit. I thought that facing that Amazon woman in therapy would help. I expected the rational explanations of my childhood fear of her would free me, not only of those memories, but from the spin-off, towards other women. But it's not that easy, is not happening that fast."

"I had that impression, too."

"I won't say I'm a bomb likely to explode, but I do have a problem that is going to muddy my water for a long time."

"And so you're telling me . . . ?"

"I'm saying that anything more than we now have would be a tremendous gamble. Certainly not as big a gamble as it would be between Frankie and me without the girls, but with the girls, well, they do make a difference to our life together." He censored the other thought – that every day he found it more important to affirm one particular set of values.

"Thank you for saying all that, so clearly. I had come to realize that was the situation as soon as you wrote that letter about your feelings. But what you've just said tells me why your feelings will be unpredictable for the foreseeable future."

"How I wish it were clearer."

"Either way."

"Yes, either way." He was silent for a long time, gently running his finger down her shoulder, breast, waist and belly, finally resting where it always seemed just right.

"Before I share something beautiful with you," he began to speak again, "There's one more thing I feel I must share. I am in the process of becoming more American than I have been in a long time. I haven't worked it all out yet, but I feel more obligated, more in debt to my national cultural heritage than at any other time in my life. What do you say to that?"

Her response was another of those kisses which said, I love you so much, just as you are, whatever you are. He had thought of adding that his move beyond relativism might be a further impediment to any commitment between them. But this was such a warmer, more acceptable way to finish that conversation. Such a statement was probably superfluous anyway.

"Now," he suggested when excitement was somewhat allayed, and they were sipping coffee by the window, "I want to read you something. I wrote it straight after a wonderful experience with my next favorite woman after you - Nicole. I called it 'Possessed by the Mountain'.

### Possessed by the Mountain

There are certainly many mountains, but there is only *one* mountain in the eyes of New Englanders – Mount Washington, crown of New Hampshire's Presidential Range, which includes peaks named to honor eight of this nation's presidents. Though only a molehill compared to the Rockies, it is a fearsome mountain. Because it rises clear above all other terrain in the northeast it creates its own weather, often in stark contrast to the conditions as near as ten miles. It takes the lives of uninitiated walkers every year, even in the summer. The world's strongest winds ever recorded anywhere have been at its peak. Even at less than seven thousand feet the summit temperature has never reached seventy, and along this Presidential Range the tree line ends at a mere four thousand feet, above which there is nothing but rock interspersed with clumps of stunted vegetation. Such is The Mountain - beguilingly alpine, but also bare and brutally unforgiving of any who fail to give it the respect it demands.

It is now ten years since I took this daughter Nicole on her first mountain overnight - up a somewhat lesser peak in this same area. As Frankie drops us off at the trailhead this balmy early fall noontime Nicole and I are filled with the excitement of a lightly laden overnight on The Mountain. We are climbing via Mizpah hut, which will save us the burden of cooking and overnight gear. After taking a farewell snapshot of us Frankie drives off down Crawford Notch with the cry, "See you tomorrow evening! And take care of your Dad, Nicole!" With absolute confidence comes her reply, "Don't worry. I will," and the two of us are into the woods.

As breathing deepens with the steady grade up Crawford Path (which will continue unabated to tree-line) we are both silent. In this silence I now review whether we have all the means of keeping warm in the worst of weather. I made a special purchase of rain-pants, and have woolen mittens, waterproof gauntlets, extra long-johns, one heavy and one light woolen sweater, a beanie, gaiters, and a windproof jacket. Nicole complained "We don't need all this gear. The weather is fantastic, Dad, and there's only a small chance that predicted cold front will reach here before we're safely down tomorrow night Silently I say, "But what if it *does* change?"

You cannot climb a real mountain without surrendering to it. "Up" means effort; the mountain demands it. "This is your first bill," it seems to say with each new irregularly-shaped "step" up. My breathing quickens, shallow at first, then deepens and gets into its climbing rhythm, the mountain's rhythm. But the immediate pay-off's! The beech forest at this level is all golden, not yet fallen to autumn showers. The world is left quite behind us in the euphoria of early fall in the New England woods. Following a long silence, we talk of how each of us handles unpleasant stuff, of what each of us wants most in life. We find it is almost the same thing: to be fully known and "accepted" (her word) or "safe" (mine). And I know that I am accepted by her, my woman/daughter of sixteen. Never have I been more intensely in one place than I am here, now. Except for one thing: if the change hits us when we're exposed! For this *is* The Mountain.

It is two hours plus , under lowering skies ("It's not supposed to rain") when the first drops hit my perspiration-wet tee-shirt. But, thank God, the hut is within sight! Safe, at least for tonight! And in the morning we *could* simply retrace our steps. We'll both be bitterly disappointed, but it could be the safe decision. The hut-master tells us "Latest from the Summit Station is that a major change is coming in. We'll know more when they radio us as usual tomorrow at 7 a.m." I fret about my daughter – but it is probably my own anxiety pretending. The sky is now dark gray, and I feel even grayer. Nicole has been so excited that we could make this "real adult" climb together. And so have I.

At 3 a.m. my bladder demands that I brave the twenty degree ambient temperature here in the hut. Operating in what had been complete darkness I find, to my delirious surprise, that a cloudless sky contains a sliver of moon telling me: "Tomorrow will be fine Eric!", as I sink back into peaceful sleep. However, at breakfast the news from the summit contrasts with that moon-sight and the warm morning sun in a crystal clear sky: "Expecting a cold front to move in this morning with wind chill of ten below zero!" But it CAN'T change, I want to believe. Yet twenty

367

years' experience tells me it CAN. Two Germans announce *they* are off to the summit, "Anyhow!" Nicole and I look at each other silently saying "Fools." One older walker, now en route ("down, thank Goodness") wishes us "Good luck!" I tell Nicole: "At least we know the dangers, can always turn back, and half-way to the summit there is another way down into the safety of forest. So let's go!" (Even if there are five hours tough 'up' ahead of us and then a five hour descent.) Somehow there's no spring in my step as I quickly fall behind her.

In spite of anxiety and the demanding climb to the top of Mount Pierce, the first of the presidential peaks, I am quite overwhelmed by what greets me as I join Nicole at this lesser summit. A full-circle view contains hundreds of ridges and peaks, and all of the closer slopes wear their autumn glory. Only one peak has a veil – The Mountain itself. Five miles away the predicted cold front has already produced total cloud-cover there, the end of our route atop this ridge. Here, the wind is freshening, light snow is beginning, and we wonder about those two Germans, already out of sight ahead of us, as we pick our way over the irregular rocks which constitute this trail, now well above the trees. As Nicole notes the tread-mark of a sneaker left in the snow by one of them she comments: "They probably don't even realize the difficulties they'll get into, or how hard it is to rescue people up here under these conditions." To myself I say, "Thank God this is snow, not rain. At least I won't get *wet*. But what of the cold? Two sweaters are already insufficient!"

Determined to go at least half-way (where the other trail can take us down to the trees) we opt to avoid the peak of Eisenhower and flank it. Some two thousand feet below us the Dry River Wilderness stretches away for nearly twenty miles. At our eye-level two weather systems are now colliding, the clouds of each joining in a frenzied dance around some invisible maypole. We watch for several minutes in complete fascination, then realize we need a snack. Which, of course, gives us an excuse to linger in awe as the almost touchable clouds go round and round, just a few hundred feet away. But the trail is now very difficult, for its uneven rocks are ice covered beneath last night's two inches of snow. The result: every step must be carefully made, lest one slip; this is no place to twist an ankle.

The prospects up ahead seem daunting. The trail stays on uneven rock along a ridge which falls away several thousands of feet each side. The slopes each side are sometimes precipitous, but usually just steep. However, keeping on the trail when it is snow-covered is a matter of spotting the next cairn – usually about one hundred yards ahead. But when they're snow-covered it is almost impossible to pick them out. To say nothing of what it would mean trying to find one in what is fast becoming a "white out". Walking is now painfully slow; we do well to cover a mile in the next hour.

With Eisenhower behind us, and on a completely open ridge the wind is now fierce. With incredible relief I shout: "Look! The junction with Edmunds Path!" The cloud is now touchable, so that you can't see fifty feet. Nearly every rock and twig has been cocooned in ice. Nicole puts it in a phrase: "This is winter!" My feeble response: "It IS different."

The Mountain has been the only thing in our minds for twenty four hours. But now our relationship to it has changed. For that time we have been coping with *our* purposes in relation to it. Now The Mountain seems to be saying, "Here, you are mine, totally. Here the only conditions are what I offer you." And there is only one possible reply: "OK."

Now bitterly cold, I'm turning onto the path that will take us down toward the trees when "Hey! Don't go yet!"

"But Nicole, it makes sense to abandon all hope of doing the three remaining miles up this ridge to the summit."

"No Dad, that's not what I mean. Look, just look all around us." So I obey, motionless, surrendered to The Mountain for a whole hour – in this one spot. It holds us in thrall. Nothing exists here, now, but grades of white, tinted with green in some places. The green is lichen on the larger rocks, peeping through at these two humans it has found the power to entrance by its almost 'not there' greenness. The rocks are topped with more snow, so that there is no distinction between them and what I could call sky, but is really the even whiteness of the cloud which is all about us. Even the wind whistling around my collar can't stop my response to the little wonders at our feet. Small alpine plants are not so much hidden as they are showcased in clear ice. Flowers have not been destroyed; they have been preserved, individually, under 'glass', every minute detail presented for our appreciation. Tufts of grass are still a warm brown under their coats of ice, and each blade trails its scarf of hoar frost, for all the world like finest silk, a full two inches long, right down its back.

We just stand there, beyond time. Then another wonder captures her attention, or mine, and we share it. No words, just a glance. Or a smile. I really don't want to go, to do anything, to say anything. It owns me.

It owns Nicole too. We belong to it – in a way beyond words. This is not something I am experiencing – as I was experiencing the demand of slippery walking or anxiety about getting down. This is something which takes away the "me" altogether. I am not "experiencing" The Mountain. Rather it has claimed me, has made me one with itself, as truly as one is sometimes "not me" but part of "the all" in the moment of sexual orgasm. When Nicole re-enters my awareness it is as another in just the same state –possessed by The Mountain. We are both "possessed", surrendering in ecstasy. And if anything could be added, it is the reality of sharing all this. (In one fleeting moment of thought there comes the notion that perhaps THIS is what keeps a man atop Everest, even unto death; and we are not yet hypothermic! Medically they call it 'disorientation', perhaps it is spiritual 'reorientation', into the state which is our destiny.)

Wistfully tearing myself from that wonderful embrace, I start down alone. A hundred paces and I am in the wonderful stunted mass of evergreens which create a safe haven just below tree-line. The driving snow now falls. Fifteen minutes and the deciduous trees start, and the 'down' starts to 'get' to me. I really walk up better that down, and even though I am not sweating as I was when climbing Pierce above tree line in the snow it is a real strain on calves and thighs, a supportive stick notwithstanding. And so, in a different way, I still belong to The Mountain, for my whole being is still obliged to operate on the terms which it dictates.

The trees are getting bigger now that we are below the area hit hardest by winds. There are voices below! Soon they materialize into puffing, sweating heaving young men who gasp, "How much further?" To where? "To the top of Eisenhower," after three more strained breaths. We smile, utter words of encouragement, and admit that that peak will take them another two hours. (A little voice inside me says: "The Mountain will exact its price – of owning you – long before it shares its richer treasures." I keep that to myself.)

Now even the 'down' is so tough that I am sweating, and the layers come off, first the jacket, then one sweater, then another and I'm down to a tee shirt with sunshine now coming down through the trees and the temperature feeling more than fifty higher than it did just an hour ago. More voices. Girls now; same crowd, struggling, really struggling to manage every steep step upwards (some of them three feet!) And they too are heading for that peak. (We learn that it's all part of an ecology course, which their instructor has integrated around Mount Eisenhower.) One aspect of being "part" of a mountain is that you feel with, and for, every other who is (by choice or otherwise) giving some of their life moments to that mountain. In response to one girl's plea: "It's not my legs it's my buns!" Nicole expresses that camaraderie by making off into the under-story of the forest and returns with two downed sticks to help these kids to get at least a bit further along. But no kindness will change the fact that The Mountain will possess them long before they can be made part of its alpine wonderland.

Back at home for dinner Nicole comments: "It's all so unreal. It seems I have been in several different worlds, all in the last twenty-four hours. There I was completely disconnected from what it means to be here on dry ground. Here it is late summer; there it is dead of winter, right now. It's as if I have been in a transporter which caused me to live three months ahead of time, and now it's brought me back here at the beginning of fall." I guess that's what it means to be possessed by The Mountain.

"Thank you," whispered the enthralled Rani. "Thank you, not only for the image of the mountain, but for letting me be part of the oneness which binds you two together."

Their parting differed from every other time. Neither verbalized the feeling, but it dominated the late afternoon drive to the airport. It hung like a giant cloud over them as they sat for forty minutes awaiting her departure. Her disappearance down the ramp took forever, with this tall man straining to catch the last glimpse of her jaunty little body as it turned into the entrance to the aircraft.

On board she found her seat, fastened the belt, and gazed out the window. Thick clouds hung low on the tarmac. The even grayness spoke to something deep within. She took out a small notebook, and as the aircraft gained speed for the take-off she found herself writing:

The flat, long horizon
Occasional buildings and low growth
Under sky large, gray and cold.
Careless of all travelers
Excited, bland, or numbed-with-sadness travelers.

How many partings
Always after discovery, reunion, union?
The joy. The pain.

Emptiness engulfs the plane, engulfs me
Surges, drowns me, numbs me.
His special, final, held gaze
Become a dagger to my eyes
Brings tears.
These tears (as with paper)
Hurt the scar tissues of other
Flat, long, cold gray, joy-pain, dagger partings.

Dark aloneness comes to craft, and me
Bringing questions, memories smiles, and what-if's.
And is that rain?

Cold blue night sky, now grayed with me
Does care.
Mixes its tears with mine.
The dark enfolds us both –
Again together.

###

August

My dear Eric

This is an anniversary card of sorts. Twelve years ago this month we met at Stanford. It was, as I believe I've told you, one of my life's pivotal events. You being there contributed <u>most</u> significantly. Feeling your arms around me when together as well as at a distance of thousands of miles has, in the last twelve years, contributed to my sense of security and well-being more than I can say. So I can just repeat what you already know: <u>I love you.</u>

Rani

###

September

My Love,

I'm sending you some details of our latest endeavor . . .

Life here continues . . . . .

Lakshmi . . . . . .

How far away you seem. But then, quite separately we have agendas which are being followed for individual emotional well-being. Nevertheless, I think of you, hold the thought close, and love you. Be well,

Rani.

### 

October

Dear Eric,

Though I haven't a great deal of clarity at 30,000 feet, this morning I do have the great inclination to write to you.

We have just buried . . . .So that is another milestone in life.

Things at the Foundation get worse . . .

During our last conversations I have felt so close and so understood by you. But I suppose you knew that. But I say it any way. You seem to be so benefiting from extended therapy- you, Frankie, and the girls. I'm pleased that your "quality of life overall" seems to be improving. Let us not see the loss – and now I speak of my experiences - of great emotional peaks and very dark valleys, which for years were the means for balancing life. Nevertheless, the Point Lobos memory lingers, as do those of Vermont, the Rockies, and many beaches.

You might remember something of my cousin who arrived from India last year. He remembered you and sends his regards.

Stay well. Peace, and my love,

Rani

### 

A card depicting several subtly different seashells came the following February:

My Dear Eric,

This "Valentine" is one I know you'll appreciate more than the red-with-hearts variety.

It was very good to hear your voice recently, though a bit frustrating that I could not talk freely. It was also the first time I recall you commenting that I'd not written recently. Perhaps I shall, if you don't mind me sorting out feelings thereby. Perhaps.

Happy Valentine's day.

My love,

Rani

### 

May 8,

My Dearest Eric,

Thank you. Thank you for helping me/us to be with each other on Tuesday. It felt right to do just as we did – the walk by the river was perfect. As brief as it was, seeing you was so necessary. I'd been in Cambridge twice and not seen you – so close. You were becoming a phone-friend. It is very good to have a recent memory of the touch and look of you. And lunch – I owe you.

Let me dwell on something, if you can bear with me trying to make sense of the men in my life, i.e. those for whom I have warm feelings – of different intensities, and of different sizes, but warm feelings, nevertheless: A-You; B-Gerard: C-My Danish "traveling friend".

As I've seen you all within the last seven days I feel able to make comparative descriptions. 1. All of you are warm giving people, and generally recognized as such by those around you. 2. A and C have deep interest in philosophy. 3. All have traveled widely, and A and C are/have been almost bi-cultural. 4. A and B have a profound respect for the natural elements around us – plants, flowers, birds, fishes (but curiously, not dogs). 4. All are intelligent – that goes without saying. I am omitting physical characteristics, for you are all alike. Now it is obvious that A is the most inclusive, doesn't it? And we can conclude that you've affected my choice of male companionship, or at least that manifest most of the characteristics I find attractive.

Oh, to get more concrete: just had a call from my friend at Brown, who says my application just made the deadline for that job. We'll see what develops. Not sure what I'm doing. Am I just in the habit of job-hunting or am I really willing/want to leave the current and potential pleasure of knowing Gerard?

Then I saw a mutual friend yesterday and she commented that she'd had a wonderful talk with you and that you seemed to be in a so much better place than you were before. Oh Eric, you and your women! (Students, colleagues, lovers) I hope Frankie is both knowledgeable of and willing to share you in some of those capacities. If she knew how you exude physical attractiveness in any of these situations she might not be. You say that you might not want her to put her hand on your penis. Question: Would she ever want to initiate such behavior?

The plane is about to land, so I'll finish.

Until we see each other again, know that I love you, am so happy that you're allowing yourself to "grow up", and am pleased to find that the "new" Eric is every bit as attractive as the "old" one was. My arms are around you.

Peace.

Rani.

###

The following Fall Eric received a bulky envelop, registered mail, at the office, bearing the Phoenix postmark. It contained all the letters, cards, and little mementos he had ever sent her. A smaller envelop contained a short note which read: I am marrying Mr B (Gerard) next week-end. I will not have anywhere that these deserve to be kept, so perhaps they can join the ones I sent you. Keep well, and happy in the certainty that you are much loved. Rani.

# BOOK V

# Chapter Thirty-Three

Eric found it hard to believe how much he had changed, how life had changed, since he met Indonesian Minah. She had been his birth. In his loving and being loved by her he had awakened. Until that telephone call asking "The Professor Johnson?" it was as if he had been a chrysalis, potentially a thing of great beauty with wings, but knowing only the confines of something less mobile than a larva, able only to inch along sightless. With her he had begun to discover, acknowledge, and enjoy so much of himself which had been there all along but hidden, perhaps more from himself than from others.

Chinese Siok Yim had entered the world of this emergent creature asking what he wanted and he, still as mute as the chrysalis, had been unable to respond. She had known exactly what she wanted – had wanted to give everything, had asked everything of him in response - and he had hidden, fearful even while wanting to say yes. Now, beyond therapy, he could explain both the yearning and the fear, but the actual feelings refused to go away. Imagining the offer and demand repeated, the opportunity there again, the yearning still filled his chest even while some of the fear still cramped his belly.

Little wonder that Rani had been such a joy, such a perfect companion all these years, which he mentally labeled "ASY" (After Siok Yim). Could it have been for twelve years that Rani had never asked for anything, but simply delighted in the spontaneous developments in their every contact?

Could a conscious drive for self-fulfillment have been the only want of this child of India, an adequate reward for such faithfulness? Only once, at that confirmation of his pro-family decision as she and he walked by the Charles River last year had he sensed there was something she passionately desired. There he realized that she wanted him as full-time, life-long companion in fulfillment. And he had chosen the semblance of 'Thanksgiving at Gran's'! But though only a semblance, a family which was "his".

### ###

It was sunset 'on Golden Pond', the last Saturday in September, 1998. Squam Lake has been gilded by the sun from behind the cottage. Now, five miles across the lake to the east a full moon was looking at them across the water. The three men had sat in silence for the last half hour, mesmerized by the tranquil beauty. From across the lake an eerie call suddenly pierced the evening and hung there, its tones refusing to sink into the water. It prompted Ahad to break the silence: "Whatever is that?"

"A loon; isn't it awesome?" responded the man for whom these environs had been his second home since birth. "But the fact that I have been hearing them all my life never takes away the sense of being called to another dimension of reality." He put down his wine glass, rummaged into the pocket of his jacket, pulled out a crumpled piece of paper, and held it so that it caught the light which slanted out from the one lit bulb inside the house. "I wrote something today, after I asked you guys to leave me behind on the trail. I'd like to share it, if you don't mind me using the loon's call to break our silence."

There was enough light now from the bigger-than-usual moon for Eric to see that Michael joined Ahad in agreeing. Each took another sip before leaning back to give him their ears, while their eyes remained glued to the moon rising over the lake.

"I called it 'My Shape':

The old root is twisted, silver gray,
Perhaps exposed for twenty years.
Furrowed, contorted, yet so uniquely beautiful
That it caught my gaze, held it long –
The product of scores of years 'alive'
Plus a score called 'dead'.

Surrounding pines grow tall
But this one's root entwined my mind, holding fast
Demanding –
But what's the question?

I wonder how my score reads, bathed here in fall sunlight.
My contortions are not nature's; I made them every one.
What say they?
What say they of paeans to freedom?
Nature's not to blame for my shape.

So I must ask:
What distortions are the product of addictions?
Which are freedom's?
And which the fruit of grace?"

"You're getting quite introspective in middle age," teased Michael.

"Little do you know," Eric responded, "I've had a life-time's introspection in the last year with my therapist Tina."

"I've been curious about that," Michael replied.

"I've wondered," added Ahad, "but felt it was much too private. I had no right to intrude."

"I'm very comfortable now to share some of it with my two closest friends. But where to start?"

"Why not start with 'your women'?" This wry suggestion came from Michael. The Iranian thought that inappropriate, but had gotten used to such banter between these two Americans.

"Actually, that is the only place to start. It was where my therapy started, and continued for many exhausting months."

"The old staying power on the wane?" Michael thought this appropriately amusing. Eric did not and scowled at him, only to find Michael's eyes still glued to the rising moon.

"You're more right than you guessed. My women trouble began with a woman neither of you has ever met or heard about – my mother." He went on to tell them about his experience and destructive fantasies as a four-year-old and how he had coped with the resultant fear and yearning, first as a boy, then as a sexually repressed youth, and in the last fifteen years by his involvement, outside his marriage, with three exotic women.

"That's quite a story. Makes you wonder, doesn't it?"

"Wonder what?"

"Wonder what lies deep within any of us."

"And why we are nice? Or nasty?"

"Or both."

Eric waited as the two of them absorbed, under the cover of those comments, what he had said. He smiled. Typical male responses, he found himself thinking, to a disclosure which goes so far beyond the norm. He loved these guys, really loved them, and had no doubt that they reciprocated. Double digit friendships are to be treasured, and can be relied upon. So he waited for some time, allowing them to be with their own feelings, himself simply being - as he had learned from Anh – with the lake.

"One of my many puzzlements," he was first to break the silence, "is about sex."

Michael once again was irrepressible; it came out before he was aware of the thought: "It's always been straightforward to me."

Eric again ignored his buddy and, badly needing their feedback on his thoughts, pressed forward. "I know you guys will agree that sex is an ever-present drive for all of us males. Maybe for both genders." Speaking out of marriages very different from his own, the other two guys quietly murmured strong agreement. "My thought is that lust should not be criticized, it should be revered."

"That sounds like a rationalization to me, especially knowing you as I do," was the immediate reaction from Michael.

"Come on, Michael. Give me a break. I'm trying to say something very important here. May I?"

"Sorry, buddy. I'll shut up. At least until you have said what's on your mind."

Having established enough space to express himself adequately, Eric did so: "Actually Michael, I'm relying on you to comment. You are the only one of the three of us who comes out of a strict Christian background, and my hypothesis is that sex is a sacrament. Sacrament is a big word for you Catholics, isn't it?" Michael nodded his silent agreement, mentally noting, as something to tell Eric later, that Catholics consider marriage to be a sacrament, but not sex itself.

"My thought," continued Eric, "arose (again a smirk crossed Michael's face, at which Ahad gave a disapproving scowl, but both were unnoticed by the presenter) "that the sex drive exists in the human animal to promote union, and union is the purpose of the universe. So it's a very holy thing, this drive that is so often maligned. I came to this place as I thought about the kind of love letters I used to write to Rani. They were HOT. So explicit they would scandalize many. Then there was the talk between her and me – such prolonged verbal indulgence concerning physical intimacies. Yet she is a very proper person, with a deep sense of the private, and profound respect for her own body. Then there was the range of sex play – absolutely everything, nothing barred, and all wonderful."

Michael couldn't resist: "We get the picture."

"The point is that all I have said was wonderful. To neither of us was any word or act anything less than that. That kind of behavior and talk preceded and followed orgasms. I am convinced that all of it deserves the adjective 'holy'."

After an appropriate pause Ahad asked: "Are you calling all sexuality 'holy'?"

"No. But I am suggesting that all sexuality has that possibility. Even the relationship with a whore has that possibility, even though that rarely develops."

"Develop?"

"Yeah. What I'm trying to say is that sexual behavior all begins with a drive within the person. Whether or not it becomes a sacrament is a matter of it being all-consuming. (I suspect that is rarely so for a prostitute.) But first, let me develop my thought about it being a sacrament. What is the technical meaning of that word, Michael? As a good Catholic you probably have it on the top of your head."

"Sure, the definition is something like this: a sacrament is the outward and visible form of an inward and spiritual grace."

"Exactly what I'm getting at! And just as bread and wine CAN be sacraments – the means by which we share in something beyond human understanding – so can sex."

"And what is the 'something beyond human understanding'?"

"Union. Oneness. Complete connectedness. They are some of the ways I would name the human experience which is ultimate, which is an experience with the transcendent. Sex is the most elemental way in which that experience – of transcendence – happens."

"Wait a minute." It was Ahad's turn now. "You're saying that carnality and spirituality are not opposites? You are saying they can be one?"

"Yes."

"That is really wild – to a Muslim. Even though we do love sex!"

"I'm thinking a bit more clearly now," Eric pondered. "What I'm thinking is that it is really great sex which is a sacrament. It is when the sex is all-consuming, so that there is no glimmer of awareness or thoughts, of anything but the two and their becoming one. In that moment, all separation is overcome. I am coming to believe that is what all existence is about - overcoming all separation, becoming one. And in the moment of, or just following orgasm, all separation is overcome. At that moment we catch a glimpse of our destiny."

"My thoughts aren't always that holy," chimed in Michael.

"And at the Mass, are they always holy, totally on the Body and Blood, as the priest describes the bread and wine?"

"Of course not! I often think how stupid the wafer is, and what lousy wine."

"So is it then a sacrament?"

"Yes."

"I wouldn't say so, speaking as one raised Lutheran. You've got to be fully into it for it to be an experience of the holy."

"That's your Protestant view. Mine's different!" retorted the staunch Catholic.

"What's love got to do with what you've said?" injected Ahad.

"I now see love as wishing this union experience were so. The union of the bodies and spirits, I mean."

"You have been thinking!"

"A professional hazard, I acknowledge. But it has put all of what critics would call my 'womanizing' into another light. And I must watch again that movie about the life of Bob Fossey – I think it was called 'All That Jazz'!"

"Rationalizations!" shot Michael.

"Maybe! But these thoughts about sex being a sacrament do tie into that experience with the root, of which I wrote."

"How so?"

"Simply this. For almost my whole life I have experienced oneness with things in nature. At such moments I cease to be, as separate from what I experience. In such moments, some of nature and I are one. Until Minah, they had been the greatest moments of my life. They are still among the greatest. Now I've added what occurred with three women."

"Alright," came from Michael. "In this whole matter I think the final word is this: it's all easier done than said."

They all chuckled, and went in to start dinner.

### 

"Breakfast's on!" penetrated Eric's deep sleep, accompanied by a smell, which seemed at one moment to be sausage, bacon the next. In less than five minutes he was dressed and seated at a table with the sun streaming across it from the same direction in which the moon had risen last evening.

"Smells like," he hesitated, "either bacon or sausage?"

"Both," announced the proud cook Michael, who had a charge in mind for his preparation of eggs benedict to go with the meats: "I expect to hear

382

some more about the results of your year's work with Tina before we go out on the lake this morning."

"What do you want to know?"

"What difference has it made to things?"

"Don't know about things! But it's made a big difference to me."

"Sure. I have noticed you are back in the land of the living; more energy, more on the ball, et cetera. But I'd like to hear how you answer the question of what difference it has made."

"I can tell you in one sentence. Then I'll enlarge on that."

"And the sentence?"

"I'm now, at forty-five, almost grown up."

"OK. Spell that out."

Eric paused for a time. You could almost see the connections in his brain firing, organizing the concepts rationally and discreetly. Then: "First, I am now fully awake, and most of the time I'm fully aware. That is true in two ways. I am aware of nearly all that is going on with myself – sensations, physical action, feelings, interpretations of what I get from others, and what my intentions or wishes are in relation to all that. The other way in which I am aware is tuning in fully to others. I have learned how to listen, with my eyes as well as my ears. And I have also learned how to empathize, how to <u>be</u> with another, so that I sense in my body what is going on in theirs."

"That's quite a lot. You say you weren't aware when you began therapy?"

"Concerning myself, hardly at all. Concerning others, just enough to trigger habitual responses, which often served me very badly. Or worse, enough to either hide or to be very manipulative."

"OK, we are familiar with that. Second?"

"I have learned to be appropriately spontaneous."

"Enough of those doctoral words! Why the qualification about spontaneity?"

"I still have the ability to be a kid, an impish little kid. But only when it's OK to be a kid. At all other times, I will be responding as people generally require in order for them to be comfortable. Or at least I will do my best to be sensitive to where they are. But don't expect me to be perfect at that for quite a while."

"And third?"

"Thirdly, in almost any situation I can pretty much answer Siok Yim's question: 'Eric, what do you want?' I'm not saying I can do so with complete certainty, yet. I'm still bugged by some fear of any strong, impressive woman, and that confuses my reading of what I want in the relationship. But I am then aware of the fear problem, and if I give myself a chance, I can move towards asking for what I know will serve my best interests."

"And fourth?"

"And fourth, I can be angry, as a situation warrants it, and express that anger without feeling guilty in doing so. At the same time, I now always know what I'm angry about, rather than feeling angry for reasons unknown, at least to me. And by being honest with myself, I don't have a shit load of anger that I will unload anywhere, just to express it, even if it has nothing to do with the situation. You know; the way I always used to be."

"Any more?"

"Just one. I am not the center of the universe. The way that comes out is that I can now tell when a comment is really about me, from when it's not about me, but about the topic, or whatever."

"That has made a big difference to the way you react in committees," added Michael.

"I'm glad to hear that. Because I now see what an arse-hole I would often be because I always saw things as being about me – when most of the time people weren't referring to me at all."

"Any more?"

"No."

"Then a very earthy question I've been wanting to ask," and Michael paused

"Yes?"

"How are things with Frankie?"

"I knew you'd get around to asking that while we were up here. It's OK. To ask, I mean. I guess the relationship is OK, too. I won't say it's great. But it's improved out of sight. And I know I want my family. Frankie is part of that. As for sex, well, the less said the better. But I figure I can't have everything."

"What about Rani?"

"I didn't tell you? She married, six weeks ago. To a guy she's known for years."

"Wrong guy, is my judgment."

"C'est la vie," countered Eric, not wishing to go there. "Let's see whether the water is still warm enough for a swim." But even as they did so, he knew that he was still avoiding feelings, rather than living them.

### 

Gazing at the dying embers in the fire late that evening a long silence between Eric and his two closest male friends was broken by his question: "Guys, how come you're both so different from me?"

"What do you mean?" came almost in chorus.

"Well, to start with, you're comfortably married, and look like remaining that way. But it's more than that. You seem - I dunno, I guess - 'settled' would be one word for it."

Ahad's brow furrowed. He glanced at his friend as if to acknowledge his comment, then returned his gaze to the fire. But Michael was more inclined to talk. His teasing smile would not be repressed. Knowing he could get away with it he suggested: "I think you wonder what makes the two of us so stable in *our* marriages."

"Maybe," Eric conceded uncertainly.

"You may be right; we are both 'settled' as you call it," Michael admitted. "I think there are a number of reasons. For both of us religion is a factor. Come to think of it, neither of us asks a fraction of the number of questions that you ask. Nor are our lives half as busy as yours. You're never still."

"But why are you so 'still' as you put it?"

"You may not believe this, but deep down I'm never worried about tomorrow, whatever it may bring."

"You're not? Why not?"

"Because nothing can change what matters most to me. Those two things are givens in my life. I mean my religion and my relation with my wife."

"I had assumed they were. But how do they contribute to you being so 'still'?"

"I'd have thought that was obvious. Both things are completely beyond doubt. Not in a debating sense, no, but in the sense of trust. I simply take them as given. The result is this basically laid-back character you see before you."

"I have to admit I've never been willing to go there – with anyone, or anything. I've always had to get on with the next thing, or to live the next development. That's been exciting. It really has. Almost every day has been a blast – even the gray ones. I've lived them each to the full. But in the rush I've missed something. That 'stillness' I guess you're calling it."

There was a long silence before Eric continued: "I've missed out on what you Mike, seem to get from your religion. You don't seem to be driving – or driven – all the time. You have a quietness and an assurance which has always eluded me – except for the minutes just following orgasm. I really hate falling asleep at that time, because the peace will be gone when I wake up. For those moments the only thing that matters is that I'm loved. With all three of my real loves – Minah, Siok Yim and Rani – that happened. With each I could just *be* – in a state of perfect peace – for that time before sleep. Tomorrow didn't matter; it didn't even cross my mind. Each of them behaved the next morning like it still didn't matter – just so long as our love continued." The other two were silent, sensing that Eric was far away, in other places, with the women who had meant so much to him.

"But not so with me the next morning," he went on. "With me it was always another day, another set of plans, doing things, getting on with it. I look back at those relationships and wonder why I couldn't just 'be in the moment' for more than an hour. But I couldn't. I can't! Their love was wonderful – beyond all imagining – for an hour at a time. Well, for more than an hour. But there was always an afterwards! What I felt didn't last. It would keep coming back – stimulated by interests, or sex – but except maybe with Siok Yim, it didn't last for any twenty-four hours. I couldn't stand the pain of her absence, but that was other stuff."

Again he was gone from the room, and returned to admit with deep sorrow: "Now, these days, as I look back, I wonder whether I'm still missing something I could have had." The attention of both friends had turned from the fire. This was a more vulnerable Eric than they had known. He looked from one to the other, appreciating their connection. They respected his continued silence, all gazing at the few remaining embers until a very quiet voice whispered: "I've been a very slow learner."

# Chapter Thirty-Four

Eric's commitment felt total for a few months after his decision to preserve his family. Not only with the girls, but also with Frankie Eric found himself involved, empathetic and caring. The values placed upon social justice and its expression in political activism were supported and enriched by each other. When Eric came home elated about the success of their web page facilitating Friends Across Differences, Frankie did more than nod her support, she gave constructive comments and suggestions. When Frankie was inclined to give up on her dreams about the education of elementary school girls about love she found Eric giving her new energy and enthusiasm.

Nicole and Jennifer were developing into young women, a joy to both parents which they verbalized to each other frequently. The occasional sacrifice "for the family", whether of money or convenience, was undertaken as positively by him as by her. Frankie was more than delighted when Eric responded, "Of course we can find the extra for a much better piano teacher for Jen."

But after eight months Eric was finding it much more difficult to meet his own needs in the limited ways he had established. Memories of all three other women became part of most days, and were certainly vivid in the context of self-satisfaction. While he carefully avoided the temptations of other women, and there were many, their power to make him dissatisfied with his married life seemed to grow with each month.

While Frankie had been delighted with "the new Eric", something was missing. Yes, she now had a committed husband, who shared homemaking and parenting to the full. Yes, she could look to the future with renewed confidence that they would grow old together and enjoy grandchildren. They often jested about that with some wonder as they noted the girls' different development. Yes, they were doing things together in which both were deeply committed, thus making a bit of a difference in the world. But the kind of intimacy she had found creeping into her relationship at work with Gregory was not paralleled with Eric. That intimacy made her feel more connected to Greg than to the man she slept with. She and Greg seemed to 'just know' what each other was thinking. She could always rely on Greg to relax her anxieties. Eric exacerbated them.

It was Eric who first raised the matter. "Something is missing, isn't it?"

"What do you mean?" she began, as if to sideline his seriousness, then stopped herself from saying more. She agreed so strongly with that one declaration, but one look at her husband stopped the plaintive words that were rising in her throat. He had tried so hard this last year, and there wasn't a single thing about which she could find fault. Except one. But to Frankie that one seemed to be all.

Truth be known, her experience had lots of similarities to his. Her friendship with Greg had been as transforming as Eric's with Minah: she had experienced a depth of connection of which she had never dreamed. For Frankie and Greg that connection needed minimal physical expression. Looks were more important than touch, presence more important than talk. The level of mutual support had grown with each year of his wife's increasing debilitation, but without any reduction of his love for the woman dying a very prolonged death of multiple sclerosis. In fact, the very need to take care of others which had led Frankie to become a nurse found expression in taking care of Greg's wife.

"You're upset," she began again, in response to Eric.

Reaching out to take her hand he confessed: "There's an emptiness in our home, and between us, which troubles me. I'm not criticizing. I'm sure it's as much me as you. But how it gets to be that way is quite beyond me. We communicate – about small things and about what matters most deeply. Yet we don't connect."

She was nodding. But neither would add to that beginning: "in the way I have connected with . . ." Did each know how the other mentally ended that sentence? Who could tell? What was clear, to them and to the daughter Nicole who passed through the room, was the sadness which both found overwhelming. It was a pressure inside each. It was a pressure upon them from the total atmosphere which filled the room.

Suddenly, without intention, both were on their feet and in each other's arms, in tears. Then slowly, ever so slowly the pressure subsided. It lessened within, and as if it had all been focused into that one spontaneous hug, it disappeared from the room. Time had no meaning as each stood there, knowing that the surrounding arms said "I care more than words can express."

To both Frankie and Eric the release was beyond belief, yet so profound that after a long time both stepped back with the other's hands in theirs, and gave an enormous sigh. It was she who broke the silence: "I think we should separate for a while." Eric simply nodded. No more words were needed. No more would have meant anything.

### 

Life in the Johnson household was different now. The girls noticed the difference immediately, but neither made a single comment, or asked a single question. With their closest friends they sadly reported what their intuition told them to be certain: "My folks are going to separate. It's so sad, but so are they, and much as they care about each other there is no real life in either of them. In fact, I can hardly remember a time when Dad wasn't full of life; but that's how he is now, all the time. And as for Mum, well she spends less and less time at home, seems to be always at the school, and looks happiest as she drives off every morning."

For both Eric and Frankie the months passed that way until the sabbatical he had arranged at Seattle University. There he would teach two graduate seminars while doing the final editing of his book <u>The Fulbright Legacy</u>, the long postponed publication based on his dissertation so many years back, but still of real interest to a wide readership within the new international scene of 'globalization'.

### 

That spring he received a call at the office: "This is Kathy Chang, Siok Yim's friend," came a now unfamiliar voice.

With deep uncertainty Eric simply murmured, "Yes?"

"How are you?" persevered his well-mannered caller.

Recovering somewhat he replied: "I'm very well thanks. And what about you?"

"I'm also fine. I'm wondering if you could stop by for coffee sometime soon."

With deepening puzzlement he acceded, and a time was made.

### ###

"Come in, Eric!" She welcomed him at her front porch. "You look great. You haven't changed one bit these (What is it?) thirteen years."

"Nor have you," he responded gallantly, then added, "but the part you can't see has changed a lot". Then, responding to her raised eyebrows he added, "I've had a major trip with a therapist."

"I'd like very much to hear about it," she offered, pouring a cup from the thermos of coffee on the square table he recalled having pushed aside one night so long ago. It was "their spot", where he and Siok Yim had made love then gazed up through the skylight at the stars. For moments he was overpowered with memory – of the effect her presence had upon him, and of what he had done to be free of that beauty which also bedeviled him. As if awakening from a trance he gave Kathy his attention, for which she had been patiently waiting out of respect for what was obviously a difficult recollection.

He realized she was speaking: "But first, there's some news I asked you here to share." Because he said nothing, she continued: "I asked you here because I did not want to tell you on the phone." Her voice had gone down to a level where it was now husky: "Siok Yim is dead. She died three weeks ago - of cancer. It was a long battle - sixteen years."

"You mean?"

"Yes. She had a lumpectomy eighteen months before you first met."

"But she never told me," came as the only words he could produce in an attempt to hide the tears that could no longer be restrained.

"I know. That was Siok Yim."

"But . . ." He wanted to say so much – to her closest friend as a kind of surrogate - but the words wouldn't come.

391

"She did get your letter." He breathed a sigh of relief. "It made her so happy. But it threw her into a quandary. She wrote me about what to do. Then the third remission came to an abrupt end and all her energies went elsewhere – until a few weeks before she died. I spoke to her on the phone then. She asked me to tell you she loved you as always, that nothing had changed, that she lived in grateful joy for what you two had together."

This was too much for Eric. Face buried in his hands, his whole strong body was shaken with sobs. Then silence filled the room, of the kind which is the sound of grief beyond words. Eventually he looked up at Kathy and saw that she too was in tears. They arose as one, finding in each other's arms some of the solace each sought.

His were the first words spoken: "I hurt her so much." The responsive nod was not condemnation, but empathy.

A few minutes went by in silent coffee drinking. Then Kathy asked: "I would very much like to hear about the change you mentioned in the non-visible part of Eric Johnson."

"Kathy, that all seems so unimportant, compared with . . ." and again, he could not finish.

He took the proffered Kleenex, blew his nose, wiped his eyes, and began: "If I were to meet her for the first time now, it would all be so different. If early on she were to ask: 'Eric, what do you want?' I would now answer: 'To explore the overwhelming feeling I have with you. It scares me, it awes me, and I want to live it, and find out if it is as important as I suspect.'"

"I have been told that you said nothing like that."

"Nothing at all. What an ass-hole! No! That's not fair to the guy I was then. Yes, I acted the ass-hole. But I was such a kid, even at thirty, confronted by the most remarkable person I had ever met. I was scared and confused and swept away, all at once. I had no idea what I wanted. Not really. Not about life, or about her."

"That has all changed?"

"Largely. My buddies say I'm still incorrigible, and I do still get into my share of trouble. But I know myself so much better now. More important, I relate to others' wants and signals, rather than simply pushing from desires inside me, regardless of the wishes or reactions of anyone else."

"If there is a heaven, I'm sure that's where she is. And as you say that, I can feel the glow that comes from her. She knew, yes, Eric, she KNEW the potential towards which I hear you moving."

It seemed there was little point in more talk. But he stayed for a long time, the last part spent listening to what they both knew to be one of her favorite concertos. "I'll be in touch," was her promise, accompanied by the warmest of bear-hugs as he took his leave.

The Eric she had just met was not the man she recalled from thirteen years back. But that was history, no matter how cherished. He was indeed what Siok Yim had seen him to be. It was the future which mattered most. She could now plan how she would honor her friend's most important final wishes, about Siok Yim's third and youngest child. Yes, she would still be Edward's legal guardian, welcoming him into her single life with wide arms, his "Auntie Kathy", when he stepped off the plane a week hence. And now, given her judgment of the man with whom she had just cried, she would also strategize the best way for Edward to come to know one he had never met, as "Dad". A big load had suddenly gone: all these years had made a fine man out of that immature person her friend had adored.

### 

"Have you read that article of Huntington's, Michael?" Eric inquired one morning over office coffee.

"I only skimmed it. I hear they are talking about nothing else at the State Department. Would you mind stating your understanding of his basic idea, so I can be sure I'm on the same wave-length."

"His view is that the big differences between the peoples of the world will not go away for generations. The ways they think and act will *remain* different. That throws a spanner in the works of those who dream of one cooperative human family, in which we will all have grown alike. He believes that a continuing tension between clans is a truer expectation than a family of humankind."

"That idea doesn't suit a dreamer like you, or me, does it?"

"No. It throws into serious doubt lots of my dreams about international understanding, peace, and cooperation. My only consolation is that it also throws into doubt all that "U.S. Imperialism" which has galled me ever since I really listened to Minah."

"What do you mean, 'U.S. imperialism'?"

"You know: We'll give them a taste of democratic government and free market economics and they'll see the light, thank us, and become just like us. Then we'll have the same interests and values, and become brothers in consumption."

"Now Eric! You exaggerate."

"No I don't. I'm confessing. That is what McArthur tried to do in Japan. That is what I had heard in Fulbright's rhetoric. It is what I have worked for in the teaching of social studies, and in that committee of Rani's, and in dozens of other things I have worked at here, with other colleges, and even internationally."

"It's what we accomplished with the Marshall Plan in Europe. That was a resounding success. So why buy Huntington's skepticism about the future?"

"Two reasons. But first let me respond to your claim that the success of the Marshall Plan in Europe after WW II proves that 'they' can become like us, politically and economically. In Huntington's view, we and the Europeans are all part of Western Christendom. We may not all be formally believers in Jesus Christ, but we have the same basic values, which stem from two thousand years of that tradition. So for the Germans to move from fascism to democracy was no great jump. And so on."

"OK. That makes sense. So what are your reasons for buying Huntington's view that we will not easily or for a long, long time become one harmonious human family?"

"First, note how the behavior of Muslims particularly suggests that although they might start to look like us, they will remain very different. The revival of Islamic thought in Iran is the best example of that. Remember how urbane the upper and even middle class were during the time of Shah Pavlavi in the early eighties?"

"Agreed, and Ahad is a perfect example."

"The second reason is a very important study of all the IBM managers, world-wide, by a Dutchman named Hofstede."

394

"Why? And what is so important about him in this business?"

"Simply this. All IBM's staff, in any country, get their jobs because they fit our American stereotype of middle or upper-level staff. They exhibit the same behavior, can operate in the same way, regardless of their birth culture."

"Of course, IBM would be crazy to employ people who did not fit."

"Absolutely. And that's what makes his findings so convincing. They all retain the values of the culture from which they came. Changes on the outside are absolutely no indication of what they value. He measured scores on four values, and on all four the IBM employees, thousands of them worldwide, were found to retain the values of he culture in which they were born."

"OK. So what?"

"Just this, and let me do it with an example. A Muslim will never put individual judgment into the conversation if the Koran contains a relevant teaching about the Will of Allah. That is true, even of a Muslim American citizen and successful professor, like Ahad. So when we and they get into a conflict of interests where it's our individual freedom versus their obedience to God, there will never be a compromise."

"I guess that's right."

"It certainly is!" Eric underlined the conclusion. He did so remembering not only the way this conflict had ended his relationship with Minah, but also how it had played out in Ahad's unplanned fathering of the child whose mother he then married, causing so much pain for so many who loved each of them.

Michael was silent for a time, then: "Do you realize that you, personally, have a third argument in support of his theory? Your women! Yes, even Rani. From what you've shared that is obvious. At least it is to me."

"How?" asked the now less-confident proponent of Huntington's argument.

"From what you shared I heard that in the case of Minah, of Siok Yim and of Rani, you eventually reached a point where one of their core values came up against one of your core values."

395

"That was true. Yes, in each case."

"And in each case you could not, or perhaps I should say you would not reach a compromise."

There was silence, and a despondent look on his friends' face, as he dropped his voice to end his point: "And so each wonderful relationship came to an end."

### 

"Eric," came the voice on his office phone, "How are you?"

"I'm well! Sorry! That's a stupid response. I have felt very, very sad these last few days, since we talked. But thanks Kathy, for calling to ask."

"Eric. I know it will surprise you to hear that I have felt the opposite. I know that makes little sense from your position. But mine's different. You see, and this is my reason for calling, the conversation with you has completely changed my expectations."

Eric was never one to be overly patient, and although she was really in mid-sentence, he had to ask: "What expectations?"

"My expectations of what it will mean to be guardian and surrogate mother to Siok Yim's son."

"Her son? But what about her daughter? But . . . I don't understand. Those two must be well in their twenties by now." He was confused, spluttering.

"She had another son. Yours."

Eric felt the wind knocked out of him. He was speechless. Usually able to come back quickly in any conversation, this time he could not. He recalled his cruel letter arguing that she must abort 'their child'. Recollection of those words caused a load of guilt to surface; his later apology still seemed unbearably inadequate. He also remembered that when he had asked her about the abortion she had given no definitive answer, but had evaded his question.

"I can guess this is a shock," came the voice in his ear, "but I couldn't say anything the other day – not until I had thought through all the implications. The changes which I heard about and the different quality there is about you now – they forced me to re-think everything. So I said nothing. Of course he must be fully your son, in practice as he is in blood. I can imagine that makes for complications. We will have to work out what is best for everyone – your wife, daughters, Edward (that's the name she gave him), you and, I suppose, myself."

"'Shock' is an understatement. I don't know what to say." His mind was racing: his delayed guilt surrounding Frankie's still-born son joined with his sense of guilt and stupidity in urging Edward's abortion. "I don't know what to say." he stumbled, "But I do know that I'm glad." She honored the silence which followed. Then: "Does he know who his father is? Will he be visiting here any time soon?"

"That all sounds like the old Eric! A dozen things at once!" he heard her chuckle on the other end of the line.

"Well I want to know, and I can't wait. Does he know about me?"

"I'm surprised that you need to ask, given how Siok Yim's straightforwardness impressed you. Of course she told him, when he was quite young. She had to when he was four, because he asked why he looked 'different'. She also told him that his father lived in the U.S. but that neither of them could see him, because doing so would hurt a lot of people. As for visiting here: he arrives tomorrow to live with me permanently."

"You're kidding?"

"Not about something so important."

"Well, when am I going to see him?"

"I've been wondering about that. What do you think about the idea of me saying, the second day he is here, that you know he is here, want to meet him, and thought the most comfortable way might be for the two of you to get together for a game of tennis? I know that he takes after his mother in both his love of the game and his competence. I saw them play in Taiwan when he was only twelve, and he was good."

"You're brilliant! That would avoid all kinds of awkwardness – on both our parts. Maybe a mother could sit down with a daughter in a similar situation and just talk, but not guys. You're suggesting the day after tomorrow - Thursday?"

397

"I had Friday in mind. He'll need Thursday to sleep off the trip- and to get ready to beat you."

### ###

Eric acknowledged the need to break the news to his family, but procrastinated on that issue. He spent the following two days in a daze. They were spent in endless repetitions of 'I have a son,' accompanied by images of that son's mother. The deep warmth she had always brought to his whole body seemed to have returned. Luxuriating in and almost anaesthetized by it, his wife, daughters and colleagues found that he failed to hear their questions.

The evening before he was to meet Edward such indulgence gave way to another set of thoughts and feelings. Yes, he told himself, I am so glad Siok Yim kept our son. But now I have to be his father. I have slowly learned to father daughters; but now a son? And a son fourteen years old? He looked at the image in the mirror: how would Edward see him? He knew that the images communicated by his mother would have been positive, but . . ., there was the undeniable fact that they had never met. Would Edward be wondering how his father could justify such an inexcusable fact no matter what his mother had said? Such thoughts gave way to doubts about himself: Will he find me lacking? Can I be adequate? Do I look like the kind of man he wants to become? Maybe he wants to be like his step-father? But I can't let my feelings and fears dominate. And so on, and on . . . .until . . .

An extremely nervous father rang the buzzer at Kathy's house. Heart pounding, stomach churning, he wiped the sweat off his hands for the second time since parking the car, held them together behind his back, then at his sides, then in his pockets, and again at his back as the door opened.

Behind a radiant Kathy stood a reserved, polished, strongly erect young Eurasian. None could have doubted that two races were joined in this youth – the facial structures said it all, and Eric knew at once that such would have caused a child of four to ask why. It seemed natural to give Kathy a warm hug before she stepped aside to allow the males to be face to face. Eric had debated with himself how to meet his son: whether to hug, shake hands or not touch, what his first words should be, and had come to no conclusion. Now the found himself uttering the words of self introduction: "Hello! I'm your father," and offering his hand.

The warm, strong shake which responded was accompanied with the simple words: "I'm Edward Wong."

The two seemed quite unaware of Kathy beaming at them  They looked long and hard at each other's face, then, quietly, slowly, both started to smile, from the inside out. With all of Eric's being he wanted to enfold him strongly and say the words which seemed to well up from his depths: 'my son'. But his emotions were matched by his empathetic sense of this young man's being in that moment. It seemed both needed to keep the hand grasp until Kathy offered: "There's a nice cold drink for you guys before you go off. Let's sit down just for five minutes."

The drive to the courts was brief; the conversation predictable, mannered, but comfortable. On the court it became another story; or we should say two stories. After his gracious "You serve first!" Eric found himself facing an earnest young man who preceded his serve with bounces of the ball which warned him that the service might be much more than he had bargained to receive from one a third of his age. It was – and more. Edward served as well as his father, and held his service for two games. Eric had done the same, finding the son as good as his mother had been. This was serious business, and it had become clear, not only that Edward wanted to win, but that Eric felt challenged in a way he did not like.

Edward bounced the ball a few times in anticipation of his first serve in the fifth game, threw the ball up, and swung. Eric also swung – and heard the ball hit the fence behind him. The ball had been so fast that he had missed completely. "My Mum said she sometimes had a hole in her racket," came from the other side of the net. Eric stood quite still, looked at his son, and burst into laughter.

"She would!" He had to reply, "But never when she played me."

Edward not only smiled at that, he started to giggle, but then joined his father in a hearty laugh. Father and son had met.

# Chapter Thirty-Five

In early July Eric found an apartment on Seattle's Capitol Hill. It was the third floor of one of that area's famous houses built during the Arts and Crafts Movement. His travels into newer parts of the country with burgeoning populations had made him distasteful of all houses called "modern." This child of Boston brownstones felt deprived and almost revolted at the sight of any dwelling stripped to the bones in its functionality. So when he visited and reviewed areas within ten miles of the Seattle University campus he fell in love with the houses which had been produced by a desire to revive craftsmanship as a reaction to industrialization at the end of the nineteenth century. The houses were usually large, with no expense spared to elaborate the forms of projecting rafters and the fretted balustrades of wooden verandahs. Enormous windows allowed the passers-by to share a little of equally gracious interiors, to which one gained access through richly carved doors holding individually designed stained glass panels. To find a short-term rental of the third floor of one such building gave him just the lift he needed at this time in his life.

But it was a new life. Even if only temporary, it held a sense of freedom which was as invigorating as it was new. In the second week, he realized with much surprise that he had never (not since birth) lived completely alone. It was wonderful. Whenever he felt like it, he could wander around the Capital Hill area where its grand old trees made a magical tunnel of each roadway. He ate when he felt like doing so - sometimes at one of the numerous restaurants within fifteen minutes walk, often from his own stove. When he needed the company of Nicole,

Michael or Ahad a phone call met most of his hunger. And not having to think about the convenience of a soul: what freedom!

Seattle does admit to lots of rain, but the fortunate arrivals by air are treated to a clear view of Mount Rainier. For a hiker like Eric its pictures had long been a temptation. Now he could walk, scramble or climb its slopes, glaciers and peaks to the limit of his abilities, for it is within sight and two hours drive from downtown. From his own tiny balcony just under the peak of a gable whose every rafter had been meticulously carved, on a fair day he could even catch a glimpse through the branches of a giant elm.

In a fresh, unencumbered environment his editor's demands were easily and quickly accommodated, with publication slated for the beginning of the New Year. The graduate students who filled the fifteen places around the seminar room were of the standard which drew the best from him, providing all the rewards which had drawn him into the teaching profession. "This is near to heaven" he told Michael during one September call.

That same month found him exploring what to him was the farther side of Rainier. Green still predominated "down below" at sea level in Seattle, but up here at six thousand feet the area aptly named Paradise proclaimed in Technicolor that it was indeed Fall. Its glory swept Eric into a state where he felt he had to write about it. But every turn gave new views, every rest stop proved to be inhabited by creatures small or large which sought his friendship. Consequently the writing about that first day in Paradise was not to be done until after he had skied these same slopes during a visit by his daughter at Thanksgiving.

I went to The Mountain expecting; But was doubly surprised.
I found myself – I lost myself – I found myself again.

It was not the white giant, never whiter, never clearer,
Its three glistening south-side glaciers ending just above me in cliffs of ice.
It was not the peaks, the familiar ridge trail,
the vistas across endless lower ridges to two other volcanoes.
It was not that Ridgeline Trail itself
With its overview of valleys on every side, below every slope
Not even the stiff climb at six thousand feet could grasp me

It was Fall on The Mountain – chiefly the huckleberries.
Crest vied for attention with crest – of shrubs, not mountains.
Brilliance contended with hue – from puce through vermilion to orange.
Variations in shade revealed the valley's sculpture,
Following the shoulders between rivulets and streams,
Dabs of hot lime shrubs for contrast, and squat, stunted, deepest green conifers.
Slowly the background registers – such slender tall penises
Worth only a moment's attention.

The screaming demands of the huckleberries
Are only silenced when from one ridge
My eye follows ribbons of their brilliance.
Down a dozen ridges for a thousand feet
Where they disappear into a dark central canyon.
I am lost - fascinated, absorbed, overwhelmed, and engulfed.
Yet my oneness remains mine.
Even during these moments – some ninety minutes plus
I am one with it all.

And now – have I climbed another thousand feet?
The switchback descent lies below
As gloriously rainbowed as the rest
But come s a memory – then a vision
A blonde of life-long fantasy
In scant attire with gorgeous body
Effortlessly striding to meet me.

The same slopes, now wintered white
Colors gone 'neath thousand inch snow
Smoothed undulations seduce our skis
Curves do their own caressing.
What matter if mismatched
And I end face down in perfect whiteness?
It's all part of paradise.

Early December brought a call from Frankie, a heads-up that the coming week's mail would bring her formal filing for a divorce. Eric was neither surprised nor upset. Soon after arriving here he had faced with fresh honesty the question: Do I want to spend the rest of my life with

Frankie? For her to initiate permanent separation was no surprise, and he had to confess it came somewhat as a relief.

The decision had come to Frankie herself as much more of a surprise. Only when Greg had proposed to her and rejected her reaction "But I'm married!' had she faced the depth of her feelings for him, and the shell-like qualities of her marriage with Eric. That marriage had been a very comfortable shell for two periods – the time leading up to the twins' births, and the nine months after Eric's heavy therapy. It had been a shell which offered protection even as it shut out a whole set of emotions. In the shell those emotions had not been acknowledged, so she had remained unaware of what their free expression would do to her, and for her. But without Eric's presence, and with the impetus of Greg's invitation, a new world had opened up. When Christine asked "How come you're so alive these days?" she had verbalized the answer which arose from her deeps: "For the first time in my life I am loved the way I was meant to be loved."

Divorce commended itself to Eric for a single reason as negative as Frankie's was positive - an end to a pattern of sexual frustration both debilitating and absurd. He had voiced his feelings about their relative sexual appetites, and she had tried. But each time, within days each one's old behaviors had reasserted themselves. Frankie's feelings were clear and consistent. For Eric, the scenario was all too predictable. Every few days he would succumb to his unmet needs. First came the thought: a friendly cuddle, nothing more. Then the question: where do you put your hand, after your arm goes around her and you conform your body to her backside? When slight finger movements on her breast bring no complaint they become stronger. "Stop it; I want to get some sleep" would then break the silence. Eventually he would turn away, more aroused, quite angry, and wrapping himself around a pillow, try to imagine it to be Rani. Fortunately, he would then tell himself, I'll have half an hour in bed after she gets up for work.

He had long since ceased to feel any guilt about his sexual needs. It was hard to separate them from the satisfaction of touch in asexual ways which had become part of the joy he found in the presence of any of 'his women'. But the anger did worry him, and he knew that would have continued and increased had they remained together. And the girls would have found more and more reasons to be 'off with their friends'. Life alone was such an improvement. And Nicole was due out for a four-day visit this Thursday.

### ###

"Come on Dad," Nicole whispered as she led Eric up the two steps into the small Eastern Orthodox chapel. "They won't mind. They just smiled gently at me when Ilga brought me here."

Entering from a dark outer world the interior seemed ablaze, yet without the use of electricity. There must have been hundreds of candles, set in six groups where, even as he watched, one more of the faithful approached, crossed himself, kissed an icon near the group of candles, and placed his offering of light with the others. The wick did not catch fire when first touched to the flame, seemed hesitant to give up its life to help the lighting of this tiny space. But in another instant two flames existed where there had been one, then separated as the devotee placed his apart, yet as a further contribution to the light which disclosed to Eric the glory of this place which his daughter had described as 'really holy'.

Nicole's conversion at camp four years earlier had not lasted long, and its influence upon him died as quickly. But today, when this young woman who meant the world to him had issued the invite/suggestion/command his face lit up as she said "I think you might find something special in this place." He did.

The space was intimate – no chance for individualism here – you could not avoid feeling you were in a group. Yet the need to move sideways into a standing space required neither words nor action: a part of the body of worshippers simply opened up as she, then he joined the sixty or so who quietly stood for most of the next two hours. The few seats were occupied by the more infirm, but even they stood up for lengthy periods throughout the service. People looked at him with soft eyes, then turned into their own experience, and Eric felt carried into that experience without understanding a word of what was being chanted by a priest or sung by a magnificent but invisible choir.

As the minutes ticked by Eric found himself looking around, and up. The structure was a simple Greek cross in plan, the arms short, the one by which he had entered acting as a vestibule of a kind, the one opposite to it being closed off by what he learned was called a proscenium. But the structure only became apparent after a veritable feast of images. Every surface was covered with them, most representing saints and apostles, but overhead, as in the Michelangelo frescoes in the Sistine Chapel, a vision of the Creator, breathing life into humankind. The importance and veneration accorded to the attached images throughout was accentuated by ornate gilt framing. The screen between the altar and the people presented dozens of images, three of which Eric slowly realized hid the fact that they were doors - which would open from time to time to give glimpses of what occurred in the holiest part of the building.

Gazing up and around, Eric realized he was inside a miniaturized version of the world's most famous Byzantine church, Hagia Sophia, in Istanbul. Like this, that building reared upwards on a series of arches and domes, but for twenty stories. Sadly, when he had visited it when returning from Singapore the surfaces displayed no images; all had been painted over by members of a faith who believed all representations of living creatures to be a form of idolatry. Now he found himself somehow transported back there, imagining every surface as richly decorated as these in this small replica.

When words are unavailable and no interpretation is given, the mind opens up to vistas unknown. It was so with Eric. Priestly perambulations, endless incense, listening without understanding, and responding to repetitious yet simple melodious chanting gave way more and more to a focus on people. All were glimpsed only by moving slightly: the ten-year-old big sister holding the hand of a three-year-old brother, as they walked across the small empty center space to other relatives; the earnest, aged woman, standing for a half-hour until she could no longer avoid sitting down; the clean, upright young man, looking so different from the driven aggressiveness of similar-aged men in any city street.

But most of all, his attention was caught by one young woman. Repeatedly he found himself drawn to her world, as it expressed itself on her face. In her early twenties, a study in gray, from scarf to the hem of her ankle-length skirt, she seemed to him the classic Slav. Sometimes her gaze followed the officiants, sometimes the family members by her side, but most of the time her eyes seemed to be looking at something afar, made clearer by almost closing them. A strong aquiline nose was barely noticeable above a generous, sensuous mouth which was wholly engaged in mouthing the words said by the officiant or sung by the choir; she seemed to know them by heart.

When she turned for a moment Eric noted the fullness of her young body, found himself tempted to mentally undress her, but was drawn back to her face. What was her world? What was it that had brought her to apparent rote memorization of a two-hour liturgy? What gave her face such a combination of peace and potential pain, a look ethereal yet earth-bound? He felt a hand slipped into his and as his glance met his daughter's something passed between them. A deep sigh welled up from within. A tear trickled down his cheek. She squeezed his hand so that he had to look into her eyes. They nodded, almost in unison.

As they walked to their car the thought came to him: Perhaps this is comprehension which is beyond conception, which doesn't need words. "I'm so glad I came," was the way that got expressed to Nicole. He wasn't even surprised, and certainly not about to counter her response: "I knew you would be. I love you, Dad."

Later, Eric found himself wondering about the centrality in his life of ideas, and of the words about them. All those elemental formulations! He had lived and excelled around the maxim: I think; therefore I am. But underlying all his thinking, his being *was*. And in that service, something *was*, without his being able to conceive or name it. There he had a sense of knowing something which he had always known, long before all that formal learning which rewarded him with a Ph D., all written in the face of the young woman in gray, and in the touch of a daughter's hand. Somehow, he told himself, my sense of values will never be the same again.

### 

Eric's evening experience in the chapel did not stand alone. Such moments occurred in a number of settings, quite different from each other. It did not seem necessary that the setting be unusual or exotic. Sometimes a similar experience occurred while going about his daily routine, when every stranger gave him a smile or a word during the three hours one morning it took to visit a supermarket, a dry cleaners and the gym. He had a similar experience twice while interacting with a class of sixteen graduate students. The realization grew that these moments had much in common with isolated times with nature and with his past loves. However, nowadays these came with greater frequency, often not requiring any special stimulus. Past reading suggested such experiences had been called severally – self-realization, peak experiences, self-actualization and self-fulfillment. Eric preferred to say that on such occasions, or days, he was "fully alive".

One "fully alive" experience stood out because of its hilarity - with two strangers on a popular trail high above tree-line on Mount Rainier. It was high summer, but snow still covered much of the popular trail up which the walkers, both neophytes and the accomplished mountain types slid, slipped and struggled, but were encouraged by the numberless panoramas which opened out differently with each steep rise or sudden bend around a rocky outcrop.

Surmounting one such steep pinch Eric came to an unexpected halt because, just ten paces ahead a woman was intent upon photographing a huge hoary marmot. This creature, lazy lover of high mountain summer sun and the roots that grow during his short months of waking, was the size of an average dog. Julie, the photographer was intent upon getting a picture of something she had never known to exist. At a distance of only six paces she was still not satisfied, so was inching closer each time the creature lowered its head and burrowed deep into the snow. Whenever it raised its head and reared up on its hind legs she would freeze, lest she scare the animal off. But twice it caught her movement, and seemed unperturbed. Each time it looked up it would stand full height on hind legs and stare at her as if to say: I'm smiling, click it and leave me to lunch. But each click tempted her to close in for better and better shots, which only ended with the whir of the camera's automatic re-wind device.

Conversation revealed that she and her girl friend were from New Zealand, were on the mountain for the first time, and were completely enthralled by it. Their approach to each challenge was a joke, their response to any failure a warm smile of encouragement, and Eric found himself a natural part of a warm, and very jolly threesome. Talk, between gasps for breath, was of this and that, of no real import except to communicate: "I'm glad you're in my life, here, today." No one said it; all felt it, even with a slide backwards on the icy trail.

When the trail leveled off somewhat they had breath to spare. Eric began to sing quietly: "I love to go a wandering, along the mountain track, and as I go, I love to sing, my knapsack on my back" – by which time it had become a vocal trio as they shouted the chorus – "Val de ri, val de ra, val de re, val de ra, ha ha ha haaa, val de re, val de ra, val de ra ha ha ha ha."

"How did you learn that?" came a surprised query.

"As a kid, camping, with the scouts!" came with exuberant smiles, as of remembered joy. With minimal pause the song recommenced, with the three swinging along at a great pace. The mountain seemed to be singing with them. They were high, with only the marmot, the mountain, the

407

sky and each other to stimulate them. A glow would reach out from one to another, be passed on, and return tenfold. Conversation became half speech, half laughter, and half song, so filled with energy were these three, so filled with all, and with each other.

Without announcement, with tentative voice and slightly flat, Julie began to sing: "She'll be coming round the mountain." The "Toot! Toot!" rang from crag to crag. The "Whoa back!" was even loader, while the "scratch! scratch!" after the flannel pajamas verse must have been approaching the noise level which can cause an avalanche, when around the corner came a young woman, resolute of stride and sour of countenance. As the first two stood aside to allow her to pass on this narrow section their warm greetings were met with stony silence. At Eric, the third, this withdrawn lady muttered, "Don't people know that some people come up here for the silence?" and was quickly gone.

"How sad!" was Julie's comment.

"Yes," said her pal, "She looks as if her world is ending. She is quite unaware of what a glorious place this is - of the joy which is so available. How very sad."

That small shadow behind them, the singing began once more, and every other hiker seemed buoyed by a brief encounter with the sight and sound of this crazy, riotous trio. Eventually, obligations to others less energetic waiting below forced them to split up the combination. But even the parting was a celebration – of an exuberant meeting, and of moments which felt as if they were 'out of time'.

Eric wondered why the event, and its feelings, returned again and again; eventually he knew they would never be forgotten - they were more moments of being fully alive. He also began to question their relation to the concept of intimacy, the shared aliveness he had known with daughters, lovers, and colleagues when they were intensely involved in the same thing, entranced by similar feelings. How strange, he found himself asking, that we should treat the activities in these moments - which would for some have to include religion, and which certainly included sex - as discrete categories, supposedly unrelated?

### 

Days at the university were rich and full. Bright, engaged students visited his office. Lunches involved faculty from a range of disciplines so that the conversations opened up new vistas. Best of all, someone from nearby offices would always be dropping by to chat, so that he felt more "at home" every day. But after a few weeks the evenings and week-ends became more difficult.

At first the times alone in his small apartment had been a new luxury – no child or spouse making demands, ever. Yes, some of the girls' need had been stimulating, their satisfaction a privilege. Meeting their needs made him feel a good father. He could choose his own TV program, listen to his choice of music, and read without interruption if he wanted to. If he felt like going somewhere for the evening he would call to find company, or just go alone. It was a bit of a downer when he wanted someone to accompany him and could find no companion, but so what?

But with time Eric found himself alone at a new level, in a new way. New thoughts about human contact arose. Reviews of his relationships began, refusing to depart. He was glad to be alone, but now asked the question: how alone have I been all my life? Sure, I have always *done* things with others. Traveling to the Southwest with Siok Yim certainly was a high. For all its frustrations, work on Rani's committee was great. Could I have asked for better buddies than Michael and Ahad? And wasn't that day on Rainier wonderful? Yet none of those memories - those images and thoughts - gives me *now* the feelings that I had then. Now I am alone in a more ultimate way than I have ever been.

But, he found his ever explorative brain asking, Maybe I was alone even then? Surely life is easier, more manageable here, alone. If so, why do I want company? If I had even the best company I've ever known, would it feel the way I want more than anything else – not to be alone? Which is more true: 'No man is an island' or 'Ultimately we are all alone'? For all that Minah, Siok Yim and Rani meant to me, there was finally a gulf between us which I could not cross: each became unreachable. Or did I become unreachable to each of them?

I hate to admit that life seems more manageable, here alone. I don't like it, but . . . I thought sex would overcome the separateness – but it didn't. I have tried, really tried to understand what has been going on all my adult years. All I have are hints; no more. I've conjured up ideas, theories about life, plans of what to do – because a man must. So what? At thirty-five they were plans for my department's curriculum; now they are proposals on a global scale. But people matter more to me more than those concerns.

409

With people I have seen hints of what really living means. With women there were moments when I had that feeling of connecting at the deepest level - with lovers, daughter, mother-in-law, even on occasions with my wife. With the first there was lots of intimacy, albeit between us who were finally acknowledged to be alien.

During one such reverie feeling deeply depressed he found himself saying: You ARE always alone anyhow, so learn to live with it! Maybe life is easier that way. He couldn't believe the thought which came up. Maybe, (who knows?) that's what happens in Altzheimers – older folks simply retreat into a more manageable world. Could it be a blessing rather than a disease? Wow? He asked himself. Have I felt that much alone in life? Has it been that hard to feel fully known?

On less pessimistic days his conclusion was this: The abiding solace and connection comes with my buddies. Those connections don't rise to level of the hints of complete one-ness I get from the women relationships. The buddy connections seem to be restricted to concepts and verbiage. But my buddy connections are symbols – of an abiding brotherhood, which transcend aloneness, even if only a little bit.

# Chapter Thirty-Six

Eric was introduced as the plenary speaker of the conference, with its publication-related title "The Legacy of Senator William Fulbright." After acknowledging the honor, and his pleasure at the opportunity of speaking to the group, Eric began:

Do you want to live **in** The Garden of Eden or **outside** it with a nature red in tooth and claw? Bill Fulbright was a great American who labored life-long to keep the garden option open to every one of the six billions who make up humankind. That is the legacy of Senator J. William Fulbright. For the next thirty or forty minutes I want to share with you what I believe it means for us to preserve that legacy at the close of the twentieth century and into the next.

In 1945, a month after Nagasaki and Hiroshima, the freshman US Senator from Arkansas introduced a bill to set up a program for the international exchange of professors and students. Many of you in this audience have, like me, benefited from his vision. He believed "that the major reason why people are willing to wage war against another people is that they don't understand the other culture or even think of the others as real human beings. It is easy for people to fight if they think all the Chinese are 'cruel' or all the Russians are 'evil'," he said. Fulbright believed that by living in another country we would come to understand them, and thus reduce the chance of new wars. This vision of world peace through international exchange and understanding became the rationale and the mantra of hundreds of programs involving persons of every age, and every ability – today ranging from Four H Exchanges to Elder Hostels.

Two assumptions underlay Bill Fulbright's plan, both of which are in question today. First, and still a matter of opinion, was the assumption that understanding of others is the key to peace. But more significant was his assumption about the parties who might get into conflict: he saw the root issue to be the clash of nations, as their particular interests came into conflict. But **now** (as we move beyond the era of nation states) a handful of much larger groups are what we must worry about. These are what Samuel Huntington, director of Harvard's Institute for Strategic Studies, refers to as 'civilizations'. He has shown that eight 'civilizations' (he also calls them 'cultural identities') are "shaping the patterns of cohesion, disintegration and conflict in the post-Cold-War world." He says that the consequence of this global situation is that, for the foreseeable future, peace "depends on world leaders accepting and cooperating to maintain the **multi**civilizational character of global politics."

I won't tempt you to go down the alley of arguing whether there are six, ten or twelve such civilizations. I would simply ask you to think about the four most obvious, each of which numbers roughly one fifth of the human race – Western Christendom, Islam, India and China. Later we will take a glimpse at the kind of clashes we Westerners might have with the other three, and what it might mean for us to accept and cooperate to maintain the multicivilizational character of the globe.

But first, a fuller picture of what Huntington predicts, and why he is on firm ground in his claim that this is the way it will be **at least for the lifetime of all of us in this place.** He says that for every one of the six billion of us living at this moment, the clash of civilizations will be a major factor in growing up, finding a job, getting married, having kids, and enjoying our golden years. How? And what will it look like? What will it feel like to the average Jane or Joe? What will it be like if the other eighty percent of the human race is in the hair of our kind for the foreseeable future - just as Iran, and many of its brother Islamic nations have been in our hair for the last twenty years?

He is saying that the spread of human rights and pluralism, and their expression in democracy and freedom, and even the spread of free market capitalism will have to **coexist** beside cultures and groups of nations whose basic values are antagonistic to some we cherish most dearly. He is saying that such differences will be at the heart of conflicts, rather than national or ideological concerns. And, he insists, such differences won't go away any time soon.

To global idealists like me (who believed that the spread of our enlightened ways was inevitable, even if it demanded patience) these predictions seemed quite unacceptable! And what of our policies requiring human rights "improvements" as a condition for financial aid or acceptance into the league of "civilized" nations? If Huntington is right, then such pressures are at best counterproductive, for they simply feed the basic antagonism of cultures which are really different from ours, and want to stay that way. Hence the cries: "Modernization, yes! Westernization, no!" and "We will be modern, but we won't be you!"

But what are the 'we'? What are the 'you' referred to in such slogans? Are 'they' really different, deep down, even when they look and behave "just like us." It is seductive to think that "underneath, we're all the same." I believe we are, at the very deepest level of being Homo Sapiens. But there are a lot of differences between them and us in the layers you meet in trying to get to that deepest level. My students like to call these differences our 'of-course-ness-es.'

> Of course the individual must be considered, we say.
> Of course people have a right to free speech, we say.
> Of course democracy is the best form of government, we say.
> Of course progress is desirable, we say.
> Of course all views should be considered, we say.
> Of course anyone can become rich, we say.

These have the most profound significance for each of us. They are basic to our identity and our sense of meaning – to the way we feel secure about who we are, and to our idea of what life is all about. A secure identity is the certainty of being the same basic persona, yesterday, today and tomorrow. Our sense of meaning is the way we make sense of all our life experiences; it is the way we feel it all hangs together. If either our sense of identity or meaning is thrown into serious question, everything falls apart.

A related note about religion. Religion seems to have a greater power both to preserve and to change identity and meaning than does anything else. This is probably because it is such a powerful source of absolutes and suggests that its adherent has the ultimate ally. When confronted with a crisis, persons often change both their identity and the way they find meaning in life by attaching themselves to a new religion. When threatened (as by modernization) persons often go back to 'the basics of their faith' as a way of preserving both identity and meaning. Little wonder then, that the response to rapid changes and challenges in every country has been the rise of fundamentalisms. They reaffirm who we are, and that the totality of things, taken together, does make sense. Examples of this abound in Judaism, Christianity and, of course, Islam.

Of-course-ness-es such as I just stated are what lie at the heart of our Western cultural identity. Such cultural values lie deep within us, and usually take generations to change. The same is true for other cultures - for other civilizations as Huntington called them. How, you might be asking, can you, professor, be so sure that they will continue? Don't they want to be as affluent etc.?

Geert Hofstede did a study which convinces me that the values underlying any cultural identity outlive most other changes. Looking at all the managers of IBM, world-wide, he measured the relative importance to them of four values. Remember that to have been hired they must have been able to operate in that company's style, which of course meant that they were all very Westernized. Yet they exhibited marked differences, in line with each one's native culture. The greatest contrasts came on the scores for what he called "Power Distance" and "Individualism". The first refers to the importance of the hierarchy of power and the amount of respect accorded to authority. On this scale scores for those in the US and Great Britain were 40 and 35 while Pakistan was 55, Iran 58, Taiwan 58, Korea 60, Hong Kong 68, Taiwan 69, and Singapore 74. The individualism scale measures the degree to which the individual is more important than the group. On this scale the differences were even greater: Pakistan, Singapore, Taiwan and Korea being scored 14, 17, 17, and 18 respectively, while the scores for Great Britain and the US were 89 and 91 (the very top). These are the differences which have not gone away, within IBM's management. I discovered a similar reality when in Singapore I tried to embrace a local manager who had been in the same program with me at Harvard. He stiffened with embarrassment, completely resisting my expression of delight, as I should have anticipated with any Chinese. So I would leave with you this thought: Hofstede's data on this large group, (correlated with many other subsequent studies by others) is powerful evidence that **radically contrasting "civilization" norms will be with us for a long, long time.**

In his book Huntington has piles of evidence to support his thesis that the heart of international politics has become and will remain for a long time the clash of civilizations. At the moment, that clash seems most evident on two fronts. The one most prominent in the media is between

The West and Islam. The more widespread is between The West and the poorer nations.

So it may be useful to list **the major areas in which we are seen to threaten the identity and meaning frameworks of other civilizations –**

The most common irritant, found in almost every non-western nation, is the importation of Mc Donald's culture – fast food, brand-named clothing and movies.

Alongside of this it is not uncommon to find a ruling autocracy with a Western jet-set lifestyle. Sometimes such have been a source of pride to the masses, but failed promises of a better life for all often lead to blaming the "westernization" as "evil and ungodly". Bitterness at their own can then be easily shifted to anger at the West, and at the U.S..

Then there have been many geopolitical "goofs" by the West. High on any such list has been the support of brutal regimes in Nicaragua, El Salvador, Guatemala and Panama, all justified by Cold War arguments, but contradicting our proclaimed desire for the spread of human rights.

Just since Huntington's publication, economic globalization has proven to have two faces. The Uruguay Round of GATT, and the one at Marrakech in '95, have stimulated counter activities aimed at publicizing the negative fall-outs of economic globalization. Globalization of the whole world economy has created affluence for a few, and disappointment for many. As the world's economic resources are moved around the globe to maximize profit a few benefit but many suffer, sometimes because of sub-human working conditions, often when the factories move on. (Esteemed brands like Ann Taylor and Liz Claiborne sometimes pay their workers as little as 13 cents per hour.) The West gets the blame, even though the globalization process is directed by no single individual, corporation, organization or nation. Where foreign investment changes a situation it is always seen to be stealing the tradition, the culture, and the young. "Who are our children now?" expresses the pain at losing all sense of meaning, and much of an ancient identity.

The issue of "environmental justice" is surfacing in a new way as people look toward Johannesburg in August, 2002. The UN Conference on Environment and Development in Rio in 1992 produced the Kyoto Accords, but the subsequent U.S. refusal to sign that agreement makes it appear that the West only wants to exploit their resources, and dump its waste in their backyards (or in their atmosphere and waters).

But the discombobulation caused by having to face other civilizations is not only negative; <u>it has a sunny side</u>. Those other civilizations have much to offer us – in terms of enrichment, wisdom, and opportunities, when we really connect. Sadly, most of us are only aware of them when they challenge us, at which times we are unlikely to find much to appreciate. Yet without learning to accept their differences and finding ways to co-exist with those differences, to connect with them fully, we will not only be in trouble, we will miss out on so much. While I could list those advantages of co-existence, I believe you will better visualize the choice before us, in pursuing Fulbright's legacy, by my telling you an allegory, about the three loves of a man called Henry.

You might think of these three loves as three roses. The first is Tropicana, vibrantly rich with its rainforest coloring, vermillion shading to orange, strikingly different from any other flower in a northern garden. This woman is from Indonesia, a Muslim, and as such represents a fifth of the world's population. The second is as refined as the first is exuberant, an exquisitely-formed bud, shading from a hint of pink at its center to a clearly defined color at the tip, Sheer Bliss, only appreciated if you linger with it, the product of colder parts of China, whose population numbers another fifth of the world's population. The third is from a world between the two – Olympiad is full, deep red and richly perfumed, all that a rose could be. And she is Indian, representing one more fifth of the world.

An outdoorsy attractive manager, Henry was thirty when Indonesia came into his life. She taught him to trust as never before. He restored that confidence in her own desirability which had been taken by an abusive husband. She freed him from New England prudishness, teaching him to laugh at himself. He brought her an intimacy of which she had never dreamed, wrapped in. excitement.

By welcoming her to be part of his very private self he became a larger person. But he was not large enough to live with the Will of Allah. In submission to that will she denied them both the complete consummation of the physical intimacy they both craved and did satisfy in all ways but one. That one, she insisted, must await marriage. But marriage was delayed interminably by divorce and custody proceedings. To him, the immediate satisfaction of their individual desires made sense; to her they were contrary to the Will of Allah. Because he could find no way for Western individualism to co-exist with Islamic obedience, all the wonder, and the beauty of Tropicana was lost to Henry. We might say he gave up all the potentially wonderful connection with a fifth of the human race.

The Chinese lover taught Henry the miracle of total acceptance  In him she found the other part of herself which she had always sought.  She taught him the intimacy which is deepest via the simplest things.  He fulfilled the romantic in her otherwise very rational personality.

By learning that love means much more than warm fuzzies, he discovered a mature oneness which was to remain the norm for all other relationships in his life —with parents, with other women, with men, with children.  But he was not able to live with her need for order.  From the bottomless well of her love he assuaged the life-long thirst which he had never been able to name.  Both of them wanted, with their whole being, to spend the rest of their lives together.  But her need for order seemed irrationally, even compulsively demanding;  her need for appropriate decorum seemed to deny him the freedom to be himself.  Conforming to her expectation of order and appropriate behavior symbolized love, in her eyes;  she saw their denial, for the sake of individual freedom, as the lack of love.  So he ended the relationship, with a lie - that it had all been fantasy.  Because he could find no way for Western individualism to co-exist with the Chinese value placed on order, all of the beauty that was Sheer Bliss, was lost to Henry.  We might say he gave up all the potentially wonderful connection with a fifth of the human race.

For a whole decade the thirty-five to forty-five year old Henry luxuriated in a long distance love with the Indian woman.  Theirs was total companionship, with mutuality of mind as well as body, of the spirit and the senses, of dedicated action and of playful delight.  She found herself increasingly fulfilled.  He found himself increasingly sensitive, in every respect.

By each being allowed to be, and learning how to just be, they had both grown —she to the point of wanting a commitment to permanency.  He had also grown, beyond the universal acceptance which was the base from which she could always delight in every option, every adventure.  He had grown beyond years as a relativist, to acknowledging his roots, as a child of the West, for whom individualism was not selfishness, but the core value.  Because he could find no way for commitment to co-exist with Indian syncretism, all of the richness that was Olympiad was lost to Henry.  We might say he gave up all the potentially wonderful connection with a fifth of the human race.

In each of those loves Henry could have gone on growing, beyond anything each could envisage, as would his partner.  In each of these loves, both parties wanted that to happen. What stood in the way was Henry's inability to live with values which were contrary to his central value. How sad. How very unnecessary. How very, very sad.

So we come now to the big question of what our response will be – yours, mine, and our nation's – to this clash of civilizations. These clashes and the irritants underlying many of them are the forces which push us apart, causing us to behave like Henry. But what are the forces and kinds of action which can bring us together? What forces can abet the process of being enriched beyond our dreams? In conclusion I will quickly suggest nine.

1. We must give up the idea that all will be well when *they* adopt *our* values particularly those that derive from our individualism. As a corollary we would cease to attach such conditions to our promises of economic and other assistance.

2. We must strengthen the knowledge of the roots and values of our own civilization. We have a magnificent heritage about which each should be more knowingly proud.

3. We must applaud and assist the spread of all religions into all countries. All teach, encourage and empower movement towards universal good, so all will benefit by closer devotion to each person's heritage or choice.

4. We must back all efforts to resolve conflicts non-violently - whether by groups of individuals, by nations, or by organizations such as the UN.

5. We must strengthen international institutions to confront and control rogue regimes that commit genocide, harbor terrorists or develop weapons of mass destruction

6. We must demand and support the increase of understanding, reporting, and entertainment which is inclusive and has a global perspective.

7. We must bite the bullet on "sustained development". This is a very painful challenge, requiring us to take seriously whether the earth can provide the sources, sites and sinks, as well as the production sufficient to give to all what presently is enjoyed by only a tenth of the world's population.

8    We must make every effort to refine the market economy model to make it more just without losing its incentive value. Without such modifications (of which taxes are an expression) there is no possibility of anything approaching global economic justice.

9    We must do everything possible to educate our own population into the attitude that "we're all human, even though we continue to be so very different and create such difficulties for each other". This while we find ever more that we can gain from each other. Then and only then will value conflicts  appear less distressing and more tolerable.

The story of Henry is sad, very sad. The story of civilizations through the twenty first century might be equally sad. But if Bill Fulbright were here I am sure he would be saying: Rather than sad, it <u>can</u> be a glad century, for all.

###

As the audience rose in standing acclamation, Nicole squeezed the hand of the Eurasian-looking adolescent at her side. "That's our Dad," she whispered to her half brother.

"And that was my Mom he was talking about," Edward added, the proud but teary face turning towards his new-found big sister as he responded to her squeeze.

A large group had gathered around the podium. Nicole and Edward stood back and watched, enjoying their father's acclamation almost as much as he.

Among those wanting to greet him was his one-time colleague, now Dean Beverly Thompson: "I just wanted to add my appreciation for your words. I came to criticize, but I'm applauding. I've been saying to myself that this cannot be the male chauvinist I used to teach with. Whatever made you change so much?"

He simply could not resist the chance of shocking his old nemesis, even though he now felt no animosity towards her. The imp in him surfaced, harmlessly he knew, and he quipped: "I guess it's because I've had great lovers!"

"You have?" came a voice which was as familiar as it was unexpected. There, to the side, half hidden by several other admirers, stood a figure which was only slightly changed from when he had last seen her fourteen years ago - Minah.

She had come out of curiosity, which had quickly changed to something more the moment he walked to the podium. Past is past, she had always said. But his first stumbling steps towards intimacy had been with *her*. And now he had acknowledged his debt to her in a very public way. He had called her a rose; how beautiful!. And the other two roses? Of course there would have been. And he sees them as lost? Well, I'm still unattached.

In response to her voice two looks met, his in surprise, both faces telling, asking, asking. Her smile was that same one which beguiled him the day they met on the plane. In it he read the same responsiveness that had awakened his senses, his awareness of himself, and a nascent ability to give of those sensibilities, without fear and without restraint, a lifetime ago, the first person with whom he had felt safely known..

He could never have anticipated what would happen next. Since they parted he had been intensely alive - to much pleasure, much pain, and much change within. Not for a moment in all those years had it entered his mind that it could all be preparation for this moment. Now, in one long look, that possibility dawned and found him wanting her to see that this was the same man, but grown to real maturity, worthy of a woman such as he now held with a smile which grew with her own.

Somehow, the smile told him that having heard his address, she was thinking almost what he was hoping she would see. As ever, she was one step ahead, and teased: "You look like the same Professor Johnson! But maybe it's just the same name?"

"And you can't be the same Indonesian I met fourteen years ago, because you're no older!" he parried.

"How can I know you're not The Pretender, posing as Eric Johnson?" She came back again.

He surrendered somewhat at this point: "Because only Eric would know of the promise he made to answer honestly whatever Minah chose to ask. And how am I to know that you are really Minah?"

"Because Minah would never have told anyone about that day in a tiny tent."

At this they both collapsed into laughter, hugged, kissed gently, then stood back. She was first to speak: "Yes, you have changed." But all the old mischief was there between them. She could not believe he had been so bold yet vulnerable as to speak of the supposedly fictional lover and his three roses. And how this man's attitude to other cultures and his own has changed? He used to be so apologetic for being an American; now he's so proud of his heritage (like I am of Islam and my province of Aceh). But he holds his heritage as one among many, and grants all the others the right to the same pride.

"So have you!"

"For the better!" came her warm acknowledgement of his growth in the years they had no contact. She had been profoundly moved by his listing of the nine factors necessary if we are to live as one global family. She agreed with every one. But that he should have grown that far! How wonderful! But I guess I knew, even back then, that he could.

"Ditto!" seemed an adequate response to Eric, although he did not quite know what it meant. Then, realizing two young faces were filled with puzzlement, he turned to Nicole and Edward with the words: "Minah, I'd like you to meet my children." Edward proffered his hand rather than accept her embrace, but Nicole responded in kind, albeit with some hesitation. She sensed Minah's need, and acknowledging her own need to share physically in the aura which grew and grew between her father and this woman she had never seen before, she returned the warm embrace. Yet for all the good feeling in the air Minah was finding herself torn. He did hurt me then, terribly. Yet he is such a hunk, and he's now so much more mature.

As crowds do, those who had come to chat with the speaker stood back, respectful of the intimacy to which they were witness. Eric thanked them, then said, "I must ask you to forgive me, but I think we will have to talk by e-mail, or something, because, as you can see, I need to be with my family right now." His use of that word 'family'; what does he mean by it? Does it include me? Why should it? And look at his family: a Eurasian son by another woman and a Yankee co-eds. What would my Aceh family say if I introduced the Johnson three as *my* family?

Turning to Minah, Nicole and Edward he suggested: "I know just the place, only a block away. Let's go!" But how to go, when the pavement won't take four abreast? The question was on every face – until Nicole came to the rescue: "You and Minah lead the way, Dad; we'll follow." Each woman seemed automatically to slide her arm into her partner's elbow, and off they went.

With drinks ordered, a child on either side and Minah opposite, Eric presented the essential information: "Minah and I were very dear friends years ago, when she was a graduate student at Tufts, and we haven't seen each other since." Nicole smiled at her dad - as seventeen-going-on-thirty girls can do - and received a smile of profound appreciation. Sensing that Eric needed 'time out', Minah comfortably engaged the other two in conversation while he leaned back and pondered the scene.

'My family' – was the overwhelming thought which surfaced first. How different from Gran's, but I feel here, now, as I always feel during Thanksgiving at Gran's. What a contrast to any specification I ever conceived! For some moments he let that feeling take charge, then found himself looking from one to the other. First, there are two children, a boy and a girl, one deeply known, one to be discovered. The uncertainties and questions which had preceded the first meeting with Edward now gone, optimism came automatically. 'Even if he does look Eurasian', he found himself adding. And this woman opposite? Can she be part of the rest of my life? Sure, she's still Muslim; I'm sure that will never change. But I am changed. I no longer see differences as either/or. This could be. Certainly, if this is to be my family, I must walk the talk of my speech. But what else have these last fifteen years been for, if not preparation to do just that?

Edward and Nicole seemed to be engaged in their own exchange, and he found Minah looking into him with that same searching gaze that had characterized their every moment together fifteen years ago. He searched but could not read her thoughts: Can this be the awkward guy on the plane back when? The guy who was so uncomfortable with anything he couldn't get his head around? He had been so demanding – delightfully so at the beginning, destructively so as things progressed. But what I've seen tonight is different. He almost cried when telling that story – which was really about us. And there were tears in his eyes as he told about those two other women: "All lost", he anguished. Yet he was laughing at himself when that woman asked how come the change. This IS my Eric, yet with a big difference. He now sees differences more like an Indonesian. Sure, he's as passionate as ever, maybe more so about lots of things. We'd probably fight much more now. But he treats the differences in others in a new way – more like the way I do. The old Eric could be made so uncomfortable, was really such a wuss.  But this Eric is so accepting and also very certain of who he is.

What am I doing here?  What do I want from Eric?  Would I want it to work out between us?  But would it work?  Yes, it would, because I see the treasure I thought was there when I was so naïve.  The man I knew and who has now become that speaker is a rarity among Yanks.  But does he want *any* exclusive relationship?  Would he now want a devout Muslim?  To her surprise, something deep down answered 'yes' to all of those questions.

# BOOK CLUB DISCUSSION STARTERS

**About being grown up**

What do we mean by that phrase?

Is it as delayed and prolonged for many men as it was for Eric Johnson?

When does it happen for most women?

Was it possible for Eric's wife to be the necessary catalyst for his growing up?

Beyond the end of the novel what else must happen for Eric to be "really grown up"?

**About being a woman hurt**

"Why did she go there?" could be asked of Minah, of Siok Yim, of Rani.

What did each of them get out of their relationship with Eric?

Would they go there again?

## About Eric's break-through therapy

Why did the first two therapists fail to be really useful to his development?

What was Eric's "problem with women"?

Can men ever grow beyond their "trouble with women"?

Why could Gran, Nicole and Rani "get through" to Eric better than Siok Yim?

Is it harder to find a good therapist than a good doctor, and how do you know you have found a good one?

Is it true that some part of any intimate will always be "a stranger" to us?

Can we Westerners learn how to keep the intimacy and live with the alien part of one we love?

What does it take to move a person who is "stuck", as Eric was?


## About what goes on between men

Could it be argued that Michael and Ahad were more important to Eric's growing up than were any of the women in his life?

What did his two buddies provide which no woman ever could?

How unusual is the kind of male-to-male conversation which occurs in this novel? Can women ever foster it?


## About partners

Which woman would make the best life-long partner for Eric?

Minah, Siok Yim and Rani are all portrayed as knowing what they want in a partner. Is that level of certainty really possible?

Is there a destined "soul-mate" for each of us, as Siok Yim believed?

## About religion

The religions of India and China (of Rani and Siok Yim) lack the demands which direct the lives of Islamic Ahad and Minah and Catholic Michael. Does that make such "comfortable" religions more or less desirable? Whose lives are more attractive to you – those of the first two, or of the latter three?

What do you think happened to Eric the night Nicole took him to an orthodox service?

Would Eric's core value (individualism) make it impossible for him to live with any partner whose religion put God, order, or tolerance first?

## Or you might want to discuss

Except for their daughters, at the end of his affair with Minah is there any other glue keeping Eric and Frankie together?

Which of the three was Eric's "best" love? Why do you rate it higher or either of the others lower? Should he have stopped running around and committed 100% to Minah? To Siok Yim? To Rani?

What does Eric really "want"?

Why do men like Eric avoid the sense of vulnerability at all costs – even though any mature woman can see immediately how vulnerable they are?

Do you think an appropriate title for Book V would be "Response-Ability"? Is that what it means to be "grown up"?

What is more important to Eric growing up: his 3-month affair with Minah, his 4-year affair with Siok Yim, his 15-year relationship with Rani, his breakthrough therapy, the fact that he was a father, or learning that he could not have it all?

Every character in the book holds a mirror in front of Eric at some point. Does that occur for most of us?

In Eric's life achievement hampers (while it sublimate) growth possibilities. So Eric keeps busy for several years after ending the relationship with Siok Yim.  Does that happen for most people in the busy years of work and family?

Time after time we see a major contrast between Eric and Siok Yim in the ability to "let go" of some irritation caused by the other.  Is this a gender difference?

## Or you might want to look at particular chapters and ask

*In Chapter 1:*

Can a woman tell if a man is married just by looking at him?

What messages did Eric convey unwittingly in the conversation about not wearing a wedding ring?

Do women consciously "mother" their husbands?  If so, is that a good thing?

Is Eric's ignorance of his wife's realities unusual for a thirty-year-old?

Did Eric and Frankie have other qualities beyond a shared Peace Corps experience and '60's radicals orientation which would have made theirs a good partnership?

*In Chapter 3:*

Can a man and a woman be "intimate friends" as Minah proposes without it getting sexual?

Why would Minah have believed that to be possible?

If you have ever experienced the level of safe disclosure which occurred between Minah and Eric what do think made it possible?

What made Minah so vulnerable at this time in her life?

*In Chapter 5:*

Minah's permissiveness in the tent seems to contradict her principles.  How would she have rationalized the apparent contradiction?  Is that uncommon among persons of strong religious faith?

*In Chapter 6:*

How would you explain an American Poli Sci prof making the mistake of equating Arab and Muslim?

*In Chapter 8:*

Therapist Kendall fails to deal with "the real issues" which determine Eric's happiness. What were they? How could she have gotten him to explore scenarios alternative to ending his relationship with Minah?

*In Chapter 10:*

What phrase would be an appropriate way to describe the Siok Yim depicted in bed with Eric at the hotel?

*In Chapter 11:*

What needs of Eric does Siok Yim intuit? How does she plan to meet them?

*In Chapter 12:*

If you had been a fly on the wall at Kathy's apartment, what words of caution would you have added to the ones she gave to Siok Yim?

*In Chapter 15:*

In connection with the two letters concerning Siok Yim's pregnancy: Can a woman empathize with Eric's thinking and counsel?

What experiences in your own life have convinced you that men are from Mars and women are from Venus?

Why did Eric have affairs? Are his reasons common to both genders?

How would a male reader enlarge on Eric's claim that "my relationship with Rani made me a better father? How would a woman discount that claim?

*In Chapter 16:*

What did Rani think of Eric the first day they met?

*In Chapter 33:*

Do Eric's answers about what he had learned adequately define what it means to be grown up?

What are your reactions to Eric's statements about sex as a sacrament?

*In Chapter 34:*

How would you have arranged the first meeting of Eric with Edward Wong?

# INTERPERSONAL RELATIONS DISCUSSION GUIDE

**A Harvard-educated attorney suggested this novel would be a convenient ready-made resource to enliven sectional meetings in an interpersonal relations course by providing numerous situations for study and discussion.**

**The parenthetical chapter references relate each suggestion to the novel.**

What messages were sent by Eric's style of approach to Minah on the plane?

Was Eric conscious of all his intentions in approaching her?

Who controlled most of the conversation between them? How?

What self-image of interpersonal competence did Eric bring to that meeting?

Was the encouragement in Minah's final quip a product of Eric's interpersonal competence?

(Chapter 1)

How did Eric's early experiences with girls influence his decision to marry?

Is Eric typical of male awareness of what is going on inside a woman?

Why did the joget and the Walden Pond walk have such a major impact on Eric?

What happened to the need for control in the dynamics of both those situations?

(Chapter 3)

During the intensification phase of Eric's relationship with Minah he discovers things about himself which he had not known. How come?

How similar or different is one's self-image from others' image of oneself?

Discuss the intrapersonal as well as the interpersonal factors in Minah's reaction when she hears that Eric has told Annette something about her.

How do you explain the differences between Eris's twins in willingness to disclose?

(Chapter 6)

Do we relate to the opposite gender differently from the way we relate to our own gender?

How is that a good or a bad thing?

(Chapter 7)

Explain why it is so easy in that committee meeting for Beverley Thompson to "win", and to have Eric's efforts dismissed.

Why is Eric more ready to accept advice from Minah than from his wife?

How is it that a woman often "knows the score" long before a man does?

(Chapter 8)

What is the significance of the *place* (a poolside) at which visiting professor Siok Yim chose to meet Eric?

How does a shared swim and spa influence interaction?

In what ways does it influence the content of conversation?

In what ways does the difference in academic status affect the interaction?

How and with what result does Siok Yim use humor and teasing with Eric?

How different do you imagine are their respective expectations of what will be the outcomes of this meeting?

In what ways is Siok Yim completely in control? What are the consequences for Eric?

What might Siok Yim have read into Eric's complete inability to answer her question: What do you want, Eric?

How does that vagueness about intentions influence all of his female relationships?

Is there any difference between what a dating man and woman "wants"?

What inhibits clarity on this matter between couples?

(Chapter 10)

There is a marked contrast between Eric's openness in Chapter 1 and Chapter 11. How much do you think Minah is responsible? How much is Siok Yim? How? Why?

How is the Johari Window useful in thinking about this matter?
(Chapter 11)

How different is the fantasy life of Eric and Siok Yim?
How typical of each gender do you consider this to be?
(Chapter 11)

At the end of Book II we read that "part of his very self was and was not his."
What is this stage in intimate relations?
Why is it so wonderful and so painful?
Is it a good thing that this is never permanent?
(Chapter 15)

How do theories about the dynamics of "approach" explain the behaviors and words of Eric and Minah as they meet at the Stanford conference?
(Chapter16)

Why, as in Chapter17, is there greater risk-taking in the pillow-talk after sex?
What interpersonal dynamics apart from sex make personal disclosure feel safer?
Does having sex together necessarily change the divisions in a person's Johari Window?
Up to the end of Book III how would you evaluate Eric's interpersonal skills?
What qualities would you place in the "blind" quadrant of Eric's Johari Window?
How does any man become aware of and competent in his "blind" areas?
Chapter 17)

Chapter 18 describes a very stressful reunion.
What was the wall between them? Why did he raise it?
Does this relate to his not being "grown up"? Or is it a typical "male" avoidance technique?
The end of this chapter describes their feelings as she returns to Taiwan for the second time. What does the contrast between their feelings tell you about the meaning of the relationship for each of them?
(Chapter 18)

Why is Eric unable to conform to Siok Yim's expectations about letter-writing and punctuality?

What does this fact communicate to her?

Are her values underlying these expectations more idiosyncratic or culturally based?

Of such failures in the most important person in her life which basis would make them more painful?

(Chapter 19)

Read Siok Yim's letter at the beginning of Chapter 20 in which she contrasts the way men and women deal with feelings. Do you agree or disagree with her analysis and the advice she gives to "her man"?

What symbolic acts would convince her that he "understands" her feelings?

What is most convincing to you that another has understood your own feelings?

(Chapter 20)

Chapter 22 contains lots of introspection by Eric about the "downs" in his relationship with Siok Yim. What is the usual pattern of working through this phase of an intimate relationship?

Why is Chapter 23 (end of Book III) so painful to any reader? What would a more mature man have done?

(Chapters 22,23)

"That avoids all this male stuff that I hate!" says Frankie in the middle of Chapter 24. How much is her comment about the inevitable roles of women as the child-bearers and how much is it a reflection of changing gender roles in our culture?

(Chapter 24)

Re-read the section where Ahn teaches Eric to mirror. Try it with a partner and check to see what you felt *kinetically*.

(Chapter 25)

Chapters 29-32 constitute "the creative crisis" of Eric's growth. These conversations with a therapist and with Rani raise several questions:

    a.   Why would such a successful guy contemplate suicide?

    b.   Could he have ever "grown up" without that traumatic experience in therapy?

    c.   Could the therapy have been possible without the support of Rani?

d. Why did he still not realize Rani was the most valuable person in his life?

e. What distinguishes what he would call "the Siok Yim effect" from his feelings for Rani: "You are my best friend and my best lover"?

The beginning of Chapter 33 describes Eric at Squam Lake with his best friends Ahad and Michael. The conversations demonstrate a humility in Eric which had been missing in all his intimate relations. Why do you think this was so?

What is it about this conversation which is "very male"?

How does your definition of interpersonal maturity compare with Eric's own, as he outlines it in that chapter?

What do you make of Eric's discovery that "he was still avoiding life's feelings, rather than living them."?

(Chapter 33)

The first segment of Chapter 34 contains very little dialog, but much is said non-verbally. What is "said"?

Could you create a dialog to verbalize what Eric and Frankie communicate non-verbally?

What are some of the most obvious symbols in a separating household?

Can you mime the way Eric would have stood in Kathy's living room a) the first time they met and b) when he made the entry described in Chapter 34.

(Chapter 34)

What other ways could have been contrived for Eric to meet Edward Wong than the one described near the end of Chapter 35?

In addition to what the author reports, what else happened to Eric in the chapel with Nicole?

Construct a dialog between Eric and Minah the day after his big speech.

(Chapter 35)

Eric had great book-learning, but learned most about himself from others. Of such learnings reported in the novel, which three or four were the most important?

# INTERCULTURAL COMMUNICATION DISCUSSION GUIDE

**A Harvard-educated attorney suggested this novel would be a convenient ready-made resource to enliven sectional meetings in an intercultural communication course by providing numerous interactions for study and discussion.**

**The parenthetical chapter references relate each suggestion to the novel.**

Eric Johnson views himself as a global idealist. That idealism motivated him to join the Peace Corps and spend a year in Singapore as a teacher of English..

In what ways did that year change him?

Can this man put himself in the shoes of a woman or of a foreigner? Why or why not?

Is his sense of his identity (who he is) much different from the average young adult?

(Chapter 1)

What do you think were the underlying needs which pushed a Muslim woman to cultivate a friendship with Eric?

How do you explain Eric's growing sympathy with the picture of Islam he gets from Minah?

(Chapters 2,3,4)

What are some of the "discombobulating" differences you have met?

Why do Minah's values discombobulate Eric when similar values he met in Singapore could just be shrugged off?

What were some of the beliefs and perspectives which you thought everyone held when you were a child?

What was your answer to the question "Who are you?" when you were 12? (The question of *identity*.)

At 12, how did you assume the world "worked"? (The question of *meaning*.)

(Chapter 7)

Re-read Eric's long talk with Michael about "discombobulating differences".

What happened with Minah interculturally which had not happened in Singapore?

Discuss the sentence: "Until I met her I never thought twice about whether they in Singapore might have a clue about how the world fits together and what the good life looks like."

How many phases in Eric's intercultural development can you distinguish?

What forms of real "otherness" have you been obliged to become comfortable with? Do not limit yourself to cultural otherness.

Isn't "cultural superiority" a necessary part of being a strong person?

(Chapter 7)

Debate the statement: "Travel is the great educator" with particular reference to what did and did not happen to Eric as a Peace Corps volunteer.

Why did that experience change neither his sense of who he was (his identity) or his idea of how life makes sense (the meaning of it all).

(Chapter 8)

Does experience support the "U-curve Theory" of adjustment? Did Eric's?

(Chapter 9)

What new did you learn about the Chinese tradition, its values, and its underlying beliefs?

(Chapter 11)

What, if any intercultural development occurs in Eric in Book II? That is, through his love affair with a visiting Chinese professor?

How do cultural values show up at the Asilomar meeting of Rani's Committee on Internationalizing Social Studies Curricula?
Can you guess what those value differences will do to her dream about that completely multicultural group in the three years of its work together?
(Chapter 19)

What were Eric's main intercultural failures at the Austin meeting of Rani's Committee?
Can you explain them? Are they excusable?
(Chapter 21)

What kind of thinking would a Latino like graduate student and Committee member Thomas describe as "So damned American!"?
Are there behaviors which also get described that way?
What should we feel when we hear such criticisms?
What can we do about such criticisms?
(Chapter 22)

What factors played into the perception of Eric by the French Canadian woman on Rani's Committee?
What stereotypes influence Americans' perceptions of the French?
(Chapter 24)

What are your thoughts on the central conception of "being" versus "doing" put forward by the Vietnamese woman?
What has Siok Yim's letter in this chapter to do with this topic?
Would our culture be richer if we gave less energy to "doing" and more to "being"?
What would we lose?
(Chapter 25)

How do experiences such as Eric's at the Indian wedding affect attachment to one's own culture?
(Chapter 25)

Consider Rani's very non-Western philosophy of life expounded in Chapter 26.
What are the inevitable tensions most of us Westerners would experience if we were moved to live by such an orientation?
The novel contains a lot about the Islamic faith and quite a bit about Indian and Chinese religion, but very little about Christianity. Yet the author believed that agnostic Eric was an exemplar of the Christian tradition. How?

Can one avoid being powerfully influenced by the religious tradition which has dominated one's culture for generations?
How does Christianity play into who Eric considers himself to be? (His identity)
How does Christianity play into the way Eric makes sense of life? (The meaning he ascribes to life)

What *non-religious attributes and styles of thinking* would stand in the way of Eric adopting the religion of Minah (Islam)? Of Siok Yim (Taoism)? Of Rani (Hinduism)?

Looking back at these fifteen years in the life of a young professor, what do you see as the components of effective intercultural functioning –
Behaviorally?
Cognitively?
Affectively?

Review the "Author's Note" about "Otherness Developmental Stages".
At what stage are you at this time as you meet Americans who are really different from yourself?
At what stage might you be if confronted by a threatening Muslim terrorist in a foreign airport toilet?

# AUTHOR'S NOTE

## OTHERNESS DEVELOPMENTAL STAGES

Much of the story of Eric's development in the fifteen years covered in this novel was guided by the following theoretical framework. My interpersonal and intercultural work since 1961 has led to the conviction that the challenges of another culture and those of the other gender are both instances of the challenge of *otherness*. One might ask why Eric is portrayed as dealing with cultural otherness much faster than he deals with gender otherness. It is not for lack of stimuli. But l*etting in* the other creates the push toward change, while *just visiting* otherness demands little and brings no change. Much of the time he *just visits* his lovers as women even while he *lets in* their cultural otherness – hence the title *Intimate Strangers*.

Development through these stages is accompanied by work on *identity* (Who am I?) and on sense of *meaning* (What's it all about and how does life all fit together?) In some stages there is modification of both; other stages only require work on one of these. Major change in either area is discomforting and demanding, both affectively and cognitively. Perhaps that is why the stimuli to the next stage are avoided if possible: then such life becomes a series of *visits* with other persons, places, ideas, and even other things. Eric *lets in* nature (profoundly), as well as ideas, his two buddies and his daughters, but with strong women the connection is largely restricted to *visiting*; hence we find him at one stage with some experiences and at a much lower stage with his lovers.

I identify seven stages of development in the way humans relate to otherness, for which the following are the best labels I can produce to date:

1. Intolerance

2. Tolerance

3. Active ethnocentrism

4. Respect

5. Modification

6. Relativism

7. Inclusivity

In the following descriptions reference to the novel's story will be kept to a minimum.

**Intolerance.**   Relatively speaking, the infant's world is a safe, predictable place, with only one set of values; anything that does not fit ought to, so we call such behavior infantile.  There is little awareness of *identity* (except 'me' and 'not me') and *meaning* has not yet become a problem.  Everything is as it's supposed to be.  Even adults are sometimes stuck in this place.

**Tolerance.**  I acknowledge there are differences, but they are inferior to my values and life-style. Because they don't trouble me, I just let them be.  My gender and my culture are superior, and I guess you just put up with the other.  The one value in otherness is that it makes very clear by contrast who I am (my *identity*) and how superior is the world-view that I got with my mother's milk (the *meaning* of it all). Eric's father-in-law is totally in this ethnocentric stage, as is Eric in relation to all the women in the first half of the novel.

**Active Ethnocentrism.**  In this stage there is a movement beyond the painless tolerance of the second stage: one's own superiority obliges action, either to help 'them' or to control 'them'.  Missionaries and empire-builders and their more recent mutations express this stage. The actors are not changed in the way they see themselves, so their *identity* perseveres. But they find themselves obliged to change the way they make sense of life: so a new sense of *meaning* and a new life-style go hand-in-hand.

The helping approach of some in this stage can be driven by a passion for justice, religious fervor or a paternalistic attitude; the controlling approach may be driven by fear, the desire for power or profit as they look out at 'the others.' In this stage Eric joins the Peace Corps and later befriends Muslim foreign student Ahad.

**Respect.** I am stimulated by those differences ("vive la difference") and enjoy them. While it occurs to me that I possibly could learn from values and lifestyles different from my own, I feel no need to do so. Yet because I acknowledge that I am part of a big, diverse world, and that the others who are quite different from me are quite happy, I have to adjust my way of making sense of the whole thing. The *meaning* of it all is thus a bit different. And my *identity* includes all of them (at least in my head), but only to the point that it doesn't demand any change in my behavior. The strangers-become-lovers do stimulate Eric, and he respects their cultural perspectives, but their persons do not become part of him until late in the story.

**Modification.** This stage becomes imperative when one identifies with the other to the point of feeling insulted when they are insulted, etc. I must change if I am to live closely with their values and lifestyles which differ from my own (that is, if I am to *let them in*). When my behavior is modified, so is my self-image and the way I define myself, i.e. my *identity*. This then confuses the way I have made sense of life, giving rise to a crisis of *meaning*. "An unacceptable invasion of privacy" and "an imperialism of the mind" are two accusations supported by Rani which Eric cannot ignore, and so he finds his *identity* changing and his sense of *meaning* in a state of limbo.

**Relativism.** While the previous stage mainly involves feelings and a change in *identity* the mind demands an explanation if this is the way things are in the universe. The answer is an intellectual relativism: the apparently contradictory values and lifestyles are completely valid *in their own context*. Because I cannot live without such diversity as part of the essence of 'me', I also find myself saying that no values are absolute, constituting a major shift in my solution to the problem of *meaning*. This stage is strongly exemplified in Hindu Rani, and is adopted by Eric just before his therapy 'work'.

**Inclusivity.** For most who do reach this stage the meaning aspect of the stage is permanent while the identity experience is occasional. The need to *explain* acceptance of otherness disappears; this conviction is as complete as it is inexplicable, but in my gut I know that oneness does not require sameness. Perhaps it arises because some experiences have manifested that as fact. **These highs of my life have been moments when I have known myself completely connected yet distinctly "me" – unique, yet integrally part of all**. This identity acknowledges, celebrates and is consciously empowered by the particular tradition which birthed and nurtured me (especially its values, supportive mythology, and some aspects of its lifestyle). Thus I appear externally to have the same *identity* as that with which I began life, but inwardly I know that emotionally it includes all others – as well as all that is 'not me'. This oneness of the wonders and perversities of others and other cultures which I feel compelled to own is beyond my comprehension, but I feel no need to make sense of it all, thus arriving at a very paradoxical solution to the problem of *meaning*. At the end of the novel Eric is fully conscious that this is the way he "makes sense of it all": but he has yet to see that he has experienced this sense of *identity* at times when he was closest to Rani and his daughter Nicole.

These seven stages thus constitute a movement from unconsidered clarity to acknowledged paradox.

# ABOUT THE AUTHOR

Sixth generation Australian Reginald Smart was a Singapore architect in the fifties, a Harvard chaplain in the sixties and a SUNY college dean in the seventies. Subsequently he has been a leader in the fields of male/female and intercultural communication. He has led numerous men's support groups, counseled hundreds of couples, negotiated inter-university agreements in eleven countries, and consulted with major international corporations such as Westinghouse and AT&T. Currently he spends most of his time writing, gardening, hiking, and mediating marital disputes at a center he co-founded in Washington State. A seasoned author of non-fiction, this is his first novel.

Printed in the United States
31316LVS00002B/160-177

9 781420 807233